WIIIS

DANGEI

BOOK 3

A.G. HARRIS

AUTHOR

Copyright

Cover design by www.amberrazzouk.com

A.G. Harris

Acknowledgments

To my fans, who have supported me even though I refuse to be chained to the algorithm of social media and post three times a day, your comments, messages, and reviews have truly meant a lot to this indie author.

To my husband, who's endured my wild ideas, plots, and non-stop comments that'll probably wind up in my books someday—I love you.

To the Cygnet Inkers, all your advice has helped me, and I hope to meet you all one day, but until then, I'm enjoying reading your books.

With love,
A.G. Harris

Whisper My Secrets

Also by A.G. Harris

Magic Borne Series Guide

Against Fate, The Rejected Mates of Magic Borne Series.

The Rites of Passage Series
Ashes to Ashes
Dust to Dust

Dangerously Evolved Series
Paint My Lies
Start My War
Whisper My Secrets

Follow me and sign up for my newsletter
https://mailchi.mp/2f14c0c70688/newsletter
https://www.authoragharris.com/
@authoragharris
https://www.facebook.com/authoragharris/

Author's Note

Before you flip through the pages of Whisper My Secrets, let's have a little chat. This is not a standalone – by now, you should have a good sense of the subjects this series delves into. But just in case you need a refresher, this dark romance isn't your typical bedtime story; it's likely to keep you engrossed and flipping pages. Brace yourself for intense themes and startling events that might raise your eyebrows higher than a Botox overdose. Don't worry; you can always close the book if it becomes too much or indulge in a glass of wine, coffee, or a sweet delight to keep the journey going.

Consider this your fair warning. The subjects in this book may be triggering, but remember, this is their story, not yours. It's a book, and if it becomes too overwhelming, simply close it. So, if you're willing, turn the page, and let's get started.

Prologue

Sol

The past.

Footsteps sound as my sister joins me outside in our vast backyard. Winter will soon approach. The leaves are turning and slowly dying.

"What are you looking at for so long?" Luna asks as she plops down next to me, mirroring my image with outstretched legs, shoulders relaxed, and palms pressing into the grass. I like to sit directly on the grass. I want to touch the earth and feel its textures.

"Death."

"What." Luna's head whips towards me. Her voice is cold.

"I'm talking about the leaves falling," I point to the trees. Luna's eyes follow my finger, scanning the landscape with a narrow precision.

"Did you ever think death could be so lovely?"

"What do you mean?" Luna asks.

I can't help but notice how her body has stiffened. I wonder if it's because of the topic. "Everyone loves fall because of all the saturated colors, but in reality, they appreciate death. The leaves are dying. It's a slow end, which should be grotesque, but no one sees it that way. They see the saturated outside, not the decay from within."

We sit in silence, the sun kissing our faces, the blades of grass tickling the tips of our fingers. "You're right. Sometimes ugly is pretty, and sometimes death is beautiful." Luna admits.

I nod. "That's because everyone tries to see the good at first glimpse. People don't think nature is killing the plants or that food will be scarce for the animals. They see the colors then the blankets of untouched glittering snow."

Luna doesn't respond but grabs her iPod from her pocket and selects a song. She turns the volume up high on her headphones. It's so loud that we both can hear her music without putting the headphones on. She plays a song I know, "What a Wonderful World" but I have never heard this version.It sounds eerie, haunting. I'm not sure if the future is going to be hopeful or melancholy, judging from the way the artist conveys the essence of the song.

"Who sings this?"

"Soap and Skin."

I wrinkle my nose, "That's a funny name."

"People choose funny things." She deadpans. Her eyes go distant and I wonder if she envisions a hope on her horizon or an endless competition.

I sit with my twin watching the leaves slowly die and fall. Moments like this are rare. Just Luna and I, enjoying nothing but everything simultaneously.

"The way she sings the song makes me feel like something terrible has happened." I tilt my head up, trying to imagine a rainbow in the sky, "It makes me feel like ashes are falling from the sky, settling." I shrug, "But where there is death," I look at the dead fallen leaves scattered on the forest floor, "There is also new life waiting to spring forth. I know that even after a harsh winter, new life will come forth. Life is resilient, even in the most terrible of circumstances."

Pivoting, I look at my twin. Her blonde hair dances over her face, and her unblinking blue eyes stare at the horizon. She's ethereal, and despite our identical features, I can't help but feel inferior in her presence. I will only feel on her level if she trusts me more.

I just want her to trust me.

I can protect her as well as she has shielded me.

A subtle twitch pulls at her lips as if contemplating a hidden secret. I don't know if it was the budding of a smile or a snarl. I'll never know with Luna. She's an enigma, a Pandora's box. You never know what is inside or what monster will be unleashed.

I grab her hand, and interlace our fingers. Luna picked this song for a reason. She doesn't listen to music like a normal person. She picks songs that reflect her darkest voice and lyrics that can speak when she doesn't know how to.

"That's our world." She admits. She hits replay, and the song begins again. We stayed outside listening to the same song for hours that day.

It was one of my favorite days.

Chapter 1

Sol

The past: The night the game began.

Location: The Cliff Walk: Grindelwald, Switzerland

Wetness spreads across my face as if it were tendrils of dread seeping through my pores. My eyes lose their gaze, scanning the ominous clouds above, seeking solace in an unyielding rain that refuses to come.

There will be no respite, no cleansing torrent to wash away this living nightmare.

If the heavens have yet to cry then why does my face feel moist? Blinking rapidly, I acknowledge the truth. The tears that stain my cheeks, betraying my inner turmoil, are my own doing.

Luna reaches out, her touch a fragile balm against the overwhelming darkness. She has always been the embodiment of strength, unyielding in the face of despair. Now, she asks something unimaginable of me. Imploring me to be strong.

It's almost comical. I've always hidden behind her. My flaw has been hiding and escaping reality. Now she wants me to face it. I'll have no shield; I must fight.

Her fingers, coated in my own tears, find her lips in a hauntingly intimate gesture. She kisses away the evidence of my shattered emotions, as if cherishing their precious memory, a clandestine intensity meant only for her. "You will emerge stronger, Sol. We all will," she whispers, her voice carrying the weight of defiance. "In the end, you will taste freedom."

But it won't taste sweet, not after what I have done.

Her words give me a tiny glimmer of hope, even though the shadows are all-consuming. Amidst the horrors surrounding me, I try to find a goal to cling to. I have to deceive myself, convincing my mind that lying to everyone I know will somehow lead to a positive outcome—a way to break free from the manipulators pulling the strings.

I'll deal with the repercussions later...if I survive. Maybe not surviving will be freedom in its own right. I won't tell Luna that. If I do, she would doubt me.

All I have wanted is for Luna to trust me with her dark deeds. I want to be her shield just as she has been mine.

Luna, my twin, has always been my courage, my rock, my everything.

As she reveals more of her plan, my mind starts spiraling. I feel adrift, like a soldier stranded in a relentless battle without any defenses. She tosses clues at me, fragments of a plan to keep us safe, but I know I'll have to figure out the rest alone. It's scavenging for survival, desperately searching for the tools to protect us.

I suppress a deranged smirk. I'm the ultimate Trojan horse, stealthily concealing the truth in the bowels of my mind. It's amusingly terrifying and comforting to be trusted with such a secret.

In one night, my life altered course. I'm the weapon they never saw coming.

How would that make you feel?

Powerful. Raw. Used. The abuser.

Does it matter?

No. Nothing matters when it comes down to survival. You will do anything.

Anything.

"How long have you been planning this?" I ask, my voice trembling with shock, disbelief... a hint of pride.

Luna smirks cunningly. Mischief twinkles in her eyes. "You don't want to know," she retorts.

"Yes, I do," I plead, trying to comprehend the enormity of her deceit.

A nonchalant shrug rolls off her elegant shoulders. "All our father ever wanted was for me to win," she says with a grin but her eyes look clouded. "All I ever wanted was for him and those controlling us to lose. I knew from the beginning that losing was my way to victory. I just had to play along until I reached the final race."

"You tricked Father this whole time?" *You lied to me, too.*

"Are you offended?" She scoffs. I know her question is a test of loyalty.

"No," I reply sternly, straightening my spine.

"Good." She chuckles darkly. "I never lied. I played his game perfectly. I reached the finish line, but I never promised to win. People see what they want to see, Sol. They paint lies. Distort reality. Don't make the same mistake. Keep your secrets tucked away from others," she leans closer to me, "but listen to the secrets as they whisper to you. It will keep you on track. Secrets are our greatest tools."

A web of deceit, intricately woven, and I never saw it coming.

She's a master manipulator, and I can't help but wonder what else she has hidden beneath her genetically engineered beauty.

She glances over her shoulder, "It's time."

Pump, pound, pump!

My head pounds as my blood pressure skyrockets. My heart beats so hard it wants to escape the confines of my ribs and display itself to her. *You have my heart, sister; please don't abandon it.*

Luna is going to roll the dice. The game is starting.

The weight of what I will witness next engulfs me, suffocating my every breath. I want freedom just as much as she does. Who am I to deny her peace?

So I swallow down my guilt and allow her to go. Ignoring the fear of losing her, of being left behind in this tumultuous world.

We will meet again.

She firmly grabs my hands. "Remember, Sol, never stop playing the game." she grins; it's genuine. It's such a rare grin that you want to cage or kill it. Like a prized hunt, you'd hang it on the wall to be admired, to brag to others that you managed to capture it.

A lone tear drips down my cheek, and I muster the courage to ask one more question. "What does this make me?"

"What do you mean?" she questions, her tone devoid of warmth, like the first sign fall has ended and winter is coming.

The toughest season to survive.

"How can I allow you to do this?" My lip trembles. "What does it say about me that I let my twin leave me in such a way? When they find out, they will hate me." *And I'll hate myself even more.*

"Stop being silly, Sol. When will you realize what others think of you doesn't matter," she replies calmly.

I feel like we are five years old again, and she just forced me to switch places with her so she could be the player in the game.

I whisper, "What do you think of me?"

She pauses, considering her words carefully.

"How do you want me to answer that?"

"I...I want to make you proud," I admit, my voice barely audible. I want to turn back time and not allow us to switch. I want to apologize for forcing you to become so devious and cunning.

"Proud?" She repeats the word as if it's new to her. "What a silly thing to seek. You should commit to achieving something that is longer-lasting than pride."

"Like freedom," I interject.

"No," she snorts. "Power." Her shoulders roll back as if reveling in the thought. "You're going to get a taste of it, Sol. Be careful; it's addicting. It distorts your mind. Stay focused." She taps her temple.

The cold wind leaves a frigid tingle over the dried-up tears on my cheeks.

Her eyes flicker to the security camera. "It's time to say goodbye." She admits. The red light clicks back on.

The recording has started.

Let the games begin.

As if this is all a fun game, she begins to skip towards the railing, Like the child she never could be. The red ribbon woven between her fingers dances in the wind as she swings her arms.

A dance of a devil.

She looks so at peace in the chaos she has constructed.

The strength that can come forth from darkness is awe-inspiring, like the universe. So much energy and mystery are still intangible to us but not to Luna.

"Luna!" I desperately call out, but my voice is reduced to a mere whisper, stifled by the overwhelming grip of despair. Why can't I talk?

My throat constricts, rendering me incapable of screaming or speaking, as if the weight of my emotions has silenced my very essence.

There is a yearning for her presence that begins to consume me. Desperate for the respite her strength provides, yet my voice remains trapped, a prisoner of my despair, echoing silently in the hollows of my soul.

What monster have I become to allow my twin to do this!

She has taken my voice with her.

A shell is left.

A puppet for her to manipulate.

"This is the only way." The wind carries her voice in a haunting whisper that pierces my ears.

She's so confident and assured.

How can she be so strong when she will end it all? Destroying everything we have ever known!

How the fuck can she be calm!

She takes her famous red ribbon and ties it to the railing. It's not an ordinary fabric typically used for ribbons. When closely examining the intricate weaving, it resembles a tightly woven net. A mixture between tulle and fine silk. Smooth and satiny, almost deceiving to the touch, as if it were a trap meant to trick the fingers.

I can no longer hear the wind. Only my heart beat as it tries to escape through my ears.

Luna's body is blocking the camera. If anyone is watching, it will look like I ran to try and grab my sister before she jumped.

It's a lie. I didn't try to stop her.

Those I feed my lies to will think I only grasped her red ribbon. A small souvenir.

You want to know what everyone will think? No, not that Luna isn't scared of heights.

See...that's me trying to find humor in all of this.

They will think she is crazy and depressed.

She is crazy; cunningly so. As beautifully disturbed as a Picasso painting.

And look how people praise his works. Maybe Luna will get the applause, the shocking gasps that steal the air from onlookers' lungs, that she deserves.

This is her only path to freedom and power. Her actions will destroy others and start a plague of grief that renders many players unable to focus.

It will also give false hope; they will think she isn't playing the game anymore. Little do they know the massive amount of pawns Luna has manipulated.

And what about me? What does this make me?

Where has my mental state gone... maybe I was never right from the beginning.

It's easier to believe that lie than accept the truth.

Perhaps, when our father designed me, when I was just a bunch of cells on a slide, he messed up. *Yes, I like that falsehood.*

He didn't make a perfect human. He made a perfect monster.

We're deadly. Dangerous.

If a normal human, one only edited by nature, can wage wars, kill millions, and create bombs that can end the world, what can an upgraded human do?

I look at my sister's back and think...an upgraded human can utterly alter the future.

And my sister will.

The science is out of pandora's box. The lid slid off the day she walked in the lab. It will never be contained again.

If I stop Luna, the world will drift into chaos; if I don't stop her, the world will grow mad.

Either way, I am on a sinking ship. I can only hope those who survive can swim and find a life boat. Find a path to protect the science my father created, so it is not abused.

The knot holding the ribbon to the railing begins to loosen from the wind; my cue. I must begin to act and paint the lies.

I push up to my feet like a robot.

I'm nothing more now.

I dare not exhale, my breath held captive, unable to escape until I clutch that ribbon.

One more fierce gust of wind, and the ribbon will be torn from my grasp forever.

My eyes are so fixed on the ribbon I don't see Luna leave me.

Blink. She is gone.

So simple yet so heart-stoppingly devastating.

Did it even happen?

It's odd, I don't remember my feet moving, but I'm standing right in front of the rail with the ribbon between my fingers.

Curling it so deep, I know my nails cut into my skin, but I don't feel it. I feel nothing.

Maybe that's best.

Time stops, and when it begins to play again, all that is left of my sister is the red hair ribbon between my fingers. My eyes look down; my body is stuck, clinging to the rails that didn't hold back her body.

I'm like a dead fly on a windshield, forced to go on the ride I never wanted to go on.

I have no options; even if I did, I would not take them. I owe everything to Luna.

Down.

Down.

Down.

My eyes narrow on a figure with blonde hair. I shouldn't look, but I can't look away.

The body looks like the birds Luna used to hunt down. An invisible arrow hit her and broke her wings. Her arrow inflicted deadly wounds. But it wasn't shot by her this time. The arrow that killed my twin was from Gabriel, from those that controlled her… from me! We are all to blame.

Why couldn't Gabriel give up his power and do as Luna asked?

He won the game our fathers were playing. Couldn't he have given this one request to Luna since she lost?

Was that too much to ask for?

They both wanted the same thing. To destroy the people who were controlling them. Gabriel and Luna each sought a different way to reach their end goal. Unable to bend a knee because they were raised to win.

Pressing my forehead into the metal fence until my flesh is forced to ripple around it, I blame them, the puppeteers. They molded Gabriel and Luna into such hell-bent creatures.

It's so silly, this entire game.

Yet we all are forced to continue to play because if we don't, *they*, whoever is controlling us, will kill us.

If it was you, would you continue to play knowing you at least get to live, or if the game was so crazy, would you end it as Luna did?

One choice makes you insane, and the other gives you peace.

I want to burn the world to the ground. I want to save Gabriel and the other pawns controlled by these mad men.

I want *them* all wiped out.

I can't do that because I have to play the game now.

So I cling to the railing, paint the lie. It's easy to paint grief and shock. That's how I feel.

The red ribbon is wrapped like a snake between my fingers. Its vibrant color helps me focus on the end goal Luna needs me to put into action. The dice have been tossed; the game has begun. My sister just took her turn, and now I must take my turn.

Tag, I'm it!

"It's all just a painted lie," I declare, the wind swallowing my secrets. Sealing my eyes shut, I whisper that secret in my mind repeatedly.

"I just have to stay focused. Allow my mind to whisper the secrets to me. Confessing the truth to only myself in the darkest of times. I can do this."

"I can do this?" I question, a flicker of doubt creeping in.

I press myself further into the fence, wishing it would just give so I could tumble down like Alice into a new wonderland.

"Yes," I swallow, trying to regain my resolve.

My mind has already become a battlefield.

Did Luna predict this? That I would be fighting a battle on two fronts?

I inhale and exhale until I'm nothing but a heartbeat, a machine.

I allow the secrets to be my anchor, guiding me through this labyrinth of deceit.

As I strive to survive and keep my sanity intact, I find myself painting the picture of insanity, all the while concealing the truth behind the painted lie.

The darkness within me and the torment around me intertwine, and I must find a way to navigate both without losing myself entirely.

Chapter 2

Sol

The present.

The oppressive ambiance of my hospital room makes suffocation seem like a more inviting prospect.

Gabriel's words hit me like a thunderclap, a deafening and jarring explosion in the room.

"Luna is dead!" he bellows.

God, his stunning face can morph into an enraged devil. Fists clenched so tightly that his knuckles turn white.

His tongue blisters with such raw emotions that it threatens to make me concede.

"Luna is dead, Sol," he repeats, the words like a relentless hammer striking the anvil of my consciousness. "She fucking killed herself!" He emphasizes each word as if they were a physical blow.

Stop!

His body trembles with anger, his chest heaving with each labored breath. His eyes burn with an intensity that sends a shiver down my spine.

He leans in closer, face inches from mine as if trying to imprint the harsh reality of his words onto my soul.

"She isn't coming back to save you," he says slowly, as if engraving it into my very bones.

Abandoned. Alone. At his mercy. *I get it!*

His words hang in the air like a heavy storm cloud, casting a dark and ominous shadow over the room. A tempest threatening to consume everything in its path.

My toes shift against the itchy hospital sheet; my skin feels grimy, but I focus on the deep inhale and exhale of his pained, labored breaths.

He's breathing; he is alive. That's why I did this.

His face is so painful that even the devil would feel guilty. Pain I helped cause.

I've been doing a lot of lying.

Eventually, one must confess. We all must face our day of judgment.

I never said today would be that day.

I look down at my bloodied hands. Deep crimson stains them. The reality of the murder I witnessed in the club last night comes rushing back.

I try to remove the stains. Chip off the guilt. The crusted red blood.

Not every stain can be removed. Some change the fabric of reality entirely.

"You've been hallucinating and talking to a ghost," Gabriel adds.

Just cut me with a knife, it would be less painful.

So what? I think defensively. *You've been hunting down and killing others. I hardly think my mind games are as heavy of a sin.*

I'm uncertain whether the spectacle of my deceit is a greater source of amusement for God or the Devil. One power contemplates how to disown me, while the other eagerly anticipates the opportunity to lay claim to my soul.

What will Gabriel do?

I know what you're thinking because I'm thinking it too. Poor girl, she has been talking to her own reflection, thinking it was her twin who left her.

Sad doesn't begin to describe it, nor does pathetic.

Grief manifests in many ways. Some ways are healing, some...a different definition of coping.

Yes, I'll admit I did hallucinate my twin.

Why? That's a two sided answer. One side will make you cringe and the other gasp.

Reason number one behind my interactions with a hallucination. Simple. Luna told me to. *Yes, I know, it's quite the confession to drop. Brace yourself because I'm just getting started.*

The objective? To portray myself as unhinged, lost in the throes of insanity and grief.

The plan was ingenious – by donning this facade, I'd effectively be rendered harmless, not even a blip on the radar of potential threats. It was all part of the intricate tapestry Luna wove.

In the end, everything fell into place just as Luna had foreseen.

I was left to navigate my grief through my art, far from the clutches of my father's laboratories. No longer a pawn in Manus Dei's game, I was cast aside, deemed unwanted – a perfect Trojan horse waiting on the sidelines, as Luna had so masterfully envisioned.

Reason number two: it was comforting. *Did you expect me to say something else?*

After everything I have been through, I think I deserve some solace.

During those fabricated conversations, I felt despair, and I allowed the figment of my imagination to feel my misery. Purged it upon a mirage.

Now, at this point, I know what Gabriel will think once he discovers the reality of all my lies.

By the way, he hasn't solved anything yet.

In the end, when he realizes the truth, he might think I'm a cruel bitch. Heck, he might think I give Luna a run for her genetically-engineered money.

I'm not! *Trust me, yes, I know that's hard to do since I've been lying, but I will confess the truth.*

Just not yet.

I can't.

Here's where things will take a turn. Yes, I've been Luna's pawn, and I've been doing a great job. A better job than I ever initially believed.

I knew I would witness fucked up shit. *Heck, all I had to do was look in the mirror!* After all, history is peppered with innovations born from the depths of adversity.

I didn't foresee the turn of events I'd bear witness to last night.

It wasn't just the murder; it was the *joy* someone got out of it. The joy other players feel as they play the game.

This game shouldn't be enjoyable.

If it is, then why stop playing?

They have to stop playing!

I was well aware that casualties were inevitable, and some, frankly, deserved their fate.

Last night changed everything, though. It was like a thunderbolt jolted me, frying all my assumptions to a crisp.

Suddenly, everything shifted. And you know what ticks me off the most? I wasn't given a single heads-up, not even a damn breadcrumb trail or a cryptic song as a hint.

I thought I saw Luna ruthlessly cut open Gabriel's throat. It was as if reality itself had been severed. There was pure ecstasy on Luna's face when she committed the act too.

But it wasn't Luna.

I can't begin to comprehend the enormity of deceit woven by Luna's hand. It's a tapestry of lies so intricate that even the most elaborate Persian rug would blush at its audacious pattern.

Luna's intentions weren't merely for me to put on a performance; she demanded that I become the part itself. To display genuine shock and profound horror, as if I had just witnessed the agonizing demise of the boy I'd shared my upbringing with, a demise brought about by his own affection, no less.

Pure shock.

Horror.

Live in the moment.

It was absolutely genius.

Admittedly, the trauma of witnessing a life extinguished forced me into a profound mental rift. But let's be real – who wouldn't have cracked under such weight?

I'm genetically engineered but I'm still human.

I can't ever allow myself to find joy in these games. That is where I draw a line in the never-changing quicksand, and if that line blurs, I will redraw it again and again.

The true definition of insanity. Repetition. *But if that shoe fits then I'll lace those fuckers up! This is a game, a race, after all.*

I've been quite the puppet in this game I never imagined I'd have to play.

And guess what?

I've played my role perfectly; painting all the lies my twin sister needed me to. I've been her little enabler.

I haven't been perfect, contrary to what my father wanted. I'll admit, I've been blind and deaf to the secrets that whisper to me deep in my mind. It hurt too much to confront them, so I chose to look the other way.

Continual turning just brings you right back to the start.

I have to face them now.

Gabriel won't let me escape the truth.

The consequences are searing through me like a scorching flame. Blistering. I can feel the burns of my complacency eating away at me.

Having a twin is like living with a virus inside your body that you can never fight. A virus needs a host to survive. One twin needs the other; our co-dependence is a weakness and our strength. Two heads are better than one...or so they say.

This head thinks it's time for a change. Don't get me wrong; I'm still going to play the game my sister wanted.

I have to.

There is no escape.

I just won't be the willing pawn and when I see a chance to change the game I will.

Yes, I have to end the game.

Me.

I must make Gabriel and Luna's pawns see that this power play is a cancer. If I fail, we all will just end up killing each other. It's up to me to fix us all.

Don't ask me how I will do this.

I have no idea, but I am a genetically engineered genius, after all. I will find a solution to the chaos. *Even if it means creating more chaos.*

One step at a time, just like a painting, stroke by stroke, the picture will become clear to me.

I hug myself, rubbing the sides of my exposed arms. I'm deep in the guts of the game. Feel the grime coating my skin. I'll never be clean after this, but we all will be freer.

That counts for something right?

I have to see the glass half full. Light at the end of the tunnel bullshit.

I swallow. It rolls down easily.

The lies are simple. Horrifyingly so.

Gabriel has no idea. None of them do.

Everything is going to plan.

Gabriel thinks he has all the power. He won our fathers' game, he is the better human, but that doesn't mean I'm weaker.

I'm stronger than he ever assumed.

Poor Gabriel has believed the falsehoods I've painted. I don't mean that cruelly. I'm trying to save him too. I hope he realizes that one day. After all, he's playing the same game now, being cruel to break me down; then he will pick me back up again.

Manipulation 101.

I must keep going, but I won't play by Luna's twisted rules. I won't be her puppet anymore. After the murder I witnessed, I know all the players need saving. I must draw a line, even if my morals and ethics are as small as a grain of sand.

A haunting memory flashes in my mind, a neck slit open wide. Red, so much red.

Forceful too.

Who would have thought death could breathe so much force into extinguishing its self?

I instinctively reach up, covering my own neck, feeling the weight of guilt that could be sliced open next.

I won't witness that again. Pretending to be Luna was one thing, but I'm not her. I feel the emotions, digest them, and they haunt me.

What's the point of being free if I'm trapped in the torment of my own mind?

It's a detail hidden in the contract that claimed my soul. The devil would be proud. The ultimate trick. Freed but caged. Tormented.

I part my lips, wanting to apologize to Gabriel. It's natural to seek forgiveness.

I can't. *Not yet...*

A haunting song echoes within the nightmare of my thoughts – "The Sound of Silence." Luna would have deemed this song profoundly fitting for the present moment.

My lips close with a tremble.

I must keep hurting him. More lies must be spun. I have to save him from himself too. We are all linked in this labyrinth of games.

The scene at the club was a brilliant plan Luna devised. I truly had my moment of insanity. I didn't have to lie or pretend.

It happened.

More clones I didn't know existed are slowly being picked off. Now I must try to remain alive. The time has come for Gabriel to take me, as Luna foretold. It's like watching a twisted play unfold, everything happening just as she predicted.

Did she foresee that I would turn on her too? *The plot thickens.*

I recall what she told me the last night I saw her on the Cliff Walk,

"Gabriel is phase three. Gabriel will try to protect you by using you."

"Using me how?"

Luna shakes her head, "That doesn't matter yet. You'll understand when the time comes. This game has many faces, and he is one of them. You're going to push him; one day, he will take away your freedom. He's going to take you but don't fight him too hard. Use him like an ally. Help him because it will also help me."

I blink, trying to focus as Gabriel corners me in the hospital room. What the hell is going to happen next?

It can't possibly be worse than the club, can it?

My mind races, desperately seeking any hint or nightmare that might give me a clue. I soon realize my mistake. This game is like my twin – constantly evolving, changing, and adapting. There are no rules, no predictable patterns.

I force myself to relax my shoulders for a brief moment, but quickly tense them again so Gabriel doesn't suspect anything.

Now that I know there are no rules, it doesn't matter if I seem insane. It doesn't matter what people think of me. The path to winning this twisted game might be the road to madness, and that realization sparks a chilling smile on my lips. I might be ahead of them all.

Gabriel notices the smile, his worry and confusion evident. In one swift move, he shoves me against the hospital bed, hovering over my face. I can't help but look into those blue eyes that once betrayed my sister and yet tried desperately to protect her.

Cutting no matter which end you grasp.

The tip of the needle filled with a sedative in his hand brushes against my exposed thigh. He's going to drug then cage me.

I grin wider, not at him but at my sister, who I pray is watching from somewhere beyond. "You killed her," That's a lie, but I speak it to hurt him. Play the part that I hate him. I can't just suddenly act one hundred percent sane and tell him I'm going to fix everything. I still need to play the broken puppet. The broken girl he wants to fix because I am the image of my twin, the woman he couldn't fix.

Grief etches on his forehead. Demons dance in his eyes.

He handles grief by giving into more darkness. *It's easier that way.*

"I killed Ethan," he replies.

Lifeless in his grasp I think of Ethan. Another pawn my sister used now killed.

I'm not surprised. A sick part of me is relieved. Ethan was suffering; maybe it's better this way. He wanted out of Manus Dei's grasp and now he is.

That's the perfect lie I tell my mind to believe.

"I will kill everyone you contacted. Everyone, Sol." *Everyone? That's not fair. Only those involved should be on the chopping block.*

"No," I whisper, my voice barely audible.

Oh, but he will use them against me. I see it in his eyes, the calculating gleam. Hazel and Wes are now leverage over my head, pawns in this dangerous game, and I can't bear the thought of what Gabriel might do to them.

"You will accept reality, Sol."

"No," I'll play along. I can't cave too easily, or he will suspect something. Naturally, I will become his puppet because it's part of Luna's plan and because I will not see harm come to Hazel or Wes.

"I'll hunt them all down. All your new friends."

I act out now. This part is easy.

A scream burns my throat as it escapes. It feels good.

Reaching up I claw at his face trying to tear off his handsome features and see the devil lurking within.

Marcus, the guard, rips my hands back. "Fucking bitch. I'm going to enjoy killing all of you." He sneers.

That's when it hits me. This guard is working for Manus Dei, not Gabriel. He's referring to the clones.

I look at Gabriel, his eyes filled with hate, nothingness, and determination as he gazes at the guard. Gabriel truly despises this man.

Interesting.

Those ocean-blue eyes turn towards me like a swelling tide. I saw his darkness when we were kids. Luna held the key to that cage. She dropped the key when she left us both. Gabriel found it and unleashed his terror. We both turned to madness, but it affected us differently.

The problem with the game is you have to make sacrifices. Luna did; she sacrificed herself. I gave up my sanity, and Gabriel relinquished his control.

Gabriel's hands grab me, digging deeper as if trying to find my soul, which isn't there anymore. "I did kill her," he confesses.

The truth is, he never got to kill my sister with his bare hands. I can see the nerve she struck. Her actions might have broken me, but I glued myself together, knowing Luna's pawns would find those who abused us. He hasn't healed, though; instead, he's become something so twisted I'm not sure I can calculate what he is capable of.

He's starting to feel.

That's not necessarily good. If he feels sorrow, then he can crave vengeance. If he feels guilt, he can create violence.

His eyes cloud darker than the depths of the uncharted ocean. *Somethings shouldn't be explored.*

Terror rises in my throat. Gabriel isn't seeing me; he's doing the same thing he accused me of. Hallucinating Luna's presence, "I did kill her," he whispers again. That is the narrative he weaves, a comforting fabrication to shield himself from the painful truth.

Deep down, a whispered secret resonates within his mind, revealing the bitter reality that the love of his life has chosen a different path, a road that makes him the enemy and her the mutineer.

The tides have turned. I'm caught in the middle of this intricate game, where love and betrayal intertwine.

Everyone seems to be fighting, choosing a side between passion and dishonor.

What is the trick to winning the game?

Maybe I don't need to choose a side to win?

Perhaps you can have your cake and eat it too. Maybe, just maybe, to win, you need to be both the hero and the villain.

That's why Luna chose me, isn't it, Luna? Me and not another clone.

I can embody both; it's as simple as painting a picture. Everyone interprets it differently; they experience varying emotions toward it. Only the artist knows the truth.

In the end, it's just a painting.

In the end, it's just a role to play.

In the end, it's nothing more than a collection of brush strokes, combining truths and lies to craft the perfect image.

Chapter 3

Sol

"I did kill her." Gabriel repeats, only this time his cruelty slips. Pain and regrets lodge in his throat.

He's feeling which means cracking. *Luna never cracked.*

Does it make me a ruthless bitch to admit it feels good to know I'm not the only one who can crumble?

His blonde hair is like a burnt golden halo, but he is no angel; he is a fallen demon created by god and summoned by the devil. He still feels and one day I hope he feels forgiveness towards me.

The room is silent; even the old heater in the window seems to have stopped humming. The lights flicker overhead, but I don't blink, nor does Gabriel. He knows I'm not ignorant anymore. I stepped into the unknown and found the monsters; the other opponents in the game. I'm willing to compete against him, even in a simple staring contest.

We are locked in a match, head to head. Gabriel wants to see me break over his words, and I will not let him. I'm no longer going to be the predictable player he wants or Luna demands.

I grin, and my fingernails dig into my palm until my skin breaks. A joyful laugh fills the room. Gabriel and I are frozen as Marcus, the guard holding my hands captive, laughs at the admittance of my twin's death.

I expect Gabriel to join Marcus in the boastful affair. I watch his lips which should be grinning any second.

No smile emerges. Instead, his face reddens, and the vein in his forehead swells like steam billowing from a boiling kettle. His eyes remain the only part of his expression that shifts as he pivots, directing his focus toward Marcus. The intensity of his gaze leaves no doubt: he's going to kill him, slowly.

Those blue eyes hauntingly look back towards me. A unspoken emotion.

He still loves Luna.

My eyes water. *I do too.*

He mouths another hidden message to me, "Don't be silly." Then, his hand begins to move.

What is he up to?

A sudden chill runs down my spine, causing the hairs on my arms to stand on end. My heart quickens its pace, thumping against my chest like a child throwing a fit.

Swiftly, Gabriel rises, distancing himself from my face, his hand holding the needle glides along the bed. His thumb exerts pressure on the needle's tip, producing a distinct snap as he breaks it off from the syringe.

Marcus doesn't hear the needle break. The fool.

What is happening? Why did he break the needle?

He's rolling the dice in this twisted game. Making a move.

I inhale sharply. Marcus thinks it's from fear. It's not. Anticipation is sweet on my tongue. You see, I know I'll play a crucial role, but as I glance at Marcus, a gut feeling tells me this fool won't. I'm looking at yet another dead pawn in this absurd game.

Gabriel brings the syringe to the side of my thigh and presses it to my skin. His blue eyes dig so deep into mine. I feel like he is reaching into my mouth and grabbing my tongue so I can not utter a word.

He needs me to stay quiet. Not purge the truth that I know.

So I do. In order to trick them all I need to continue to be the broken puppet. The unnoticeable one.

I feel the liquid of the sedative run down my leg. Without the needle, he can't penetrate my skin. The injection is useless. A trick.

Marcus's eyes start to leave mine as they slowly drift toward Gabriel's hand. "Fucking hold her, Marcus. She is trying to move." He hisses.

That's a lie. I wasn't trying to move. Gabriel doesn't want Marcus to know he isn't giving me the injection.

I jerk my arms against Marcus's hold to act out the falsehood. He quickly moves his face back to mine and readjusts his grip.

Gabriel stands, rounds the bed, and pushes Marcus out of the way. His hands wrap around mine, replacing Marcus's. "The sedative is kicking in." He fibs to Marcus. "Go tell the others we are ready for transport."

Marcus nods and begins to leave. "Marcus," Gabriel calls. "I don't want any fuck-ups during the ride; double-check everything. If anything happens, if you overlooked anything…." He lets his threat hang in the air like a noose swaying in the wind or, in this case, a snare. It's a trap, and Marcus will walk directly into it.

He nods. Less confident this time, "Yes, Sir."

Both Gabriel and I listen as his footsteps fade. The elevator opens and then closes from down the hall. We both hear the gears in the motor begin to lower the elevator. Then once I know we are alone, I speak.

I pull my hands out of Gabriel's hold and sit up. He allows me to. "What game are you playing?" I eye the broken needle on the bed sheet.

"Finally woken up. Snapped out of your mental lapse, I see," He mocks. "If only you could have done it sooner, you wouldn't be in this mess."

"I'm sorry if it took me longer to mourn my sister than you did."

He stills. His eyes peel up my body till they reach mine, skinning me alive.

I feel his loathing over my statement. He is grieving Luna, he just shows it differently.

I want to feel his hate. I deserve it. I welcome it because I'm not just Luna's puppet.

No, not anymore.

I'm her little monster. I might not have murdered with my own two hands but the deeds I have done…they are chilling. Heart stopping so.

And Gabriel doesn't even know the half of it yet.

I lick my lips and inhale, trying to summon my courage. I've waited for this moment. For months, I've wanted to ask him, "Why?"

He leans closer to me. His hand reaches out and I curse myself when I flinch. He doesn't strike me. He was never violent towards me in that way, but I can't trust anything or anyone now.

"Why haven't I cracked, acted out like a petulant child, why haven't I given them a reason to kill us all? Is that the question you seek, Sol?" He drops the needle into the trash, then turns to me.

I snort. "It's a start."

"You think this is a game." His jaw clenches. "Gambling your life for answers you don't even understand."

I throw my hands in the air. "Then help me understand so I don't keep breaking." I stride forward and grab his chest, digging my nails in deep. "Yes, I do think it is a game." I sink my nails deeper. He doesn't flinch. *Where is your blackened heart?* "A game you, yes you, and Luna trapped me in."

"Always the victim," Gabriel scolds me.

I shove him away. That's his mistake thinking I can only be a victim. It's a mistake that will cost him the game because in the end I'll change spots. A victim no more.

He laughs. It's heartless but full of pain all at once. "You've kept me busy, you know," his words sliced through the air, a mix of frustration and cruelty. His hand press his shirt flat from my claw marks. "Cleaning up the mess you've left in your descent into madness. But isn't that what you wanted, Sol? To divert my attention away from winning the game, from fixing everything. Congratulations, you've succeeded. My focus is solely on you now." That's a threat if I ever heard one.

"Maybe I wanted your attention because I don't have Luna's." I dare.

His eyes assess me anew. The room shrinks smaller as I watch the calm rise and fall of his chest.

He shakes his head, but a grin tugs on his lips, "I explicitly warned you to stay away from the game, but you couldn't help yourself, could you? And now, we're in this mess. You've fucked it all up. But don't worry; I'll utilize your blunder." A folded set of clothing catches his attention on the chair beside the medical waste bin. His grip tightens as he picks it up.

"There's not much time for explanations," he snaps. "Get dressed. When Marcus returns, you're going to pretend you're asleep. For your own damn sake, Sol, you better not fucking flinch during the trip. If Marcus suspects something then you can add witnessing another murder in less than twenty-four hours to your memory."

Our eyes lock. *What has this game done to you?*

He glances away from me, gripping the clothes tighter. "You keep painting me as the villain, but I'm not. There's someone far more sinister out there. Someone who makes me look like a saint. They're willing to wipe us out, erase everything. Your notions of madness, of good and evil, of testing limits and making sacrifices – they're about to be rewritten."

I toss my hands up, "If you truly didn't want to be cast as Luna's villain, then why didn't you just yield to her?" My mind feels exhausted, and I still have so much yet to do, "It's painfully clear, Gabriel, you're still holding on to her memory. Even when Marcus taunted her name, you wanted to strangle him. You're still in love with a specter, a mere ghost." *So am I.*

A bitter sob escapes me. His face remains unphased. "How could you let her down like this? Push her so far from your trust? This mess – it's all on your shoulders. You had the chance to mend it, to make things right." My anger, dormant until now, finally erupts.

I know it isn't entirely fair to heap all the blame onto him, but the release feels cathartic. My breathing grows ragged as I deliver the final blow. "And why, for heaven's sake, couldn't you have relinquished that power? Why not obliterate it all, just for her? You two could've forged something new, a fresh beginning. Instead, you're left with nothing and no one. Believe me, Gabriel, I'm well-acquainted with the gnawing ache of loneliness."

"I didn't tell her to jump!" He roars. Alone tear falls from his blue eyes.

I'm sorry. Hurting you numbs my pain and I need a break, Gabriel.

"But your lust for power did," I jab.

"I was never after power, you silly fool," he retorts, his back straightening. The tear seems to evaporate off his cheek as he regains his composure. "I was after control."

"You wanted to control her."

"Someone had to," he utters with cold cruelty. He runs his hand through his hair, then wipes the sweat off his forehead.

I nod. "Someone did have to. Someone needed to control you too. You both trapped each other. Now you have no bounds. It's a dangerous world, Gabriel. Be careful."

His eyes narrow, and his head tilts slowly, as if he's sizing me up. He's calculating me now, wondering why I had been acting so strangely in my grief, questioning if it was all true.

I might have misstepped just now. So I pivot, taking a deep breath and urging myself to stay focused.

I approach Gabriel until his shadow consumes me, "Why did you look at Marcus that way? Why do you want me to think you are helping me?"

He jabs his finger at me, "I am helping you. I'm trying to protect you, but you keep stepping in front of a bullet." He shoves the clothes at me and lowers his torso, so he is looking me in the eye. "I did want to kill Marcus. I. Will." He confidently states with a wicked grin. A regal beast. "I wanted to kill him right there." He points to the side of the bed where Marcus stood.

"So why didn't you." My fingers dig into the clothes like a bulletproof vest.

He snorts, "The last time you witnessed someone being killed in front of you, you had a mental breakdown."

My heart palpitates.

I noticed the scar on the clone's eyebrow. I should have known then it was all a game.

"He had a scar." I whisper. How many more of us, our reflections, are there in the world? "The scar was on his eyebrow. It was small, but I noticed it."

"Of course you did." He snickers. "You've always noticed too much, but now you whisper the secrets that should have remained hidden. When you voice something, Sol, you must take responsibility for it. Now you will. This is my game; you will be my key to ending it." He shakes his head in dissatisfaction as he evaluates me now. It makes my toes curl in like a snail that wants to be hidden. I cast my eyes down at the hospital title floor, unable to hold his glare as he speaks. "You're so much like your father. He created the science and ignored how it was being used. Like a commissioned piece of art, he only cared about painting it. Dorian never questioned why the painting was required or where it would hang. It's time to wake up, Sol. The science we designed has shaped the world, and we must ensure humanity doesn't destroy everything with it. The only way to do that isn't to destroy Manus Dei but rather to take control of it."

It's a compelling speech. I have to give him credit.

What he doesn't know is that I am taking responsibility for the science I created by playing my sister's game. I am paying her back for protecting me as a child.

I'm also going to protect all of them from what we created. Ourselves.

My lips tremble when I speak," You knew your clone was going to die," *Can't you see you need help, Gabriel?*

Without betraying a hint of emotion, he confesses, "I hoped."

I hug the clothes to my chest and step back. *Oh, Gabriel. How am I going to fix you?*

I remember what Luna told me on the Cliff Walk,

"I don't trust someone who could kill themself, Sol. Gabriel will continue to do that because he is trying to trick them. I won't kill for them to destroy them. Gabriel doesn't want it to end. He wants it to continue. He wants to take their power and make it his own."

"You have killed our clones before." I whisper the secret. "You betrayed Luna when you killed the clones that looked like us. Would you trust someone who could kill themself?" I voice Luna's words to him.

That's what pushed her over the edge.

I understand it now.

"Would *you* trust someone who could kill themself?" He rebuttals.

Ouch. That hurt. My throat begins to close from his verbal slap.

"The clone in the club wasn't the first." I swallow and continue, "That is what drove Luna to madness. You have killed other Reflections of yourself before. Luna told me they only wanted to spare a few of us after you won. You agreed and killed the others."

"I won the game. There were no boundaries or morals. Luna knew the rules. This is war now, Sol. Soldiers die, and some deserve to. Stop thinking like a normal human. You're not!"

"You both were in love! You could have found a way to work together. You could have hidden away the clones Manus Dei wanted you to kill. But you didn't. You went along with their request, making them think you were the perfect winner. You both wanted similar things, Gabriel. You wanted to be safe and free from Manus Dei. Why couldn't you agree with Luna." I snap. "How can you kill someone you love?" I shake my head.

"How can you kill someone you love?" he mimics like the perfect puppet. "Ask Luna that. She killed you, after all, didn't she?" He points at me, his eyes judging my current state. "The old Sol is dead. Twisted and fucked in the head now. Your sanity is there, but your insanity," he hits the side of his head, and I jerk, "which is controlled by your memories of Luna, is stronger."

You swallowed down my lies whole.

His fists shake by his side. Hands that have killed. Murdered his own face. "We need the power to keep us safe. Luna failed to see that. Manus Dei's name has so much significance in this world that it can tip it off its axis. I can't rebrand. I cannot destroy it all. I don't have time." Desperation traces his features.

He's scared.

If the big bad wolf is worried, then you better bet your ass I am. Scared shitless that somehow I will fail and not be able to end the game. Terrified that I will fail and hand it all over to the wrong player.

He speaks slower now, "Vultures will swarm and try to fight for the remains of Manus Dei's power. I have to contain it. That is the logical alternative. Use the name but change its aesthetics and ideals."

My eyes bounce around the room. I've fallen so deep into the rabbit hole I don't know which direction is up anymore.

His point sounds valid but his path to reaching it isn't.

He relents. Shoulders roll in. His armor is cracking. Showing signs of wear and tear. "I was never going to kill her or you."

Wow! I jerk. Is that his saving grace? "But what about the others that look like Luna and me?"

He shakes his head, "You'll never understand. Some of us were made to be monsters. Some needed to die." He pounds his chest, "I did what had to be done, Sol. Not every monster can be tamed, and some can not be caged. I did kill some of us. Some looked like me, and others looked like Luna. I had to win. I had to win to keep Luna safe. Luna thought I couldn't draw a line." His blue eyes look down. Guilt. He grinds his teeth as he tries to fight away his demons.

Just how many has he killed? "Can you?" I question.

Dear God, what did Manus Dei make him do?

He tilts his head and looks me up and down. Digging deep into my mind. *Don't look there, Gabriel. You won't like the lies but the truth will be even more disturbing.* My mental state, my inner turmoil. Sanity versus insanity. Grief versus coping.

"You're still alive." He replies.

"Why?" I'm not sound of mind and it's clear that other clones who had been corrupted by upgrades were put down. I remind Gabriel of the love he lost. I echo all his pain every time he looks at me.

It should be simple. I should be killed.

So why haven't I been?

What details did Luna leave out? Why do Luna and Gabriel need me?

Why me?

Chapter 4

Sol

There's no point in asking Gabriel why he needs me. I mean, come on, it's like asking a cat why it's being mysterious – you'll just get a blank stare.

But hey, who needs his reply anyway? I'm more than capable of figuring it out all on my own. That's what I've been doing.

Gabriel parts his lips. A mere second of hesitation, a chink in his armor. It's a peculiar turn of events, like witnessing the devil himself having a peaceful chat with God.

That's a fantastic point; God and the devil were once on the same side, just as Gabriel and I were.

"I want to be better. I'm too selfish to stop creating the science. It's too addicting." He releases a cold laugh. "I want to keep the world evolving. We have to. The only way to keep going forward is to keep Manus Dei on top. If they fall, a war of genetics will start, Sol. That's why I have to keep Manus Dei intact. I have to control them, make them better, so no one else suffers like we did." His words slip from his lips in a hushed whisper. A confession.

And you know what? I'm on the verge of actually buying into it.

Well, fine, I already have.

Unlike Luna, who's all about veiled enigmas and cryptic tunes, Gabriel's got a straightforward approach. He's upfront, raw, and in your face. It's just that he's got more faces than a Rubik's Cube, and I'm stuck deciphering which one is his "true" face.

Why so many confessions?

I tilt my head. Is he offering an olive branch. Perhaps he hopes it will push me to his side.

It might.

My arms are yanked wide, and my skin feels like it's about to split. One end, it's Luna pulling, and at the other, it's Gabriel. Two damn genetically engineered clones that I'm inexplicably attached to.

It's almost obscene, the way I adore Luna and Gabriel despite the trail of betrayals and exploitations they've left behind. If I didn't care for them this much, I'd throw in the towel. But no, they've been my twisted protectors during some of my most vulnerable moments.

So, here I am, caught in this absurd tug-of-war, unable to play favorites. You see, it's like being a parent who can't abandon their star-child. I can't forsake Gabriel, no matter how much I resent his hand in Luna's dramatic exit. Luna isn't the victim either; she is just as guilty as Gabriel.

Duty's a demanding mistress, and it's got me tight in its grip. I've got to offer a hand to both of them, no matter how messed up that sounds. I'm going to save us all.

How do I help them both without betraying my morals and having to commit the crimes they have?

"Better," I echo.

Manus Dei deemed Gabriel the better human. Luna wanted better too. That is why my sister started this game.

Gabriel, Luna and Manus Dei think better is having more control over others.

It's not control they should seek. It's an end. The big ta-da, over the hill, light at the end of the tunnel.

They think control will end the games but power is just another game. Never ending. The sad irony is they were only ever taught how to play these games.

Someone has to teach them how to end it.

Someone like me.

I thought I was going to be the flawed hero, the perfect pawn to help defeat Manus Dei. That wasn't what Luna wanted. I see that now. That is why she has lead me into the depths of this dark world.

I was never meant to be the hero.

I was molded to be the villain.

***

The night the game began.

Location: The Cliff Walk: Grindelwald, Switzerland.

"You are not God, Luna," I stress. "You don't have to do this alone."

"I'm not," she deadpans. "I have you and others doing it for me."

I exhale. I can't crack her armor. No matter how hard I try, she has made up her mind. She has only confessed partial truths to me about why she is determined to do what she is about to do.

I can't stop her. If I try, she will completely shut me out. I lose her either way.

So, I have to exert blind trust. It's what I always have had to do when it comes to trusting my twin. So far, it's kept me alive.

So far...

I understand why this game has to be played. We can't be controlled any longer. That's not all, though. There is so much more she isn't telling me. It's her style. She never reveals everything.

Where is the fun in that?

A war is coming for us all. Everyone, even those who are not playing the game. One day we all have to play. World war has a way of affecting absolutely everything.

Luna has planned everything out. So many hidden details, like the Mona Lisa's smile. You can't stop wondering, watching, holding your breath.

What is she thinking?

I don't want her to die as a martyr or a memory whose image is painted and hung on the wall for viewers to be left guessing about her true intentions.

But I fear that when the game is finished, that is exactly what will happen. Some factions will hate her, while others will praise her.

She shrugs as she turns her head to look off into the distance. Her body language seems at ease. When we first arrived here, she seemed manic. I thought she had gone insane. It was so unlike her that I didn't know what to do. Luna has never acted out of control. Emotional.

It makes me wonder if it was the truth or a lie she painted for me to believe. To push me into being her puppet. As if I needed a push. I owe everything to her.

I grab her hands, needing to feel her touch to stop my mind from spinning. They are cold but dry. No sign of worry.

"I wish we could have more time." I whisper as I grip her hand in mine. Time I used to talk to Gabriel. To see what else I could uncover. To discover if there was a less dangerous way.

She scoffs, "There's no saving me." She keeps her head facing away from me but it's her eyes that pivot towards me. Like a silent plea I don't fully understand yet.

"You're not the villain, Luna."

She laughs. It sounds dead. "You know what is funny? Heroes and villains are the same. They are fighting to save the world. The hero's world versus the villain's." She rolls her eyes. "Everyone praises the hero for saving the world but did they ever think that maybe the villain was trying to protect the world too? The villain just envisioned a different world to save. A new future. Things are broken here,"

She drops my hands and points out to the landscape. "I might be the villain, but I am trying to save them all. If Gabriel's side wins, the world will continue to break. The power will corrupt him. Sometimes the hero is so blinded by the praise he can't see his faults. I'm going to show them their faults."

Maybe if I could talk to Gabriel, I could help change his mind. I bite down on my tongue instead. Whatever has passed between Gabriel and her is done. Luna made up her mind; it seems Gabriel has too.

She begins to stand.

That's the problem. There are too many games that are about to collide. Luna doesn't have time to talk to Gabriel; I don't either. The dice are thrown, and now gravity is pulling them down. They land on the game board, telling my sister it is her turn. The next roll will end up being my turn.

The games have begun.

Some will lose.

Others will lose more.

The hero will triumph in some battles, while the villain will emerge victorious in others. It's a seesaw of power and conflict, a relentless struggle where the line between right and wrong blurs, leaving us all grappling with the shades of gray in between.

I look down at my now empty hands. I physically will no longer have my sister.

I have to play.

I must win; I must lose less.

I turn my palms over; I'm unsure if I am this game's hero or villain.

Only time will tell.

***

What are you, Gabriel?

The villain or the hero? Both? None at all?

Time will reveal your true intentions, just as it will mine.

Gabriel rolls his shoulders, his blue eyes attempting to soften, a challenging task for him. He only revealed his heart to Luna, and now he's striving to show me the broken pieces, hoping I won't resist him.

"You can't slip back into your mind. Paint lies that make you feel better. There will be no room for errors, Sol. One wrong move, and you'll be the next dead clone. Do you understand me?"

"So I had one mental slip." I run my tongue over my teeth.

"One?" His eyes narrow.

"One, two."My left shoulder raises, "Does it matter?"

"Yes! When others are monitoring you, it matters!" He yells.

My right-hand curls into a fist. The dried blood on my skin cracks under the pressure. "What was I supposed to do?" I bite my trembling lip, revealing my true pain to him. "I thought I had just watched Luna murder you. I was shocked." Shocked she didn't give me a heads up about what I would witness.

"You slipped. Cracked. Gave them the perfect reason to have you killed." He grabs my hand and uncurls it. Eyes lingering on the blood, "Play wiser," he murmurs as he jerks my hand in a plea, "Play. Play every side, all sides, every angle." He squeezes my fingers with a force that feels like a desperate attempt to prevent me from jumping off a cliff; a grip determined to keep me from falling into the abyss of uncertainty and danger.

"You can't back out now," his eyes fixated on the tattoo inked on my wrist. "I can't always be there to save you now. Everyone is playing for a different outcome. Luna didn't understand why I had to keep the power. All she saw was red. I couldn't make her see the other colors we could mix into it." His thumb brushes over my tattoo, and disappointment fills his eyes as he traces the ink.

It's a gentle touch. Did he touch Luna like this?

"Gabriel."

His distant eyes blink. He imagined my wrist was Luna's.

When his eyes clash with mine again, I see the smallest light of hope, like dawn's early light trying to reach the ocean's depths.

"She forced you to paint her color, but you can change that, mix in a new color, and change the image's focal point. After all, you're an artist."

I see what you're doing, Gabriel. You want me to think I have a choice. But I don't. You will use me regardless. It's easier for you if I come willingly and not kicking and screaming.

Luna never gave me a choice, either. It's not in their nature. Predators don't offer options.

Do you know what the villain would do? Keep playing Luna's game, be Gabriel's willing pawn, keep my enemies close and those I love and want to protect trapped in my web of lies. Then, when the finish line is in sight, I will turn the table against them both.

Wow, it's startlingly easy to think like the villain. In a way, the villain and the hero think the same. They will go to great lengths to get what they want. A villain just goes further. I just needed to push myself. I'm not scared anymore, not after what I have seen.

It's time to end this; after all, Luna and Gabriel started this game because they felt. Yes, they felt. They were raised differently from me. Molded to be cruel. Sculpted to be cutthroat.

Maybe that's a bad analogy after what I witnessed last night. Or maybe it's the perfect analogy.

Somehow, along the way, they became sentient. They fell in love. Unbeknownst to those who created them, the allure of a crown and the ruling seat would not be enough for Luna or Gabriel. They wanted more.

Now I want more.

I don't just want my freedom. That would be ignorant, and I'm no longer the clone I once was. I don't want Manus Dei's power, and I'm not silly enough to think I can destroy all the science. I want my family not to be tangled in this web of falsehoods and frolics.

I only see one way to do that.

Chapter 5

Sol

Have you ever felt trapped in a web with a predator looming closely? Well, that's what this scene looks like. Me, the helpless prey; Gabriel, the predator trying to manipulate me.

That's the lie.

He has no idea he's trapped in *my* web, and I, the spider, spin the snare wider to trick them all.

"I'm good at painting," I mock him, feeding him what he needs to hear. Lying so he thinks I'm so broken I have no other options.

It's sweet he's trying to make me think I have a choice. In the end, he's going to take me regardless.

He nods. A hint of relief makes his skin glow. "I hope for your sake you are. I'm going to need you to paint something for me." He flexes his fingers then balls them into a fist. Not because he is incensed. He's eager. I've seen that excitement in Luna. I witnessed it right before she guilted me into playing her game.

Yes, I said guilted. I felt like I owed it to Luna to spread her lies.

Yet, seeing how Gabriel and Luna use me so easily makes me wonder how thick blood is. How many times can you dilute it until it changes substance? Until loyalty is a matter of question and not fact.

You know what's so silly? I would give my life for them, but they would take my life and play with it just as easily.

These games must stop.

The only way to end the game is to finish it. I have to keep playing so I can finish it.

I fear my new strike of revolt has shown on my face. It's hard to hide anticipation. I'm not the doll that listens to them anymore. The strings that connected me to their control have been cut.

Shot down like the birds Luna used to hunt.

I must find my own path in this rebirth.

Gabriel clears his throat. He's trying to tighten my leash, showing that he controls me and that I owe him a great debt.

"I am the one keeping you alive. You are a ghost walking. Marked for death. It's because of me you are living and breathing. So next time your mind snaps, you better break and crumble entirely. That way, when they order me to kill you, I will feel it is a mercy to you and Luna's memory." He warns. He's trying to be the bad guy. Force feed me with fear till I have no choice but to swallow some down. Then when I'm scared and shaking he will be there to scoop me up.

A smile graces my lips, but it's tainted with bitterness and sorrow. To him, it appears deranged. "Sol," his voice is firm. He thinks I'm slipping back into the depths of my fractured mind.

I'm not. After all, that was merely an act, a mask to conceal the turmoil raging inside me.

"When I was in Alexanderplatz, this man was singing." A snort escapes me, "He wasn't good, but the song was. Sometimes, it's not the person behind the voice that matters; it's the message that holds the true significance." I don't dare look him in the eyes; the game would be over if I did. He would see right through me. "Don't you want to know what he was singing?"

"You're slipping into Luna again."

"What? I can't appreciate music also." I sneer and cross my arms.

"We don't have time for this," he urges, shifting his weight to his left foot.

I shake my head, but my gaze remains fixed on the door. "No, we don't. Our time is running out." The room around me blurs; I recall the haunting melody. "I think Luna would play the song he was singing at this very moment if she was here."

"She's not here," His voice breaks, his eyes lowering, tormented by his demons and regrets. "Get dressed." He turns his back to me, guarding the door.

Reaching back, I exhale as I fumble with the strings of the hospital gown, each tug a reminder of the filth and despair that has stained my existence. Dirty in many ways. I chuckle softly, finding a strange solace in my imperfection. I'm far from the perfect human Manus Dei sought to create, and in that imperfection, I find a strange sense of beauty and peace.

"Don't you want to know the song?"

"I don't give a fuck." He growls.

"You will," I whisper, knowing his upgraded ears heard me.

"You can turn," I declare, my voice steadier now, "I'm ready." *Pull my strings. Make me your puppet now.*

He steps closer, eyes appraising me as if I were an old, rusted antique he wasn't sure he wanted to purchase but couldn't pass up. I might be valuable or a total waste of money.

I can see the weight of his regret and helplessness when his pupils dilate. Now he's going to be the good guy. He's always fought both roles. Helping Luna but also competing against her. It's tore him apart.

His lips part. Is that a struggle I sense? Another crack in your armor? "I wish... if I could have saved you from this, I would have. I would have saved Luna, too."

Don't worry. I'll save you in the end.

The elevator doors open, the sound a grim reminder of our impending confrontation. Gabriel scoops me up in his arms, his embrace a mixture of protection and desperation. He's trying to shield me in his own twisted way, as if he can still salvage a fragment of what once was.

I keep my eyes closed, body limp in his arms, allowing the weight of my vulnerability to manifest. With a tender gesture, he sweeps the hair off my forehead and cups my face to his chest. It's an intimate moment of connection, bittersweet in its rarity and complexity.

"I'm sorry," he whispers, his voice barely audible. "I'm so fucking sorry." It's the apology neither of us had the capacity to offer when Luna left us, a shared symphony of remorse. He hugs me tighter, and in that embrace, he chooses this moment to declare his apology because he understands that I cannot reciprocate. I must continue to play my part, not move or speak. He will be left to endure his suffering alone, once again.

We rarely spoke after Luna left us. He remained a shadow in the corner of my room. We never voiced our grievances to one another. It would have led the way to blame, and that would have led to more deaths.

"Me too," I croak. *I'm sorry I must keep hurting you, Gabriel, but I am doing it to protect you. Just like Luna hurt me to keep me safe.*

I hear Marcus's shoes getting closer, the footsteps echoing in the corridor like a ticking clock counting down our moments of respite.

"What was the song?" Gabriel asks. I'm happy my eyes are closed so I don't have to see his grief.

"Daylight," I whisper, knowing when he listens to it he will feel the pain, pride, and the profound reason why we continue to play this dangerous game.

Our time is up.

Secrets were whispered, lies were untold, and a new game has begun.

Just as Luna foresaw.

I can only hope Luna never anticipated me wanting to betray her followers.

The scary question is what if she did? What will be waiting for me at the finish line then?

I'm not even sure I care about the finish line anymore, only about those running the race. The rare few I hope to protect.

I have to start my own game in this labyrinth. Be the puppet but also the puppeteer.

I will plot a way to make Gabriel and those who follow Luna realize that the only way to survive the power the science radiates around it is to work together.

Our time for peace talks is up. I have to play wiser, and that means, at the moment, putting faith in Gabriel. He didn't give me the sedation for a reason. He is allowing me to learn.

***

One, two, three, four…

I count again, each passing second feeling like an eternity. It adds up to a torturous thirty-three minutes.

The car moves at a painstakingly slow pace, lulling me into a deceptive sense of safety. With cautious curiosity, I crack my eyelids open just a sliver. Gabriel's protective arms cradle me in the back seat, and Marcus sits to my left. Our driver remains a shadowy figure, his face concealed from my view, but the road ahead reveals a chilling truth – we've left Berlin far behind.

A solitary car leads the way, as though it's clearing a path in the desolation that surrounds us, though there's little to clear.

Marcus grunts. He has done this four times. I can't see his eyes, but I feel them on me. "Are we going to kill her right away?" He finally speaks.

I hear the hiss of Gabriel's heart. "What would you like to do, Marcus?" He asks; his words are frigid like the devil offering a contact you know is a trick to plunder your soul.

Marcus doesn't respond right away. Not many would. When he does speak I hear a slight tremble but his greed outweighs it as he confess his fucked up fantasy. "Play with her. Make her suffer. She looks like that bitch."

"She also looks like your leader." Gabriel growls.

What does that mean?

Gabriel moves his forearms to hug me closer. His readjustment covers the goosebumps that spread over my arms. "We will play a game," he admits.

I can feel Marcus's anticipation, but he is too foolish to observe the situation.

I remember Gabriel's words and his promise. My stomach, which used to be filled with caterpillars burrowed away in their cocoons, is now fluttering with butterflies.

How quickly things can evolve. Fear morphs into anticipation. Ignorance into the quest for knowledge. The will to play a game into the need to end it at all cost.

Just weeks ago, I was in a haze of passion with Wes, and now every day is getting darker. The kisses he seared onto my flesh are now distant memories. Soon they will be nothing but ghosts whispering to me every now and then. Haunting me.

I'm to blame. I allowed his lips to collide with mine. The sensation was like a catastrophic symphony of desire, a crescendo of emotions that had been pent up for far too long. It was a magnificent song that can never be played again. That's why I welcomed it, savoring the taste of his lips as they met mine, the warmth and tenderness, the utter madness of the connection we shared. I had begged him for this, the unspoken yearning between us now fully realized.

As our lips met, it was as if time itself stood still, and the world faded away, leaving only the two of us in that moment of pure intimacy. A pause.

No more pausing now. No more Wes.

The hole where my heart once roared for him is now frozen over. It's easier to play the game this way.

The murder in the club was just the start. Luna warned me as much.

How much more blood will I see?

Gabriel's body had remained relaxed for the first forty-eight minutes, even in the face of Marcus's taunts. But now, something has changed. His muscles tense like a coiled spring, and his grip around me tightens. His right hand shifts, as though he's subtly readjusting how he's holding me, pressing my cheek against his chest with a painful intensity.

Then, he exhales slowly, his voice barely rising above a whisper. It's so low that my upgraded ears nearly miss it. But they catch the faint vibrations, transmitting them to my brain. "Get ready," he whispers, a cryptic warning that sends a shiver down my spine.

That warning spikes adrenaline into my blood as my brain shouts at my body to prepare. Fight or flight kicks in. The small aches in my muscles are forgotten as I focus and zero in on the death threat coming my way.

Then it happens.

A deafening bang shatters the air, an explosion of chaos, as a tire blows, thrusting the car into a frenzied dance of uncontrollable spirals. Gabriel's body is violently slammed against the car door, folding inward as he instinctively cradles me in a protective embrace. The metallic screech of twisted metal reverberates through our world as another vehicle smashes into ours.

Amidst the tumultuous collision, a gunshot rips through the air, a sharp, penetrating note of danger that pierces the chaos, amplifying the intensity of the moment.

Everything stops, if only for a mere moment.

I force my eyes open, and the first thing that greets me is the unsettling sight of more blood shed inside the car. The unforgiving sunlight reflects off the crimson droplets, creating an eerie tableau that resembles stained glass.

Desperately, I try to think of it as some form of morbid art, a coping mechanism to preserve a semblance of sanity. However, in the grim reality of the moment, I am starkly reminded that in reality, the driver just took a bullet wound to the head.

It's not art; it is death.

Our car doors are ripped open. In the chaos, Gabriel is calm, he steps out of the car, still holding me tightly. My eyes follow my arms till they reach my hands which are clinging to his shoulders. I should let go but I can't.

I twist my neck to observe the unfolding scene. The air is punctuated by more merciless gunshots, each echoing like a deadly drumbeat. Two men, shrouded in all-black attire with masks concealing their faces, carry out a ruthless execution of the occupants in the car ahead of us. In an instant, a simple pull of the trigger ends their lives.

A haunting silence descends upon the scene, a momentary stillness that hangs in the air like a fragile promise of peace, a promise that slips through our fingers, leaving us in the abyss of uncertainty.

Marcus's shouts break the peace.

"I'm going to set you down," Gabriel informs me, then eases me onto the ground slowly, giving my legs time to adjust from the shock of the impact. I lean against the car, pressing my trembling fingers into the door. I need the sensation of touch to ground me, to remind myself that this is all still real.

As my fingertips make contact with the car's metal, I feel its cool surface, the smoothness of it beneath my touch. It's unmarred by the violence that has just unfolded. It's like the opposite side of the coin compared to the carnage on the other side. Bent and twisted metal, bullets, and blood. It just goes to show you, you never know what someone or something is hiding.

A man, eerily matching Gabriel's size at six foot three, emerges, clad entirely in black. He drags Marcus into our line of sight. Battered and bloody, Marcus has a stream of crimson trickling down his head, his broken nose grotesquely twisted with exposed cartilage.

"You fucking traitor!" Marcus bellows a venomous accusation. "I knew your kind could never be trusted."

"It's funny," Gabriel grins as he pushes up his shirt sleeve. "In my eyes, you're the traitor."

Marcus's throat slowly rolls as he struggles to swallow.

"You wanted to play a game, didn't you, Marcus." Gabriel laughs. "Let's play."

Marcus's cheeks suck in before he lets loose spit that lands at Gabriel's feet.

Gabriel shakes his head and looks at the masked men. "Pathetic."

The masked man chuckles a dark melody that does something to my insides. It's haunting but tempting, like a haunting house you want to venture into.

He pulls out a gun and presses it to Marcus's temple. It's chilling reminder of the dire circumstances we find ourselves in. Our lives are in someone else's hands.

Every single one of us.

"He's mine," Gabriel tells his masked friend. He looks over his shoulder at me. "Close your eyes, cover your ears." He orders. Eyes linger, waiting. When I don't move, he grins like a proud father.

I can't hide from this. That means watching Gabriel kill Marcus. My sister sent me one postcard at a time, like breadcrumbs. She fed me slowly, leading me like a parent holding a child's hand. She was preparing me for this. First the club. Now this.

I don't want to commit murder. It's my line in the sand. It isn't Gabriel's line.

Gabriel seizes the gun from the masked man, tense anticipation electrifying the air as he steps forward to face Marcus.

I press my hands harder against the car, wishing I could slip through and peek out the window like a child sneaking around again. Things weren't simpler back then, but it was easier to paint over the truth. The masked man tilts his head up, his eyes the only feature left uncovered. Yet, from my vantage point, I'm too far away to discern their color but not their target.

Me.

I exhale a shaking breath. *Why is he watching me?*

I feel like prey sensing a predator stalking it. Ready to pounce and devour me.

I narrow my eyes on his. Daring him. No more hiding. His watchful eyes note my subtle movement, and I can't help but feel his concealed satisfaction, as if a hidden smile tugs at the corners of his lips behind that ominous mask.

"You wanted to play, Marcus. Let's play. If you don't scream, I'll let you go." He declares, then raises the gun and fires, the shots ringing loudly. My back slams into the car as if I were the one just hit.

Red blooms on Marcus's pants. It's like watching a live painting as the blood spreads into an abstract composition. The bullets found their mark on each of his legs.

"Was that a scream I heard?" Gabriel jokes, then fires four more bullets into his stomach.

"Yes. That was indeed a scream." Gabriel bends down, "You always liked to hear your woman scream. Tell me, "he pressed the hot barrel to his cheek. "How does it feel to be the one begging."

The screams swiftly transform into desperate pleas and anguished cries, a haunting sound of suffering that I fear I will never be able to forget. His face contorts into a grimace of cranberry-shaded pain, a gruesome picture of torment.

Blink, come on blink! Look away! That's what I tell myself I should do. It's a lie I can't swallow anymore. This is what I always wanted.

The truth.

This is what has been going on all along.

Death.

My eyes remain wide open. Like a hapless insect glued to a windshield, unable to avert my gaze, I'm forced to witness the unfolding events with a sense of helpless fascination. My eyes widen, absorbing every detail, every twist and turn. The gravity of the situation holds me captive, transfixed by the unfolding drama, my heart racing with anticipation and apprehension.

Just kill him! End it.

I step forward. For a moment I want to grab the gun and kill Marcus just to end his suffering.

Welcome to the darkness. A wicked voice whispers in my fractured mind. I stagger back and redraw the line in my sandbox. This is how it starts. Killing to end suffering until it becomes normal. Then you kill to kill.

"Luna always hated you." He laughs tipping his head up to the sky, "She is going to be so jealous that I got to kill you and not her." He aims and fires off three bullets into his chest; then, he stands with no hesitancy.

The masked man speaks, and I finally look away. "That was a mercy kill," he tells Gabriel, but his eyes are still on me.

Mercy!

"I didn't have more time," Gabriel admits. He hands the gun back to the masked man, then turns to look at me. No words are exchanged; they aren't necessary. In that moment, I understand that while one round of this twisted game has concluded, another is just beginning. The dice are rolling once more, and the outcome remains uncertain, casting a long shadow of dread over me.

Time seems to stretch and elongate, slowing down to a languid crawl as my eyes take in every detail of the scene before me. The sky overhead is a vivid shade of blue, a serene canvas that momentarily eases the tension coiled within my muscles. A gentle breeze caresses the air, tenderly brushing over my clammy skin and bringing a welcome sensation of coolness. The sun, obscured behind a drifting cloud, casts a diffused, gentle light that illuminates the surroundings with a soft, almost surreal glow, revealing every intricate detail with a crystalline clarity.

The other men who attacked our lead car prepare to leave now. As they drive away, their tires make a loud sound that fills the air. It sounds like an injured animal.

I shift on my feet, and the gravel under my toes makes a distinct sound as if it were a demon chuckling at me. I never got shoes when we left the hospital. I can feel the texture under my toes, but it feels like an out-of-body experience. I'm numb from everything, yet this game, Gabriel's game, is just beginning.

At least Luna's game didn't shed blood till months into it. He showed me blood less than an hour in.

Gabriel turns his back to me and nods at his masked friend. The faceless man who's eyes are still fixed on mine. Watching and waiting for my reaction.

A knot of unease tightens in my stomach. My eyes narrow when the masked man raises the gun, slowly pointing it toward us. *What the hell is he doing!*

The masked man, almost tauntingly, wraps his index finger around the trigger, tilting his head ever so slightly, his eerie eyes still piercingly focused on me, provoking a reaction. A surge of adrenaline courses through my veins as I become acutely aware of the imminent threat that hangs in the air.

With a swift motion, the assailant directs the barrel of the gun towards Gabriel, aiming with lethal intent.

My feet edge forward, and I trip when I hear the gunfire. The palms of my hands hit the pavement. The tiny pebbles cut my flesh, but the pain doesn't register in my mind. My chest heaves. It feels like an elephant sits on my back, trying to crush me flat into the road.

It takes all my power to tilt my head up. When my eyes look, I stress about what I will see.

Was Gabriel just murdered again, was it him, or is there new trickery at play?

Chapter 6

Sol

In a world where reality itself seems shrouded in uncertainty, where can one find trust?

We dwell in an age where deep fakes have become a commonplace spectacle, where clones of the very individuals I cherish and protect are being systematically eradicated right before my eyes.

Now, don't misunderstand me – I'm no saint; saints were not perfect, and after all, I was genetically designed to be perfect. Luna and Gabriel were further engineered to reach perfection, continually evolving.

I've woven my own intricate web of deceit and continue to do so. But I'd like to believe that it's all in pursuit of a greater cause, a grander truth, and an end to the distorted pursuit of humanity.

My eyes follow the trail of blood dripping down Gabriel's perfect body. He let the man shoot him! My narrowed eyes become barrels, loaded and aimed like guns themselves.

I must admit the art of deception has its own peculiar allure, doesn't it? I won't deny the satisfaction it occasionally brings, the thrill of navigating the treacherous labyrinth of falsehoods. There's a certain, undeniable temptation to it all. After all, we wouldn't indulge in deception if there wasn't at least a modicum of pleasure to be derived from it.

It makes me wonder what the fuck Gabriel wanted me to feel when the shock subsided? Why not tell me he was going to take a bullet?

Yes, he's broken, his once impenetrable walls now revealing hairline fractures. Luna's departure inflicted considerable damage upon him. My lies further seeped into those cracks, slowly eroding him more. *I'm so sorry, Gabriel.*

I had momentarily overlooked the predator in him. His display of emotions and pleas in the hospital concealed the beast that still lurked within. A master manipulator. Not as good as Luna; he's the runner-up in that race.

He is a wounded animal, and wounded animals, as desperate as they are, can be unpredictable and dangerous.

He's also an emotional sadist. He thinks before he acts; Plots and plans. He knew exactly what he was doing and how it would affect me.

That is what he relishes in, the aftermath.

Gabriel is still standing, undeterred, not unharmed. A small hole cries bloody tears down his back. It was a calculated shot, meticulously planned by the masked man. A shot Gabriel could have warned me about, but chose not to. He wanted me to hear that gunshot, to feel its reverberations deep within my bones, intensifying my anxiety with each passing second. He wanted me to see, to feed off my anxiety.

He removes his shirt with barely any struggle, then wraps it over his shoulder to cover his wound. "Get up, Sol." He orders.

I curl my fingers into the road inflicting more small cuts into the palm of my hand. What I want to do is scream. "He just shot you."

"Good, you didn't mentally slip again. See you're playing better this round, seeing reality." He replies. Gone is the man who showed me an ounce of emotions. He's guarded in front of these new comers.

I push to my knees, palms pressing flat, feeling the pavement, the only thing that seems solid in my world. "Why didn't you tell me? Why did you let me worry for you?" My voice quivers with frustration, the emotions bubbling up to the surface.

His fingers brush against the bullet wound without so much as a flinch.

My shoulders slacken when I realize why he didn't react. He must have undergone a genetic enhancement that rendered his pain receptors impervious. Not a single bead of sweat trickles down his forehead, no cry of agony, no acknowledgment of the bullet tearing through his flesh. His gaze remains fixed on the blood staining his fingertips, his expression void of remorse. There's an eerie, calculated calmness about him.

"I need to make sure you still care about me," he deadpans. His words hang in the air, leaving me bewildered and unsettled. Then, those cold blue eyes slowly lift to meet mine. It strikes me like a sudden revelation – he wants me to care about him. He fears I will leave him too. This is why he has been watching me all along, not merely following Manus Dei's orders. It's about his conscience, his last link to Luna, the sole surviving memory he refuses to relinquish. More than that, he's silently beseeching for me to care, to help him cope.

Dear God, Gabriel. Why can't you just be upfront and ask? Because that would make him weak, and he wasn't raised to be weak. Neither was Luna. They can't simply ask. They have to test.

An overwhelming urge wells up inside me. I want to rush to him, to assure him that everything I've done, was for his sake, for all of us. To rescue him from the clutches of this insidious game.

I can't. I have to keep lying, to play my part until the game reaches its conclusion once and for all.

I fake fury as I shout, "What?" My legs feel too weak to stand. "You orchestrated this to test my loyalty?"

Watching his stance relax further as he stands with a gunshot wound, surrounded by dead bodies, makes me want to smack him. "Congratulations, you passed this round." He quips.

I stand slowly, like a boiling kettle billowing with steam. "You fucker." Then it hits me, and all my steam is replaced with enlightenment, "You want me to hate you." He craves my hatred because it's the only emotion he can truly feel in the absence of Luna. He wants me to help him survive, not move on. I'm a constant memory that will cause him to be perpetually tormented.

My head shakes as I widen my stance, "I won't. I will not hate you. I'll save you." I declare.

His blue eyes darken, "There's nothing left to save." He snorts.

The masked man steps closer to him. *Does he care?*

"Then why keep playing?" I challenge. Why fight so hard for Manus Dei's power?

His eyes meet mine in a silent answer. He's doing it for me, for the other clones. It's his redemption.

When does he get a reprieve? When can he begin to heal?

My eyes find the pavement splattered with blood. *That's a silly question, Sol; why would he want to heal?* Healing means you allow yourself to feel. He doesn't want to feel; he doesn't want to move on. He's trapped in the void of Luna's absence. The only way to fill that pain, to soothe the festering wound, is to keep playing mind games. If you play enough, you eventually become lost in them, never having to face reality.

"Will you ever be able to stop these games?"

He seems to ponder that question with curiosity, his gaze shifting slightly. For a moment, a flicker of contemplation passes over his features, hinting at a depth I hadn't seen before.

"The games are all I know. It's in my DNA." he replies.

I shake my head, "Bullshit. You can change that trait."

The way his body suddenly freezes makes my brain scream that choosing either "fight" or "flight" might be a brilliant survival plan right now. I've hit a nerve. His chest leans forward, and his fists clench. "Careful, Sol," he warns, a hint of sarcasm in his voice. "Starting to sound like your father, aren't you? A little tweak here, a modification there, and soon enough, you've unknowingly engineered a deadly monster."

A shiver courses down my spine, "I won't become what I despise. I hope you can do the same."

He murmurs, "I have protections in place. I won't rule alone. Too much power has driven many to madness." Finally, he uncurls his fist. "The line between light and darkness can blur easily. Just remember, sometimes the most dangerous monsters are the ones that hide within ourselves. It's important to surround yourself with people you trust."

I snicker, "You shouldn't trust me." My impulse to expose my true intentions stings as soon as the words leave my lips.

"I don't." He grins, taking two steps towards me. The blood begins to seep through his shirt now. "That's what makes me a wiser player. If I were you, I'd rethink who you trust, Sol. Where are Luna's pawns now?" He opens his arms as if to welcome them as his eyes scan the landscape.

They are not here. I'm alone. It's cruel, but it's his way of showing he cares for me.

"They don't care about you. They want control, and you are the key to gaining it." The sound of his shoes on the pavement draws my attention. Looking down, I see they are covered in blood. Why are the people I care for always covered in blood? "Stop allowing yourself to be used."

I snort, "Sounds like great advice, especially when it's coming from the one who plans on using me."

"To free us."

"Makes no difference." The bitterness seeping into my words can't be concealed, "If this is your way of caring for me, I'd hate to see how you treat those you don't care about."

His gaze shifts towards Marcus, the unspoken answer lying on the pavement.

"Come on," He begins to walk to the car the masked men arrived in. The front is damaged from impaling our car, but the engine is still running. Broken but useable. My perfect chariot.

I slowly follow, passing and studying Marcus's dead body. It's been only minutes, but his skin is ashen. It is a color I never want to see on my palette.

"Sol." Gabriel presses.

I don't listen. It's time to teach him a lesson. I bend down, searching for a pulse on Marcus's neck. I know it won't be there, but searching for life in death is normal. This is why I must find a way to end this. The competition has led him to believe killing is normal if it gets you to the next round of the game. This convoluted moral compass is how all the other clones I have met think.

I must teach them right from wrong again.

The weight of my task bears down upon me. I toil to stand, to push away from the dead body, but I can't. I need to remember what I am fighting for.

Footsteps approach. "Marcus would have done terrible things to you," Gabriel admits. He touches my shoulder in such a delicate manner you'd think he was picking up a chipped teacup. Such a discrepancy from the monster who lurks inside.

Maybe my definition of a monster is wrong. A monster is just another beast, an animal. What does every animal, even man, want?

To survive.

Gabriel thinks this is the only way for us all to prevail; Luna thought her way was better, and now, I think my way is best.

Does that make me a monster now?

"We don't have time to waste." He persist. It wasn't that he derived pleasure from the chaos, but rather a cold determination to survive propelled him to continue to commit such violent acts.

I closed Marcus's eyelids, a small act of mercy he didn't deserve but one I chose to bestow upon him. I must rise above those I conquer, not sink to their level of cruelty.

I stand and begin to follow Gabriel to the waiting car.

"You need to get going," he instructs the masked man. His hand still rests on my shoulder in a protective manner that makes me hesitant.

Who am I being handed over to now? Which puppeteer is this?

"Why did you let him shoot you?" I ask Gabriel.

"Be wiser, Sol," he replies cryptically. "You tell me. Plot it out."

Blood fills my eyes as I look at his gunshot wound. We were attacked but it was planned. A realization strikes me. "You're not coming with us. You're painting yourself as the injured victim," I say. It's brilliant. "It's a calculated act to deceive Manus Dei, to make them believe you were caught in the crossfire. But in reality, it was a deliberate move, a part of your grand design."

The right side of his lip tugs up, a glimmer of satisfaction sparks in his eyes. "Not the silly little sister anymore, are you, Sol?"

The second masked man joins us, dressed differently in a maroon suit with a black shirt, tie, and shoes. He was part of the group that attacked the car in front of us. His hand swiftly reaches for his mask and tears it off. I know that face.

His well-defined Roman nose draws my attention up to his striking jade eyes. Hair cut and styled in a manner that would make a Calvin Klein model jealous.

War.

His smile, devoid of warmth, slowly stretches across his face, sending a clear silent message: "Keep your mouth shut, Sol. You don't know me."

More secrets.

My fingers touch my right hip, where my bag usually is. Where I kept War's tie pin.

I don't have any of my tokens.

"Everything is all set," War tells Gabriel.

Gabriel trusted these men to save us and shoot him. I stagger back as the realization hits me like a train derailing. My gaze shoots to Gabriel. Instinctively, I place my palm over my chest as a palpitation throws my heart into a new rhythm.

"You... You are one of them." My fingers clench, grasping at the fabric of my clothing, but the flimsy material proves no match for my anxious grip. My nails dig in, struggling to anchor myself amidst the tumultuous revelation.

"I'm one of many in this game, Sol."

I shake my head, "You're a Horseman," The truth now laid bare between us.

He reaches out, forcing my hands to unclench my flesh, exposing my heart to him. "Run a full scan when you arrive." He instructs War. "We need to be certain everything has developed, and the upgrade she gave herself didn't fuck it up."

Deep in my mind, I register his odd words but don't think about them. All I think about are the Horsemen. I've met them all now. That means Gabriel is Conquest, a fitting name for what he wants to do with Manus Dei's power.

The man that shot Gabriel inches closer like a shadow that wants to attach itself to my soles. The wind carries his scent to my nose, a mixture of gunpowder and pine. Pine is a scent my mind remembers, like a forgotten note stepping out of a ghoulish shadow.

He reaches for his mask, and when he starts to pull it off, I see him grinning wide.

Death is about to reveal himself to me.

Pushing forward on the balls of my feet, I eagerly wait to see the truth I have lied to myself about. I've prepared for his revelation and knew it was coming.

Death always said he would come for me. Today seems to be that day.

My mouth slightly gapes as I let out a laborious breath. Gabriel notices it all; he turns his body toward me, his forehead creasing with concern, wondering why I seem so eager for Death to stop hiding, why I can't wait for him to reach out and pull me deeper into the game's shadows.

I glance towards War. He's grinning, but he is watching Gabriel. He knows something Gabriel doesn't know and wants to savor the reaction.

I can't focus on that. All I feel is the tingling fire that is tickling the tips of my fingers. My lies are about to be unearthed now and I'm not sure how Death will react.

I've always known who lurked behind that mask. I've harbored the truth about Death's identity all along. I've dropped clues along the way this entire time, hoping it would make him admit who he was.

He didn't.

Neither did I.

I've always said this was a game within a labyrinth of games. The moment Death snuck into my room and wrapped his hands around my throat I decided to play my own game with him.

Chapter 7

Sol

Warnings are constructed for a reason. They are supposed to make us hesitate and think. We must observe the possible outcomes of either heeding the warning or ignoring it.

My vision goes blurry, but my mind recalls his warning to me. A warning I purposely pushed aside.

"I don't know how not to break you, Sol. If I give in to us, I will only hurt you. I will crush everything you ever thought you knew about me. You'll never trust again, Sol, and a person who can't trust can't live. They can't have dreams or a future."

"Wes." I state in a calm manner.

The truth stares back at me.

In the midst of shock and betrayal, a hefty dose of self-reproach smacks me right in the face. I can't help but feel like a royal fool, like I've won the grand prize for willingly participating in my very own circus of deception.

The hints were there all along, subtly woven into our interactions, but I chose to play the "ignorance is bliss" card, wearing blinders crafted from my own desires and the delusional hope for something genuinely extraordinary. *Bravo, Sol, bravo. Give yourself a round of applause for this spectacular performance.*

It's true. I lied and chose to believe my own lies. *You shouldn't be surprised.* Deep down, I always knew the truth. That's why I slept with Wes because I knew Death could never truly kill himself. Wes and Death are one and the same.

You didn't think I actually would have risked an innocent life. That I would have dragged Wes into my game with Death? That I would have used Wes, fucked him, only to hope my stalker didn't kill him?

Having a relationship with Wes only served to provoke Death, and what do I do best?

Provoke.

I wanted Death to be jealous, to step out of his dark shadows and collect my soul with a fancy scythe and a hooded cloak. I embraced my inner con artist, painting elaborate lies in my mind and gobbling them up like candy on Halloween. *Well done, Sol, well done indeed.* I am a reflection of my twin, after all.

I wasn't the only one playing a cruel game of temptation.

Wes wanted me to admit the truth, to confess that I knew who he truly was. That was why he pushed me away, why he tested my loyalty. He hoped I would stop lying and face the reality of our situation. But in the end, my time ran out. Our passion consumed us, blinding me to the darkness lurking beneath.

The unsettling grin he's flashing me right now speaks volumes, unraveling untold secrets and hidden intentions.

"It's time to confess your sins to me, little mouse." He purrs. Hearing his voice again makes something deep inside my body hum. It's not butterflies, more like fireflies flocking to a light in the darkness. That's what he is, a flicker of light helping me navigate the shadows.

"I wanted you to be normal; I wanted my first love not to be involved in the game." I admit. "I wasn't the only one who ate up the lies. You liked the escape, too."

His jaw twitches. "You were never an escape. I hinted at my true nature all along. I kept waiting for you to accept it. Accept your fate. Stop running from us." He tilts his head, eyes dancing with anger, "You think I would have let another man fuck you. Touch what was mine; hear your cries. Your pleas are only for my ears; no one else will ever hear them." He laughs, "They were always mine, little mouse. Always."

My next swallow gets lodged. Was it all a game? Wes made me feel loved. Death makes me feel used.

Reality rushes back, and I realize that Gabriel and War are listening to every dirty detail.

I've felt a lot of things since Luna left me; I've done a lot of fucked up shit. Half of which none of them have yet to figure out yet.

I've never felt humiliation. I don't like it. I hate myself in this moment. Hate that I allowed myself to live in a dream that turned out to be a nightmare.

It has always been a nightmare, a warning Luna gave me long ago.

Self-blame surges within me, overshadowing any resentment. I chastise myself for painting a picture of normalcy that could never truly exist. I allowed my desires to cloud my judgment, to create an illusion that shattered under the weight of truth.

"I was never just going to be your first love, little mouse," he declares. "I'm your first and your last. I'm your inhales and exhales. I'm your heart, the beating power that keeps you alive."

He is.

I became infatuated with him when he snuck into my room and didn't kill me. Then, my infatuation turned into obsession when he killed for me, protected me. That obsession evolved into trust once he started to help guide me in the game.

I've always yearned for someone to love me, to rescue me from my cage.

Life is never as simple as our childhood fantasies paint it to be. It's intricate, filled with details, not just stick figures on a canvas. Within those intricate details lie both beauty and unsettling truths. Life is like a twisted rose, with thorny stems and soft petals. It's a mixture of good and bad, pain and passion, all woven together into a complex tapestry.

Gabriel takes a decisive step toward Wes, his emotions fueling an explosive surge of determination. He delivers a powerful punch to Wes, but it seems to have no effect. Wes remains unfazed, even as blood drips from his mouth. He stands tall, emanating an enigmatic aura of invincibility. *My dark knight.*

"You were supposed to watch her. Not fuck her!" Gabriel roars.

I can't paint away honest emotions with lies. They show on my canvas, my face. Gabriel sees the truth. I lived the life of a fool in love. Wes indulged me.

Wes chuckles. The sound is one I will never forget. The hairs on my arms rise, and my heart reverses a beat. Watching someone be killed in front of my eyes was sickening, but it was nothing compared to the devil playing with my heart. Nothing is worst than knowing I offered him my heart to play with.

"I will crush everything you ever thought you knew about me." His warning was accurate, but I didn't think of the effects it would have on me. It's bone crushing.

Why did I lie to myself? Why did I make myself think I could have one night with a normal man?

He's not just after my heart, he wants something else. That's why he didn't tell Gabriel all the details. He's only just revealed his cards.

Obliteration sparks in my core, engulfing me whole. I know what it feels like to touch the sun, to feel the heat of passion because it burns you irrevocably. Leaving no ashes or bones behind.

Nothing.

Absolutely nothing.

"Come on, little mouse, no hard feelings. You were playing me too." Wes replies with a chilling, unsettling tone. His eyes flicker to Gabriel as if trying to convey no hard feelings.

"I told you I would help you navigate the shadows. I was always there, watching you, protecting you," He states.

"Did you ever really care, or was I just a fun fuck to pass your time?" I try to make my voice cold and detached, but I can't. My throat tightens, as if it's trying to knit its own sweater.

"Be careful," his green eyes turn black.

"Why, worried I'll mend my heart with another man that isn't you." Just to provoke him, I glance at Gabriel.

"Keep spreading lies, little mouse, but remember, I see the truth. I see what no one else does. That's why you spread your legs for me, and that's why if I dipped a finger between your sweet thighs, I'd find you soaking wet for me."

"Well, now you've done it." War chuckles as Gabriel lunges at Wes. I watch numbly as they fight each other until War finally has to step in between them, holding Gabriel back.

Huffing but still wearing the panty-dropping grin, Wes says, "You lied to me too. Sometimes you have to lie to see the truth," he raises a brow, daring me to confess that I always knew who he was. "You're attracted to the danger and darkness in our world. Admit it. Stop running. Runners don't win."

"I never wanted to win." I bite. Little do they all know Luna spoke those same words.

I can't deny that I did learn a lesson, albeit a painful one. I'm much more like my twin than I ever dare to admit.

Gabriel's eyes assess me as a new player, no longer the puppet.

Admitting the truth, both to myself and to others, feels like stepping into uncharted territory. Yet, the realization dawns upon me, acknowledging the darkness within may be the key to finding my way out of this labyrinth.

Why the lies and games? Why can't I admit I'm drawn to the shades of grey covering Wes?

Because we are human, genetically modified, but our core DNA is still there. Man can't resist the temptation of a game.

"I should kill you both!" Gabriel hisses, trying to stop the bleeding from his bullet wound that is now dripping more profusely. "I don't have time for this."

Wes shrugs, his eyes never leaving mine, drinking me in, stripping me bare, "But I do."

I want to pluck his eyes out, but that dark, insane part of me wants to run into his arms because now I can see him for who he is. The only man who can guide me in the dark. The only man who can make all my fears vanish.

War steps between them again, "I'll keep them on track." He claims as he adjusts the lapel of his jacket. His tie pin is missing.

"You are already walking on thin ice." Gabriel snaps.

War taps his feet like a dancer and smiles, "I'm a master at finding balance on uncertain soil, brother." He pats his shoulder over the bullet wound, "Have no fear; War is here." He curtsies with dramatics.

I can't describe the need that is surging through my body. I just need a moment's break, a mere second to compose myself. It's not just the Horsemen I need a break from but also the chaos within my mind!

I know I can't truly escape, but the silly fool in me still makes the choice to run. I abruptly turn, my heart pounding in my chest as my feet propel me forward. With each stride, I am consumed by a desperate longing for liberation, a fervent desire to break free from these twisted games.

From my lies, falsehoods I still have to pretend are true.

That darkness inside of me chose to run because I enjoy being chased. There, I admitted it to myself.

As I sprint through the open field, I find myself whispering to the wind, "Chase me."

I like that he pursuits me; even when I'm so fucked up, he still seeks me out.

I fixate my gaze on the tree line, a distant sanctuary beckoning me. Is this how the birds felt when Luna hunted them? She let them think they got away and found refuge, only to claim them.

Leaving the paved road behind, my feet sink into the unforgiving earth, its coarse texture mirroring the harsh reality I am trying to escape. The farmland, untouched and unyielding, becomes my canvas for liberation, where the taste of freedom intertwines with the sting of pain. My arms pump and swing forcefully, driving me onward as I push myself to outrun the suffocating entanglement of this game.

Amidst the pounding rhythm of my footsteps, a new sound reaches my ears—running steps, growing louder and more relentless with every passing second. They echo with an intensity that sends a chill down my spine.

Arms grab me. Hands that tackled me into my bed just weeks ago. They hold me for a different reason now. His body rolls, shielding mine from the impact of hitting the ground.

Everyone is deformed and mentally disturbed. They want to drag me under but also try to protect me.

My back is pressed against his strong chest, fitting together like two puzzle pieces that were always meant to be.

Peace and turbulence.

Sanctuary and a cage.

Patience and passion.

In a fluid motion, he rolls us over, hovering above me. My cage and protector.

As our eyes meet, I see a glimmer in his gaze—a blend of desire with a newfound intensity that wasn't present the last time we found ourselves in such a position. In this moment, the world around us fades into insignificance, and it's as if time stands still. The tender touch of his fingertips against my skin sends a surge a heat down my core. My body relaxes as my mind becomes fuzzy. The passion between us crackles in the air. It's tangible; with each inhale, neither of us can deny it.

Our eyes meet in a moment of shared vulnerability. Neither of us is used to baring our hearts, but we can't help it; it's as if our hearts have thumped so hard, breaking free from the confines of our ribs to embrace one another. In that instant, a darker kind of romance blooms, igniting a fire that burns with an intensity we can no longer deny.

"Run for me, my love," Wes whispers, his voice filled with longing and desire as he gently lowers his lips to meet mine. My love. He's finally admitted it. Our sickly beautiful love. "I will always chase." His lips tenderly brush against mine, seeking a response, but I remain still, neither rejecting nor encouraging. Not a rebuke or cheer. Nothing. That tickles his feathers. Death likes a chase; he wants a response.

I'm still the coward that can't admit I like this depraved passion. I close my eyes. "Stop."

"Why? Why can't you be loved, chased, cherished."

"Owned." I spit.

"You're word not mine. Is that what you want, little mouse, for me to own you."

"I want to be free."

"We gave you freedom, and you ran back home into my arms."

"Aspen was a trick."

He snickers, "A lie you helped weave. No more lies, little mouse. Admit you need this." He claims my lips, swallowing the air I'd need to reply. Taking my words and replacing them with his taste. God, his taste!

Where I find the power to twist my head away is a mystery. I swallow and shake my head. *I don't deserve you; you don't know the half of what I have done, Wes! What I still am doing. And I can't stop the lies because if I do it will all be for not. You don't understand the picture I have to paint, Wes. When you see it you won't chase me anymore.*

I cautiously trace my tongue across my lips, savoring the lingering taste of him—a taste that has become both my poison and my addiction. His essence, like a curse, has seeped into the depths of my being, staining my desires with an unsettling allure. Once a decadent treat that flooded my senses with euphoria, has transformed into a bitter elixir that both repulses and entices me.

The game didn't shatter me, but he did. How can I crave his touch, which has hurt me? I lust for his lips that have lied to me. He is a sin created by god but used by the devil. The perfect weapon. A combination I can not go up against because it's like going up against myself.

"You did warn me," I mutter. A warning I did not heed. I've damned myself.

His handsome face, sharp and angled like a faceted diamond, holds an irresistible allure, a sparkle that no one can resist. Those peach-colored lips, as they twist truths like the devil's serpent, evoke both fascination and trepidation. His arms bear the strength to lift his body above me, a display of power I once craved as my shield. But now, it has become my cage, confining me within its grasp. Trapping me until I confess the truth…that I love him; crave him.

Protection has a way of tricking you. You think you reached safety only to realize you backed yourself into a corner. Your enemy has you surrounded, and there is no escape. Nowhere to run.

"You're mine now." His hand traces up my shoulder until he gently caresses my neck. The heat his touch leaves behind is like the humidity from the sun on a boiling summer's day. He melts my defenses. Brings everything to a boil. I can't think when he is touching me; that is exactly what he wants.

Strong fingers, callous to the touch, caress my swan-like neck. When we first met, Wes was Death, a horseman. He held my neck, my life in his hand. He snuck into my bedroom, I thought Death was going to kill me, but it was just the start of a personal game with him. When I met his other face, Wes, he kissed my neck, showing me the difference between life versus living.

Wes is the embodiment of Death. He can show me the meaning of life and the sentiment of living without it; that makes him stronger than his other side.

Wes has killed me in every way.

This might just be exactly what I needed. A dose of brutality tinged with passion. It's toughened me and turned me into a more deceptive player.

Turned me from a puppet into a puppeteer.

Did Luna know this when she allowed Death to stalk me? Was this all part of her plan to make me ruthless and less empathetic… more like her?

Just when I think I have a mind of my own, that I can create my own game, I'm left wondering how genius Luna was? How upgraded was her mind to be able to plot out even the smallest of details, to know not only how everyone around her would think but how they would adjust and operate along the way?

Chapter 8

Sol

The heat of his body envelops me, squeezing me tightly like a suffocating blanket meant for a child. I squirm, desperate to escape its constricting hold. Yet, his piercing green eyes keep me pinned down, unyielding and resolute.

I refuse to yield. I can't tell him I love him back until I fully understand him. So, I do something that will provoke him. I wipe the pain from my face and resemble Luna – emotionless, cold, calculating.

A furrow forms on Wes's forehead as he senses the deception. "Don't look at me like that," he protests.

How well did he know Luna?

"This is who I am," I assert.

"No. You're Sol, not Luna. No more evading, little mouse," he insists.

A wicked snicker escapes me, fueled by the knowledge that I am playing with his perceptions. "You think you hold all the strings, Wesley," I challenge him, my voice dripping with venom. "But the truth is, you control nothing. It's all an illusion. Perhaps I am Luna after all." I am a monster just like my twin.

"Stop!" he interjects. "Luna is dead. I know who you are. I understand the game you're trying to play," He declares boldly, exposing his motives. "You don't want to play a mind game against me, little mouse."

"I could conceal her from you if I wanted to. I could never show you Sol again. I could always pretend to be Luna," I taunt, testing the limits of his power, and mine. How evil can I be? Can I deny myself passion?

He leans closer, his lips grazing my ear before nibbling on it. It makes my body shudder with need. "But you won't," he whispers seductively. He sucks on my earlobe, eliciting a response I try to suppress. "You want to know why?" He pulls away, beaming with a warrior's manic grin. "Because you crave me. Me. Luna never craved another; she only lusted after power. That's why you can never truly pretend to be her in the long term."

I feel like a balloon that was just popped with a needle. The power dynamics shift as desire and manipulation intertwine, and I am left grappling with the realization that in this game of control, neither of us truly holds all the cards.

"How does it feel?" I whisper, arching my chest so my nipples brush against him. We both feel them pebble under the friction. As I speak, I bring my lips directly over his, but I don't give him the pleasure of kissing him back. "Knowing you deceived me. Captured me," I provoke.

His chest rumbles with a low growl, the sound resonating through his body. I can feel his arousal, his hardness pressing against me, caught between my legs.

I continue, "Do you like me better now that I can see in the darkness?" If you can't fight them, then confuse them. I'm playing wiser, not smarter. A smart player wins one round, and a wiser player wins the whole damn game.

My sister led me into the darkness, and Gabriel took my hand and pushed my feet down the path. Death showed me how to see in the shadows. Wes showed me how they could feel.

I'm giving him a taste of it right now.

How does that feel, Wesley?

I know how it feels, like a frigid chill scraping over your exposed skin. It burns you and breaks the raw skin out into hives that blister to the touch. The only salvation promised is to keep going. To sink deeper, plunging into the gloom. At first, you suffer and feel so much you think your feet can not budge another step.

They do.

The mind has quantum strength, as does the body. The more you push, the more callus the mind grows. Like a diamond, under pressure, you evolve into something that can reflect even the most minuscule amount of light. You keep walking, and as you receive more wounds, you also start to feel the healing medicine only darkness can provide. Your senses bud with a new numbness. Only wicked blooms can produce such a fragrance. Your pain lessens, as does your sensitivity to everything.

This feeling is what drives the hero to become the villain.

It makes me stronger, more than that, it makes me want vengeance, not against Wes but against the games we have been forced to play against each other.

Wes's fingers squeeze my neck over my pulse. The beat surges with added intensity, sounding like a rushing river in my ears, a current that delivers my heart directly to the palm of his hands. "Be careful, little mouse," he growls in a low rumble.

"I think I'm done being careful. I evolved into someone who isn't scared of pain."

His jaw clenches like a gator that won't let go of prey too big to swallow.

"Hurry up," Gabriel shouts from a distance.

I snicker like a child who got the biggest piece of cake. "Seems your time is up. How does it feel to have to obey someone else, Death."

These men are all pursuing power and control but often overlook their interconnectedness. Their actions affect each other, creating a web of manipulation and deception. Wes deceived Gabriel when he stalked me and stole my heart. War manipulates all his brothers, and Famine has joined my sister's cause to dismantle Manus Dei. Then there's little old me, The player who is benched and broken, lost in her lies.

Little do they know, I'm the most dangerous player because they view me as the weakest.

I was never lost.

The secrets always whispered back in my mind.

Those secrets are my power.

The underdog has teeth, too, and soon I'll use them.

I reach up and run my fingers over the shadow on his jaw. It's sharp and prickly, just like his heart.

His hand leaves my neck, and his index finger grazes my lips, tracing them or the memory of them from a past time when they kissed him back.

I wanted to hate Wes, but that wouldn't be playing every angle. I need them all to think I have bent a knee and accepted the yoke they hung upon my shoulders. We are allies, meaning we use each other for self-gain.

Before Wes pulls his fingers away, I swipe my tongue over them. I taste the salt off his skin. Savory and sweet.

I will play all sides and angles.

I understand Gabriel's end goal. He wants to take over Manus Dei. I know Luna's; she wants those she trusts to create something new, without abusing the science. I know Wes desires me.

What about my goal? That's easy, end all the games, but not just that – I want to be selfish. I want Wes, but not as he is now, not wearing two coats of armor. I want him as my own, mine, just as he claims to want me. I want him as my soldier in this game.

Luna told me to make allies, but fuck that. I'm going to build an army of my own after I seize the power for myself. Luna warned me that Gabriel would take me, use me to get his hands on the power, and then her pawns would strike. So here's my plan: right before the exchange of power, I'll make my move. I'll bury away the science until I deem those left standing worthy enough to control it. It might be Gabriel's side, Luna's, or no one's. I never said I had to keep the science alive.

But what if Wes refuses my vision? He might, but that's okay. I'll survive. I can always paint over my pain with another lie. It's what I've always done, and I can do it again until these games are done. Just like Luna, I don't have to feel; I can always choose to ignore it. *I hope it doesn't come to that, but these games must end at all costs.*

Chapter 9

Sol

What monster have I become?

That's easy; I'm the same monster I always was. I just don't lurk in the depths of my mind anymore. I'm uncaged, out in the open, in the blinding light of the truth and lies of the game.

Now I'm surrounded by the other monsters. The players. My own kind.

Wes's state of genetic upgrade is still unknown to me but I'll discover it eventually.

My monster.

My love.

My beast.

My tamer.

He sits in the drivers seat ready to steer us into the next labyrinth of the game. A new destination awaits. Not Luna's. It's Gabriel's roll of the dice now.

Eventually it will be mine.

War stands next to the open passenger door waiting for me to be ushered inside. The sun is shining bright now; no more clouds can hide its light.

The car Gabriel and I were driving was set on fire. Blood still drips from Gabriel's bullet wound, but it has begun to slow. I don't ask him if he will be ok. He's been upgraded to heal faster. I remember when my sister was injected with the ability to regenerate small portions of herself. I'm sure a clean bullet wound is easy to recover from.

Gabriel touches my shoulder. "I didn't know." His eyes drift to Death, his brother. "If he hurts you…."

He's baring his heart to me. That's good. I can use this to try to peel open his mind and find his true intentions.

"What will you do to him and yourself?" I poke. Gabriel has hurt me just as much as Wes has. Little do they know I am going to hurt them to save them.

His blue eyes hold mine hostage. He sees my pain. Good. I see his too. The hole where my heart once beat with trust is now empty. "Luna always wanted you to have someone."

"What good is having someone when they betray you?" I quip. That's the pot calling the kettle black, after all he and Luna betrayed one another. That's what got us *all* in this huge mess.

Love is a sickness that runs deep; a dangerous virus that mutates. Even I am not sure I can find the cure for it.

"This is how we were made. We were meant to be calculating."

Is that his defense? It's laughable.

I shake my head. The ground shifts beneath my feet, "We can change how we are made now. Wether it is by nature or nurture. I taught Luna how to feel. I know you helped with those lessons. You showed her love, and she loved you back, even if she could never voice it. So what excuse will you try to use now."

"I am trying to fix it. I need the power to keep us safe. We need to keep the science under our authority. Others will abuse it as our fathers did," He leans back on his heels like a seesaw, trying to edge me up and into the car. So eager to play his game now that he has me.

"You want a world order?" I ask, trying to dig beneath his heroic words. If he were so noble than why didn't Luna agree to his demands. What are you hiding Gabriel?

He looks like he just bit into something sour as he sweeps his tongue over his teeth, eyes narrowing slightly. "Not a world order in the traditional sense," he begins, choosing his words carefully as if he were playing hangman. "Rather, a system of governance that ensures the responsible use of scientific advancements. We have seen the devastating consequences of unchecked power and knowledge in the wrong hands. We must protect humanity and prevent further harm. I will make that order under Manus Dei's name." He assures me.

"And Luna didn't want that?" I question. It sounds like they are singing the same tune. So now the question is, who is lying? Did Luna lie to me, or is Gabriel? Whose nose, other than my own, can rival Pinocchio's?

"She wanted to start over." He swallows, eyes holding mine. He's telling the truth...I think.

There must be a catch. What did Luna see that I didn't? Because now, I wholeheartedly concur with him. I share his belief that the science can't be contained, but it should be controlled to prevent its abuse.

"Is protecting the same as controlling, Gabriel?" I provoke him.

His expression remains serious, "No, they are not the same. Protection involves safeguarding and guiding, ensuring that scientific progress is used responsibly for the betterment of society.

Control, on the other hand, implies dominance and manipulation. It is not my intention to wield power for personal gain or to exert control over others. My aim is to create a balance where science serves humanity without causing harm." His voice deepens, "We have done good, Sol. We have cured and saved—"

I interrupt him, "Just as many as we have deemed unworthy and killed."

"That was under Manus Dei's rule. Mine will be different."

I tip my head up to the sky.

"Let me prove myself to you. Just help me get to the point where I can." He pleads.

It's odd to hear a plea leave his lips, like nails on a chalkboard. My shoulders twitch up to cover my ears.

"How can I trust you when one moment you care and the next you lash out."

"Look in the mirror."

I grin. He's got me, but part of my actions is an act to maintain the illusion of my deception. At other times, it's simply satisfying to challenge those who hold power over you. Then it hits me: I hold power over him, and he doesn't like it, so he lashes out.

I meet his piercing blue eyes, rivaling the heavens above. My eyes still reflect determination as I continue to play the role of the reluctant puppet that is being swayed by his words. "And you believe Manus Dei's name will grant you that power? You think the people who follow them will readily embrace your new ideals?"

"Yes," he hisses, a hint of frustration in his voice. "I won't give them a choice. Now get in the car." He grunts.

"That sounds a lot like controlling them," I counter.

"I'm protecting them!" Grabbing my forearm, he gently shoves me to the door. "Don't push me into a defined definition, Sol. I aim to protect, but my protection will have its rules and boundaries." And there it is. "Think hard, Sol. Consider the potential consequences if governments without ethical considerations obtain genetic upgrades or other powerful technologies. You know the tip of the iceberg; you helped create some of it. You don't know what lurks under the surface." My eyes look at his bullet wound. He never felt the pain. That's what he's hinting at. Upgrades I know nothing about. Genetic modifications that make even his corrupted mind hesitate.

His shoe nudges my foot to take a step, "You're right, I won't give them a choice. Now get in the car." A slow exhale leaves his mouth like a tire that is slowly deflating. "I miss the girl who was scared and followed orders." His lips tug up, "But I'm proud she has vanished. You're going to need a thick skin."

I pause for a moment, absorbing his words. I look out past his shoulder at the open land. If his last statement comes true, those trees in the far distance will be covered in fire. The world will fall. I understand his flight, but I also sympathize with Luna's. Some evils are lesser; you just need to decide which side is the lesser evil.

"I understand," I admit. I do and so far Gabriel is giving a good argument I just don't like his actions to aching it. After all Marcus's dead body is still laying on the road.

I Don't like Luna's either. Which side is the lesser evil? Time will have to tell. I'll make it.

His eyes drift to his brothers, "They will instruct you. I need you not to break." He shakes his head, eyes no longer meeting mine, "Luna is gone, Sol." Hearing him speak those words is like having my nails ripped off. Torture. I gasp when he cups my cheek as if saying goodbye to my sister. "She's gone." He swallows. Then his index finger brushes over my temple; he taps it twice. He is worried about me continuing to speak to a ghost.

Don't worry; it was a lie you gobbled down. I knew the truth.

I never used to fib so freely. The idea of using my talents to deceive so many people was once inconceivable. Luna taught me how to paint sinister images and weave convincing lies for the world to believe, all to further her own agenda. These lies remain hidden, secrets yet to be unraveled by anyone.

In the beginning, I lay awake at night, tormented by guilt over my actions. One such lie I had to paint and present to Gabriel haunted me—the image of me dressed as my sister, conversing with her apparition. It pained me to think about how it affected him, but with time, my remorse dwindled. I changed and evolved, becoming desensitized to the art of deception. Now, I've even concocted my own elaborate scheme, one I hope Luna never suspected.

My new life is akin to stepping into a video game. It's fascinating how, when playing video games, many of us tend to gravitate toward taking on the role of the villain. Numerous studies have delved into this phenomenon. Why is it that we find it not just acceptable but liberating to embrace our inner villain when immersed in a game?

Because when we play a game, it isn't real, so we have the excuse to explore the dark parts of our minds.

Luna and Gabriel lost sight of reality. That's how I feel now. My wrongdoings are...ok. I even feel a surge of dopamine when I act on them now. It motivates me more, and that scares the shit out of me.

These games are real. I have seen the blood. Witnessed the hearts stop beating.

In war, morals are erased; the excuse is warfare. It makes everything alright. It makes lying, murder, insanity, and deception very reasonable.

Dear mental Journal,

It's been a long fucking time. Sorry I was busy. Lost in my lies. Kept too many to myself. But here is a confession. I'm prepared to tell you a secret Luna asked me to do. She asked me to lose my sanity that night.

"I need them to think you are insane because they think madness is broken. It's not. They don't realize how genius insanity can be. So talk to me whenever you need to."

I did talk to Luna, Journal. I played them all just as she asked. I even played myself. I found comfort in my folly. It helped me focus and see the details covered by the lies. Talking helped me solve so much of the puzzle.

Now I know what you're thinking, Journal, because you are my mind, after all. I did break at times. I did indeed have a mental lapse. Maybe I was method acting?

It doesn't matter.

What matter is that I'm doing everything Luna asked of me. Even more.

Luna thought starting her game would save us, but it didn't. It only created another turn in the labyrinth.

I see how to save us all now. I must remember that my reality isn't a game or a simulation. Every action I commit has consequences when this game is finished.

Luna has been fighting this war much longer than I have. She started as a child, but now I must bear her flag and continue as an adult. It makes sense why Luna was so polluted as a kid, why she hunted and killed birds and strived to learn the science to manipulate it.

Every waking minute, I find it easier to think like Luna. I once felt so different from my twin, but the further I go into this game, the more blood I see, and the easier it all becomes.

How quickly a tossed coin can change sides.

As Gabriel's eyes flare with concern over my prolonged silence, he remains unaware of the internal turmoil within me. He doesn't know that during that moment, I was confessing a terrible deed inside my mind. I was told to feign insanity, to make him believe that he could fix me, use me, and protect me.

"It's time." He grabs the car door.

As I get in, I see the look Gabriel gives Wes. It is a warning; I wonder if Wes will heed it. I know Death won't.

I buckle my seatbelt, and the sound feels like the click of the game starting again.

Tag, I'm it.

I'll play; I have no choice but to play multiple games at once. I need a bigger canvas and more paint because I have a lot of ground to cover, so many lies to paint, and secrets to whisper.

Chapter 10

Sol

The past: Thirteen years old.

"Please, can we watch it? Please, please," I beg the new nanny, Gretchen, to put on the live interview my father is about to give. He's the star speaker at a bioscience convention.

Gretchen agrees, easily swayed by my persistent requests, and goes to fetch the laptop. Meanwhile, Luna approaches me and slaps me across the face as soon as Gretchen leaves the room. The sting hurts, but it's nothing compared to the pain of my twin hurting me.

Luna has changed since she started playing the game, turning into the one who inflicts pain.

"Don't ever beg, Sol," Luna hisses, her eyes filled with disdain as tears well up in mine. It's unclear if she despises my display of vulnerability or if she hates that she is the cause of it. Deep down, I know Luna doesn't enjoy hurting me. She's trying to toughen me up. Lessons come in different forms.

"I have access to the labs twenty-four-seven," Luna admits. I'm aware that Luna has more access to the labs than I do, a result of us switching places. I could have been in her position.

Luna bristles when I don't respond, "If you can't handle a slap, you could never handle our future." She criticizes, crosses her arms, and sinks into the sofa.

Gretchen returns just as I wipe away my tears, oblivious to the red handprint on my cheek. Setting up the live stream, she becomes engrossed in her phone, smiling while texting her boyfriend.

I yearn for a smile like that, hoping to find someone with whom I can escape with.

The live stream starts. My father stands behind a blue backdrop with the convention's logo patterned behind him. A woman holds a red microphone close to his lips. Father looks old; more stress lines detail his forehead now. The sides of his hair are almost completely gray.

"Dr. Eklund, it's an honor to have your time. Can we ask you a few questions?"

Father smiles and nods, but I can tell by how his lips are pursed that he wants to decline the interview. We missed his long lecture; Gretchen didn't let us watch that because we had our biology classes with Dr.Victor online.

"Your lecture showed the world a new future that looks like science fiction. You are managing to convince the world to bend to your side. Your company Exodus Technologies has successfully implanted patients with 3D-printed organs made from their cells. You have chipped away at the organ donor list and made ungodly advancements. How do–"

Father holds up his hand. "The choice of your wording implies I am tricking the world. Science is no trick; it is not science fiction. Does science fiction help inspire scientific advancement? Certainly." Father quips. "Results are facts; The results showed more than we could have ever anticipated. It's a very promising future." He looks off to the side of the camera.

Who is he looking at? Why does he look so distant.

The woman leans forward, "What would you tell the people who don't trust science yet? To the people who don't believe you can continue to crack more codes of genetics."

Father responds without hesitation, "In the 1980s, many reporters voiced sentiments similar to yours when personal computers emerged. The news industry was rife with attempts to stoke fear," he remarks, a hint of a grin touching his lips as he recalls history. "They painted a picture of personal computers as both the harbinger of a bright future and an ominous intrusion into our daily lives. The world resounded with apprehension, but that apprehension gradually subsided as people witnessed the transformative power of personal computing. Let me pose a question to you," he turns the tables, fixing his gaze on the interviewer, "Would you willingly part with your cell phone?" Father's question hangs in the air, and the reporter responds with a resolute shake of her head.

"No, you would not willingly part with your cell phone. Just as you can't imagine living without personal computing, there will come a time when gene editing kits become an integral part of our lives. This, my friends, marks the next phase of human evolution," Father asserts, his gaze now directed squarely at the camera, as if addressing a wider audience. "We already use technology daily for personal entertainment, and this leap in gene editing will follow a similar trajectory. It's not a question of 'if' or 'when.' This is an inevitability, much like the rise of personal computing. The foundation for gene editing technology is already firmly in place, and it's only natural for us to strive for something better, just as we observe in the animal kingdom, where males often exhibit brighter colors and plumage than females. It's a display that not only attracts potential mates but also serves as a means to identify and select the fittest partners. Gene editing functions along similar lines, but with an added dimension of benefiting everyone. This technology offers us the unprecedented opportunity to level the playing field."

"Most critics argue it makes the playing field steeper. They fear that designer babies will be genetically designed and only those who can afford the technology will have access to it."

Father snorts, "I guarantee you, designer babies are the last subject I care to discuss. I'd much rather stay on the topic of what my studies focus on, like the genetic manipulation of disease resistance cells. Cells that can be engineered to repair themself." Father raises his brows, "Stopping cancer before it spreads. The cat is out of the bag, Mrs. Baldwin, gene editing is out there, and it will never go away. You can use nuclear energy to power a city or destroy one. I will use my developments to benefit others, and I hope the media will help keep other scientist in line to do the same." He grins, "There is only forward, not backwards."

I glance at Luna, who looks at me at the same moment.

We are designer babies but were not created to be boasted about. My twin and I are hidden.

Why did father make us?

"So you plan on making this new GENESIS SL1 kit accessible to all?" The reporter questions.

Father glances down. He is about to lie, "You can't hand over nuclear power to everyone, Mrs. Baldwin. We don't want another cold war. My science will be in the hands of those who understand it and will not turn it into a weapon." He blinks. "Many governments agree with that statement. They are already having conversations about how to apply it. With this discovery, we can edit bacteria to consume plastic and not dump it in landfills. We can change the genetic makeup of salt water to have a lower pH so the human body can drink and process it. A world without diseases. Without problems." Father stresses. "The possibilities only have to be dreamt up then created." His eyes look into the camera again. I feel like he is speaking directly to me. Father has groomed me to create and dream.

Luna slams shut the laptop. "Did you believe that?" she questions me.

I nod, "We are proof of his science."

"No!" Luna hisses, "Did you believe that father has created this, us, to better the world?"

I chew my lip, "Why else would he? Curing diseases is a sound reason." Luna and I know this. We edited the genes of mice to be resistant to malaria just two years ago. It was a project father assigned us and gave us one month to complete without his help.

"A sound reason." Luna laughs. She holds her arms up at an awkward angle and begins to move them. She's pretending to be a puppet that a puppeteer controls.

"You think we are puppets?" I suggest. Father is directing us, but he is our parent; That's his duty.

"No, think again." She presses.

I look at the laptop, "Father is a puppet?" My forehead wrinkles.

Luna grins. A wicked smile makes the hair on my arms stand to attention. She reaches forward and smooths out my furrowed brow. She wants me to hide my confusion. "Ask a smarter question, Sol?"

I lick my lips and reply, "Who is father a puppet for?"

Luna nods.

"The people in the tunnels?" I ask.

Luna drops her arms. "Don't ask too much. Greed is a sin, sister."

Chapter 11

Sol

In a state of delirium, I somehow snatched a few hours of shut-eye during our scenic drive to Munich. It's almost surreal how the whirlwind of chaos and uncertainty in my life managed to lull me into slumber.

But now, I'm wide awake and brimming with anticipation. I can't help but pace the floor of my new room.

I scrutinize every detail of the space; my nose turned up like a stuck-up influencer unhappy with the reviews from their latest upload. The walls are a dark gray with a subtle blue undertone, almost resembling the rugged texture of slate or stone. It's not warm and cozy. A splash of color and some throw pillow could go a long way. There's an old bed that squeaks whenever I shift on it and a dusty bookshelf, its faint, musty scent indicating infrequent use.

The whole house seems frozen in time, as if abandoned, devoid of any artwork or photographs that could inject some life or emotion into its dreary ambiance.

My feet carry me to the bookshelf; I run my fingers over the books, leaving a path in the thin layer of dust on the spines. I once wanted my life to be as adventurous as the books I read.

Be careful of what you lust for; sins have a way of being deceptively sweet and wicked deadly. Too much sugar can kill; hope has the same ending. Hope can lead to insanity, delirium, and Death.

I must be a masochist because I can not heed my warning. I'm ready to continue my journey into the darkness, no matter how much the anxiety consumes me. I welcome the monsters because they will help me end these games.

I carefully slide a book from its spot on the shelf and bring it closer to inspect. The pages have aged to a delightful shade of yellow, and as I gently flip through them, I notice the faint wrinkles where someone had once marked their place. These books aren't my usual reading material; they all revolve around history, detailing the exploits of great generals and the battles they fought.

These subtle clues point to an unmistakable conclusion – this house must belong to War. It starkly contrasts the custom-made suits and impeccably polished exterior he presents to the world. The discrepancy makes him even more intriguing. I just found a new side of him that contradicts the persona he carefully cultivates for others to see.

Upon our arrival, War escorted me to this room and gave me a simple directive: clean up and get some rest. Wes remained in the car as he took a phone call. I expected him to return, to sneak into my room and do all sorts of dirty things to me.

I laid on the bed waiting, hoping, fuming. The crisp white ceiling soaked in the grey walls' reflection making it look like a thundercloud ominously hovering above me.

I place the book back and run my fingers down my clothing. I'm still wearing the hospital gown with the scrubs over it. I look at my palms, which are still stained faint red from the blood that soaked them during the club.

Footsteps sound up the creaky old stairs. I know the weight of those steps, how each foot resonates when it plants its weight on the floor. "Sol." Death voices as he opens the door.

I wait for a bated breath before I turn to face my monster.

There he is in all his well-slept glory, eyes gleaming with a clear conscience that is laughable. He even comes with an offering, a tray of food filled with breakfast delights that turn my stomach.

"You didn't shower." He states as he kicks the door shut with his heel. He places the food tray on the bed and crosses his arms as he studies me.

His feet are bare; he's dressed in sweatpants and a white undershirt. He looks so fucking normal. Stunning but normal. It's such a wasted lie.

I look at my palms at the dried blood that would make a naive person think I just ate a bowl of strawberries, "There is no cleaning what stains me." I confess. I don't want to clean it off. I need it there to remember what is real. What I don't want to become.

He strides forward. I hear the fury in his steps as he grabs my hands, pulls me into the small bathroom, and turns on the shower. He is so tall that it feels like I swallowed a pill to make my stature smaller.

"Get in," His eyes watch me, his gaze filled with a twisted, dark sickness. They take note of my defiance, relishing in the challenge. "I'll make you," he grins, his words dripping with anticipation.

He cups my face, his palm firm but the tips of his fingers gentle, two sides of the coin, caring yet claiming.

I lean into his touch. *Don't judge me. You would too.*

His body purrs. It makes me want to cuddle closer to him like he's a kitten. Even kittens have claws, Sol.

He tilts my head up, forcing me to meet his gaze. "Are you Death or Wes? Which side do I find myself entangled with now?" The line between his two identities blurs, leaving me unsure of which version of him holds sway over me in this moment. Which side can I try to manipulate to join my cause?

"Are you Luna or Sol?" He rebuttals. "Neither, both, you don't know anymore?" He pushes, taunting me to question my own identity.

To admit it.

I attempt to step back, but his fingers tighten around my jaw, preventing my escape. "Don't lose yourself in this battle, little mouse," he warns, his grip a painful reminder of his control over me. The struggle between the different facets of my being threatens to consume me, but Wes's words serve as a chilling reminder to stay grounded, to resist getting lost in the darkness that surrounds us.

"What if I never knew who I was, to begin with?" I confess. The truth of my identity feels elusive, as if it was deliberately obscured from me. The teachings and guidance I received from my father now appear to be nothing but a web of lies. My entire foundation was built on deception. I was meant to be nothing more than a tool for Manus Dei.

"What if you knew all along but were too scared to confess it?" he states.

He knew precisely which button to push. No one else has seen what he has. No one else knew that I was as drawn to the thrills that lurked in the tunnels of my house, just as Luna was. I was just cautious; I had my trepidations. This caution made them all think I was a coward. But Wes he sees the truth. Some creatures just need coaxing to step out of their hiding spot. He's got me standing wide out in the open.

It's the truth. When I was five years old I was scared to play the game my father played with Hans. That didn't mean I didn't want to play! Luna manipulated me, made me think I was weaker so she could claim my spot. Ever since that day I've been hiding my true desires.

"Light is blinding; it is hard to discover who we are when we cannot see," Wes muses, "But darkness... darkness is freedom. It doesn't blind the eyes. Your sight adjusts, and in the absence of light, you begin to perceive shapes, to explore, and uncover who you truly are in the darkest times." His words brush against my heart, sending a surge of warmth through me. "You will admit what you want, Sol," He assures me, his hand drifting lower until our fingers intertwine. The touch makes me feel safe and loved. "I'll be there, holding your hand whenever needed, and I'll be by your side, teaching that same hand how to fight."

My heart hums, maybe I can turn him into my soldier.

With a slow, hesitant touch, his fingers grasp my clothing, and I lift my hands in surrender, allowing him to strip me bare. True to his promise, he doesn't make me face this vulnerability alone; he undresses himself as well. His magnificent body, adorned with scars and tattoos, a testament to his experiences. Some tattoos bear the mark of Lumenis ink, while others are done in conventional permanent ink.

Taking my hand, he leads me into the shower. With the bar of soap in his hands, he begins to wash me. It's so intimate that my knees shake. He doesn't just love me, he cares for me.

His touch is gentle yet thorough, washing away not just the physical grime but also the remnants of my struggles, including the crusted blood under my fingernails. Each finger is meticulously cleaned. He further tries to undo me when he kisses the tip of every single finger before he moves onto the rest of me.

I watch him closely as he tends to me, his eyes lingering over my body, yet never crossing the boundaries of respect. A deeper connection forms between us, one that goes beyond physical desire. His care and attention makes me feel cherished and renewed, as if the act of cleaning is a metaphorical purification, washing away the stains of the past and creating space for a fresh start.

But I'm also not the naive little mouse I once was.

Every action is a manipulation.

Wes is playing me, trying to convince me that Gabriel's side is sounder than Luna's. He wants me to think he will keep me safe as long as I am the perfect pawn for Gabriel and him. And by allowing him to wash me, I am manipulating him into thinking he can bend me anyway he wishes.

I'm going to try to make him my soldier, one loyal to me and not Gabriel.

There is always the question of if I fail. I pondered that when he never came to my bed last night.

I've learned that I don't need others to keep me safe. I'm wise enough to realize I can keep myself safe and bold enough to try to protect everyone else, including the man who deceived me but also stole my heart.

Chapter 12

Sol

How can everything go from hot to cold; why isn't there a simmer button I can select when it comes to Wes?

Passion to cruelty.

Bitterness to compassion.

Where is the middle ground? Maybe we need to make it?

Wes left to reheat my breakfast and to give me privacy to change. That considerate nature is what drives my mind insane. I want him to either be an asshole or a caring person. Not one or the other.

But then, would you be attracted to him? His crazy shifts are what drive you toward him.

I shake my head, determined to silence my inner thoughts. I redirect my focus to the present moment.

A set of nondescript clothing is left on the bed. A plain gray undershirt and matching sweatpants. I grab the shirt and hold it up; It's a man's shirt, no doubt his. *Laying claim, are we?*

I bring it to my nose, inhale deeply, and smirk. Yep, it's unmistakably his scent. Like s'mores, smoky yet sweet. I take another luxurious inhale, unable to resist savoring it once more.

How morally corrupt am I now? I crave a man who stalked me; I love a man who twisted truths to seduce me. I've become my twin. My relationship with Wes mirrors Luna's and Gabriel's.

Deep down, I wish for a different outcome in which Wes's love for me is stronger than his desire for games and control, unlike Gabriel and Luna's ending.

I slip on the shirt, and it instantly makes me feel safer because it belongs to Wes. As I raise my leg to step into the sweatpants, I realize they're a bit too big, and I have to roll them four times to keep them from sliding off me. Without a hairbrush in sight to comb out my knots, I resort to using my fingers to rake through my hair.

I go back into the bathroom and look at the empty counter. I have nothing here, not even my makeup, no paints for my lies. My reflection stares back at me; I reach out and touch it. "You are always with me," I tell my sister. My index finger traces my image then taps it. "Never stop playing," I whisper my sister's words. No matter the emotions that come my way.

"I'm sorry I can't do everything you asked. I have to end this, Luna." I press my palm flat against the reflection. "Maybe that is what you wanted all along. I hope it is, then my actions won't be a betrayal." My hand slides slowly down until it rests on the countertop. "I don't know how I'll do it, but I will find a way to stop the games."

The stairs creak. Wes is coming back. Those stairs will make it hard to slip from my room without notice. Even falling dust from the air causes them to squeak.

As I exit the bathroom, I spot my Horseman holding a tray of food and holding one of my treasures. Tucked securely under his arm is my Prada handbag. Instinctively, I move towards him, longing to reclaim my prized possession. Just as my fingers are about to touch the smooth leather, he pivots his shoulder, using it as a barrier between me and my bag.

"Eat first," He orders, eyes skimming down my body. "You haven't eaten in almost two days." He places the tray on the bed.

I curl my hands into fists, but I reluctantly listen. To manipulate Wes effectively, I realize I must make him believe he has control over me. It's a delicate dance because, in truth, he does have control over me. The challenge will be finding a way to mold that control to suit my purposes and not vice versa.

I pick up a slice of bacon and sink my teeth into the crispy, oily flavors. Wes chuckles, but his laugh fades when I lick the oil off my lips, and his eyes glaze over with heat that sparks a flame inside my belly.

"How did you get that?" I glance at my handbag, which he shouldn't have. You see, Gabriel had claimed I didn't possess a bag, yet I vividly remember wearing it in the club where his reflection was mercilessly murdered. My bag is an essential part of me, a constant companion I never leave behind. Gabriel's lack of knowledge in the hospital didn't escape my notice, but I chose not to confront him at that moment.

Why did you hide my bag from your brother, Wes?

He slowly opens the bag; the expensive leather stretching back emits a suspenseful creak. My eyes remain fixed on the postcards tucked neatly inside. A wave of anticipation washes over me, intensifying my heartbeat, which now echoes like a wild stallion trying to escape being caught and tamed.

"My brother, Famine, sent you the postcards," He confesses. His tone is absent of anger or surprise. It only makes my palms grow clammy. I need a clue to know what he's thinking. "Famine has been loyal to Luna all along." He sits down, and the bed dips, forcing my body to slide an inch closer to him. His nostrils flare finally tells me he's upset, "But what I want to know is," he reaches inside. I see the flicker of metal shine between his fingers as he grabs a new item, "how did you get this?" War's tiepin is clutched between his fingers.

Oh my, are we jealous? Yes, we are.

I'm exposed, caught in the tangled web of secrets, but so is Wes. I grin, unable to suppress it. After all, he has my bag, which means he was in the club. I didn't hallucinate Death speaking to me before I passed out. He was lurking in the shadows all along.

He must have taken my bag before Gabriel arrived.

"Be careful, little mouse," He warns.

He's right; I must take carefully planned steps when I paint this story for him. I mentally grab a paintbrush but not any brush, one that has a fine tip for details. Whatever I confess will reveal War's lies to his brothers. I can paint War as a traitor, or I can paint him as something else...

"Have you talked to War?"

"Strike one," he says, amusement flashes in his green eyes, fully aware of my unsuccessful attempt to mislead him. He crosses his arms. Muscles flex. A lion bracing to pounce.

"He gave it to me," I reply, licking my lips and tasting the bacon on them.

"When?"

Ah, this is where I must tread lightly. War followed me that day in New York, the same day he met with Famine, who was working with Luna. Makes one question: which side War has a higher bet on? Until I know for certain, I can't expose him. So, I think of the perfect falsehood.

"In New York," I confess, finally revealing the truth.

"Strike two,"

"That's the truth!" I exclaim, frustrated. I drop the bacon onto the plate.

"I know," Wes grins, shifting closer. "I want details, Sol. I want everything." His words pin me down. "You know I crave that, but you're playing a game. Lie to me again, and you'll see what happens."

"That sounds tempting," I mutter.

"What was that? It sounded like a little squeak," he remarks, reaching out and lightly tugging my bottom lip with his thumb. "Speak up, baby. Tell me what you want," he encourages, leaning in closer. His warm breath tickles my ear as he adds, "And if you're good, I'll give it to you."

Oh, I have a feeling you'll give it to me either way.

"I was shopping," I fabricate, "War approached me. I thought he worked at the store. He was dressed so impeccably. A man in a suit does have a certain appeal."As I speak, I can see the flicker of jealousy in Wes's eyes, causing him hands to begin to roam.

"You don't like a man in a suit, little mouse," he snaps. His hand skimming over my shoulders sending shivers down my body.

I pivot towards him. "I'm not sure what I like," I lie.

Refusing to give Wes the upper hand, I press on. "I noticed his tie pin. I've never seen a man wearing one before. So he took it off and insisted I keep it. He said it would bring me luck."

I dangle the bait, watching as Wes eagerly takes it. Jealousy can be a cancer, spreading from within. I observe the red flush that tinges his tan skin, a clear sign that it's already starting to consume him.

He forcefully shoves the tray off the bed, causing the dishes to shatter on the floor. His heavy breath reverberates like a battle drum, fueling my adrenaline and preparing me for the impending clash. He seizes my shoulders and claims my lips without hesitation, his tongue asserting dominance and setting my soul ablaze.

It's utter bliss.

His taste.

His touch.

His wicked tongue.

His hand presses against my spine, merging our chests together as if he desires our hearts to beat as one. *I want that one day, baby, If I survive.*

My back hits the bed as the breath flees my lungs. His weight, a delicious presence hovering over me. A throbbing begins in my intimate depths. In one swift motion, he removes my pants, then his own, still caging me from above. I clutch his hard biceps, my fingers gliding up and down the grooves of his muscles.

We're flesh to flesh now; the scorching heat is almost too much to bear. "Wes," I moan as I buck my hips up. Fuck I missed him. Missed this passion that I had to deny.

He grinds his thick cock over my lips, his tip nudging my swollen clit. I'm Ravenous. A hunger for more consumes me. He keeps a slow motion, never pushing in, just up and down. The grin on his lips spreads like a cat that got the cream as he watches my body become delirious for his.

Another flush of wetness coats my thighs, my cheeks burn from embarrassment. "Don't hide from me, little mouse." He nudges my chin, "I want to see what I do to you. I want to engrain what no one else will witness."

His weight bears down on me, pinning me firmly against the mattress, yet I've never felt more secure. With each gentle push, I yearn to draw closer to him.

It's never going to be enough.

Never.

Never deep enough. Never long enough.

My hands cling to him, nails digging into his flesh with an intensity that threatens to break the skin. He halts, meeting my gaze. Thick lashes frame eyes that have haunted my dreams and tempted my nightmares.

It is in that moment that I realize I hold the power. He's waiting for my permission to fuck me, and he won't proceed unless I grant it. He may be a monster, but he maintains control over his inner beast.

He respects me; when a soldier has your respect, he will fight a perilous cause. Will Wes leave behind his brothers and run away with me once the games have finished? I'm too scared to ask. I want to feel something other than the constant plotting in my mind. Forget everything for a few minutes.

My hands trail up his back, my fingers dig into the groove of his spine, eliciting a moan from him. "Fuck me," I taunt. "Make me forget."

He shakes his head, "I'll make you remember." Then he thrust his thick cock so deep inside me that I think I died and touched the stars. All I see is light, blinding, hot, beautiful explosions.

Our lips collide in a passionate frenzy, and within an instant, I remember the craving I constantly felt when I saw Wes. From the first moment our eyes clashed in the art gallery, there was passion, a primal need to taste each other.

That need grew into a delicious pain. An exquisite pleasure.

"Fuck I missed you." He pants, "Missed this tight wet pussy. I should punish you for running, for lying to me. Maybe I will." He slows.

"Don't you dare stop."

He chuckles, "That's it, beg me, beg for my cock."

This is new. Wes never spoke to me like this but I'm not fucking Wes am I. This is Death, my Horseman. I crave both the gentle lover but also the raw, carnal side.

My core pulses around him. "You like that. Fuck, I can feel how much you like it." He reaches down and adds his fingers, circling my clit. A reward. My legs squeeze tight as I chase my orgasm. "You're so tight. So perfect. Mine."

And I want you to be mine, not your brothers. I want you all to myself.

I clutch his hair, the intensity of our connection sending shivers down my spine. My voice trembles with a mix of emotions. "God, I hate you," I moan, pulling him closer.

"I love your hate," he growls, his fingers adding more pressure, his thrust hitting a new depth. Leaning down, he tantalizingly traces his tongue in a slow, teasing circle around my hardened nipple. My back arches in response to his skilled touch. "But I will cherish your love even more," he vows, then sucks my nipple into his hot mouth.

Fuck.

I'm ruined.

I surrender to the overwhelming sensations. My body bows as my mind unravels, waves of pleasure washing over me, momentarily erasing all else from my mind. And then, Wes follows suit, roaring with such intensity that it feels as if the very foundation of the old house might crumble around us.

We lay there, entwined and breathless, both recovering from the intensity of our connection. He's still deep inside me. It feels so natural. He's still hard, too, because once isn't enough.

The outside world fades away as we bask in the afterglow of our shared desire, our hearts beating in sync.

"This isn't normal," I whisper. "It's too much."

"It will never be enough," He whispers, his voice husky with desire. He dips his head, trailing kisses, nibbles, and passionate bites along my neck, sending shivers of love coursing through me.

"Now ask me," he purrs as he slowly withdraws, leaving just an inch of himself inside me. I arch my hips, craving more of his touch. I don't want to be empty yet; I don't want to return to the game.

"Ask you what?" I moan as I push my hips up, forcing my sore body to stretch around his thickness again. It burns, but I know he can chase away that discomfort and turn it into bliss.

When I attempt to thrust again, he shakes his head, his dark eyes locked on mine. "Ask me to make love to you now." He pushes against my opening, teasing me. "Tell me you love me."

My heart races, and I swallow hard; my cheeks are flushed from his prickly jaw.

He's two men; each has a distinct role. Death fucks, but Wes loves. He will always be two men until he hears the words leave my lips. I'll never have all of him until I stop lying and admit I love him.

"Say it," he demands, his jaw grinding.

"Make love to me," I whisper, only giving into part of his demand. There, I've conceded a little. I don't want to utter those words until he's fully mine. My soldier, my lover. Not a Horseman who is chained to Manus Dei's power.

"It's ok. I won't back down." He whispers as he begins to move again. This time it's a mixture of slow and fast. He pulls out so gradually that my body trembles. I feel every single long and hard inch of him, every vein on his thick velvety cock. Then he pushes in brutally before he switches to slow and gentle. He's giving me a taste of *everything* I can have if I just say the words.

I want to scream! It feels so good I think I will die.

Who needs fucking or love making when the crosshairs are so divine.

Dying like this? The best way to go.

These games will devour us whole. Any time we can seek peace or pleasure, we have to take it. I'm taking it now as I squeeze my legs around him. Matching each thrust he brutally gives me.

I'm so close to coming again. Wes knows it. He slows, not allowing me another orgasm, but I'm so sensitive now I might just come again with the shifting of my hips. I try to claim it, but he pushes his weight down, pinning me; he grins and shakes his head.

"Don't stop," I beg, turning my face into the pillow.

"I want to see your face," he purrs.

"Then let me come." I tease.

His exploration continues, kissing my lips, jaw, and neck before finding his way to each of my nipples. With each touch, he fuels the fire of my longing, fully aware of the insatiable desire that consumes me, a desire that intertwines with the dangerous allure of his own identity as Death.

"How do you want to break, little mouse?" He pulls out, shifts down, and licks my pussy, "On my mouth?" Oh God! That's too much. I'm too sensitive.

He shoves three fingers inside of me, "On my fingers?" My back arches, rivaling the curve of Cupid's bow

Games. He's playing a game.

"On my cock?" He grabs his dick and starts to pump it hard.

My eyes can't look away. I nod.

"Words, I need words."

How can I speak when you've got me wound so tight? I can play this game, too. Slowly, I glide my hand down the center of my chest till I thrust two fingers inside my soaking wet core.

His green eyes turn molten. He snatches my hand and licks my fingers clean, "That's mine." He growls, and then he buries himself so deep inside me that the bed slams into the old wall.

My nails rake up his back until I try to tangle them in his short hair, but there is nowhere for me to hide. I can never hold him tight enough. It's torture. Self inflicted.

"Wesley!" I cry as pleasures ricochet through me. It's pained from the force of him but soothed by the satisfaction.

His jaw clenches, his control teetering on the edge as he commands, "Look at me." Through the haze of passion, I struggle to open my eyes and meet his intense gaze. "You belong to me." He says, punctuating his words with a powerful thrust. "No matter how far you run, I will always find you. You can jump, but I will be waiting to catch you at the bottom."

A tear slips free from my eye. He licks it away. Steals it.

He circles his hips with each thrust hitting a new part of me I didn't know was even there. I come apart.

It is explosive.

Fireworks is too small of a word to describe what it feels like. More like the big bang. I'm destroyed and created anew. A void of dark matter and energy.

My body slackens as does his. Only our breaths and beating hearts can be heard now. The chaos of our aftermath.

His verbal warnings echo in the absence of my mind. They mingle with the whispers my sister told me so long ago. A clash of two titans fighting for my attention.

I press my lips over his scar from the heart surgery. It's rough and raised under my lips. Unlike my twin, his scars are visible. He doesn't heal as pretty as Luna did. He wasn't designed that way.

His scars tell me he is a defensive player. He will take the bullet. Death is the perfect Horseman for me. I need someone willing to die for me and my cause.

There's always a catch, isn't there? Saving a life means you owe your life in return. Death thinks he's saving me, and in return, he wants my life. I wonder how he will feel when the table is reversed when I save him and come to claim my favor.

Chapter 13

Sol

The past: The night the game began.

Location: The Cliff Walk: Grindelwald, Switzerland

Luna divulges more and more of her plan. It crinkles my mind.
Covers my skin like a rapid rash. Just fucking stop talking, let me
catch up. But don't stop talking. Our time is almost up.

How can I keep this all a secret? It's too much to bear.
Pandora's box, and I can't resist opening the lid; to take a bite of
the apple. Humans always choose sin when it is placed in front of
them. That's what got us into this mess. Man versus god, the devil
versus man. We are all fighting for the attention of a higher power.

"You can do this," Luna stresses with a smile. It's her real
smile. A confident and wicked grin.

"I'll slip along the way."

"No. You will not." Luna hisses. Inching closer to me.
Threatening yet supportive. Essentially her. "You are an artist.
That means your craft consumes you. A master of any medium. You
can paint my lies; paint them for others and yourself." She knots
her famous red ribbon around her fingers. Trapping herself in it. Is
she hinting at something? That she is trapped or that this is a trap
for others? "Become a liar. Do whatever you have to do to make
sure my secrets are whispered in your mind. Let my whispers linger
like a wind blowing through a fallen tree. Some of your leaves will
tremble, and some will fall. You might feel dead when all your
foliage is gone. Stripped bare. But your branches will feel me on
the wind. You will remember this conversation and every truth I

told you. Whisper my secrets." How can she make her cruel plot into a poetic temptation?

"You're asking me to throw away all my sanity." I pinch the bridge of my nose, "My mind is the only thing I have control of." I confess. Through all the experiments father did on us as kids, my thoughts kept me grounded.

"They can take that from you, Sol." Her smile drops. She is empty, like a bottle adrift at sea that holds no message of hope inside.

What have they taken from my sister's mind? Is that why she was so unaffected as a child? During those experiments, did father try to take the freedom of her mind?

Her body jerks, "Take it yourself. Claim your sanity and insanity. Take everything and use it to trick them."

I reach out and touch the red ribbon. It tangles between my fingers now, binding us both together. "What if I lose sight of what reality is?"

"There are people to guide you along the way?" She promises.

"The man that night, the one in my bedroom. The killer. You knew him," I state. She has skated around this, but she can't run anymore.

Luna begins to play with my fingers, "I can't stop everything."

"So you knew he was coming?" I press, remembering the feeling of vulnerability in that moment. I remember how he trapped me from behind, his hand snaking around my neck, gentle yet so firm it made my thighs clench. His body was so warm and hard it made me feel things I never felt before. Fear and...anticipation. No man had ever dared to claimed me like that.

I always thought I was stronger and more evolved. At that moment, I felt fragile. I felt as if every other human on earth did.

I want that again, but I won't admit it. I crave to meet that mysterious man. It's a secret I have kept to myself.

I've kept a lot of secrets.

Luna pulls out her cell phone, opens her music app and plays a song, "House of the Rising Sun" by The Animals surrounds us.

"No. I didn't know he was coming that night, but I knew he would come for you. You ensnared him." She bites. Am I to blame? "I was going to kill him when I figured it out, but then I thought about all the angles." She admits. I still. She has never talked about killing so openly. This is new. "Having a monster hunting you is not a bad problem, Sol. Monsters hunt and they give chase. He will keep others at bay. He's powerful, and his family is too. What he wants, he gets. Once this all begins, when it is your turn to roll the dice and play, he can protect you in ways I can not, but he also can hurt you in ways you'd never imagine."

Her fingers still on the ribbon. Her laugh sounds more like a strangled cry. "Love ruins everything. It changes the very meaning of what life is. When you feel and taste real love, you will do anything to taste it again, like sweet ambrosia. Love has ruined me, Sol. It has ruined so many. Don't let it ruin you."

Chapter 14

Sol

The water's caress barely lingers on our skin, washing away both the grime and the remnants of our forbidden desires. But as Wes steps out of the shower, leaving behind the steam-filled sanctuary, my mind snaps back to reality.

Droplets cling to my skin briefly, cascading like shattered dreams from my curves as I step out of the bathroom. The game is about to begin again.

My gaze falls upon Wes; he's dressed and points to a pile of new clothes for me. His jaw is stiff as if he's numb from having a cavity removed. I was his sweetness, and now he must also return to the maze of lies.

"We are leaving in twenty minutes," he states. A tingle crawls up my spine, signaling a shift, a change in the game we play. The once tender dance between us has morphed into a precarious tightrope, and I can feel the weight of uncertainty pressing upon me.

"I thought we were going to talk," I utter, my voice barely above a whisper, my skin prickling with anticipation. Secrets linger, unspoken and unyielding, casting a shadow over our connection.

"We have much to discuss and a lifetime ahead of us to do it. Now isn't the time."

A lifetime with him…that sounds like a fairytale. That's the problem. I want real. I want to devote my life to a man I don't have to lie to. A man who isn't engaged with Manus Dei.

"Where is my bag?" I swallow. I always looked at the gifts from Luna before I started my day, before I lied. They were my good luck charms.

"I'd give you the world. Just say the words." His lids lift in hope.

So that's the stick up his ass. He thought two good fucks would crumble all my defensives. *You're going to have to try harder, Wes. I'll enjoy the side effects of your efforts.*

The smart player would utter the words, hoping he would comply with my wishes. However, the wiser player recognizes that temptation is best savored slowly. With that in mind, I provoke him further, "It's time to play the game."

He nods, accepting my challenge, "You didn't think I would let you keep your weapons, little mouse," he grunts.

"They're mine." I step forward till I'm toe to toe with him. "The gifts my sister left me are not tokens to be barred with. If you seek my love this isn't the way to gain it." I seethe.

His eyes glint with a mixture of amusement and authority. "You're mine," If he had a hot branding iron in hand I'm sure he'd use it on me. "And that means the bag is mine too. Behave today, and I might just let you have an item from it back."

"Fuck you."

His lip tugs up, "I can again if you'd like." His hand reaches out, slipping under my towel; chills erupt over my damp skin. I try with a fool's hope to squeeze my thighs shut, but he forces his hand between them easily as if pushing into butter. Like a master marksman, he finds his target, swiping my folds. My next inhale is painfully sharp. His eyes smile now as he traces the hard tips of his fingers up and down but never pushes in. Temptation 101.

"Already wet for me, little mouse." He slips his hand free and then sucks his fingers into his mouth. It's...primal.

"Addicting." He purrs as he licks my essence.

"Maybe consider rehab." I bite playfully. Bending down, I grab the clothes, dropping the towel I begin to change in front of him, letting the fabric tease my skin.

His eyes roam over me, his voice lowering to a sultry tone, "It's too late for that. The only cure is a daily overdose."

"Are we going back to Aspen?" I slip on the jeans. They fit perfectly.

Wes's laughter fills the room, echoing with a touch of incredulity. "Levi would kill me if I brought you anywhere near Hazel," he remarks.

I feel him at my back like a blanket that's so cozy you never want to wiggle free from it. His warm hands on my hips, tracing my curves, makes me want to strip bare so I can feel his touch my skin, marking me, bringing me to new heights I've never explored before.

I push back, my neck surrendering to a relaxed state. He bends down, inhales my wet hair, and then kisses my neck.

"Does Hazel know?" I ask. Was she a lie also? I thought she was a true friend.

He shakes his head as his lips continue to gently kiss my jawline. "Sometimes ignorance is bliss, little mouse." He mocks my words back.

It pisses me off so I jerk my ass with force into his groin. He grunts. "I didn't think you'd mind a little pain." I joke as I turn.

"This is a new side." His voice is husky.

"I hope you don't like it." I grab my shirt and slip it over my head.

"There's not a molecule about you I don't like," he responds. "I want to hear you say the words."

"I'm surprised you know what a molecule is." I snort. Has it been months since I stepped foot in a lab? It feels so freeing. I never want to create a tool for Manus Dei again.

He sucks my neck before stepping back, his eyes on the mark he left behind. "You'll admit everything to me one day."

I roll my eyes. On the inside I'm jumping for joy. My plan is working perfectly. Each time I push he pulls and soon he'll pull himself over to my cause. *I hope.*

"Is Levi like you?" I question. Hazel had mentioned that Levi and Wes served in the Navy together. Is that even the truth?

I'm irrevocably in love with a stranger.

Wes crosses his arms and leans against the door frame, "There are only four Horsemen. The others will never be like us."

I flip back a wet strand of hair, "That doesn't answer my question."

He shrugs, having won this round, but before he leaves, he gives me something; his words are a sign that he struggles to deny me. He is slowly wrapping himself around my finger. "Levi is a Rider. You will learn more about Manus Dei and those they have working under them. A Rider is an assassin, and Levi is one of the best."

He leaves without even staying to watch my expression. Maybe he feels like he is betraying his side by confessing this to me.

***

I press my back against the wall to stay hidden. It took me nearly five minutes to carefully walk down the old creaky stairs without making a sound. An impossible task for a mere human.

"Is she almost ready? We need to get going; we only have a small window cleared," War asks Wes, his voice tinged with urgency.

A sudden thud resonates through the room, followed by the sound of a footstep that reverberates against the old, creaky walls. Even the snow on the roof seems to tremble in response to the disturbance.

I peer out from my hiding spot, my eyes widening as I witness Wes gripping War against the front door. Wes's broad back shields his face from view, but his towering presence exudes a fierce, simmering anger. War, however, manages to catch my fleeting glance, his eyes briefly meeting mine before darting away.

Wes, consumed by his own wrath, is oblivious to the exchange between War and me. I wait for War to admit I'm spying on them, but he doesn't.

Why is War playing his brothers? Who is he loyal to? Perhaps it's himself; War has a different motive in the labyrinth of games I have yet to discover.

"You followed her to New York," Wes growls.

So he believed my lies. I grin.

His left elbow presses firmly against War's chest, causing the fabric of his three-piece suit to crease. In his right hand, a gleaming knife is held precariously close to War's throat.

War's lips curl into a defiant grin, like a naughty child who knows they're about to break the rules but revels in the thrill. "Someone had to step out of the shadows," he retorts, his tone filled with a mix of audacity and hidden intentions.

"Why did you give it to her?" He sounds insanely jealous and I like it. What I don't like his how his grip changes on the knife in his hand. He pushes it harder into War's neck as if determined to slice through the wrapping of a valuable package. His skin ripples around it, threatening to break under the pressure.

"I thought she needed it," War replies. He's quick. Not revealing too much incase he fucks us both. War knows I lied but also kept his lie hidden.

"You questioned my loyalty, and now I'm questioning yours," Wes sneers, and suspicion sways in the thick air like a noose hanging from a skeletal tree. Swinging back and forth, waiting for it's next victim.

War attempts to shift his neck, trying to inhale deeper. He's denied. His voice reflects his insult now, "I didn't question your loyalty, brother. I merely questioned the cause you were willing to die for. Are you certain we are not loyal to the wrong side?" His hand rises, pressing against Wes's scarred heart, the very heart that beats because of the science I helped create.

War's eyes search Wes's for understanding. There is a plea in his gaze that jolts me.

That's a look of love.

I feel like an intruder in this intense and private moment unfolding before me. My fingers grip the edge of the wall, desperately trying to find stability as the tension thickens in the room.

"We should all be working together," War whispers, his voice filled with a sense of longing. "We should be willing to take a bullet for one another."

Take a bullet.

Narrowing my eyes on War's hand covering Wes's heart, I connect more dots. Did Wes take a bullet that was meant for War? Is that why War feels torn to stay with Wes but also aid Famine?

I seal my eyes shut.

War wants his family back together.

I lick my lips understanding why War allowed me to stay hidden. He wants what I want, his family whole again. War isn't working against his brothers but rather for all his brothers.

He wants to end the games.

My eyes water as I witness his pain. I understand his motives. He's causing them to question their loyalty, hoping they will come together and be loyal to one another again.

"Famine had his reasons. We should hear him out." War urges.

The silence between them is painfully palpable. When the blade pushes deeper into his throat, the room fades, and the music of the club returns. I don't see reality but rather the memory I can never erase.

Blood seeps out from Gabriel's neck.

"Why aren't you trying to stop it, Gabriel. There's so much blood." I reach out and try to stop it…or are my fingers painting in it? The blood only seems to smear. I didn't mean for it to spread. I was trying to stop it, but in doing so, I only made it worst. "Like playing the game. Luna asked me to play so it all would stop, but it's only causing more games to begin."

"Sol! Fuck." Wes shouts. "Why didn't you tell me she was there!"

"It won't stop," I mutter to myself.

Why am I so hot? Sweat covers me.

"Sol!"

I startle, my eyes blinking rapidly. I glance up and there's Wes. I'm back. I'm no longer lost in the depths of my own mind. That's the third time I've snapped. Truly snapped. First was in the club, second in the hospital, the third now.

PTSD. I can't allow this to become a persistent problem.

Wes pushes me against the wall. The knife that was in his hands is on the floor. I see the light reflect off of it in a rainbow of colors. "Weapons can be so alluring. Luna was a weapon. I am too." I whisper.

"Sol," His voice firm. A determination in his eyes that seems to cut through the fog of my mind. "Remember, you're not alone in this. You're stronger than you think. Ground yourself. Engage your senses." His words resonate, a strong tether in the midst of the storm.

I nod, taking a deep breath and focusing on the tangible - the color of the walls, the feel of the wood floor beneath my feet, the lingering taste of my coffee, the soreness between my legs. "I'm here," I whisper, an attempt to anchor myself in the present.

"It was real, not a lie," I tell myself. What happened in the club was real. It happened. I'm not painting a lie right now. I'm just myself, my broken yet stronger self. I'v never been so unmasked before. Tears fall from my sky-blue eyes. Like rain on a cloudless day, it is beautiful. It's a taste of life when the games are finished.

Honesty. One day I won't have to lie.

So I keep talking, purging it from my recollections because, at any moment, my mind will remember the falsehoods I must resume to paint. My lips will shut, and my tongue will contort my words.

"I saw it, Wes," I say, my throat thickens. "I saw him. I saw Gabriel."

"It wasn't Gabriel," Wes insists, his palms pressing gently against my face, cradling it like a lifeboat. *Oh, Wes, how I long to be in your lifeboat. But where would we sail to in these tideless waters? There is no island or safe haven while the games are still being played.*

"But it was his face! I saw the life drain out of him as she...Luna's clone...silenced him forever." The memory of that night, the event that triggered my post-traumatic stress disorder, is as clear and terrifying as if it just happened.

"He was a terrible clone, Sol. If you knew what he did..."

If you knew what I did, what I still am doing, would you kill me so easily?

I shake my head sharply, cutting him off. "Don't make rational reasons for murder, Wes. I don't want the monster right now. I want the man that listens and helps guide me."

He leans closer. Nose to nose. His steady breaths force mine to follow. "It's ok," His words like a balm against the pain of my past. Our lips touch in a tender, comforting kiss. "You're here with me."

His reassurances should comfort me, but I can't shake off the reality of the past. I pull back slightly, looking into his eyes. "You were there. You took my bag. You saw..."

Wes drops his gaze, a flicker of guilt crossing his features. Fingers trail lightly over my skin. His voice is heavy with emotion when he finally speaks. "I told you I would help you see in the dark, not cover your sight," he admits, "I was there with you. I've been there all along. No matter how deep you fall, I will find you."

A tear slips from my eye. Sometimes he is so much like Luna it sickens me. My twin used to think the same. You must fall to learn how to walk; Luna, let me fall. She let me bleed so that my skin scabbed and grew back thicker.

"I understand why Luna never killed you, Wesley." I tell him. Luna had to leave me, but she knew I would be safe with my stalker. A man who won't stop me but rather help me navigate the depths of my dark soul. I'm stuck in this game, and a game means you have to make moves. Wes is going to be there to push me and watch me move.

His green eyes soften to a shade of wet moss, the closest to crying he will ever show me. "One day, you will understand why I never killed you either."

A throat clears, "As cheery as your fucked up romance is, we need to move on." War states. His hands move to flatten out the wrinkles of his suit. His eyes look sharply at me.

"Wesley found the tie pin you gave me when you followed me into the store in New York. He didn't take it too well." I tell him.

Before Wes turns to face his brother, War nods thanks. I just filled him in on the lie. We're working on the same side. To save those we love, but that doesn't mean I can trust him completely.

Wes grabs my hand, interlacing our fingers. He opens the door, and I inhale.

Tag, I'm it again. Where will this next round of the game take me?

Chapter 15

Sol

I don't know if it's divine intervention, fate laughing at us, or maybe, just maybe, someone else intervened. As we drive to an unknown destination, the radio plays a song that seems to pierce my soul. Mocking me, taunting me, understanding Wes and me.

"Bottom of the Deep Blue Sea" by MISSIO. I think Wes feels it too because his eyes keep finding mine in the rear-view mirror. Each blink of his eyes burns my skin.

He reaches out to change it.

"Don't," I snap.

His hand drops as if he were a fly I swatted. Flies always return, and so do his eyes observing me. My back hits the seat as he presses the gas harder, but we can't outrun this. We're all trapped, stuck in the car, and caged in the game. There's no escaping the magnetic pull between us. It's fatal in a way that rebirths you.

The road stretches out before us, a ribbon of uncertainty leading us deeper into the unknown. Questions linger in my mind, clawing for answers. What awaits us at our destination? Will it hold the key to unraveling the truth or present more riddles to decipher?

Each passing mile builds a sense of urgency within me. Closer, one step closer to untangling the web that traps us all.

One step closer to no longer having to weave it.

My thoughts race, trying to connect the fragments of information I've gathered so far. Luna's revelation echoed in my mind: Gabriel's intention to use me as a pawn in seizing control of Manus Dei. Among Luna's pawns, Famine, one of the Horsemen, appeared to play a pivotal role in her absence. His strength and leadership made him a suitable successor to Luna's power vacuum. It had come down to a battle of brothers: Gabriel versus Famine for control of Manus Dei.

As the puzzle pieces fall into place, it becomes abundantly clear what my mission entails: intercept the power transfer. But here's the kicker – I just realized that this power they all want is physical. Gabriel needs me to get it, and so do Luna's pawns.

If it's something you can grab hold of, then you know what that means. I can steal it before I hand it over. That's how I will stake a claim and try to end these games. I'm a puppet being used, but I'll cut the strings at the most opportune moment, when I have what they all want. Then I use that as leverage, forcing them to end the games or else.

I don't feel betrayed that Luna conveniently left out that juicy tidbit. Everything she did was with purpose. She wants me to figure this out myself. The question is, why? What does Luna imagine I will do once I get to this point in the game?

The air crackles when I inhale. I taste the thrill of the unknown and all the mysteries surrounding my twin's true motives. A smile creeps across my face, but as Wes's eyes meet mine in the rearview mirror, I wipe it away, revealing nothing. In an instant, I painted the image of a willing pawn, ready to carry out their orders.

As we enter the highway, the sound of passing cars surrounds us, amplifying the silence that hangs between us. Unable to bear the quiet any longer, I finally break it, directing my words to Wes. "Gabriel said you would explain things. Explain."

A snicker erupts from the front seat, grating against my nerves. "Look who's getting feisty," War remarks, casting a quick glance at Wes. He swivels his head to face me, meeting my narrowed eyes through the rearview mirror. "Why don't you fill us in on what Gabriel has spilled, so we can fast-forward to the juicier bits, Lovely?"

Lovely? Oh, he really likes to stoke the flames of conflict, doesn't he? Kindling the fire, relishing the embers crackling under the heat motivates him.

Wes focuses on the road, a sigh escaping as he responds to War's attempts to push his buttons. "Oh, brother," I can hear the grin stretch over his plump lips. It's power, and he's about to yield it. "I know all your dark secrets, too. You see, Sol, we have an obsessive tick. We can't let some things go. Isn't that right, brother?"

War shrugs, "I won't leave my brothers behind,"

Wes chuckles. It's the sound of the upper hand. "I'm not talking about you still communicating with Famine. I'm talking about her. Your little bookworm."

Leaning forward in my seat I drink up every bit of gossip and possible leverage I can gain. My eyes play ping pong off their backs, absorbing the unfolding dynamics. War adjusts the lapel of his suit, his tone shifting. He's uncomfortable. "I have a lot of women in my life. None as lovely as Sol."

Wes shakes his head, "I never thought *she* was your style, but opposites attract," he retorts.

War fidgets and unbuttons his jacket, dropping his playful demeanor and revealing his true nature. I watch his knuckles move and notice the many scars on his skin. It's clear he's been in quite a few fights and a part of me wonders if they were all by choice. I recall our first meeting in New York when I discovered he didn't like the idea of a cage.

The past.

I can't help but smirk. "A cage doesn't frighten me, War. Yet it appears it does unnerve you." Oh, I know your weakness, alright. I know exactly where to twist the knife.

War's irritation is palpable, visible in the twitch of his features. "You're skilled, but you need to be better," War retorts, adjusting his cufflinks with a deliberate air. "But remember this, little mouse," he sneers, spitting out the pet name Death has given me with sheer disgust. "I hold the key to the cage." His grip tightens around my wrist, his fingers digging in. "You don't."

He might hold the key to his cage, but Wes knows which buttons to push, and each shove sends War closer to the cage door.

"What are you implying, brother?" War's aggression surfaces like a cat edging away from the hellish bath it is forced to be dunked into.

The conqueror's grin on Wes's face tells me that's all he's going to give me. Tidbits to keep me involved in there family dynamic. A family Wes wants me to be part of. "I think you should answer his question, Sol. What has our brother told you so far?"

I allow the seatbelt to snap me back into my seat. I don't reply immediately. I study War, taking in the visible tension in his neck.

Who does War want to keep hidden?

"Love drives us over the cliff, doesn't it, Sol," War sneers. His chuckle is cruel, the words purposely meant to inflict damage on my psyche. He's provoking me to hurt Wes too.

War is right; love makes us do things I could never have imagined. It's a sickness and a cure all wrapped up into one endless maze.

"Luna didn't just do what she did for me. She did it for all of us." I whisper. No one will understand how unselfish Luna's actions were until I stop painting the lies. Until then they are stuck believing the falsehood I show them.

Here's a confession, brace yourselves. Are you ready?

What Luna did was the most unselfish thing anyone could ever do. She sacrificed herself for her cause. Yes, I said it. I mean it. She benched herself so no one would suspect I was sane enough to function as her player. A pawn devoted to her cause. Luna wants to free everyone from the power that sickens us. The sad part is Gabriel does, too. They are too stubborn to join sides, bend a knee, and follow the other. They did what they did best and turned it into a competition. It's the after they can't imagine, but I can. I must.

With narrowed eyes I target the Horseman who might be the only other player in this game like me. War just wants his family together and the only way to accomplish that is to end the games and make them rule together.

Is one ally you don't fully trust enough to end the war?

I hope so.

War snorts at my reply. I'm not sure why he is playing the bully now. Maybe it's so Wes doesn't suspect War is helping me. "Luna didn't help us. She fucked with my brother's heart. Killed it the same night she threw herself over a cliff; Gabriel is struggling to hold on. A king without a queen is just another heartless ruler. That's not what we need. Your fucking psycho twin screwed with your mind, and for some insane reason, you still cling to her cause. You talk to your reflection—"

"Enough!" Wes roars. He jerks the car to the left. It sends War sliding into the door, where he bashes his head.

"Fuck you!" War mocks as he slide back into his seat.

I slap my palms onto my thighs, feeling the sting and pain. I try to focus and get us back on track. "Tell me why Gabriel needs me!" I holler. My voice is assertive. So forceful it silences the bickering brothers.

Green eyes flash in the mirror as they glimpse at me. Judging me. I'm not slipping, crying or snapping back. I'm here and ready to play. Wes begins, "Gabriel needs you to be your sister."

War pivots in his seat, a devilish grin spreading across his face. "It should be easy for you," he taunts, his tone dripping with mischief.

I stumble over my words, feeling a knot of unease tighten in my stomach. "My sister? Gabriel told me to stop being Luna."

War's expression turns into a disapproving tsk. "Uh-oh," he responds, sick amusement bubbles on his tongue. "You went backwards, not forwards, little mouse. Do you want to tell her or me?" he asks, directing the question to his brother.

"Tell me what?" I demand. My toes curl inside my shoes as I brace myself for the impending revelation, my heart pounding in my chest.

"Not Luna," Wes's voice is gentle. Here it comes, a new revelation. "Your other sister." A new light shines on the tangled web of secrets that surrounds me.

I bite my lip, and tears well up in my eyes. The scientist in me knew this. You don't just test on one subject. You test on many. Many that are one and the same. Only days ago, I admitted the dark truth buried in my mind. Luna and I were not the only clones. I witnessed one of *my* other clones murder Gabriel's clone at the club. Me in the same body but a different mind.

How different I am is still a question I am battling with because with each lie I tell, it seems I am much more like my sisters than I ever imagined.

If so many of my clones are capable of murder, how close am I to committing the act I sore I would not succumb to?

It still feels like a right hook. Another sister I never knew, perhaps one I don't want to know. "I only know Luna. Luna is my only sister."

Wes nods, "You're going to have to meet and pretend to be another one." A moment of hesitation makes me hold my breath. "One even more deformed than Luna."

"Luna wasn't deformed. She was who she was raised to be. No other option was given," I whisper. I rest my head on the car window. The slight vibration relaxes me. Numbs me. "Why do I need to be her?" I question. I'm going to have to delve into darker depths of my mind.

War's eyes gleam with anticipation, and I feel like I'm cotton candy being spun while he's the eager kid, bouncing up and down, waiting to grab hold of me, sink his teeth into me, and then lick his lips once I've dissolved away.

"Sol doesn't understand it all yet. Can I help her?" He briefly looks at Wes and then chuckles before adding, "Alright, I suppose I can. We need you to become your sister, Sol, to gain access to a place we can't. It gets interesting once you're inside because we don't need you to be your sister for long. Once you're in, we need you to be yourself," he explains, grinning from ear to ear.

"Myself?"

"Oh, don't play dumb, Sol. You must have wondered why *you*. Why was one clone kept on the sidelines as a backup in case all the others who were upgraded broke." His brow raises, "So many did."

"I was the control in the experiment. I was meant as a guideline to compare."

"Bull-fucking-shit. You never really believed that lie, did you?" War spits.

"The queen always had a backup whether she wanted one or not. The Masters ensured that. You are the key, the thorn in her side that will very soon pierce her heart."

My throat begins to close. I glance at Wes. He nods. Fucking nods.

"Didn't you ever wonder who you were cloned after?" War jabs.

The weight of his words settles upon me. It has always been a lie, my entire existence. The only solace I can find is that it's no wonder I'm so good at lying.

War's enjoyment in his confession is undeniable, and it becomes clear that his intentions are veiled in layers of complexity and hidden agendas. He is a very dangerous ally to try to align with.

Skip, jump, thump! Goes my heart as it skips a beat. My hands are so clammy that when I wipe them on the leather seat a little squeak emerges.

"Oh, come on, little mouse," War beams. He's my friend and foe.

"War," Wes hisses.

He rolls his eyes, "Ok, no more fun. Just facts." The smile drops from his face so suddenly. He reminds me of Luna. Her outward emotions were all an act, a trick to seduce others. "Once you are inside, we need you to be yourself, be the person you were cloned after. You were not just a control for the science, Sol. Your father and the Masters kept you as a weapon against her."

"Who," I ask. My voice shakes, and I feel nauseated. Who am I cloned after and why did War refer to her as a queen?

"Your mommy dearest," War replies.

Chapter 16

Sol

Did he say mother?

I banished the idea of knowing my mother a very long time ago. My mother was nothing but a donor of DNA that my father then genetically modified so much that her donation didn't count.

That's that.

Or at least it was.

A wave of heat rolls over my body like a boiling summer's day. Nausea soon joins. Blinking rapidly, I judge that this is real. The car isn't fading. This isn't a dream or hallucination.

I have to ground myself, so I look at my surroundings. I look at the dark leather seats which are holding me. I study the stitching on the edges of it. I look outside the car at the grey, snowy world around me. This is real, but what War said can't be factual.

I shake my head, "I don't have a mother."

"You do and you don't, little mouse," Wes replies.

"What the fuck does that mean?"

"It means you are a clone of her." He replies.

"That doesn't make her my mother. Just a donor."

"I agree." Wes states.

My nails dig into the leather seats. War didn't have to use that term because it doesn't apply. He just wanted me to feel abandoned, dangled the idea of a mother who never existed. He wanted me to need the Horsemen, him in particular.

War continues, "She is a Master, fighting to keep her genetics in play. But she is more than that. She is the last Master left standing."

"You said she was a queen."

"Eager to take her crown, are we?"

My eyes turn to daggers.

War tips his head back and laughs, "Oh, come on, ask me more. I know you're curious to know about the original. The last Master left standing, the bitch that tried twice now to steal the crown and was sly enough to lock away Manus Dei's knowledge without them realizing it until it was too late."

"You're loving this." I sneer.

His smile drops, "I love that I can anticipate tasting the ashes from our final battle." His nostrils flare as if he can smell the cinder, "I adore knowing soon the air will have the aroma of a rusted metal tang once her split blood. I love knowing that her death is imminent."

My next inhale is shaky; Gabriel is close to achieving his goal. One more Master to kill before he can take over all of Manus Dei. In a sick way, the last Master is me since I'm her clone.

She is the original.

War is right; she is my mother in a way. She gave her DNA to create me.

My eyes seal shut, trapping the lone tear that tries to escape. Another piece of the puzzle just slots into place. A reason behind Luna's motive to use puppets. Dear God... "I know why..." I shut my lips as the words slip out. I understand why Luna is using Gabriel. It isn't solely to steal his power. That's all a lie, a mask to hide the rare emotions Luna did possess. It wasn't just that he betrayed her and chose his own plan to destroy the Masters.

I'm starting to think the true reason Luna started this war was all a lie. It's a trick I have just begun to figure out.

Until I solve this new puzzle I know one thing for certain, Gabriel is her bullet, Famine is her gun, but I'm the trigger man.

Luna didn't just construct a Trojan horse; she built a war machine, and I'm a part of it.

She said she could never kill her reflection. What she meant was her clone. She drew a line just as I did. She found ways to use others so she didn't erase the line in her sandbox.

She tricked Gabriel into believing he was the only player left so he could kill the original. After all, Luna told me that Gabriel had killed his reflections before, so killing Luna's reflection should be easy for him.

I feel a deep, gut-wrenching empathy for Gabriel, yet at the same time, I'm overwhelmed by the pain I feel. It's as if a dagger has been driven through my heart. They each used each other for selfish gains, hoping their advances would protect their love. But in the end, the web of lies and betrayal only slowly killed them. They destroyed what they were trying to preserve.

It's excruciatingly painful, to the point where I want to flee from the very concept of love. I glance at Wes, and deep down, I fear that he and I are mirroring what Luna and Gabriel did— reflecting their mistakes and their tragic ending.

Maybe that is actually why Luna put Wes in my life. Instead of giving me a song to understand her feelings, she gave me the real thing. A tragic love story.

"The last Master was backed into a corner when your sister released Subject 52." Wes states.

"What is a Subject 52?" I ask, diverting the subject of my mother so I can accept that I was cloned after an actual person.

"Subject 52 is a weapon Manus Dei was working on. A new soldier. Your sister released him when she lost the game."

I nod, remembering that Luna mentioned that she released a weapon to back all the Masters into a corner. She succeeded.

"You met him at the club," War adds. He's relishing in my shock. I can hear it as he hums with glee.

"Gabriel's Reflection that was murdered?"

Wes nods. I remember seeing the absence of a soul in that Reflection's eyes. Yet even though he was a monster, I felt a heavy grief when I watched him being murdered because he was like Luna, and deep down, he was like me. Designed and abused for someone else's gain. Luna used Subject 52 for her gain, and he died because of it.

Suddenly I see my fate. Will my twin lead me to death just as she did Subject 52?

I'm a puppet; I never signed up to be an executioner. That's how I feel right now. Looking at my hands, I see the blood still on them. His death is my fault.

Why would you do this to me, Luna? Is this the price I have to pay for allowing you to take my place as a child?

I forcefully rub my palms together, and for the first time in my life, I question if obeying my sister was the right decision.

I feel like a soldier on a battlefield surrounded by death. I can smell its pungent odor and hear the flies as they buzz closer. Some land on me, knowing I'll join my fallen sisters and brothers one day. As this soldier, I ask myself, what the fuck am I doing? Why am I a soldier in a war for those using me? I never asked for this as a child. I never knew the cost I'd have to pay my sister.

I want to be done! I want to swat the flies away from me so they can't feast on my flesh because I know these games will claim me one day.

It will never be enough, even if I somehow outsmart everyone and end the games. You become who you surround yourself with. Man influences man.

I can't remain around these people when this is done.

That's when I make a new decision; after I end the games, if I somehow survive, I am done!Finished with the science that created me but also tried to kill me.

I'm walking away. Cutting the strings that force my fingers to pull the trigger.

I will leave my family behind. I'm choosing me and not them.

Blood has been spilled, it's gotten thinner, and it's no longer thicker than water. I forgive Luna and Gabriel for using me. All they have been taught is how to extort.

I was on the sidelines, observing it all. I learned how to manipulate others as well. But as a spectator, I also learned to feel a wider range of emotions than the original players did. It transformed me into a new kind of player.

A cage can be unlocked, the door open but it's up to the person locked inside to step out. To decide to be free or remain trapped in their madness. I can only hope the others will make the right decision when I walk away, but I won't give up my life to enable them. To keep them on the correct path.

I pray that the love Wes has for me is enough to convince him to leave his family behind and make a new family with me.

I nod my head, and my blonde hair brushes against my cheeks like gentle fingers, guiding me onto this new path. My decision settles deep in my mind. My shoulders relax, and for the first time, I feel like there is a light at the end of the tunnel in the depths of the darkness. I must stay sane enough to see it and use it as my compass.

Chapter 17

Sol

I hear the gear shift as Wes parks the car and looks at War, "Get out." He orders him.

"Brother, haven't I—"

"I said get the fuck out!" He roars, shattering the tense silence.

War waves his hand in the air, "Fine, fine," he replies; he opens the door, and a cool breeze rushes in and chills away some of the sweat beading on my brow. He slams the car door shut, and I'm trapped with the man who seems to have a front-row seat inside my mind.

How do you hide something from a person that sees everything?

You don't.

That's the trick, the other angle you have to play. You show it to them, which I will do to Wes. I'll offer him a choice to come with me when this all ends.

Wes unbuckles his seatbelt; the click startles me. I've faced countless demons, but this fear isn't just about danger. It's the worry that games and power could eclipse love. I'm haunted by the thought that Wes might not choose me in the end, and if I somehow manage to survive, if I succeed in ending the games and then break free from my family, I would be truly alone... alone with my mind. No compass, no guiding light, just the tumultuous sea ready to whip me at every turn.

Eyes that have haunted me, eyes that served as my anchor, keeping me tethered to sanity even when I successfully convinced the world I was insane, gaze back at me. He is strikingly handsome, rugged in a way that momentarily takes my breath away. There's a shadow on his square jaw, his skin has been kissed by the sun with a warm glow, and hands calloused by life's harsh realities, capable of both destruction and crafting poetry when they turn gentle in moments of intimacy. These eyes see through all defenses, and in their gaze, my mind falls silent, granting me a moment to inhale his genuine beauty, unburdened by the lies that have consumed me.

I want to tell him I love him. God, how badly I want to. It's just three simple words, the ones he longs to hear.

I don't.

Now, I'm the coward. If I confess the truth and he picks the others over me... well, I won't survive. There would be no point. So, I bite my tongue until it bleeds, savoring my pain. I can only confess the truth once he picks me, but once he knows all the truths I hold, I know he'll side with his brother. I've damned myself, tasted the passion of truth that has tangled up love, and one day, it will all be nothing but an ashen memory.

I'm still going to try because it's my nature. To survive, to strive, to make my love keep beating with a strong rhythm until the very end. I'll keep trying to manipulate Wes to my side until the moment I have to betray them all.

The drivers door jerks open, he exits and opens my door. He stares down at my frozen state. "You stopped asking questions, little mouse."

I nod. I rake my fingers through my hair and take a moment to itch my scalp. I see the finish line, but I still have to play until I cross it.

So I play, asking what Wes assumes I would. "Why do I need to be this woman? There are clearly other clones that could play this role. More ruthless ones too."

His eyes fix on my chest, and he continues, "There are aspects of you that were not upgraded before birth. This woman possesses those same genetic mutations. All your other sisters were changed after birth, so they can't pass as her." His sharp inhale delivers a blow, "You are her twin more than you are Luna's, Sol." I shake my head, but he continues, "When Subject 52 was released, a killing spree began."

"He killed my father." I fit the puzzle together.

"Yes, and he kept killing, as did we."

I look into his mossy green eyes. He regrets nothing. "You killed to protect me. Why did Subject 52 kill?"

The struggle in his eyes is palpable; he wants to protect me like he always claimed he would, but protection isn't blinding the person you love. That's what separates him from everyone else in my life. He doesn't want to lie to me; over time, he won't; he will tell me everything. He was honest when he said he'd help me see the darkness.

I hope that someday, I can do the same if he's willing to listen to me after he uncovers my lies and betrayal.

"Subject 52 killed because that's all he was raised to do. That's why he had to be stopped. He wanted Manus Dei destroyed, but he wanted to kill everyone. Even you, and that's why I don't care that he died, little mouse." Wes cups my cheek, and I instinctively lean into his touch, feeling like a part of me will always stay with him, like peanut butter that never quite gets completely scraped off hard toast. We've left our marks on each other. *I love you*, my mind whispers. *I hope I can say it to you one day.*

"Will you ever stop playing the game, Wesley?" I blurt out. It's a test to see if he can ponder the idea of leaving his brothers behind.

His eyes lock onto mine, like a telescope tracking the path of a shooting star. *Don't let me pass you by; come with me*, my mind cries.

"How can I end a game that keeps you safe?" he asks.

I pull away from his hold, bewildered. "Safe?"

He nods. "Yes, safe. Manus Dei has the power to keep everyone else away from you. Fear goes a long way in our world, Sol."

No, please don't continue. "Science is our double-edged sword. It's keeping you safe, but I can also see it destroying you." Then, as if he knows my endgame, he adds, "I'll free you from it."

You...not himself because he thinks Manus Dei can protect our love.

A lone tear escapes from my eye, tracing a path down my cheek until it falls. He reaches out and catches it on the tip of his finger. Our eyes reflect our shared anguish, glistening. The question escapes my lips, laden with a mix of longing and uncertainty, "What will you do when I am free from it?"

Wes's grin unfolds slowly, unhurriedly, as if he possesses a crystal-clear vision of his future. "That's easy, little mouse. I'll chase you," he responds. Lifting the finger with my tear, he licks it, savoring it.

"Why do you think I'll need to be chased?" My throat is thick, filled with the turmoil that threatens to suffocate me.

"Because you're going to learn more things that I can't protect you from," he explains gently. I'd rather his hardness. It's easier to hate cruelty than hear honesty. "And when you do, you will want to run away from it all. Seek solace in solitude and express yourself through your art. But your paintings will haunt you, forever reflecting the past. That's why I have to chase you. I need you to see that there is a future. A new life beyond this, where you can have everything you want. I'm going to make sure of that."

His words wash over me, a bittersweet mixture of comfort and uncertainty. The idea of a future, free from the constraints of the game, brings both hope and trepidation.

More tears fall. I allow myself to envision a future with him. I cling to his promise, the belief that he will be there, chasing me toward a brighter path, helping me discover the possibility of a life beyond the shadows that have consumed us.

But deep down, I know it's a lie. He will choose Manus Dei's power over me.

He watches me cry. His fingers continue to wipe away my tears, soothing me but not trying to make it stop. "I'm always going to be there, little mouse."

My lip trembles, "I know." *So will the ghosts that haunt my mind, so will the games that surround Manus Dei's power.*

War shouts, "We should go,"

"This is just a routine checkup. That's all for today. Tomorrow you will start learning more about the woman you need to reflect." Wes tells me, reaching for my hand he has to pull me form the car.

Deep down, I feel so incredibly numb. A part of my mind wants to turn off and wrap itself into a shell so these emotions can't affect me. *Is this how you felt, Luna?*

***

My sneakers crunch into the muddy snow outside. "I'll get you boots," Wes announces, eyes looking concern.

"These are fine."

"No, they are not." He reiterates. He wants every part of me safe and protected. Even my toes from the wet snow that will seep past the canvas fabric.

Inhaling deeply, I gaze at the building in front of us. The back door, rusted from years of use, has an ID badge reader and a security camera above it. A small placard reads "Exodus Technologies," my father's legacy, now in Gabriel's hands but truly controlled by Manus Dei.

The door clicks open, and War enters, but there's no one behind it. He salutes the camera mockingly. I step into a dimly lit hallway. "Is Gabriel watching?" I ask.

"Yes," Wes confirms, stepping in front of me, and War pressing closely against my back. They both brandish their guns, holding them high and poised for action. Confusion sets in, "If Gabriel is watching, why do you need guns?"

Wes turns, his dark figure casting a protective shadow over me. A shadow I love to be swallowed in. A darkness that I welcome every time it hovers over me. "I won't take risk with you." he replies. He didn't even need to voice it. I saw the truth in his eyes.

We step into an elevator that's been hacked, the doors sliding open without needing ID badges. The ride is short but tense, and we emerge into a well-lit hallway. From there, we enter a lab, where a tall man in a lab coat greets us with an air of importance. He towers over Wes, who's no slouch in the height department. What truly catches my eye, though, are the man's long dreadlocks, streaked with silver, like moonlight on dark water. It's either early-onset gray hair or the stress of running this place. A hint of his dark brown skin peeks out from beneath the lab coat. Let's not forget the pièce de résistance—the footwear. He's sporting his signature flip-flops. Today's choice: highlighter yellow and lime green stripes.

I'd know Logan anywhere. He always looked like he belonged on a beach. You would never guess the man was a genius. Naturally born too. He graduated from Yale at fourteen years old with a doctorate in Biochemistry and Molecular genetics. My father recruited him to work for Exodus Technologies when he was sixteen. Logan was just a few years older than me, but I loved when I got to work with him because he felt like an escape. A taste of a normal world I rarely got to see.

I beam. "Logan!" I push between Wes and War. I almost jump into his waiting arms.

Logan was the first person I considered a friend, and that's because he risked his career for my sister. He was a head scientist in the clinical trials for 3D-printed organs. I was under his guidance when we worked on the technology. It was Logan and me who first watched the printed heart take its first beat.

Nothing stays pure, untainted, for long, though. Logan got more involved in my father's work, and he discovered the genetic upgrades that my father did to Luna and me. His job shifted as we aged, we worked alongside him, but he also studied us. Unlike Ethan, who carried guilt after he left, Logan cleared his conscience as he still worked at my father's company, helping Gabriel and Luna as much as possible.

His arms embrace me, but when I hear Wes stride towards us, I break from the hug. "He's a friend," I tell Wes. I stand between the two of them. Wes doesn't regard me. His killer eyes are trained on Logan.

"Clearly, or we would have killed him," War states. "We only have two hours." War tells Logan.

Logan seems stressed, "Gabriel wants a full analysis." He shakes his head. Even though I know two hours is not enough time to run every test.

"Work your magic," War grins, hopping up to perch his tailor-suited ass onto the lab table.

"Let's get started with the MRI first. We will run a functional scan." Logan opens his hand to guide me, but Wes steps forward. This is a peacock show, but Wes doesn't realize that Logan would be more attracted to him before he was interested in me.

We all follow Logan in silence. Our feet sound off the floor like tiny drums. Memories echo in my mind. This isn't the first time Logan has guided me into the lab to run this same test. The last time I had to pretend to be Luna.

The past...

With gentle fingers, I adjust the scope, my focus narrowing on the view of the cancer cells. However, my concentration is abruptly shattered by a sudden bang. Startled, I turn to see the source of the commotion barreling through the door. It's Gabriel, striding towards the electrical panel on the wall. His face is flushed, an unusual display of anger that makes his once-golden blonde hair appear more burnt than shiny. With a forceful motion, he reaches out and yanks the master plug from the MRI machine, cutting off its power. His fists are clenched tightly, and he inhales deep, labored breaths.

"Dammit, Gabriel!" Logan joins us, standing with his hands on his hips. Bright pink neon flip flops catch my attention. I wish I could wear shoes like that. Father would never allow such a display.

Another deafening bang reverberates through the room, and Luna storms out of the MRI chamber. Her eyes quickly scan Gabriel's enraged state, and she recognizes the mounting tension that has caused his shoulders to inch up toward his ears. It's a level of strain I've never before witnessed in him, leaving an atmosphere charged with volatile emotions.

What's even more chilling? Seeing Luna's eyes flicker with anxiety before she masks it.

My palms sweat as if held over a roaring fire. I've never seen my twin look so worried.

Never.

"It's ok." Luna's voice is gentle as she speaks to Gabriel. She shows him a side I never get to see. She's a submissive to Gabriel. She can finally relax. I didn't think it was possible.

Gabriel bears all her worries…except now.

"It's not ok! You're failing!" His words feel like a cold slap to the cheek. He walks to her and shakes her shoulders, "You're failing!" He roars.

Logan steps forward, but his feet are hesitant. So are mine. I hear Gabriel's words, but I can not decipher them. They are foreign to my mind. Luna doesn't fail.

"I need time."

"We don't have time! Time is up. When she went psycho, it took all your time away. You have to prove to them you're not the same." Gabriel shouts. His face reddens, making the entire lab seem too small to contain him. However, his eyes are not angry anymore; they look desperate.

Luna's eyes find mine, and mine must mirror some of Gabriel's worry. She chases away her failures in a second, putting on a brave front. That's my sister, always covering up things that make me anxious. Luna is my rock, but as I am witnessing, rocks can crack…they often sink.

I don't know what Gabriel is talking about, but I know there is no point in asking Luna. She keeps so many secrets from me now.

Logan looks at Luna and then at me. "Switch." He deadpans.

Gabriel pivots to him, "What?"

"Let Sol do this test. It doesn't have to be performed in front of them. They want the results. Sol can do the test, and when I submit the results, they will never know it wasn't Luna. Sol…" his eyes find mine, "she can think as I would."

"I don't need Luna to think like you." Gabriel spits. He grabs the back of his neck and squeezes it.

Logan rebuttals, "Yes, you do. You need that part of her brain to be signaled. To prove to them, she won't snap. That she can be affected."

"Not as much as a normal human." Gabriel quips, "They will know the results are falsified."

"That is why Sol is perfect. She is above average, half of Luna but lesser. Her mind can trick the results."

My eyes fall and hit the polished tile floor when his words register. It hurts. Hearing Logan voice that I am lesser shatters my affection. All I see are my plain sneakers against the laboratory floor. Am I plain next to my sister?

"Watch your words!" Luna sneers.

They are all watching me when I look up, "I'm here." I state as I walk forward, annoyed I'm not only left out of the loop but being spoken about like I'm absent. Like I'm a dumb fool!

Luna steps forward, but Gabriel grabs her hand. They share a silent look until Gabriel concedes. She looks down, unable to meet my eyes, and her voice carries a hint of embarrassment as she says, "I can't fake something, and you don't need to fake it."

I tilt my head, "You can't pass a test." My words sound like I am rubbing her failure in, but I'm not. I'm not cruel. I'm shocked. Luna has never failed.

Logan interrupts, "After Luna's last upgrade, she is having trouble processing some emotions properly."

Gabriel shifts and touches her lower back, "I'll fix this. I'll create a cure." He whispers.

"I don't need a cure." She steps out of his touch. Her blue eyes flick to mine, and I see the lie at that moment. I witnessed her pain

and suffering. Luna wants a cure. It's so clear in the way her pupils dilate, but she is denying herself it.

Why?

What is she up to, and why is she keeping it from Gabriel?

Gabriel steps in front of me as if Luna's attention is a competition.

"What upgrade are you talking about, Logan?" My eyes find her pinky finger. I remember when she was upgraded to regenerate faster. Father tested it by cutting the tip of her finger off.

How did father test the upgrade they are referring to?

"Your father aimed to rectify some cognitive enhancements such as cognitive reasoning. Emotional influences can indeed obscure rational judgment, and his objective was to refine these aspects. However, the haste with which he pursued the results..." Logan's voice trails off, his unease palpable. Shifting uneasily from foot to foot, he struggles to complete his sentence, aware that he's revealing more than he should.

"Father tried to change how you think." I state, dumbfounded. He attempted to alter my sister, a core value that defines who she is. I feel sick. I thought her upgrades were more focused on the physical aspects—cancer-resistant cells, faster healing, heightened cognitive abilities.

Silence.

I shake my head. "No."

"Oh, fuck this!" Gabriel snaps. "We don't have time for catch-up." He tosses his hands in the air.

I step forward, "Tell me the details of the genetic upgrade. I want to help."

"Help!" Gabriel sneers. His cruel laughter makes me feel as small as an ant that his shoe is about to step on. "It was you who got her in this situation in the first place. Little Sol, always coloring away her fears with imaginary lands and heroes. Where are they now, Sol? Where are the heroes you devoted your childhood to painting?"

My bottom lip trembles. How easily he can shatter my fragile defensive walls. Luna hisses, desperately trying to intervene. "Gabriel, stop!"

"Stop defending her, Luna! One day she will have to defend herself, and when that day comes, she will be wholly unprepared," he retorts coldly.

Swallowing hard and blinking back my tears, I muster my strength, pushing away the vulnerability threatening to consume me. I look to my sister, seeking support and hoping for her to speak in my defense, but she remains silent.

In that moment, I have been abandon, left to face Gabriel's harsh words alone, but I fear what else I will have to face alone in the future.

She finally speaks, and I cling to her words, "Remember when I told you I had friends in the tunnels that disappeared when they didn't play the game smart enough."

I nod.

"My latest scan is showing too many similar signs. I'm a risk, and a risk is eliminated. Gabriel will win if I can not pass this test."

For the first time, I hear the worry in her voice. Failing has never been an option for Luna. Only winning in whatever way necessary.

My eyes flip between Gabriel and Luna. They have been locked in a head-to-head battle with one goal.

Winning.

Bound by a deep and complex love, Gabriel and Luna find themselves in a perpetual conflict of wanting their counterpart to triumph, even as they strive for victory themselves. This delicate balance sustains the game, but what happens when the inevitable end arrives and the distinction between winner and loser is unveiled? How will they navigate this critical juncture, where their desires to save one another clash with their own aspirations?

"Where is father?" I ask, my frustration evident. "If he messed this up, why isn't he fixing it?"

"Yes, Luna, where is Dorian?" Gabriel quips. That gets me thinking. I haven't seen my father in well... three months and twenty-six days. It's not uncommon; at the most, Father went almost seven months without seeing us. In recent years, his dedication to his scientific pursuits has demanded much of him, with extensive travel to his labs and catering to the press.

My forehead wrinkles like an old, cracked leather chair. If this is a matter of winning or losing, why isn't she confessing to save herself? We want to help her; we don't want her to lose. I don't understand.

"This is my game, not my father's," she glares at Gabriel. "Don't ask me again." She warns him. It's a button he's pushed many times before, so many times that the button looks ready to break or stop responding.

Logan looks at his bright orange watch, "One hour before I need to submit the reports. I'll restart the computer and note a power failure." His eyes look at mine, "Why don't you get Sol set up." He instructs Luna.

Five minutes later, I am lying down in the MRI machine where Logan will perform a functional MRI. "Answer the questions how you think I would. A little more emotional, don't overthink or plot, just answer as a normal human would."

Nodding, I lick my lips and pivot my eyes to my twin, "Father would not get rid of you, Luna." Some nights the knowledge of the game keeps me up at night. Conversations I overheard haunt me like ghosts, making sounds deep in my head. If a subject breaks then don't waste time fixing it; we move on because we have more.

Luna told to forget what I heard, to paint a new picture of the truth, and believe what I created. So I did. I painted a lie that my father and Luna were talking about a lab mouse named Herald. It's silly and childish but allowed me to sleep without fitful nightmares. I believed my lie, but the truth was always there. My mind whispered it to me like a secret every time Luna disappeared into the tunnels to receive an upgrade or perform a test.

How many lab mice did my sister witness being killed?

Luna presses her lips firmly together. Under the dim lights in this room, her face looks more contoured. The shadows dip into the hallows of her cheeks. Her eyes have dark circles, and I can see the small bloodshot veins in the whites of her sclera. "Father isn't in control when I enter the tunnels." She admits to me.

"Who is in control? Who is seeing these results."

Luna releases an exhale I didn't see she was holding. Her full lips part open, and mine mirror the same movement. Is Luna going to reveal the truth to me? I find myself trying to sit up, but the equipment of the MRI halts me. "Man–" Luna starts to say, but she can't finish.

"Luna!" Gabriel shouts. "It's time." He stops Luna from confessing.

Man? What man?

I won't know. It's a seed that will either be watered or never nourished.

Fifty-three minutes later, the test is complete. I passed, but no thanks came from Luna or Gabriel. Relief doesn't settle on their frames.

Advancing only adds more pressure.

They huddled outside the room, but I can see them through the window that looks into the lab. Gabriel rubs Luna's arm. He is trying to reassure her. Pulling her into his chest she inhales deeply.

I step forward toward the door, but Logan clears his throat. "Best to let them be. They will solve this. Gabriel never fails."

But my sister did.

I wonder if she has failed before. Has Gabriel had to falsify other tests to keep my sister alive?

I join Logan and hover over his shoulder as he submits the false results. "If my father finds out what you did, he will ruin you."

He continues to submit his findings, "I'm not scared of your father."

"Who are you scared of?"

He clicks enter, and the screen closes. What's done is done now. He turns in the chair and looks up at me, "Myself." He smiles sadly, "I was young and hungry for knowledge. They gave it to me, but I'm not willing to sell my soul."

"Does helping my sister redeem you?"

Logan turns his back to me, "I have many years ahead of me until I feel the light of redemption warm my face, Sol." He stands and walks to the door. "I know you can not trust your father, but I will not turn you away if you ever need my help."

***

Logan saved Luna's life that day. He submitted the false result, and in turn, the game continued. It wasn't the first time or the last. Gabriel and Luna had danced that line before, covering each other when they fell short. They ensured that every test, every round of the game of perfection, remained tied until they had gathered enough knowledge and power to take down Manus Dei. That's when the real game began. Unfortunately, by then, they had chosen different sides.

I remember the despair in Gabriel's eyes. That wasn't the look of a man who would kill his love to win a game.

Yet that night on the Cliff Walk, Luna wanted me to believe he had. Why was she lying to herself? She knew Gabriel would do anything to keep her safe, but she pushed him away. Shoved me into the game. Her true motives are still blurred. They might always be.

When will all the players in this perilous game realize that winning isn't everything?

Sometimes, love is.

We finish the fMRI scans, and then Logan physically examines me. It's not invasive. We don't have the time for that, and I'm not sure Wes would allow Logan to examine me more intimately. Logan's hand pokes at me with haste. Wes is breathing down his back, and it's starting to irk me.

"Can you step back?" I assert, my voice directed towards Wes. I need some space to breathe, to focus on the task at hand. There's something Wes and War don't know, a secret that's about to be revealed, but I can't disclose it until I'm alone with Logan.

As Logan approaches with the needle, I sense the tension in the room heightening. Wes's deep, heavy breaths seem to linger in the air like a suffocating presence.

Logan's fingers tremble as he presses the needle to my vein to draw blood. He knows the secret too, and he isn't as skilled as I am at concealing it.

Everything in the game is coming to a head. The finish line is in sight, but that's when most players stumble, just like Logan is doing now.

Logan misses his mark, and Wes growls—an actual growl.

I turn towards Wes, hissing, "Can you please give us some space? Your restlessness is making me nervous, and I've endured a million pokes before. Logan knows I'm yours! This isn't a pissing contest."

War's deep laugh is the only sound that fills the room.

Wes looks at Logan and steps back an inch. He crosses his arms, and his muscles flex.

"Any noted physical or mental changes." Logan swallows and looks down, "Beside the hallucinations." He mutters slowly. Trying not to embarrass me.

"Gabriel has kept you informed." I sneer. I'm not embarrassed about my conversations with my sister's memory. It was an act that sometimes came true. It helped me cope and play the game.

He clears his throat and adds, "I'm aware these symptoms began before you gave yourself the stolen upgrade. What I'm asking is if it is all because of grief or a side effect?" He looks at me with an expression resembling a disappointed parent. In response, I roll my eyes like a bratty teenager.

"Yes, I started to talk to my sister when I went to Paris," I admit. "It was not a side effect from the upgrade."

Wes steps closer. His shadow an invisible form of support. "You don't have to be embarrassed. Some of the strongest men I know cope in different ways." He touches my lower back, "Some choose not to cope too." He whispers.

I don't respond. Everyone thinks Luna could not cope with losing. They all think she ran. I have to bite my tongue not to shout out the truth. That Luna started the game over, only this time, she controlled other players to make moves for her.

"Any other problems I need to take note of? Gabriel sent you here for a reason, which wasn't due to your hallucinations." Logan adds. He levels me with a serious tone.

I lick my lips and look at Wes and War. "Can I speak to Logan in private?"

"No," Wes replies swiftly.

War laughs.

It was worth a try. I'll have to try something else because Wes and War don't know that I knew I'd see Logan again.

I knew it would be soon.

My sister warned me. It was all part of her plan. Unannounced to the Horsemen, they are helping me fulfill Luna's plan perfectly, and unannounced to Luna's pawns, they are helping me get closer to ending the game once and for all.

The past.

"The only way you will win is to believe the lie. You have to live a false life, Sol. Throw away sanity and lose your mind to the void. Gabriel is shrewd. He can smell a rat. If you act, he will know it is fake. You have to live a lie and believe the lies. Then once Gabriel takes you, let my secrets echo in your mind. Don't forget the truth. Turn those echoes into voices, then turn the voices into shouts." Luna tells me, her fingernails digging into my skin, like etching words on a stone tablet, leaving marks that may heal on the surface but not as deep as the indelible mark her words will leave on my mind.

Chapter 18

Sol

Dear Mental Journal,

Luna knew all along that Gabriel was using me as bait. She knew Gabriel would be watching, using me, and protecting me in his own twisted way. I was the cheese, and Gabriel was the mouse that gobbled up all my lies. Everything is right on track.

Luna confessed so many details to me that night on the Cliff Walk.

She also didn't tell me enough.

This was one of the things she did tell me, "You will see the man who helped me cheat. He's helping us all cheat still."

Now I'm with Logan just as Luna planned. This means her plan is still on track. Gabriel is close to winning, but so is Luna. They are head to head, neck to neck, yet again.

***

I need to get Logan alone. I exhale in frustration, feeling Wes's hovering presence creeping up my skin like an overzealous paparazzi, hungry for the latest scoop.

Logan shifts his chair to the left, blocking Wes, "Tell me about these heart palpitations."

I shrug, not caring about that. "I've been under a lot of stress."

Wes edges closer. I can't escape him…I don't want to.

I don't want to admit it, but I like his stalking presence. It gives me peace and lets me close my eyes and dream at night.

How will I sleep without him? My body slumps in the chair like a wilted flower needing some serious sunshine.

Wes leans forward, his voice edged with impatience. "Enough with the nonsense. Sol's heart palpitations are getting worse, and you're supposed to run the test. We're running out of time."

Logan shakes his head, "Change of plans. Didn't Gabriel update you?"

Wes cracks his neck, then turns to face his brother. "Bearer of bad news here," War grins to himself, savoring the moment. "We lost our heart doc. Gabriel needs a few days to find one we can trust."

The rumble of Wes's next inhale sounds like a monster is creeping out from a dark cave. It sends chills up my arms and makes me clench my legs.

"Sol," Logan calls me, his tone calming. "Tell me more about this change. Did it start after you took the upgrade?"

I shake my head. "I've had them before. It's stress related." I admit. I never told my father about this flaw. I was too worried about what he would do. I also never told Luna. She had enough on her plate.

Logan raises a brow, pushes back into his chair and crosses his bright flip-flopped feet. "I need you to be more specific. Did they start after your sister," he clears his throat, "left." His face pales, and I can see the sorrow in his eyes. Not even his help could save her from the game.

"Sol." He stresses.

"I think it started before that."

"You better think fast, Sol." Wes hisses as he looms in front of me now.

"I never told Luna. It happened when I was sixteen," I confess, my voice tinged with frustration. "Not often, but now it's happening more frequently. It's stress." I shoot a pointed glare at Wes, a sarcastic edge in my tone as I quip, "I wonder why."

From the corner of my eye, I catch War's sly smile, and it's clear that my confession provides him with a peculiar satisfaction. It's not shock or worry; it's something different, something that seems to genuinely please him.

There's something I'm missing here, something that War and Wes appear to be infuriatingly ahead of me on. My revelation about my heart condition obviously isn't news to them, and it only adds to the growing frustration and ache in my chest.

"Would either of you care to enlighten me, or is this just another piece of the puzzle you've conveniently kept to yourselves?"

Before they can respond, Logan interjects like an angry parent, "You've never mentioned this before!"

I shrug, "It's always been fine during the tests father gave. Nothing ever caused alarm," I reply. My eyes look at War again, who is biting back his grin now. I've never wanted to smack a pretty boy as much as I do right now.

"You know better than this, Sol," Logan scolds sharply. "We needed to make a note of any changes. This could be a serious error in your and Luna's biology. Your sister never had this condition." His voice rises in frustration. "You know that, Sol! As a scientist, you understand the gravity of this situation. What were you thinking? This didn't just affect you; it could have impacted any upgrades Luna received!" Even his usually dark complexion has taken on a shade of red in his anger.

"She's fine. We'll get the doctor, and we'll get the test done. Now, finish up what you need to do," War barks.

Logan looks at his watch and then at Wes, "If you get me more time, I can try to run a preliminary scan without the cardiologist here."That's the perfect bait Wes needed to hear. He's a dog salivating over a bone as he storms from the room.

"Now you've done it." War sneers at Logan. "Brother wait—" He follows Wes, and I'm finally alone with Logan.

As soon as the door slams shut, I speak, "Logan–"

He interrupts me, "Are you lying?"

"No."

He licks his lips. The worry on his face makes him look five years older. "It's good to see you. If there is something wrong, I'll fix it." He nods to himself.

There are too many wrongs for Logan to fix. "It's good to see you, too," I reply. I want to cry, but he shakes his head.

"Luna told me I'd see you again."

Logan smiles, "I found redemption by continuing to help her cheat." He whispers. His eyes widen with hope, "You are so special, Sol. Not only for the reason Gabriel will use you for, but for much more." Raising his hand, he taps his temple, "Everything you need is in your mind. Please stay focused; I'm not just helping Luna or Gabriel. I did this for *you* because I know you can do what needs to be done. Don't lose sight of reality."

An elephant lands on my chest at his warning, but before I can respond, shouting erupts from outside, and then there is a loud bang.

The door to the room swings open, and I have the urge to shout, "No! I didn't have enough time."

War and Wes stride in. War positions himself by the door, while Wes approaches my side. "We can't make it tonight. Ten minutes left, Doc. Do what you can until we reschedule." He glances at me, running his hand over his jaw, the sound of stubble scratching against his fingertips. "You'll be fine. I know it," he states with such unwavering conviction that it feels like he's either a god or possesses a glimpse into the future.

Something's gone down on Gabriel's end, and it's got the Horsemen tied up tighter than a pretzel.

"We'll run a full test to make sure nothing has exacerbated once we get a man we trust."

My eyes narrow at his choice of words. Exacerbated. That tells me that Wes knew I had this issue. He isn't startled by the news, just annoyed that I have this small glitch.

Who's the lier now, and how the fuck does Wes know what I haven't told anyone?

War adjusts his tie with a smirk. "It hasn't. She's a clone," he snickers. His eyes briefly flick to me, that dark sparkle gleaming in his irises. It's evident he relishes having a secret advantage over me. Crossing his polished shoes, he practically salivates, anticipating my reaction to the news.

Friend and foe.

The true definition of warfare. He benefits and pillages you. Gives, but also takes. It's like signing a contract with the devil. He'll give you the knowledge of the world in exchange for your mind, and you know what that means – the deal you struck was useless because the devil always has the upper hand.

I don't react. Rather, I curl inside my mind and ponder the mystery. I assumed my problem was caused by stress because Luna never had palpitations. Therefore it was a singular anomaly within me and not the other clones. However, War has suggested it isn't. Another clone has this same problem.

Logan sighs, "I need to check her vision. To make sure the upgrade she gave herself is working properly. I'll get the equipment." He stands and leaves.

Wes tips my chin up. He scans my eyes as if he can see my heart. "Someone else has this issue. One of my clones." I mutter to him.

Instead of nodding, Wes shakes his head. "Not a clone, little mouse."

His phone rings, and expectancy spreads over his face. His thumb brushes over my bottom lip before he swipes his hand away. He leaves the room to answer it, keeping more secrets from me.

War pushes off the wall and stalks toward me. His dress shoes make an expensive sound that ricochets off the tile floor.

War and I are finally alone. I waste no time clarifying his motives in the game, "You're working with Famine. Famine is working with my sister."

"Shouldn't you be referring to her in the past tense?" His words sound like a warning of unshed secrets.

"Don't waste time with formalities." I hiss, "Are you helping me or not?" Whose side are you on War?

His hair shines under the light. His posture is relaxed in the midst of the chaos. He looks like a male model. Sculpted of marble and polished to stunning beauty. His suit is tailored to hug his defined body like a second skin. It should make it hard for him to move, the fabric should not bend to his will, but it defies the laws of physics. When he moves, the fabric stretches like silk over a statue in a museum.

War is perfection in its most deadly form.

"Or," he says. My brows furrow and he delights in my reaction. "I will help, *or* I will not." His smile drops, his eyes look out the window where Wes is on the phone. I can tell from the redness on Wes's face he is arguing with Gabriel.

"You're worried about Wes." I read between his words. "You don't care about who controls the science. You only care about your brothers not about ending the game."

"I won't leave my brother behind." His eyes grow distant.

"Now you're speaking grammatically incorrect. Don't you mean brothers? Plural. What about Famine and Gabriel?"

War points a finger at me, "I never swore allegiance to your sister's side. I love my brothers. I will fight only for them."

"You're tearing them apart by playing them. You need to choose a side or you will find yourself alone."

War shakes his head and unbuttons on his jacket, "What you see as tearing apart, I see as sewing back together. I'm trying to make them realize we are better together. Jointly we are organized chaos; separate, we are a brewing storm."

My eyes narrow into slits, and if I were looking in a mirror, I'd say I resemble Luna's cold glimmer.

He inches closer to me, "You know that nature always finds a rhythm. It will always sync." He points to Wes, "What you see as madness, me playing my brothers, I see as syncing. It's harmony, and we will all be together again one day." He crosses his arms over his chest. No stress weighs him down.

War is right; he refers to the second law of thermodynamics, which states that everything in the universe tends to be in disorder. Chaos is the norm. Yet the universe isn't messy because there is a spontaneous order. A synchronization. Like fireflies that eventually sync and begin to all-flash together or a crowd of people clapping. In disorder, we harmonize. War thinks somehow, in these games, in disarray, we will all sync and find our way back to one another.

My irritation turns to sympathy. I view him as I did my twin. Like Luna, War is a million steps ahead of everyone.

He's not looking at me or the enlightenment on my face. He is still watching Wes. He must feel my eyes burning into him because he finely pivots his glare at me. "It's not what you think. I love my brother, but not in the way you're implying. Everyone has a favorite sibling." He steps back, putting distance between us again. "Do you know how he got those scars? He stepped in front of bullets for me. Not singular. Plural. Bullets." War stresses as he parrots my previous words.

My throat thickens, hands grow clammy. War's pain is still so fresh I can feel it cut me. "Conquest and Famine are trying to save my future, but Death saved my life. Without life, we have no future. I can not turn my back on him."

My shoulders hunch, my mind feels heavier than a ton of bricks. I understand War's loyalty. I respect him for standing by his convictions.

I'm going to stand by mine.

"What about Famine? You'll turn your back on him?"

A glacial expression targets me. "I can either lose one brother or two, Sol. It's the same fucking outcome no matter what side Death remains on. Famine will not change, and neither will Conquest." The tone of his voice is slightly higher. The subtle shift in his tone lets me know he's still not leveling with me. There's definitely something else concealed in his tailor-made bag of tricks.

War gazes out of the window right as Wes ends the phone call, his words hitting me like a sledgehammer. "Time's slipping away, Sol. Once Gabriel's done with you, things will shift. If you play this next round, you're aiding both Gabriel and Famine, each with their own agendas for the power. If you lose, you're aiding the last Master. But if you run... oh, if you run, I'll give you a head start in return for pretending this talk never happened."

He thinks I'm the scared little twin I've painted myself as. Everyone is always viewing me as the underdog who follows the bigger dogs. "And what if I win?"

He tilts his head, uncrosses his arms. A single groomed brow lifts in curiosity. "Then this conversation doesn't matter. May the most patient clone win."

Chapter 19

Sol

War's choice of words lingers in my mind like a haunting melody: "Patient." What is he concealing behind that cryptic statement, and why is patience suddenly the most crucial quality? I'm left with unanswered questions, unable to pry for more information, as Wes returns to the room, his tension palpable. Each of his heavy footsteps feels like an ominous drumbeat, and War's devilish grin, swiftly concealed, hints at secrets that even Wes remains ignorant of.

Gabriel was unable to grant them more time for the procedure. I think the only way to calm the storm in his mind would be for him to see my heart beating and then to cage it so only he could see it.

My eyes tracked the demon I love. Torn between two people, Wes, who cares for me, and Death, who plays with me. With his short black hair and sculpted muscles, Wes looks like a gladiator ready to battle, but his opponent didn't show, so we were all left with his sour mood. A mood that is distraught because he cares about me.

I loved that I affect him so strongly, but it's also dangerous. Wes could break me as easily as I can him. Passion knows no bounds. Obsession is a dangerous ally.

Logan turns the lights off so he can test my vision. I lean forward and look into the small binocular-like machine. It looks outdated but between the small rings are sensors that are reading the dilation and movement of my eyes. "We don't have much time left, so instead of reading the lines, just let me know if any look blurry. I also need you to count the lines. Tell me how many are written in Lumenis ink. Let me know if the ink is clear and if you can see the letters. This way."

I blink, adjusting to the light, trying to regain focus. War's hushed words to Wes momentarily distract me, but as my eyes fully adapt to the scene, everything changes. The standard ink I expected to see is there, but alongside it, the Lumenis catches my attention with its distinct features.

"Can you see the Lumenis?" Logan asks. His voice shakes slightly.

"Yes," I reply. It's not a lie but it's also not the whole truth. I also notice the hastily scrawled Lumenis writing at the bottom of the slide. It's a message that Logan has just added to the flashcard. That's why it took him so long to wheel the machine into the room.

"Some of it looks faded," I reply, attempting to gain a bit more time to acclimate my eyes and decode the minuscule letters. Despite my enhanced vision, I initially struggle to read the sentence. Slowly, it becomes legible.

Use the restroom. Under the trash bag. Take both. You'll be sick. You're strong. You have to be strong, Sol.

"How many lines, Sol?" Logan inquires, his anticipation palpable in his tone. He's going to give our secret away if he doesn't calm the fuck down.

"Six."

"Times up, doc." War chirps.

The lights turn on abruptly, causing me to blink rapidly and readjust my vision. "Are you okay?" Wes asks.

Nodding I exhale loudly and pinch the bridge of my nose, "I'm tired now." I rake my hand down my face. That's a lie; my body is being pumped full of adrenaline. I feel like a live wire next to the open ocean.

Wes takes my hand, our fingers intertwining before he kisses our knuckles. It's as if I'm holding a freshly cut rose, its thorns poised to dig deep into me at any moment. "You're done for today," he declares.

I'm just about to get started.

I snort. In one day, I learned more than I have in the past few months. My head is hurting, and I want to escape now. I want to press pause and fall asleep in the arms of the man trying to turn me into a traitor. But I can't; I'm not done yet.

"I need to use the restroom before we leave." No one thinks twice about my request. It's normal for a woman to have to use the bathroom. Before I enter, Wes looks inside and ensures the room is clear. He lingers for a moment, "I'm not peeing in front of you."

His eyes look around the bathroom again.

"I really need to pee, Wesley," I stress his pet name, playfully flipping my hair over my shoulder.

He reaches for me, and I initially think my plan has just failed. However, instead of stopping me, he kisses me. It's a gentle kiss, and I melt into it like chocolate on a warm day, slow and sweet. A complete mess.

I respond back, hands reaching, gripping his hard body. His tongue pushes past my lips, and his hands snake around me. We swallow each other's moans. The kiss ends too soon, and he presses his forehead to mine. The passion and need are replaced with guilt. As much as he loves me, he still allows Gabriel to use me. "Make it quick," he whispers.

A mischievous smile crosses my face covering my pain, "I'm going to make it longer now."

He responds in a soft, purring tone, "There's my little mouse; I don't know which side of you I like better. The side that needs me or the side that tries to push me away."

I shrug, "Ponder it well I take my time." I close the door in his face. Turning the lock, I scramble and search for the trash can. A steel box attached to the wall catches my eye. Bingo. I open the lid and spot a brown bag. My fingers grasp it, and I dump out its contents. Two auto-injectors roll into my hand.

The sound of my own heart pulsates like a hummingbird's wings, resonating in my ears. I push my shirt up and bite down on it, preventing it from falling and obstructing the process.

Gritting my teeth, I remove the lid from the first needle and swiftly jab it into my lower abdomen. I hold it there, waiting for the satisfying click that indicates the release of the contents. Almost immediately, a sensation of ice-cold burning spreads under my skin, resembling the searing of acid. Despite the discomfort, I suck it up and continue.

My attention shifts to the next vial, and with a flick of my thumb, I knock off the lid. I pierce it into my stomach once more, the coldness of the liquid even more pronounced this time. The burning sensation intensifies, causing tears to well up behind my closed lids and escape down my cheeks. Shit, that hurts!

My head knocks back against the wall as I pull the needle out. Two small drops of blood slowly sink down my stomach.

How much blood will I have to shed for these games to end?

"Sol," Wes knocks.

I rush to the toilet and flush it, then I hurry to hide the needles where I found them. There is no mirror for me to check my appearance. I splash cold water on my face and try to paint a beautiful picture filled with lies.

***

After we arrived home, I managed to eat dinner, take a shower, and crawl into bed. Wes quietly entered my room just after midnight, having wrapped up his conversation with War. Normally, I would have attempted to eavesdrop, but I was too drained to muster the energy for it. The exhaustion settled in like an unwelcome guest, brought on by the avalanche of information. My body protested with a chorus of aches, and all I yearned for was a sweet embrace with sleep.

My eyes snap open, and I'm catapulted from the depths of sleep into a heart-pounding reality. It's like I've been dropped into the center of a whirlwind, my senses in a frenzy. My chest rises and falls like a rollercoaster, desperately seeking air after a wild ride. A glistening sheen of sweat coats my body, my skin feeling like a slippery fish, while an intense wave of heat emanates from my core. Oh no! My stomach drops, I'm going to vomit!

I attempt to move, but a searing pain clenches my stomach, threatening to turn my world upside down. Fighting the discomfort, I roll off the bed and rush towards the bathroom.

Wes transforms from a peaceful sleeper to a guardian angel in the blink of an eye, his powerful presence erupting like a storm. He springs out of bed, his body poised for action as I reach the bathroom just in time to avoid a mess. I don't want him here. I don't want him to see me like this.

I have no retort or control as my body revolts. He holds my hair back, his hand tracing soothing circles along my trembling back. In a hushed, comforting tone, he reassures me, "It's okay, Sol. I'm right here with you. I've got you."

He gets a cold cloth and places it on my forehead when I am finished. My body slumps onto the cold tiles in my bathroom. Deep green eyes loom over me, "What's the matter, little mouse?" His words are full of concern.

I want to cry, to burrow into him and allow him to be my shield.

I can't just yet. Wes and I are fighting on two opposing sides, and I can not allow him to block the bullets flying my way. My sickness can aid me, though. When you nurse a creature back to health, you are more attached to it. You never want to release it back into the wild. I want him to join me when I step away from the game. I want him to chase me.

"I think the food was bad." I lie. I have no doubt this is a side effect of the two injections.

He feels my forehead, "You're burning up."

"I'll be ok." *I hope so.* I don't even know what I was upgraded with.

He moves to lift me, but I shake my head, "I want to stay here." My fingers brush over the bathroom cold tile, "It feels good." My voice shakes.

He brushes my hair off my face, then bends down and kisses my cheek. I cringe, "I'm gross."

He pulls away and readjusts the cloth on my forehead, "When are you going to understand? I don't care how you crumble; I will always pick you back up and glue you back together."

My heart palpitates, and my already watery eyes cry more.

How can a person love you so strongly yet oppose you so vastly?

Is this how Luna felt when Gabriel helped her cheat but refused to give up the power that made them both sick?

Chapter 20

Sol

A deep wheeze fills the room, it makes my heart spike, but my next breath is even more labored. The wheezing is coming from me!

My mind paints an image; I'm standing out in the cold, snow falling around me. My deep breath shows in the gray air as the tiny snowflakes fall. Each inhale burns from the cold draft that surrounds me. I should be cold, but I can't feel the arctic chill. I feel numb. Everything feels far. My mind's image is now covered in a round glass globe. I'm trapped inside the snow globe as the snow and numb air consume me.

"When did this start!"

"Wes said she had food poisoning."

"You fucking tell me what is happening, Gabriel! Fix her! If this is the heart condition then I want it fixed. We will find another way inside."

"This has nothing to do with a heart condition."

"It wasn't my cooking." A new voice playfully jokes.

Arguing ensues, more shouts erupt; the floorboards squeak under pressure; I struggle to clear the fog from my mind. I run to the edges of the snow globe in my mind. As I run, my deep painful breaths fill the air and fogs my vision. I press my palms against the snow globe's glass, but it is too frosted to see out, so I begin to pound on it, but it refuses to break.

Hands touch me, trying to grab me back into the globe's center. I groan everywhere I feel their pokes. My entire body feels tender.

The pain behind my eyes throbs so harshly that I begin to sob. I can't open my eyes to seek help or move my tongue to plead.

"It's ok. We're going to fix you." I know that voice. That is Death. He sounds shaken but hearing him trapped with me in the fog helps comfort me.

"Sol, open your eyes for me." That voice, I know too. "Sol!" That's Gabriel.

My body shakes again. My jaw aches as my teeth quiver uncontrollably. The bed dips, and my body is forcibly pulled against something hard. I'm on my side as a hand rubs a gentle circle on my back. It's the last thing I feel before the fog swallows me whole again.

***

A hushed conversation rouses my mind. Whose voices are these? Who is talking? Think! You know these voices. Yes, that's Gabriel and... Wes and Logan.

I tentatively move my index finger, checking if the ache in my body has subsided. My fingertips brush against the soft sheets beneath me. What happened? Why am I so sore? Then it clicks, the reaction to the injections.

If Logan is here, does that mean the Horsemen found out about the upgrades?

I lay still and listened so I don't mistakenly give any information away.

"Have you ever noticed this severity before?"

"Gabriel," Logan sighs. He sounds weary, like a worn-out engine sputtering to life, and I can sense the frustration in his tone. "You've never had food poisoning because you've been upgraded, but Sol hasn't to your extent. The nanobytes inside your body work 24/7. They alert your cells to an invasion like this. Sol doesn't have that same upgrade, so she has to allow her body to rest and fix itself."

"I don't need to be lectured on a science I created," Gabriel states, his voice as stern as a judge's gavel striking the bench.

Logan clears his throat, "Her symptoms are a typical food-borne illness. This is normal. It needs to run its course. She's dehydrated; we are treating that. Her body will treat the rest. There is nothing else I can do. I'm not God, and neither are you; we don't have a crystal ball, so we must depend on the facts." he warns.

"If you say that she is fine one more time," Wes booms.

"Calm down and listen to me!" Logan's voice crackles with urgency. "Her body is stronger than the average human. It's purging the illness from her. She's more evolved, not immortal. If you cut her, she will bleed. If you shout at her, she will react. Stop projecting your fears onto the science," he retorts.

"Make her immortal." Wes snaps, and the room grows quiet.

Logan snorts, "I'm a scientist, not a god."

"Enough!" Gabriel seethes. "I need her better. She doesn't have much time to prepare as it is."

"Her body needs rest. Give it another day. With the added medicine and fluids, I am sure she will be back on track." Logan responds.

"You better be." Wes growls.

"Fine!" Gabriel snaps, "Give her the fluids and meet us down stairs. Wes I need to speak with you in private." The room quiets, and footsteps fade as they leave, but I still sense someone. I open my eyes, having to blink rapidly to clear my vision. There is a raw pain behind my eyes making my vision feel ultra-sensitive to the light.

"Sol!" Logan whispers a gasp.

The slight pivot of my eyes toward him throbs. He rushes to my side, dropping to his knees beside the bed. "I don't have much time," he whispers urgently, his gaze fixed on the slightly ajar door. I know the Horsemen are lurking downstairs. "How are you feeling?"

"Everything...s-sore," I croak.

He reaches for a glass of water, and I swallow every last drop. He watches me, his eyes studying my face, my eyes in particular. His dark complexion seems more ashen than it should be.

"W-what...give...me?" I'm still so thirsty. I want to ask for more water, but I fear I will not get answers if I do.

"I gave you the Regeneration upgrade," Logan hurriedly explains, his words tumbling out with urgency. "It's a genetic enhancement that will turbocharge your cell regeneration." He shifts and pulls out a small Swiss pocket knife, flipping through the blades until he has the smallest one out. "I need to test it. Somewhere Wes and Gabriel will not notice."

I nod. I have no other choice. I'm curious if it works too. Deep down, I fear how Logan will test it. I remember my father took the tip of Luna's pinky finger. I curl my fingers into fist.

He pulls the bed sheet back and takes out my left arm. "I'll make a small cut near your armpit. They shouldn't look there." His movements are gentle as he makes a small cut that barely stings. "It should heal within the hour. If it heals, it worked. If it doesn't…." He gulps, "you'll need to be cautious then."

A heavy exhale leaves my lungs, "What else?"

"The second upgrade will help you see as a predator would. No more shadows for prey to hide. Your sister has most of her followers in the—" Logan halts his words. I want to scream, but I don't speak, either. The front door closes loudly, footsteps start to make for the stairs. "You will need sharper vision."

Our time is up when Wes and Gabriel enter the room.

"You're awake!" Wes gasps. The relief on his face makes a knot of guilt in my stomach. I did that to him. What of the fury once he figures out I'm still lying? "Why didn't you get us!" He seethes as he approaches and shoulder shoves Logan out of the way.

"She just woke up. She hasn't said anything. I just gave her water."

Wes brushes my cheek. A lover's touch. His eyes are framed with dark circles, and the green lacks its saturated color. His dress shirt is only halfway unbuttoned, his open heart surgery scar runs thick and red down the center of his chest.

"Little mouse," His shoulders soften as he speaks my name. "How do you feel?"

I tear my eyes off his scar. "Better." I gulp. It burns. "More water, please."

"Get her water," He orders Logan.

Another dark shadow encroaches upon me and in my weaken state I tense. Gabriel looms like a god ready to cast judgement

upon a lesser being. His gaze analyzing. *Show me a human,*
upgraded or not that wouldn't feel chills under Gabriel's scrutiny.

"Are you cold?" Wes asks.

I don't look at Wes. I keep my eyes on the blonde archangel
who looms over my bed. I fear he sees everything. I don't want
him to hurt Logan if he finds out the truth.

"I don't ever want to eat roasted pesto chicken again." I joke
as I stick to the story that I had food poisoning. Gabriel's eyebrows
knit together. He doesn't speak. I don't know if that is good or bad.

Wes shifts and positions himself on the bed, creating a
protective barrier between me and Gabriel's prying eyes. Grateful
for his presence, I extend my hand, searching until I find his. "I
have some chicken soup for when you're ready to eat," he informs
me.

"Thank you," I respond weakly as Wes helps me sit up.

Logan chimes in, "I'll return to the lab now. If you need
anything, Sol, don't hesitate to ask." With that, he exits the room,
and I can finally release the breath I didn't realize I was holding.

Gabriel steps closer, moving with deliberate slowness that
sends shivers down my spine, like a predator closing in. Fear
clenches my heart, and my fingers tighten their grip on Wes. His
green eyes remain locked on me, his muscles tense as he prepares
to shield me from whatever may come.

My lover senses my fear, and my heart races as he defends me.
"She is not training for your damn game right now."

"My game?" Gabriel counters, and the room falls silent. I hold
my breath, awaiting the next exchange.

"Don't play word games with me," Wes snaps back. "I've been by your side through thick and thin. You're more family to me than my own blood. Don't test me on this, brother."

"Then don't make me test you," He retorts, his voice raised. Footsteps approach, and War appears in the doorway. Our eyes meet, and I see a deep, old pain in his gaze. He's been watching his family fall apart for some time now.

Gabriel runs his hand through his golden hair, his Adam's apple bobbing as he swallows. "Fine," he concedes, "She will train tomorrow."

"If she is ready," Wes adds, firm in his resolve.

Gabriel turns to leave, but before he exits, he snaps over his shoulder, "You are letting your emotions guide you. Don't make the same mistake I did."

His words provoke a prickling sensation on my skin. "Maybe you should let your emotions guide you, Conquest," I spit out. "If you had, perhaps my sister could have chosen a different path to walk down."

Gabriel stands still, shoulder to shoulder with War, who grabs him by the bicep to hold him back. He keeps his back to me. "A path that ended with a jump?" He challenges, "Your sister chose her own path. No one, not even you, could change her mind. Not even right before she turned her back on you and jumped off a goddamn cliff." Then he turns. I know I pushed a button that set off a nuclear bomb headed right at me. The fallout will affect us all. "What did you two talk about that night, Sol? What did you say that motivated her to jump?" His eyes turn accusing.

I jerk. "I didn't tell her to jump!" I cry, but my weak, dry voice sounds more like a parched fish.

"Leave!" Wes roars. "She needs rest."

Gabriel looks past his brother at me, a brow raised. "Rest?" He chortles, "I think she has been resting for a very long time. Since she was five years old when she allowed Luna to take her place."

"If I hadn't, you never would have had Luna," I counter.

"That's enough!" Wes hollers, striding forward; he shoves Gabriel hard in the chest.

"We will start tomorrow," Gabriel bites before War grabs him and slams the door shut.

I stand, and my legs wobble. That got out of hand, but it deflected Gabriel from prying further into my sickness.

He thinks I motivated her to jump? Is that what they all think? My hands clutch my stomach. *What did you expect, you silly fool?*

I shouldn't have pushed him," I admit the truth. But I had to to cover up my lie. I have to keep hurting.

His hand reaches out, tugging me into our bathroom, where he turns the shower on but doesn't start to undress me. His caring face morphs into a furious one that has me inching away. He rolls his lips, breathes slow and deep as if trying to wrangle an inner beast. I swallow and reach out for his hand. He cocks his head in question, making me hesitate.

My hand drops, I back up, but my butt hits the sink. He steps forward, trapping me. I look at the water as it swirls down the drain. I understand now; He turned the water on to drown out this conversation. His calloused fingers guide my face back to his, his right hand wraps around my neck. Wes always holds my neck when he's struggling with his emotions.

His left-hand reaches for my baggy shirt, tugging it up but stopping halfway. It becomes apparent that he isn't undressing me but revealing something hidden. My gaze shifts downward, my eyes fixating where his hand pauses. My heart beats into overdrive. There, on my flat stomach, are two faint yellow bruises in the exact location where I had administered the upgrades. Auto-injector needles often leave behind bruises or rashes.

I'm caught.

"What did you do, little mouse?"

Chapter 21

Sol

I try to swallow, but the gulp lodges in my throat. I feel like a mouse that ran into a hole too small to escape through. Now I am lodged in it. Stuck and trapped as I wait for the predator to snatch me in his claws. Hands I know all too well, fingers that I love to hate and hate to love. Fingertips that have caressed every inch of my genetically modified body, hands that made me feel normal yet so rare and endangered.

I choke, but Wes doesn't release my neck; he only grips me tighter. I struggle to inhale. He watches me. Studies my every flinch and gesture.

"Be very careful what you say next." He warns. The green streaks in his eyes darken to emeralds buried deep near a volcano.

I mentally try to find a paintbrush and ink to create a lie that he will believe. My mental hands stretched out wide, grasping for purchase, but no surface comes.

"My shy little mouse," He pushes into me, his pelvis traps mine. A weight so devilishly sweet, it heats my core. Lips brush in a ghostly whisper over the pulse point on my neck. My legs quiver as my core grows wet. "I'll go first. I will tempt you into my darkness." He purrs before he sucks painfully on my pulse. Marking. Claiming. "I'll show you how it can be addictively sweet or sinfully painful to those who lie to me."

What about those who betray you? Will you push me out into the light where it's so blinding it burns my heart into ashes?

"Wes!" My yelp turns into a moan. The grin on his face could make a nun turn against her ways and praise the devil.

Eye to eye he begins, "You did something naughty again. My little mouse likes walking past predators. You like to tempt us only to run away." His hand snakes around my lower back till he cups my ass. Fingers kneading. "You can't tuck your tail this time. You injected yourself with something. Two things. The question is who, what, when, where, and why, little mouse?"

My tongue darts out to wet my lips as I prepare to speak, but Wes doesn't allow me to utter a word. He's baiting me, leading me further into his trap. My heart pounds in my chest as he brushes his lips over mine, momentarily closing his eyes.

A small moan escapes my parted lips as I push my tongue inside his mouth, hoping to distract him, to divert his attention away from this dangerous pursuit. I want to persuade him to let go of this relentless hunt and focus on something else, anything else.

Wes responds to the kiss, but there's a hint of amusement in his lips, a smile against mine that tells me he sees through my trickery. He's not falling for it. My kiss turns desperate. The intensity of the moment hangs between us as he pulls away, baring his teeth. It sends chills down my exposed skin, and I try to look away, but his gaze won't release me.

"Let's start from the bottom up," He says, his voice laced with a dangerous edge. "Why? That's easy. You are greedy; you upgraded yourself." His words hit me like a punch to the gut, and I feel a wave of defensiveness rise within me. I didn't do it out of greed, but out of a deep-rooted desire for self-preservation.

"Where and when? That's also simple," he continues, his tone cutting through the air like a sharpened blade. "It must have happened when we took you into the lab." The mention of the lab sends shivers down my spine.

"And now the most important question," He declares, his eyes locked with mine. "Who? Who gave you the upgrades, little mouse?"

"I did," I respond, my voice steady despite the turmoil within me. I hold his gaze, refusing to let fear dictate my actions.

I'm pushed back and plunged under the cold water of the shower. The icy water pelts down on me. I cling to his warm, hard body like a life raft.

"Answer me!" he roars, his demand echoing in the small bathroom. My back hits the cold tiles, his hard cock brushes the apex of my thighs.

He's torn between lust and protection.

I'm torn between the same.

I'm doing this for you, to save you all, because I love you!

My body shakes from the cold and fear of losing him in the end. Instinctively, I move closer, his hard thick length now pressed tight against my core. Seeking warmth and solace. Instead of providing me comfort, he turns the knob even colder. I pound my fist against him, feeling the sting of the freezing water against my skin. He's trying to scare me, to break me down, make me think he is my protector. *You have the shoe on the wrong foot, baby, I'm doing this to protect you.*

With trembling fingers, I reach out and grasp his wet shirt, the fabric clinging to my hands, thick and heavy. His strong, towering presence remains unyielding under the torrent of water. Droplets cling to his skin as they rake down his strong muscles. *I never thought I'd be jealous of water.*

I push up on my toes and hesitantly kiss him, my tongue exploring his mouth tentatively. The cold water continues to run down our faces, adding an extra layer of sensation to our interaction.

"Sol," He presses. But his fingers curl into my ass, gripping me. Never wanting to let me go. He tugs me up high so I'm forced to press into the very tips of my toes. A punishment with a reward.

"I did it for us," I confess in between kisses, my voice barely audible over the sound of the rushing water. I deepen the kiss, swirling my tongue around his, hoping to convey my sincerity. His muscles flex beneath my touch, a sign that the power I hold over him is slowly working its way through. I cling to him, gripping his wet shirt with more force, as if he is my lifeline, my savior. "Let me have you." I whisper.

"You can't sway me with your body," But his words contradict his actions. He lifts me effortlessly, and I instinctively wrap my legs around his waist, my body molding against his. He adjusts the water, turning it to scalding hot, as we continue to kiss. The warmth gradually envelops us, but amidst the temptation to lose myself in him, I remind myself of my purpose. There is no more room for hesitation, running, or escaping. I need to seize this moment, to grab hold of him and convince him to see the light at the end of the tunnel.

"I had to be stronger. The upgrade was the only way." I hint.

He sinks his teeth into my neck, growling a mixture of desire and frustration. "Don't lie to me," he warns.

"Regeneration upgrade," I confess.

He hisses a deep breath and presses his forehead to mine. He's upset, but deep down, he's happy I'm not as fragile. "Logan gave it to you. That's who. There is no other option. You were never alone. He slipped it to you somehow," he asserts. "What was the second upgrade?"

Now I have to lie because I don't know what the second upgrade was. All Logan hinted at was "seeing," so I use that truth and merge it with the falsehood. "The Lumenis didn't fully take. It should now," I say. With my legs still wrapped around him, I cup his face.

"Why don't you want me to be stronger?" I ask. Little does he know my question is meant to provoke. I need him to see this as a good outcome.

"I want you safe."

"Being upgraded makes me safer."

A droplet of water rolls off his thick brown lashes. I watch it, witness the worry in his eyes, "That's how it starts. An upgrade here, then there. It's a rabbit hole and I don't need you to tumble down another one."

"Then trust me." I plead, pressing my forehead against his. I want him to come with me, to follow the light that beckons. Luna and Gabriel couldn't turn against their training and their need to win. Can Death?

"You said you would choose me when the games ended. You said I would run from what I see and discover. You said you would chase me." I remind him. Vulnerability seeps through my cracks.

"You're twisting my words, little mouse. I said I would keep you safe; once Gabriel is finished with you, you'll fight me and try to run. You're addicted to the chase now. You always wanted to be normal, but after you witnessed life in Aspen, you didn't like it, so you kept digging deeper. You still can't admit you like the thrill. That's why you will run. I'll catch you, pin you down," his cock rubs against my pussy, "and I'll make you confess everything you desire."

"I'm addicted to you. You were the thrill, not the games." *That's why I want to end the games, so it can just be me and you and our fucked up attraction.*

His lips briefly brush against mine in a tender kiss. "What game are you playing now, little mouse?" he questions. His eyes search mine, as if trying to unravel the truth hidden within.

"When all this comes to an end, will you walk away from it all for me?" I ask bluntly, my words hanging heavy in the air. I fear I already know his response, but I need to hear it from his own lips.

"You will leave the Horsemen, leave Manus Dei, for me," I state this time. A order, test of loyalty.

My eyes wide, legs clench tighter, fingernails dig.

No words come.

Power is the most dangerous beast of them all. It's like Medusa. Everyone wants a look, a taste, but it lasts as long as smoke on a howling wind. Then it claims you, devouring another soul.

"Wesley," I plead. I want the answer that my heart yearns for.

Silence prickles our skin. It feels like we both tumbled into a thorny bush, stretching out into an agonizing pause. The warm water continues to trickle over us, but I've never felt so dirty, so uncertain. Each passing second feels like an eternity as I wait for his reply, my heart pounding in my chest.

"I will do whatever I have to do to keep you safe," he answers. He's avoiding a direct yes or no. I see through his response and find the truth. Death, like Gabriel, suffers from the same affliction, the same unyielding nature that plagued Luna. A predator will always be wild; you can never truly tame them. Luna couldn't change, Gabriel couldn't change, and Death will forever be bound by his role as a Horseman and the games. He knows I will run, for I am nearing the end of my journey. But his own end is never in sight.

His large hand presses against my broken heart. *Do you feel the destruction of my shattered chambers, Wes, feel the off rhythm beat because our love wasn't enough?* "I choose the side that I *know* will keep you safe," he continues, touching my heart. "That will keep this heart beating for me."

"Beating against you," I murmur. Unclasping my legs, I slide down his body and step back, creating a physical distance between us.

He shakes his head, eyes blazing. He's ready for the chase. "Beating either way," he bites, he pushes the shower door open, and a cold wind chills my abandoned skin. "If I squash your dreams, you will hate me. You have to fall, Sol. That's just the kind of person you are. I'll be there, as I have always promised. When you stand up and run from me, I'll be there to drag you back here again. I'll keep you safe. I'll give you everything you need."

"But not what I want," I retort sharply. I want a future with him, free from the constraints of the games.

With a heavy inhale, his shoulders inch up to his ears, his voice filled with pain. "What we want doesn't always keep us safe.

Wanting in our lives is foolish. It's what we need. I need you by my side, *alive*."

"And I need you by my side, alive," I mock. "These games will take everything from us, Wesley. Everything! You think the games will save me, but what will be left of me?" I touch my chest, digging my nails into my flesh. "What will be left of my mind? My heart which is being pulled by too many puppeteers." I shake my head, overwhelmed by the weight of it all.

Nothing will be left. We will be hollowed-out shells.

Together but so empty.

"We will evolve and adjust," he argues.

I snort, "Not everything evolves, Wes. Some things die."

Droplets of water from the shower continue to cry like tears over our bodies. We stand and survey one another, the spoken truth hanging heavily in the air. Sometimes, the truth can be more harmful than a lie, but that doesn't mean it should go unspoken.

Reaching up, I cup his face, feeling his strong jaw clench beneath my touch. "You always see the horizon. You should learn to look back at the setting sun," I say. He's so much like Luna, always moving forward, never looking back to see the destruction left in their wake. No conqueror does; it's how they justify their dominance.

He steps out of my touch, but I grip his hand tightly and tug him back under the water. He turns, and water drips down his sharp face. "Logan will be safe," he mutters. Death will bend to make me happy, but he won't break.

"Why didn't you tell Gabriel?"

"I don't want him to see you as Luna," he bites. "A person who betrayed him and risked her own life because she couldn't handle losing." The pain of Luna's actions resonates within his voice. "This is a one-time pass. Next time, I will not be as forgiving." He closes the glass shower door, his silhouette fading as he exits. Hot water continues to beat down on my body, but I feel cold, trapped in my own personal snow globe once again.

I stay in the shower until my skin prunes, thoughts swirling in my mind. Eventually I step out, grabbing a thick navy towel, wrap it around my body and dry off. But as I run the towel over my arm, I pause.

The cut!

Flinging my arm out, I inspect my armpit where Logan had cut me. I run my fingers over the skin multiple times, disbelief coursing through me. I push my torso closer to the mirror, wiping away the condensation from the hot shower. Reflecting back is perfectly smooth skin. The cut has vanished, fully healed, not even leaving behind a scar.

"Holy shit... it worked," I gasp, but there is no joy in my voice. I may be a tougher human now, but will my stronger skin be enough to keep my heart safe?

Chapter 22

Sol

I move closer to the mirror, my gaze fixed on the perfectly healed skin. Tentatively, I probe it with my fingertips, amazed that there is no tenderness, no trace of a scab. The regeneration process is seamless, leaving me awestruck by the wonders of science. The urge to rush to a laboratory and dissect the intricacies of this newfound ability tugs at me. Scientists are always driven to push boundaries, never content with the status quo. We create solutions only to hunger for the next breakthrough, the next level of improvement.

Resting my forehead against the mirror, I touch my eyes, recalling Logan's words about the second upgrade and its promise of sharper vision. Already, I can decipher the invisible Lumenis ink. What more lies beyond the threshold of my enhanced sight? What does this upgrade truly offer and why do I need it?

A shiver runs down my spine, coursing through my veins. It's the sensation of falling further down the rabbit hole of genetic upgrades. Alice never did want to leave Wonderland, why would she? That's why they all want the game to continue to exist. The pursuit of what's next, bigger, better, more deadly. It's what humanity craves—fire, a gun, and then the thermonuclear bombs. The relentless quest for power and advancement, even at the risk of self-destruction, is a twisted part of our nature.

Cautiously I press my eyelids, "You are going to witness so much more. I'm sorry," I whisper, a sense of reverence directed at my own blue eyes and the depths of my mind.

I sweep my gaze around the room, searching for any signs of heightened vision. I wonder how much more I can develop. My eyesight is already better than that of the average person.

A voice within me echoes Luna's words, reminding me that one can never be good enough. There is always room for improvement.

As I enter the kitchen, I spot Wes and Gabriel outside. They are arguing, like two bulls going head to head. They talk in a hushed silence. Their breath mingles into foggy puffs in the cold air, forming ghostly plumes that add to the haunting atmosphere befitting the Horsemen.

Gabriel lingers by the driver's door, preparing to leave. Unnoticed by both of them, I observe from the window, studying their interactions intently, searching for any clues or hints of changes since the upgrade.

Squinting my eyes, I strain to improve my vision, furrowing my brows in concentration as if they were a magnifying glass searching for details. I make several attempts, hoping to discern even the slightest difference, but to no avail. What did I expect, a miracle to emerge from my gaze?

You're acting silly, Sol. I .

Maybe I've been barking up the wrong tree. Perhaps the upgrade is all about getting up close and personal. I eye the kitchen countertop which is made of old butcher block. The surface is adorned with intricate ringed details and cut marks. Leaning in, I run my finger over the wooden patterns, narrowing my eyes. Hidden lines within those minuscule grooves are clear to my upgraded eyes. Those details have been with me since birth, since my father designed me. This vision isn't new. Did the second upgrade not work?

"You keep looking at that wood grain as if it is going to sprout up and grow into a tree again."

I swiftly turn to find War leaning casually against the far wall, his ankle crossed over the other, a relaxed and amused posture. I hadn't even noticed he had been watching me. That was a mistake; I can't focus on just one thing. I need to see the entire game board if I want to remain alive.

"I am not," I retort defensively.

"Are too," he grins mischievously.

There's an endearing quality to War's demeanor, as if engaging in friendly banter with an old acquaintance. It's disarming, causing me to lower my defenses, knowing full well the potential for manipulation that lies beneath his three-piece suit and perfectly styled chocolate brown hair. At first glance, he may appear less menacing than Death and Famine, but it's precisely those qualities that make him all the more ruinous.

"What do you want?" I ask, crossing my arms over my chest. His widening smile confirms his awareness of my unease as he pushes off the wall and moves closer.

"What were you doing?" he inquires, rubbing his chin thoughtfully.

"Studying the wood grain for a painting," I lie, eager to end the conversation.

War steps closer, his expression a mask of contemplation. "It's a curious thing," he muses, before continuing. I feel a jolt of anticipation mixed with caution. My hair stands on end, and I wrap my arms tighter around myself. I glance over my shoulder; Wes and Gabriel are still deeply engrossed in their conversation. I'm alone with War.

"My brother stole a few trinkets before he changed sides," he reveals. "Famine was…" He pauses, and a dark gleam crosses his steel-blue eyes, the color of a knife's edge on a thunderous day. So perfectly fitting. I wonder if he was as designed as I was? The origin of the Horseman is still a mystery I have yet to delve into.

He continues, "insatiable for things he didn't even need—possessions he already had. Quite curious, isn't it?"

My pressed lips slacken. What's his motivation for sharing this? He's caught in a precarious game, attempting to aid both sides, hoping to save all his brothers.

Hope often leads men to madness, and the day will come when War must choose a side.

We all do.

I did.

He rubs his chin once more, his gaze fixed on his brothers through the window. "Famine loves the sun. It nourishes life and facilitates growth." His fleeting grin fades, replaced by a distant pain filled with worry—as if he was a parent concern for a child venturing into the world alone.

I unfold my arms and take a step forward. "Why are you telling me this?"

His focus remains on his brothers outside. "I can't begin to fathom the suffering Famine has to endure now. It's so dark," He stresses.

He just dropped a breadcrumb.

"What do you mean?" I inch closer, seeking clarity. My abs clench, and my palms press over my core like a shield, bracing for my stomach to either plummet or constrict from this knowledge.

"There is no light where my brother is," He finally turns to face me. "For some, it is a struggle to see in the dark, but for others, it is as simple as breathing. Is it simple for you now, Sol?" He raises his right brow.

"Wes has been helping me see in the dark," I reply, trying to solve his cryptic message. Is that what he means?

War shakes his head, "The darkness Death has cloaking his wide shoulders is nothing," He spits as if this is all somehow my fault, "compared to what you will have to navigate."

He drums his fingers on the countertop, "Cat got your tongue. What, no more questions?" He mocks.

"You're going to have to pick a side."

His index fingers nail the wood with a hard beat, "So are you," he quips. His nostrils flare wide.

"Why can't you just cut to the chase? Tell me what you know. We could help each other." My eyes flash to Wes, "We both want the same thing. To keep everyone we love safe."

His fingers swipe over the countertop before he raises his hands to inspect his nails as if we have all the time in the world, "Actions affect people differently. You say you want to protect us all, but one little move could alter that. Plus," He drops his hand, "it's more fun to watch you figure it all out. So tell me, little lovely mouse, what have you discovered from this little chit-chat."

I could refuse him, but I need him just as he needs me. Our alliance is a give and plunder, not just a take. Negotiating with War is like dancing with a hungry lion. One wrong ship, and I'm his next meal. "Famine stole the upgrades and gave them to Logan,"

His eyes grin, "Logan doesn't have access to trinkets like that. Some weapons are kept under lock and key."

As the clues align, I draw a conclusion. "I can see in the dark now?"

War merely shrugs, leaving the answer open-ended. "You tell me, Sol."

If Famine continues Luna's mission, then following the postcards should bring us both together very, very soon. The next postcard is from Norway—a place where certain parts experience months of darkness.

"You expect me to go to Norway?" I question. That means I will run from Wes, but it won't be easy unless…War helps me.

"It's a beautiful place for some; hell on earth for others. You see, hell doesn't have to be brimstone and fire. It can be silent, empty darkness," He replies, his voice carrying a solemn tone, akin to a lone drummer atop a hill, gazing upon the devastation wrought by the battle. "Darkness can be a powerful ally, but it can also be a merciless adversary. Should you choose to venture there, you may find answers that elude others."

His words hang in the air, their weight bearing down on me like a heavy anchor sinking into the depths of my understanding. The vast amount of secrets he hints at is not lost on me. He holds knowledge that could shape the course of my journey. The seriousness in his tone leaves no room for doubt—this is a strong warning.

"How will I get there? How will I escape Gabriel?" I question. *And how will I trick them all along the way and take the power for myself so I can end everything?*

He opens the palms of his hands. A showman on his stage, the mistress to the limelight he craves. "I am but a message in a bottle. I am not the ship to carry you across this treacherous sea, Sol," He states matter-of-factly, followed by a chuckle. "Your sister must possess the power of Jesus to convert so many believers to her cause," he remarks, his gaze momentarily diverted to the window. "Or the allure of the devil. After all, the devil loves the game of trickery."

My heart skips a beat at his words. "Why would you suggest that?" I ask, my voice slightly higher than it should be. He's dug deep into my lies, or perhaps Famine has confessed the truth to him, a truth his brothers are unaware of. It's a truth that could derail absolutely everything. The delicate balance of secrets and lies teeters on the precipice, and I'm left wondering what War wants in return for not whispering all my secrets.

His eyes scan me, assessing me with an enigmatic gaze. "Luna was a marvel when it came to keeping her true plans under lock and key, her plans encrypted in her own code. Up was down, down was sideways. The truth was just another fucked-up lie," He leans closer, "It was her lies that held her twisted truths. If you listened closely, you could hear the secrets her lies whispered."

My next inhale is pained, like a knife to my ribs.

"Who knows the real meaning behind her motives," he muses. Leaning against the counter with complete ease, he exudes a cocky confidence that practically dares me to challenge his knowledge and intentions. "Maybe the reason we are all playing this game isn't what we think it is."

What is that suppose to mean?

I feel like I've just been shoved down another rabbit hole. His words hang heavy in the air, casting doubt on everything I thought I knew. Luna's legacy is a web of mysteries, and untangling it may reveal a truth none of us are prepared to face.

"What is the reason then, if not for the power Manus Dei holds?" I press, desperately seeking answers.

But before he can respond, the sound of a car door closing interrupts our conversation. Gabriel drives away, and Wes begins his approach towards the house. War's smirk widens, a deceptive grin that leaves me with more questions than answers. "Time's up, little mouse," he replies cryptically, evading my question once again.

My fist ball, nails digging into my palms as I watch him retreat into the shadows, his impenetrable presence lingering in the air like a rare flower that only blooms during a full moon.

The mysteries surrounding Luna, Manus Dei, and the true nature of this game continue to elude me. If I choose to trust War, then that means the actual reason for Luna's game was just another shocking lie. It also means that buried within one of these lies is the truth, waiting to be set free.

Why else would Luna force me to play this game?

Chapter 23

Sol

The sun has risen, casting an eerie glow upon the world as the next day dawns. I'm still alive, so there's that. It's just the damn ground beneath me that can't seem to make up its mind. War's hints kept me tossing and turning all night. The Bastard. With dark circles under my eyes, I'm about to dive headfirst into Gabriel's twisted game. No longer a passive observer, now I'm his puppet — or at least that's what I need him to believe.

I wipe away the eager smile that tries to creep across my face, maintaining the facade of a cooperative canvas, ready to paint a perfect lie. I must be careful not to appear too eager or excited to start. A delicate balance must be struck - a subtle defiance, a simmering frustration, and a calculated display of emotions to keep Gabriel unsuspecting.

Water cascades over my body, cleansing away any trace of vulnerability. I dress in plain jeans and a gray sweatshirt, devoid of the trappings and adornments that would shield me from the blows of this game. Stripped down to my bare essence. I have none of my items, and it makes me anxious. Nothing I can use as a mask to shield myself from the blows of the game. No makeup or designer labels.

Just me and my skin.

I hope it's thick enough not to feel the pain.

A creaking sound interrupts my thoughts, the bedroom door opening to reveal Wes. My clammy hands instinctively rub against my thighs as I sit on the edge of the bed, my heart racing. With measured steps, he approaches, crouching before me. No words escape his lips, but his touch is both familiar and charged with unspoken meaning as he cups my face and plants a kiss upon my lips.

He pulls away, and for a moment, our contrasting gazes collide. Green eyes meet blue; Earth confronts water. The unspoken question lingers in the air, which force is stronger?

His voice breaks the silence, a plea disguised as a command. "I need you to be strong." *And I need you to be a traitor, but you won't.*

I lick my bare lips, the taste of vulnerability lingering. I have endured tests, grief, lost, love, pain inflicted upon me at every turn. Yet, the concern in Wes's eyes stirs an unsettling mix of emotions within me. Why is he, my Horseman, so nervous about what Gabriel needs me to do?

"Can I have some of my items back? My makeup, clothes, and my handbag." I have played my part, obeyed their rules. It is time for him to yield to my demands.

He stands, his words laced with resistance. "You don't need any of that."

"But you said I could have my bag," I protest. Every word I utter is carefully calculated, the performance of a grieving sister yearning for the objects that once drove me to the brink of madness. I must embody the role flawlessly, convincing Wes of my supposed attachment to those haunting artifacts.

His hand emerges from his back pocket, clutching my sister's red ribbon. "You can have this." He holds it just out of my reach. The longing to snatch it from his grasp courses through my veins.

"If this memory becomes too alluring, if it threatens to lead you astray into hallucinations, I will take it away."

I snatch the ribbon, "How dare you," I sneer, hugging it tightly against my chest. This is the Wes I detest, the one who inflicts deliberate cruelty upon me.

"I want the rest of my items!" I demand.

"I told you I would give you what you need, not what you want," he retorts, his tone icy. "You don't always get what you want, little mouse. Did you think I would reward you after you betrayed me and accepted the upgrades from Logan?" His words strike like daggers. "Did you ever stop and consider that Logan could have been working for the Masters? He handed you a loaded gun, and you shot yourself."

"This isn't Russian Roulette," I joke, "Logan has always helped me,"

"And Luna used to always take the bullets for you, but she can't anymore. War changes things, Sol. Your friend may now be your most ruthless enemy."

And, your lover might be the one who stabs you in the back, but she might also be the one to mend the wound and save you in the end.

"In the world of Manus Dei, loyalties shift like tides. They are ever-changing. Weather can change in seconds, and so can alliances," he warns, his tone laced with a veiled threat. At that moment, a flicker of unease surges through me, fearing that he may be aware of my clandestine plotting, my hidden agenda to forge my own ending.

"But not your loyalty to the Horsemen. You'll choose them over me," I bite.

"I chose them to protect you. There is a difference," he retorts. Spoken with such conviction. It's compelling but not moving.

"That sounds like a lie you tell yourself," I counter, unable to resist the impulse to provoke.

"Don't fight with me, Sol," Wes pleads. "You have just stepped into the inner workings of our world. It's a place you cannot survive alone. One day, you will understand that *everything* I have done was to protect you."

"I could say the same," I interject without thinking, the words escaping before I can contain them.

His eyes narrow like a detective on a caffeine high, suspicion tap-dancing in the spotlight. I change gears, quick and sly, "You swore no harm to Logan," I whisper.

"And I kept my word," He shoots back sternly. "But that doesn't mean I won't punish you. You went behind my back and seized something that could have brought about your demise." His eyes trace over my makeup-free face. "Besides, you don't need makeup. You're perfect just as you are."

"Perfect," I scoff. Ugh, that word. Nails on a chalk board. "I don't use makeup to feel perfect." My expression darkens. "I use it to paint."

Another step closer, "You use it to hide." Eye to eye, we challenge one another. "No more masks. Not with me. I won't be your enabler," he shakes his head.

"But you will be my captor."

He takes my hand, grip firm and reassuring, tugging me toward the door. "I'm your shield, little mouse. I'm here now," he says, "Don't fight me. Allow me to take all the bullets, all the hits, and blows. There is a mental battle on the horizon. Gabriel's training will push you. Prepare yourself and trust in me to catch you, hold you down, and keep you sane."

And who will take the bullets for you?

His lips descend upon mine, swallowing my response.

Taking so much more.

His tongue speaks a desperate language; I can feel the urgency in every breath of mine he inhales and steals.

Consuming.

He's terrified of what I will endure as Gabriel's pawn, and his anxiety ignites a fire within him. I respond with equal fervor. A passion-filled confession, an apology, we each can only show, not tell. A moment I am etching into my long-term memory because one day, one tragic day, I won't be able to kiss him. One day, I'll be running, and he will be chasing me, and if he catches me, we won't be the same two star-crossed lovers we are now. Everything will be tainted because that is what time does; it erodes, calcifies, and deteriorates love that is forced apart into a twisted hate.

Time stand still as the kiss lingers, and I am reluctant to let it end. I long to remain in his embrace, to find solace and strength within his arms. But eventually, reality crashes down upon us, tearing us away from the sanctuary of our embrace. With a gentle tug of my hand, he leads me forward, down the stairs, and towards the path that awaits me as Gabriel's puppet.

Each step reverberates with a sense of purpose; the echoes are a reminder of the journey that lies ahead. His fingers tighten their grip, symbolizing the delicate balance between strength and vulnerability, where the boundaries between ally and adversary blur, and the true nature of our roles will one day be revealed.

He pauses, his gaze shifting downward to meet mine. "All the strength you need is here," he says, touching my temple gently. "You create the barrier you must climb. You possess all the power. Your sister knew that."

He thugs me again down the stairs, further towards our demise. Further into a game that is ripping our love into jagged pieces, sharp enough to kill.

He slows his steps, retrieving a vintage iPod from his front pocket. Its white frame and small screen carry a sense of nostalgia. It was Luna's. "War tweaked this for you," he says, avoiding eye contact, a veil of guilt lurking beneath his gesture. "It's linked to music apps. I wasn't sure which one you'd like."

I take the gift, feeling its significance. Luna had a special connection with music, using it as a means to communicate her emotions when words failed her. Often, she would leave me a song to capture her mood and thoughts.

"How did you know my sister?" I inquire, realizing there is still much about Wes that remains a mystery to me.

"If you stay strong and work with us, I will tell you," he promises.

"Will there always be a give and taken in our relationship?"

"You tell me?" He rebuttals. I'm guilty too.

I walk past him and continue the rest of the way feeling his eyes digging into my back.

We reach the basement of the old house, War stands in the far corner, holding a tablet. Wires run along the walls and up to the low ceiling, made only of large wooden support beams. Cobwebs litter every corner. The wires dangle down from above, ultimately connecting to a headset placed prominently in the center of the room.

"You ready?" War looks at me, his usual three-piece suit replaced with trousers and a light blue dress shirt. His sleeves are rolled up, and the top buttons of his shirt are undone. His gaze then shifts to Wes, and a sense of unease settles within me.

"What's going on?" I ask. Eyes tracing all the wiring and the headset.

Wes closes the door, his sturdy frame blocking the only exit. Footsteps echo, drawing my attention to War, who moves to the center of the room and retrieves the headset.

"The murder at the club was just the beginning, Sol. We need you to see more. See what she saw," he admits. No boastful grin. No pleasure. He's worried too. "In order to become this other sister, you have to understand her." He takes a step closer ready to catch me should I try to flee.

Now I understand why Wes intended to give me the iPod later. A gift of solace after today's events. Through music, I could find temporary refuge, just as Luna had. I have to embody this new sister, a sister who took delight in murdering Subject 52, Gabriel's reflection.

Can I portray that? Become a person who enjoys killing?

Wes's fear reflects in his eyes, worried that I may blur the lines. Lose myself in her darkness.

War hands the headset to Wes. Each stepping closer to me. Trapped, caught between two predators circling around me.

My gaze drifts towards the headset again, its technological design suggesting a virtual reality experience. A new form of torture.

It's like looking at a book on a shelf; the cover is compelling, but the genre isn't your cup of tea. I want to know this sister but don't want to understand her. Nonetheless, you can't resist grabbing the book, looking at the cover, excitement bubbling. Slowly, you turn the first page, knowing that by the end of the book, your mind will be fucked.

"I am here, by your side. Even if you don't see me, little mouse, I am here," Wes assures me, his voice a steady anchor amidst the mounting uncertainty. With a final gesture, he extends the VR headset towards my waiting fingers.

Chapter 24

Sol

"This is a Virtual Reality headset," Wes begins, his voice carrying a tone that sounds like the first eerie notes of a haunting melody. "It is an older model. We managed to pilfer it from the facility's archives without anyone noticing." His hands stumble as he fumbles with the straps, struggling to maintain his composure. "The latest models... they go far beyond what you see before you. They immerse you entirely, scent, touch, and pain."

"Lovely," I jest. "I suppose a thank you is in order since I don't have to experience the latest version."

Nothing.

Tough crowd.

The cables dance in the air, like a rope swaying in the wind. Wes continues, "We set up a perimeter, a boundary grid that illuminates once you approach the walls. You're free to roam within the confines of the playing scene, but our focus lies in observation, not unrestricted motion."

My fingertips brush against his palm, finding refuge in the calloused terrain that has both taken lives and offered salvation. "Why do you harbor such fear for this new sister of mine?" I question, aching for clarity within his gaze.

His response is resolute, "I am not afraid of her or any Reflection, Sol," he asserts firmly. "My concern lies in the aftermath, in how this Reflection will influence you. You and Luna, flawed as your father may have been, possessed something she never had. Your father cared about you and Luna in his own distorted way. This clone never had that. She was but a tool, imprisoned by the very woman from whom you were cloned. She is a weapon, Sol. I need you to see her as a weapon and not a broken doll you want to try to fix. She isn't Luna."

"But you, too, are a weapon," I remind him, "You are capable of love if given the chance. People can change, Wes."

His exhale is like the swing of an executioner's blade. Final. "Not everyone can change, Sol," he counters.

This is the root of the problem with everyone in the game. They don't want to fix the problem; they want to erase it; paint over it. "You judge her for her actions when you should blame the person who raised her, who shaped her into this grotesque reflection. The creator and those who exploit her should take responsibility."

He tenses, "There is no place for compassion in the heat of battle. The moment you give it, the enemy will strike you down. This clone idolized Luna, and Luna used that to her advantage. So can you." He tugs me to his chest, eyes slipping to mine, "You want to know why I'm scared? Because I fear the hope that flickers in your eyes will evaporate once you try to become her. Sin is addicting, no matter the taste. Love or murder. One taste changes your palette. And I'm asking you to become the absolute worst Reflection of Luna but remain the woman I love."

He presses his forehead to mine, eyes closing like a silent prayer, "You can still be affected. Don't lose that. Focus, little mouse." He replaces his warmth with the cold headset. "Remember to stay on the path. You can not help this sister, but if it brings you comfort, know that someone is attempting to save her. It is not your fight. Leave it to another."

"Will she suffer the same fate as Ethan?" I reply. I thought he was going to be saved. Maybe his death was his gift. No more suffering. But I'm no longer ignorant. I want to know all the details.

"No," His voice firm. He's not lying, but he's not relieved either. Sometimes, living is a worse fate than dying. "Someone is working to show her that she is worthy of affection and care."

"But you're not going to tell me who?" My eyes look at War. Is she the woman he is trying to hide?

War flashes his devilish grin for the first time today, "I'd cut off my manhood before I touched that clone. Sorry, love, but I'm attracted to a different kind of beauty. Not conventional."

"We need to get started." Wes interrupts.

War nods as do I. Suck it up and roll the dice, Sol. The next round is about to begin.

"You met this clone in the club," War begins as he taps away on the tablet. "She is the Reflection that killed Subject 52. Her name is Klara, Klara Karlsen."

War turns the iPad toward me, displaying a picture. It's me, or rather, Klara, a clone. There's something unsettling about her gaze, a darkness that mirrors Luna's twisted essence. Buried within the void is motive. None of them see it. I saw it in Luna's eyes. If someone has motive then that means they feel. It might be a tiny spark but it's there. Maybe she just wants to be loved or maybe she just likes to kill. Only time will tell.

A wave of unease washes over me, a memory resurfaces. "Klara was happy when she killed Subject 52," I recount. The realization strikes me with a chilling clarity— Klara saw Subject 52 as nothing more than a weapon, just as Wes views her as a weapon. To her, destroying a weapon is an achievement. You out smarted it. Proved your worth.

The image of Klara nonchalantly pocketing the bloody knife flashes vividly in my mind, a seemingly mundane yet profoundly unsettling act. I refuse to succumb to the darkness within her, within me. I was created, designed for a specific role, one I adamantly refuse to embrace.

My hand reaches out, trembling slightly, as I carefully place the headset over my head. The moment it settles into position, a surge of electricity courses through me. It's as if a veil is lifted, and the virtual world engulfs my senses.

As the room transforms around me, I stand tall, finding solace in the knowledge that Wes is by my side. Even if I can't see him, even if he will eventually betray me in favor of power, I still cling to his presence.

Some people like rainy days, enjoy the sound of thunder; it's a cool, numbing presence; others prefer bright, clear, sunny days. I'm ready to admit that I prefer the rain, the thrill that courses through my bones when thunder erupts is exciting. Unlike the sun, which burns, rain and thunder comfort. They cling to my senses, drowning out everything else. Storms knock you off your feet, forcing you to see life from a different perspective.

That's what I need to do, see everything from a new angle. Wes's presence feels like a shield, a comforting anchor to his strength. I sense him leaning closer, his fingers lightly touching my shoulders, grounding me in this uncertain reality.

My dark knight.

Darkness engulfs me, plunging me into an abyss of uncertainty. Then, like a flickering flame, a room materializes before my eyes. I stand alone in a vast expanse of white, a blank canvas yearning for life's tapestry to be woven upon it.

Strong hands anchor me, their touch on my shoulders a reassuring presence. "I'm here, Sol. If it becomes too much, take it off," he whispers.

I take a deep breath, steeling myself for what lies ahead. This is my moment to immerse myself in Klara's world, to observe her interactions, and navigate the distortions that await me. With Wes as my anchor, I step into the virtual realm, ready to uncover the truths and confront the horrors that lie in Klara's mind so I can pose as her and not be caught.

"All we need you to do is become Klara, Sol," War explains. "Observe her. You will witness her interactions with people, delve into her world."

Curiosity burns within me as I pose the question that lingers in my mind. "How am I seeing through her eyes?"

Fingers press firmly into my shoulders, grounding me in the moment. "I'll explain later. For now, focus," Wes assures me.

War interjects with a sardonic note of caution, "Some of the uploads may be distorted. The visuals and sounds might pixelate or fade during Klara's early years. Just do the best you can. Learn her tics, how she walks, regards others, and how she thinks. You're all clones, but each is unique, each monster a different beast."

I raise an eyebrow and tease, "Careful, War, you're starting to sound sentimental."

War chuckles darkly, "Everyone in our world has a different definition for emotions. I never said I didn't care. Maybe my problem is caring too much about those who have been copy and pasted. If only I could turn my back on you clones and focus on mere humans."

"If only," I mutter.

The white room flickers, its sterile walls dissolving into a whirlwind of fragmented images and swirling darkness. In a breathtaking surge of adrenaline, I am thrusted into the depths of Klara's mind, an immersive realm teeming with untold secrets and haunting memories. The transition is disorienting; my senses overwhelmed by a cacophony of sights and sounds that converge in a kaleidoscope of emotions. The air crackles with anticipation as I find myself standing in the midst of Klara's tumultuous world. I'm one step closer to becoming her, to stealing the power and ending the game.

Chapter 25

Sol

Ashen stone walls loom before me, an imposing presence creating a tingling sensation up my back. Each stone is massive, a formidable weight that hints at the strength and fortitude required to construct a castle. My gaze sweeps across the ancient blocks, their weathered surfaces bearing the weight of centuries of history. The stones exude an aura of timelessness, as if they hold secrets whispered through the ages.

Taking a tentative step forward, I feel a subtle shift in the virtual reality, a ripple of pixels dancing at the edge of my vision. The world around me flickers and transforms, the shapes coalescing into tangible forms. The room I initially perceived begins to reveal its true nature, stretching and morphing into a long and narrow hallway that reaches into the unknown.

"Hurry up!" A new voice enters. An image flashes, streaks of light, and new pixels appear before they take shape. The pixels swirl around like swarming bees. I want to stand and watch them paint their image, but reality continues to move. It's easy to forget I'm not here. I look down and see small black dress shoes on my feet. The feet of a child. I'm in her body.

A tall, slender woman rushes past me. Red heels clap loudly on the stone floor. She looks so tall that I have to tilt my head up. I finally glance at my hands and see how tiny they are too. I'm a child in this memory. Not mine, but Klara's.

With this technology, we have achieved what was once deemed impossible—truly walking in someone else's shoes.

"Klara!" The woman pivots, her blonde hair swirling around her. She glances down at me, her harsh demeanor making me want to run. My feet instinctively back up. The room flickers, and I'm pushed out of Klara's body now watching the scene unfold outside of her eyes. Like a ghost clinging to the pixelated walls. I take another step forward, and sudden streaks of light flash. In an instant, I find myself no longer inhabiting Klara's body but instead watching her from the outside. Then, with another flash, I'm back in Klara's perspective.

"Don't fight it. The headset senses your movement. You need to move as Klara does in this memory. We will watch each scene twice. Once from her point of view, and then you can move freely and watch from the sidelines," War instructs me.

With a fast inhale, I relax and roll on the tip of my toes. The room stabilizes, and I see a woman enter. Her beauty I remember most, just as well as her cruelty when I first met her. "I know her." I gasp.

"That is Astrid," War informs me. The scene pauses. "I can pause the memory anytime you need me to. In case you want to study details."

"Are you seeing this on your tablet?" I question.

"Yes." He clarifies.

"I'm right here, little mouse." Wes voices again. His breath kisses my right ear. He is Death, hiding in my dark corners, ready to protect me.

"I met Astrid before, when I was a child," I tell the Horsemen. I first encountered Astrid when I was just five years old, and in that moment, she seemed like a celestial being. Her presence exuded a radiance that captured my young imagination. With her mid-length, platinum blonde hair cascading around her like a shimmering waterfall, she appeared as if fairies had sprinkled stardust upon her locks. Her porcelain skin, smooth and pale as an ice skating rink, gave her an ethereal quality. And her eyes, oh, her eyes were a mesmerizing shade of blue, resembling glacial waters mirroring a pristine blue sky. Everything about her seemed magical.

But every fairy tale turns south. The enchantment quickly crumbled when Astrid spoke. The sweetness I had perceived was replaced by cruelty and spite. She reveled in causing pain, even making me shed tears. It was Luna who came to my defense, kicking Astrid in the shin. Astrid, a benefactor at Exodus Technologies, my father and Hans's company, would occasionally visit my father's lab. Her presence was always foreboding, lurking in the shadows like a malevolent force. Her angelic face twisted into a permanent scowl, devoid of any hint of warmth or ease. I never witnessed her smile or show any kindness. Marble statues had more personality and warmth.

"I'm going to continue," War responds.

Young Klara follows closely behind Astrid, her presence almost ghost-like as she shadows the woman's every step. The hallway stretches on, seemingly endless, and I can't shake the sensation that I've been here before.

The realization hits me like a lightning bolt. "Am I in the tunnels?" I whisper, my voice barely audible.

"Yes," Wes admits. The confirmation sends a chill down my spine as I recall the countless times I watched Luna disappear into those tunnels.

I'm finally inside! It's been a long awaited desire but look what I had to go through to get to this point.

Concealed beneath my father's Swiss estate, those tunnels were perpetually a forbidden treasure. Their mysteries teased my curiosity, leaving me eager to unveil their hidden truths. In these tunnels Luna and Gabriel played their game. It's where monsters roam and beast are born.

Now, through young Klara's eyes, I finally get to explore them. As Klara's fear and curiosity meld within me, I tread cautiously through the dim passages. Aged stone walls bear the weight of history, marked by the passage of time.

Each step I take resonates through the tunnels, creating an eerie symphony that fills the empty spaces. Shadows play tricks on the walls, their forms flickering and distorting in the dim light, adding an element of mystery and suspense to our journey. It's as if the tunnels themselves are holding their breath, waiting to reveal their secrets. So, let's see what they've got, shall we?

A labyrinthine of passages. Twist and turns that will require me time to memorize them. Fascination envelops me. Intricate details, hidden alcoves, and the subtle signs of occupation by Manus Dei.

With each turn and corridor, I can't help but wonder what truths lie concealed within these walls. The tunnels have been a witness to the clandestine meetings, the plotting, and the conspiracies that have shaped the world of Manus Dei. Now, it is my turn to walk in Klara's shoes, to witness the transformation that awaits her under the tutelage of Astrid, the artist who molds her like clay.

The darkness of the tunnels surrounds me, amplifying the sense of anticipation and adventure. My heart quickens with each step, knowing that the secrets I am about to uncover will have far-reaching consequences.

The room shakes and flashes a blinding white that blinds my eyes, "What's happening?" I reach out, feeling off balance. Wes steadies me. "You're doing good." He whispers. I feel his lips kiss my shoulder.

"These older memories are not stable. It's going to be patchy for the first few days until we get you up to speed. This version of virtual reality has been created with enhanced graphics. It helped render the images to make them clearer and more believable."

Wes releases me, the room materializes again, only this time, we are not in the tunnels but a lab I know all too well. It is my father's lab in the basement. The first person I see materialize is my sister, not Klara or any other Reflection, but Luna.

"Luna!" I call out desperately, my voice echoing through the virtual tunnels. The longing to be reunited with my sister intensifies, but as I attempt to run toward her, the boundary grid materializes, its illuminated lines barring my path. Klara's memories hold me captive, preventing me from reaching Luna.

I stand frozen, trapped within Klara's mind, my heart aching for the solace and comfort only hugging Luna could provide. The absence of Luna, forever beyond my reach, bears down on me, intensifying the feelings of isolation and yearning within this digital domain.

It's torturous to see my sister but not touch her.

This isn't my reality. This is Klara's. I repeat until my throat doesn't feel as thick.

Klara is with my father and Luna. I know it is Luna because she has a red ribbon in her hair. She only appears to be five years old. The age our father first started to experiment and perform upgrades on her. My father looks younger as he stands with a tablet and talks with Astrid.

"Well, sister," Father's voice gleams through the virtual simulation.

"Pause!" I shout, and the room freezes in a suspended state. "Astrid is my aunt?" I utter in disbelief, my mind racing to comprehend the revelation. *But I'm cloned after her...*

"Don't lose focus, Sol," Wes's voice cautions me. "You need to stay on the path, observe Klara and her interactions with people."

I lick my lips, my gaze locked on Astrid, the cruel angel who is my father's sister. It dawns on me that my Father never mentioned anything about having an aunt. And Luna knew all along, but she never revealed the truth about our familial ties.

As the simulation resumes, my father's triumphant declaration echoes through the corridors of my mind, a chilling reminder of the game that unfolds before me.

"I won this round." Father gloats.

Astrid's posture stiffens, her voice dripping with a hint of menace. "For now," she responds, a cold smile curling upon her lips. I watch as young Klara instinctively retreats, her small figure shrinking back in fear. "Remember, brother, I can take all your pets away whenever I want." With a swift motion, Astrid seizes Klara, her grip harsh and forceful, causing Klara to stumble in her grasp.

No! Stop hurting her! I want to shout. Stop this from happening, but this is the past. There is no altering it. This is the mold that shaped Klara.

Cruelty.

Now, I comprehend how a villain is made.

I'm not referring to Klara.

I'm talking about myself.

Right now, a burning desire for vengeance is igniting within me. That's what worried Wes. Vengeance engulfs me as I bear witness to the agonizing transformation of this child. The weight of her suffering fuels my determination to bring down the Masters, to tear apart the oppressive system that breeds such cruelty and destruction. In this moment, I understand Luna more than ever—the void of emotions, the lack of sympathy towards those who have harmed us. I yearn to unleash justice upon those who orchestrated this twisted game, to ensure that no more innocent souls are subjected to such torment. The fire of retribution consumes me, igniting an unyielding pursuit to dismantle the very foundations that enable their heinous deeds.

Like my twin, I don't want to kill, but that doesn't mean I won't load a gun and watch as it is fired. That line I drew in the sand, the line I said would fade, but I would draw again; well, in this circumstance, I'm going to let it fade more before I redraw it.

How could I not?

Is this how it starts, how a villain develops? You go against your morals just one time. One time! One excuse, reason, and cause...then maybe one more time, then again and again.

Fuck it, I'll deal with my guilt later.

Wes was right. In the midst of battle, compassion cannot be afforded. Not everyone deserves to be saved. Murder isn't my style, nor was it Luna's, but it was the style of others. That's why Luna didn't intervene to stop them. I understand Luna now. It's not my style either, but it is the Horsemen's, and I won't do anything to prevent them from putting an end to Astrid. It's why Luna pushed her pawns into committing the act, how she meticulously plotted their every step to ensure its achievement. She understood the necessity of sacrifice and the cruel realities of our world.

People can easily be turned into weapons; you just have to know what type of weapon they are best suited to be. Once you've solved that, your unstoppable.

I can't help but see the twisted wisdom in Luna's actions. Perhaps, in this dark and dangerous game, it's the only way to save what remains of our shattered world. Fighting evil with evil, forsaking morals to preserve morals.

It's a haunting realization, but I must embrace the darkness within me if I am to stand a chance against the impending threat. If I am to protect those I care about and ensure a glimmer of hope survives amidst the chaos, I must become a force to be reckoned with, for in this twisted battle, the lines between good and evil blur, and survival becomes the ultimate goal.

Chapter 26

Sol

I feel the headset's weight resting on my head as it prepares to immerse me in another memory. The virtual reality world begins to unfold, but this time, I remain an observer on the sidelines, watching Klara's experiences play out before me. War had explained that we would be switching perspectives, first seeing the memory through Klara's eyes and then rewatching it as an observer to capture all the details. I can't help but think that Manus Dei must also employ this technology as a weapon for evil purposes. Good and evil are inseparable in this twisted game, and Manus Dei is the master of manipulating that balance.

"It's a tie," my father's voice resounds in the virtual reality simulation.

Young Klara underwent a test, pitted against my sister Luna. Some tests are physical, but most are mental, challenging their skills in solving equations and puzzles. My aunt Astrid crosses her arms, "That means they both lose."

"I wouldn't draw that conclusion, sister," my father retorts, tilting his head. He regards his sister in a perplexing manner. A look that's like a riddle I can't quite decipher. It's a mix of caution and love, worry mingled with commitment, as if he's trying to figure out the most complicated puzzle in the world.

Today, they are not alone. Another older man accompanies them, along with a young boy who keeps glancing toward Klara. The older man seems to act as a judge or viewer of sorts.

After reviewing the results, my father and Astrid retire to a separate room with the other man, leaving the door ajar. The young boy positions himself by the door, his back turned to the adults, his gaze fixated on my sisters. Klara sits on a small round stool, her eyes cast down, but she steals glances at Luna, whose feet swing back and forth on an adjacent stool. Klara's eyes inch upward as if drawn to Luna but hesitant to meet her gaze fully.

When I gaze upon Klara, it's like looking into a mirror of my childhood. Unlike me, Klara didn't have the luxury of a twin who would willingly exchange positions with her. A twin who protected her, even during those moments when truth be told, I didn't want Luna to be my shield.

Luna's eyes light up with a devilish grin as she pounces, "Boo!" she exclaims, startling Klara, who jerks in response. She hops off the stool and confronts Klara, hissing, "You need to stop it."

"Stop what?" Klara asks, bewildered.

Luna reaches out and pinches her. "Ouch!"

"That!" Luna presses her index finger to Klara's lips. I snort and shake my head, recognizing Luna's peculiar way of helping.

"Stop showing your weakness," Luna whispers to Klara. "I won't help you next time."

Klara's gaze shifts towards the door, where the young boy continues to observe them silently. "What do you mean?" she asks Luna.

"You think we tied?" Luna raises an eyebrow.

Klara stares at my sister for what feels like an eternity. A proud shock courses through me as I witness Luna's subtle guidance.

Despite her disturbed nature, as her sister, I know that Luna is trying to protect all of us. She tied with Klara so Klara would not be punished. By doing so, Luna risked her own skin in the game.

Slowly, Klara rises from her stool and stands alongside Luna. "Testing makes me anxious," she murmurs.

"Get over it. Fast," Luna orders, her voice sounding strangely wise and hardened. She reaches out and takes Klara's hand. "Do you know why they created us?" Luna asks, shaking her head before Klara can respond. "Shut up. I'm going to tell you the truth. That woman you call mommy is the reason they created us. I don't matter, my father doesn't matter, and neither do you. Astrid is the only one that matters." She grins sinisterly. "Or so she thinks."

Klara chews her lip before asking, "Why are you telling me this?"

Luna closes the distance between them once more grabbing her shoulders. "Because you'll never gain mommy's approval. The sooner you accept that, the easier this game will be. You have more power than me. You live with the monster. I only live with the creator. You can be so much more than this pathetic version of yourself, Klara. Tick, tock, time waits for no one, so you'd better start growing up and accepting your fate. When you're ready, I'll be waiting. And if not, so long and goodbye." She shoves her away.

The room fades, and the virtual reality dissolves around me. I leave the headset on momentarily, trying to process everything before I'm forced to return to reality.

"Are you okay?" Wes's voice breaks through the lingering echoes. Without hesitation, I remove the headset, avoiding his gaze. I know that both Wes and War have watched everything unfold on the iPad, and that unsettles me. I feel a need to protect Klara, and these intrusions into her memories feel like a violation.

There's another reason I have to watch these memories from both inside Klara's shoes and as an observer. They don't just want me to understand Klara; they want me to become the woman I was cloned after. The puzzle pieces are aligning. Klara always appeared alongside Astrid. Gabriel needs me to assume Klara's identity to get close to the woman I was cloned after—the last remaining Master in Manus Dei. My mother, but also my aunt, and also... myself. I am a clone of Astrid, after all.

"Is Astrid the woman I was cloned after?" I finally voice my realization, cutting to the chase.

"Don't ask a question when you already know the answer, little mouse," Wes responds with a touch of cruelty. By now, I've come to understand that he can be cruel when he intends to be empathetic. It's a tactic Luna and Gabriel employ when they want the person they care about to develop resilience. When you love someone, you want to protect them, but being their shield can ultimately weaken them. Love comes in different forms, and sometimes that love is callous, sharpening you like the edge of a finely crafted sword.

I make my way toward the door, stating firmly, "I'm done for the day." Climbing up the stairs, I retreat to my bed and close my eyes, shutting out the questions swirling in my mind. I don't dwell on why my aunt wielded such control over my father or why he cloned *her* repeatedly. I accept the knowledge that Astrid, my father's sister, is the woman I was cloned after—a Master in Manus Dei.

As my head hits the pillow, I close my eyes tighter and see the flickering light at the end of my tunnel. There is a new darkness within me, one I must embrace if I am to navigate this treacherous game. It should be easy; after all, the woman I was cloned after is the definition of evil.

Chapter 27

Sol

My fingers trace over the trident tattoo inked over Wes's open heart surgery scar. I haven't been able to paint the tattoo but tracing his scar calms me. I tilt my head up and watch him. He has one arm over his head, the other tucked around me, his fingers resting on my naked hip. His eyes are closed, and all the darkness that usually clouds him has vanished.

He crept into my room well past midnight, woke me up, stripped me bare and made me forget everything. Sex was my balm. Now we rest in the aftermath. A new day is starting, and soon we will have to wake. I'll have to start training as Klara again, and Wes will have to begin his inner battle with himself and Death.

I wish I could press pause and remain in this moment, but instead, all I can do is capture it in my mind. Study and observe every detail, from the gentle rise and fall of his hard chest, to the stubble growing thicker on his jawline. His body is so at ease, like a sleeping predator I stumbled upon. His muscles are not flexed, they are so sculpted I can trace the outline of his abs perfectly. My finger dips in the grooves of each muscle, and I stir the beast. He exhales a hum of approval.

I skirt my hand up and trace the three small bullet wounds. I watch as I do so. Each time I touch these scars, his body tenses as if they are pained.

"I want to know your story."

"You can't even handle your own story, little mouse," he retorts.

Undeterred, I push myself up, meeting his gaze with determination. "Maybe I can handle yours," I counter. "I won't know if you don't tell me." Leaning closer, I press my lips against each of his bullet scars, feeling the subtle tension ripple through his body. The skin is raised and hard, but it's still skin no matter how it was changed or deformed. "Please," I persist. I want to understand the beast that lured my heart into the palm of his hands.

His lips part with hesitation, and though his eyes remain closed, he guides me back down with a gentle touch. I rest my cheek directly over his heart, feeling the steady rhythm beneath my skin.

"My father heads a black-site program. Like your father, my family is very powerful," He reveals. "My father was born into Manus Dei, trained and groomed to be influential in the US government. His power in the US is monumental, but in Manus Dei, my father is considered low on the totem pole."

I listen intently, my fingers tracing delicate patterns over his chest. I can sense the complexities of his family dynamics, the conflicting loyalties that exist within their world.

"He never held deep-seated loyalty to Manus Dei," Wes continues. "For years, they approached him because they wanted me. I was a perfect candidate to become one of their Hunters. But my father continued to refuse them, trying to protect me. It was something my grandfather didn't extend to my father."

His words paint a picture of sacrifice and defiance, of a father's unwavering determination to shield his son from the clutches of Manus Dei. I find myself silently honoring the strength it must have taken for Wes's father to stand against such powerful forces.

"I was in the Navy with Levi and War," Wes reminisces, a wistful smile playing on his lips. "We joined the SEALS and were trained with the best the US government had to offer. After three years, War and I found ourselves on a mission that went terribly wrong. We completed our objective, but amidst the chaos, I spotted a small boy hiding under a broken table, holding a gun. In that split second, he aimed it at War, ready to take his life."

I listen, my heart aching for the weight of the decision Wes had to face, the unimaginable choices thrust upon him in that fateful moment.

His gaze fixates on an unseen point in the room, and his hands clench the bedsheets tightly. "I had the shot," he starts, his fingers gripping the fabric like the rifle's trigger. "It was simple for me, just pull the trigger, and the boy would have never been a threat."

His voice quivers with the weight of the memory, and his body tenses. "But I froze," he admits, "I couldn't take the shot." His fingers tremble slightly, mirroring the turmoil within him.

His gaze shifts to the ceiling briefly, as if searching for answers in the shadows. "I couldn't kill a child," he whispers, his voice strained. His hand moves to his forehead, his fingers pressing against his skin in frustration. "But I also couldn't bear to watch my brother die." His palm rests over his heart, as if trying to soothe the ache that memory still brings.

My eyes snap to the bullet scars that mark his body. He leapt in front of those bullets, risking everything to save his brother and the boy who had threatened them.

As our eyes lock, the unyielding resolve in his gaze speaks volumes. "I would make the same choice."

"I know," I reply softly. He will do anything to protect those he loves, whether taking a bullet or putting them in a cage. "What happened to the child?"

"He ran," He answers, his gaze distant. "And just before I passed out, I ordered War to let him go." His words hang in the air, heavy with the weight of the consequences that unfolded.

"I was left in a coma, hooked up to machines. The bullets were removed, but my chances of survival were as slim as a toothpick. I needed a heart. And guess who came swooping in to save the day? Gabriel, offering my father a deal he couldn't refuse. He promised to whip up a brand-new 3D-printed heart for me, using my own cells, so I wouldn't have to bother with meds or organ rejection. In return, he demanded my father's division help him and for me to become a Horseman."

"So you were born normal."

"Opposites attract, little mouse." He jokes.

"Yes they do."

"My father accepted because, like Gabriel, he despised the leadership and the distorted future Manus Dei sought to create," He explains. "Within hours, a 3D-printed heart was ready for me, and from that point on, my path intertwined with Gabriel's. I became a Horseman, an enhanced soldier who followed orders."

"So how did a soldier come to view a clone as his brother?"

"I never really saw Gabriel as just another clone," Wes states emphatically. "You see, when people start ranking themselves, thinking they're above or below others, everything goes to hell. So, instead, I judged Gabriel by what he did. I liked what I saw. He recognizes the immense power that Manus Dei wields, but he also sees the corruption and bullshit that accompanies it. His goal is to take all that science and turn it into something that benefits everyone. That was Manus Dei's original vision, you know? It's a big damn challenge, but I genuinely believe he's the only one who can pull it off."

"Why him?"

"It takes someone who knows the depths of evil to truly control it. You see, the science, it's both a force for evil and a force for good, Sol. It can mend just as much as it can break. It's that classic double-edged sword scenario. The question is, which edge do you want to wield, to present to the world? Astrid wants destruction, but Gabriel, he wants salvation."

"If it's a weapon that can be flipped like a coin then why not destroy it all. Wouldn't that be safer. A restart."

His gaze turns unyielding as it locks onto mine. "I get your concerns, Sol. They're valid, and I've battled with them myself. But the science is out there, beyond containment. You can erase their library, but folks will always find a way to connect the dots again. At least, under one name, all that knowledge is somewhat centralized. Controlled. Darker forces are lurking out there, ready to exploit it for even more nefarious ends. The devil you know is better than the demon you haven't met yet. Manus Dei stays, and Gabriel will lead it."

"You paint such a pretty picture," I quip.

"Don't get pissy with me. Imagine a world where Manus Dei's knowledge and technology fall into the wrong hands. I've been a soldier in war. Seen the death all for the gain of power. Gabriel understands the dangers of allowing such power to be wielded recklessly. By maintaining control of Manus Dei, we can prevent the misuse of its capabilities and ensure that it is used for the betterment of humanity."

I tap his scar. "Many causes start out noble."

"No government is entirely good, Sol, some are so corrupt and evil that even Luna's cold heart would shudder at their deeds."

"You might have known my twin but you don't understand her." I bite.

"Neither did you."

Touché. I didn't.

"I want to live in a world where every soldier gets access to a 3D printed heart, not just one who sells his soul to the devil."

I nod. "I want that too."

"Then help us make it happen."

"I don't have a choice."

He kisses my forehead. Pain evident.

"When did you first meet my sister?"

"During all of my upgrades. In a way, Luna was my creator." He begins to play with my hair.

"Luna performed the upgrades?"

"Yes, Luna and Gabriel lead the Horsemen project." A slight grin tugs at his lips as he reminisces. "The first time I laid eyes on Luna, she had bright red headphones resting on her shoulders, her music was blasting so loud it filled the room. I thought she was the most stunning woman I had ever seen. When she walked into my hospital room with such confidence, I felt alive again."

Jealousy pumps through my veins at hearing this.

"Don't worry, little mouse," he reassures me, a hint of amusement in his eyes. "My initial infatuation with her was short-lived. Luna drove me to the brink of madness, fucking insane, and not in a good way. You're nothing like her. I've never met a woman like you, and I know I never will. That's why I can never let you go. You are so fucking precious to me, Sol." He pulls me tighter to him. "I can't even describe what I feel for you. Can't find the words. My actions are all I can show you, and you might not like them at times, but I know deep down you know it's from a place of love. Love so strong it has changed my very soul. Bound me to you."

My throat thickens. *I love you too.*

When I can't voice it back his fingers grip me tighter. "You will say it one day. I know you will." He whispers into my hair. Then he continues, "For the first couple of months Luna rarely spoke to me or acknowledged my questions. I was nothing more than her fucking lab rat. Always had on those goddamn headphones, blasting so loud. They were like her shield, blocking out the world, including me. I grew frustrated, and one day, in a fit of anger, I snatched her headphones off her. I demanded that she answer me. Instead, she handed me her iPod, selected a song, and slipped the headphones onto my ears. I realized she wanted me to listen to the song for answers. After the song played, she took back the headphones and told me, 'It took you long enough.' Then she punched me in the nose."

I laugh, "That sounds like her. She was testing you. Finding your buttons."

He nods. "When I recruited War for our cause, Luna started to view me differently. I thought she looked at me as her equal. A friend and not her pawn. She started to speak to me more and not just through songs." Darkness clouds over his face as if he tastes something bitter. "Sometimes I wish Luna didn't talk. She spoke in haunting rambles. Nothing made sense, yet everything did. It makes a person feel as if they are going mad."

I smirk. I understand exactly how Wes feels.

"She told me I would have to watch Gabriel's back but also protect his mind."

"She loved him," I murmur.

"She was planning to leave. I realize that now. Making me her pawn to watch over Gabriel."

"I'm sorry."

He shakes his head, "Don't apologize for her actions. They are not yours."

Oh, my love, you have no idea how wrong you are.

His hand glides up and down my spine pressing his warmth into my soul. "Gabriel and Luna have experience things no one else has. Their definition of love is complex. It's something neither you are I can understand." He adds, as his fingers slow. "I often wonder how it's possible for two people to love each other so deeply, willing to do anything to save one another, but ultimately end up destroying the very love they've worked so hard to preserve."

My heart skips a beat, "I wonder that too." I mutter. My lips kissing his chest. *I wonder how you can't see it happening to us.*

For the next few moments, I listen to his beating engineered heart. It's stunning and so precious.

"Something started to change with Luna," He states. "Her behavior became increasingly unstable at times. I thought it was because the game was coming to an end. Gabriel assumed that theory as well. I followed her. I wanted to ensure she was loyal to our side and not the Masters. That's when I first saw you." His voice elevates to pure lust and happiness. It spreads like a virus to me. His fingers drum gently on my hip bone.

"I wanted you from the moment I laid eyes on you," he murmurs, his voice filled with a twisted kind of love. "You were the purest thing in my life, a beacon of light in this sea of nightmares. I watched you through the scope of my rifle, observing your every move, your every expression. Your eyes, they held a depth of emotion, a whirlwind of conflicting feelings that I yearned to unravel. I wanted to possess you, to mark you as mine. See your smooth skin turn red under my touch. You were this angel living amongst monsters, completely oblivious to the true danger that lurked right next to you. I wanted to protect you at all costs, shield you from the horrors that awaited you. You had no idea who you were living with, what your sister was capable of, or the sinister experiments your father was conducting."

An unsettling mixture of dark and twisted passion fills the room. It should give me pause, make me question his motives and intentions, but instead, it stirs something deep within me, a desire to cling to him even more tightly.

So I do.

Shifting my body I straddle him. His hard thick cock settles between my bare thighs. Our eyes lock, and I can see the intensity of his emotions, raw and unfiltered. Feel the strength of his unspoken words right between my core. I rock my hips, his head tips back in pleasure. "Fuck," he moans. Hands lock onto my hips, guiding me, caging and controlling. The tip of him teases my entrance.

"I didn't want to risk losing you," He starts to push inside of me slowly. Invading me. Caressing me.

"Wes," I gasp; my hips slow. He's so thick each time feels like the first time.

"Relax," He commands and I find my walls growing more slick. Craving him. "You were made to take me." So I do, I grind my hips pushing him another inch deeper.

"Yes," he purrs, "That's it. So fucking tight, but you bend and break only for me." Another inch.

"Don't stop," I beg. I want him like this, in a state of confessing but with a loose tongue because he's driven mad by pleasure.

"Everything was shifting, Sol," he pants as I clench my core tighter. Testing and teasing. The next shift of my hips has him buried deep within me. Tearing me in half, but also making me feel whole. My mouth parts. He grins and shoves himself impossibly deeper.

He's breaking me. Just like he always wanted.

Cracking me open. Pushing himself inside.

I wasn't brave enough to confess this is exactly what I wanted. All those years of reading romance novels in my study were a lie, a forced fabrication. I tried to make myself believe cotton candy romance was what I should crave.

It's not.

Who wants cotton candy when you can savor the taste of salted caramel? Bittersweet, sinful, and utterly irresistible.

This pursuit, this chase—it ignites a passion so intense that words alone cannot describe it. So like Wes, I revert to actions.

"Plots were crashing together, chaos was unfolding. It was Gabriel versus Luna, versus Manus Dei, versus Astrid. Dorian and Hans's game was coming to an end, and that's when Luna disrupted everything." He steers my hips up and pulls me down, pausing so deep within me that my body pulsates around him. It's the most delicious way to learn about him, cast a drift in lust and confessions.

"Wes," I pant. It's too much, he's too thick.

It's not enough.

I'm completely free, unchained from expectations.

Liberated.

Loved.

When we were flesh to flesh, I wasn't a genetically upgraded human, a twin used as a puppet, or a player in the game. I was the version of me I always dreamed about.

A soft groan rumbles in his chest, urging me on. My hips rock with an insatiable need, his thrusting up, meeting my every demand.

I love you. "More," I plead, nails digging deep, not wanting to lose him. *But I will.*

I try to prolong the moment. One day, Wes will be a memory that haunts me because he won't just choose me. My heart throws a tantrum worthy of a drama queen, begging me to shout the words he longs to hear, pleading with me to allow my body to come.

Feral eyes clash with my grieving ones, "Don't," He growls as if he senses my every thought.

"Come," he demands. I lose all sense of time and restraint as I comply with his order, clenching and shattering around him. The little death, as the French call it. The best way to die, to taste a heaven I might not be welcomed into.

As if I were shot in the heart by Cupid's arrow, I collapse on his deep, heaving chest. His hands hang lazily over my body, keeping me pressed to him.

Then reality comes back. The pause button untapped. I breathe a labored breath, "Keep telling me your story."

I hear the laugh within his lungs as it escapes his lips. "Do I have to?"

"Yes. It was a moment of pause, but you and I know there is no escape until these games end."

"It won't always be like this."

"As long as you call yourself a Horseman, it will be. You belong to them, the science. You won't share me." His fingers dig into my ass. "Don't expect me to share either."

"Jealousy can be a good thing," he purrs, satisfied. He loves that I'm territorial over him. It must have been torture when he acted as two separate people, knowing that I was sleeping with Wes but also tempting Death.

That misery was my doing. I wanted to hurt him because I knew he would hurt me one day. Cage me. From the first taste, when he touched me in my room as an intruder, I knew our love was toxic. One taste was going to poison me, sicken me. Nothing ever tasted as satisfying again.

That's why I fought him, like a child who didn't want to swallow down the medicine they needed.

Propping my chin on his chest, I look into those forest-green eyes. Eyes that beckon me yet frighten me. His forehead is covered in a sheen of sweat; our bodies still remain as one as we fall back down to earth, into the maze of lies and more lies.

"Until it cages you," I bite.

"Some cages are meant to protect, not trap."

"Any wild animal would agree, a cage is still a cage."

His fingertips interwind with my hair, "You're not as wild as them, Sol."

"But I have to evolve to be if I am meant to be Gabriel's puppet. I have to become Klara, reflect Astrid."

"A reflection doesn't have to be the embodiment. That's why I'm protecting you."

"I'm not that pure light you fell in love with, Wes. This game has changed me. Now I'm just another monster roaming in your nightmares. How can you love that?"

"How can you love me?" He challenges.

"I never said I did." A cold hearted bitch would have sounded more empathetic than I just did.

His chest flexes. "Keep lying. One day you'll run out of fabrications, and I will hear the truth," he coldly bites.

A deep exhale escapes from his lungs before he continues his story. "Luna decided to play the good cop and released most of the subjects marked for termination, causing chaos. Astrid went into hiding when the other Masters started disappearing or getting killed."

"So the other scientists who were killed, they were Masters?"

Wes confirms with a nod. "Exactly. Astrid knew her time was running out. Either one of her creatures would come after her, or another Master would pull a Brutus and stab her in the back. But she didn't just hide. No general worth their salt willingly backs themselves into a corner without leverage. She was secretly encrypting all the data from Manus Dei for years. It was her job to protect the data, but she was actually rewriting it so that no one else could access it. Just before she went into hiding and locked herself away, she flipped the switch and encrypted all the data. The encryption codes are stored on a set of hard drives she has. Without those hard drives, all the servers with access to the science data are useless. Now, she holds all that knowledge and power. Leverage. Astrid believes she can seize control. She may not have been destined to rule Manus Dei, but she's ready to shake things up and take that throne no matter the cost," Wes confesses.

My mind stills, and the air in the room thickens. What do you do if you want to claim a crown that is more powerful than the people surrounding it, than the kingdom and profits? Astrid didn't care about the scientists, Masters, soldiers, or clones, not the power or money. All of that could be rebuilt if she had the most valuable thing.

The data.

But she had to protect the data. You can't transfer it to just one server or thousands tucked away in the tunnels. The knowledge is too vast. So you do the next best thing: lock it up and hide away the key.

Encrypt it.

Make your own Rosetta Stone, a secret code only your key can unlock and decipher.

Now I know what Gabriel and Famine are after. Encryption code stored on hard drives. Drives Astrid has hidden away with her in the tunnels.

It's clever. A chess move that could claim her the win. She has the king cornered, checked with very little moves to make for escape. Now I understand why Gabriel had to play ball with her, why he had to pretend to be loyal and stay close to Astrid.

I sit up and cross my legs, my hair brushing forward, covering some of my nakedness. "You said I was more Astrid's twin than any other clones were. More identical to Astrid than I was to Luna."

He nods, pushing up on his elbows, his eyes sweeping over my breasts before they meet mine, "You're starting to understand," he replies, the corner of his eyes softening, sensing my grief.

I nod again, feeling like a bobblehead on a rocky dashboard. "I have to be Klara to get inside those tunnels because Klara is her dog, which she allows to come and go. Klara went to kill Subject 52, making it safer for Astrid." I grunt, "That is why Gabriel allowed Subject 52 to roam for so long. He was waiting for Klara to leave the tunnels to hunt him down. He needed her set free so he could catch her. That's why he waited to take me."

My eyes tilt up to the ceiling as if it were a holy light. *It all makes sense now, Luna.* "Now, Gabriel will make his interception. Klara won't be going back to her master. I will be."

"We thought about ambushing Astrid, but we knew she would have wiped the drive clean by the time we breached the tunnels. This is the only way to get close enough to kill Astrid without alerting her and causing her to delete the key." he confirms.

"And Gabriel doesn't need Astrid alive anymore because he has me. Her genetic clone. A clone more genetically like her than any other clone." And that's why Luna's pawns allowed Gabriel to take me because not even Luna herself could have passed for

Astrid. Only me. I was a key all along. A key that unlocked more than one door.

Goosebumps blister my skin. Wes's hands begin to rub my arms, soothing what he thinks is fear when it's the onset of knowledge.

"I'm guessing that Astrid has hidden these encryption codes away with biometric security. Only she or I can get inside," I confirm.

Wes sits up fully, his shadow covering me like a plate of armor, "Yes. And after you get inside, unlock the security and get those hard drives with the encryption code," his voice lifts, "you'll be free."

"Free in your cage."

"You'll be mine."

I roll my eyes. A question lingering on the tip of my tongue. What about Klara? Because if there is one thing I have learned well reliving her memories it's that she idolized Luna not Astrid.

Holy shit… That's when the puzzle clicks. Klara isn't Astrid's dog. She isn't just a way for me to trick Astrid. Klara is a different kind of weapon. Gabriel and Wes have no idea, and I can't tell them that either.

"What is it?" The back of his hand presses against my cheek, "You're cold," he states.

That's when I have to change the subject so he doesn't figure out what I just stumbled upon."Did you ever try approaching Klara to see if she could be turned? Gabriel must have worked alongside her from time to time."

He shakes his head, "Klara is a loose cannon. For years, Astrid kept her hidden; even Luna couldn't reach her. We had no way of knowing whether she would align with our cause or Astrid's. So, we had to work around her."

I listen intently. "That's why you were watching me at the club," I interject. Realization dawning upon me. "You couldn't intervene when Klara killed Subject 52. You and Gabriel allowed it to happen. You needed her to earn more approval from Astrid to stay close to her. You didn't fully trust her not to harm me so you lurked in the shadows. When she fled Gabriel continued to track her so that I can take her place."

His hand caresses my cheek softly. "Yes, Sol," he murmurs. "It's all part of the plan. We have to play our roles carefully, maneuvering through the web of deception. And you, my little mouse, have a vital role to play in bringing Astrid down. That is why I could not tear you out of this game. I had to teach you how to play." His index finger traces the curve of my breast, his cock growing hard between his thighs. "It's much easier to see shapes in the darkness than the blinding light, isn't it, little mouse."

It is.

Chapter 28

Wes

I lie in bed, my senses attuned to every movement around me. A blessing and a curse that keeps me up at night. Inhaling, I smell the scent of our passion still lingering on the warm sheets. My palm spreads wide where the sheets are still indented from the shape of Sol's hips. A slight warmth still lingers on the sheets.

She slipped out of bed ten minutes ago after she watched the even rise and fall of my chest. My little mouse thought I was sound asleep.

I can almost feel the hushed footsteps, like whispers, against the floorboards as she paces the bathroom, just like a mouse running about.

Rolling onto my side, I watch her shadow sweep back and forth under the slightly cracked door. A grin on my lips; she's always been skilled at sneaking around, effortlessly navigating the shadows.

We share this understanding, Sol and I. Both mice who were played with, changed and altered. That made us observers, watching and studying. However, our motivations differ, like two sides of a coin.

Two days ago, I confessed to Sol how I first met Luna. I didn't go into all the details; I didn't want her mind to wander or think about Luna for too long.

It's cruel. I don't care because it's also constructive. Sol is sick, and I'm the only medicine that can cure her. That's a fact she has proven time and time again. I am the one person who can pause her lies and free her of her mental torment.

It's guilt making her still run from me. A deep-seed culpability to still help Luna.

My fingers curl the sheet. I wish it was her under my palm.

I will uproot that weed Luna has planted in her mind and replace the hole with my love. I will nourish and watch it grow, digging deep roots, wrapping her up in my vines.

She's mine.

Sol thinks I want to cage her. I will, but she won't be trapped. *Yeah, there's a difference.*

I want to watch her grow. I just need to know she is safe.

You can thrive in captivity. Heck, it's all Sol has known.

Look how the wild has treated her so far. She can't survive alone. That's why she escaped into her mind. That's why I have to keep her from slipping into her memories. Ground her here and in the moment. Therefore, I am letting her solve the puzzles herself. If you decode a problem, you'll never forget the solution. The bullshit about believing in yourself is actually true. Sol has to believe the truth we are guiding her to see. I need her to see my side and not her dead sister's.

If you follow the dead, you'll fall in their grave.

There's no way I will allow that to happen.

Sol will escape the games, and I'll give her a future. A path rooted with my brothers. Our world may rotate on an axis, but it runs on power. Pure, emotionless dominance that only a few possess. Morals and ethics are only in place to make the common men think the power hungry have a conscience.

They don't.

If you think the rich donate to charity because it makes them feel better, don't bother conversing with me. Everything is a take in this world. The rich give only to take a tax write-off, which gives them tenfold more than they donated.

It's just how the world works, how man has evolved.

Dog eat dog.

In the end, it's man versus man. We will do whatever we can to up *our* odds at surviving. *Not yours.*

I know the man who raised me. He cared about two things. His family and his power. The rest was a chess board to be gambled with.

If I were foolish enough to turn my back on my father or brothers, Sol and I would have the life span of freshly fallen snow on a warm spring day. We'd be piss yellow and belly up before the sun had reached its high point.

It was inevitable that others would eventually try to seize my little mouse, restrain her, and dissect her in pursuit of deciphering her father's science. Sol may perceive the world as bleak, but she's oblivious to the extent governments will go to secure cutting-edge weaponry. The science inside of her makes her a weapon just as much as I am.

That's why I have to keep her tucked under my side. Always.

I've given Sol time. Watched her eyes light up when she tried to convince me to fight for Luna's vision. Observed the light dim when I remained against her.

Those who follow Luna are dead men walking. That's why War is acting like a desperate groupie trying to make us all a happy family on tour again.

The band has split up. Whether it is temporary or long-term is up to Famine and how far he is willing to try to fight for a ghost.

I'd trust Famine with my life, but I'd never support him to be the leader of Manus Dei. He's missing what Gabriel's got. The will to toss everything aside, even love, for the greater good. I *don't have that trait also. Not since I found Sol.* Gabriel's our best shot, no doubt. Sure, he's a bit messed up in the head, but hell, all the top generals are. That's what enables him to think outside the damn box.

Gabriel is the living embodiment of the science. He gets it like no one else except Luna, but she doesn't matter anymore. He's weathered and abuse from power-hungry men trying to harness that knowledge, making him vengeful enough to not exploit the power.

His reign? It's all about control, not taking advantage.

Now, Luna, she had this freaky gift of foresight, I don't know if it was just natural or some upgrade she got. Frankly, I'd rather not peel back the layers on that one. I'm a fan of my beauty sleep, and her tweaked genetics would make even God scratch his head.

Luna is like a sleeper cell. She's a Minesweeper game. She planted landmines all over the board, just waiting to knock players over. She's the only person who knows where to step without getting hit, and since the dead can't talk, we have to play defensively. Take the blows and adjust accordingly.

We have, and it's gotten us this far.

The complexity and reach of Luna's influence is staggering. It casts a shadow of uncertainty over every mission. But a storm on the horizon doesn't stop a ship from sailing. The show must go on. We just have to navigate the waters with more caution.

As a soldier, I've got a clear understanding of the importance of singling out the main threat amid battlefield chaos. And right now, that threat is Astrid. She's at the top of our enemies' pyramid, an old hand at this game, toughened by years of mind games and deceit.

Astrid wields the deadliest weapon in her arsenal—the key to unlocking centuries' worth of Manus Dei's knowledge. That treasure trove of information and power puts her in the big leagues, making her the most dangerous player on this twisted game board, far beyond Luna's landmines.

Gabriel, he'll never turn into an Astrid. I'm not scared of the leader my brother will become in the heat of battle. What keeps me up at night is the leader he'll evolve into when the games are over, and the dust finally settles.

A king without a queen is just another madman waiting to be born. Everyone needs a counterpart, whether that person is the devil or angel on your shoulder. You need a weight to balance your scales. Clearly, Luna was the devil whispering in my brother's ear, but even the devil can make the most roving soul see reason. That's why he has claimed so many, the master manipulator. The all-star sales agent, turning hell's real estate into the hottest market to own land in.

The sound of running water seeps from beneath the door, its ceaseless flow breaking the oppressive silence. I can sense the heavy shroud of familiarity draping over me as I rise from the bed, each step measured and cautious. Beyond that slightly cracked door is a haunting image I've grown accustomed to.

With deliberate slowness, I nudge the door open, my gaze locking on the scene before me. Sol is at the sink, her hands submerged in soapy water, scrubbing away with relentless determination. It's a ritual I've witnessed many times, a desperate attempt to purge the stains of our sins, to unburden herself from the weight that clings to her soul.

I prefer my way of cleansing her soul, making her come, screaming my name until she shouts that I'm her god.

I understand what she sees in those hands, the haunting reminders of the atrocities we have committed in the name of our cause. Unlike her father and sister, she was never raised to be a soldier, to carry the weight of our dark deeds with unwavering resolve. She grapples with the guilt and the remorse, seeking solace in the act of washing them away.

But for me, I chose a different path. Learned to embrace the darkness within; let it seep into my being until it becomes an inseparable part of who I am. I made peace with the stains upon my hands, for they serve as a constant reminder of the sacrifices we must make for the greater good.

Luna never revealed this vulnerability, and as much as I hate to witness it—the fracture in the woman I love—I embrace it, for it sets her apart from the rest of the players in this twisted game. The day she starts acting like an emotionless robot is the day I know I have truly lost her.

That day will never rise on my horizon.

***

The past.

Luna pulls off her bright red headphones, allowing them to rest on her shoulders. I never wanted to smash an object so badly. Her chin is slightly raised, an air of power hangs around her like a rich Parisian perfume when it should make the air scent sour. Fucking genetic editing.

A savior and a curse.

With a tug, the red ribbon she always wears falls loose, her hair cascading behind it. Botticelli would have worshiped her.

Instead of sitting in the office chair across from my hospital bed, she strolls to the far wall and locks eyes with me. I return the fuck-you glare, eyeing her as she slides down the wall like a stripper pole until she sits cross-legged on the floor with her tablet.

That's what irks me: the abnormal behavior. Why isn't she sitting in the empty chair? That's what gives her the power, because she likes to keep people guessing.

I relax my eyes as if I don't give a shit, but I'm a late player to this game. It won't always be that way. I'll learn her ticks and how to decode her.

I just got another upgrade, and as usual, Luna's here to assess me. I've never encountered a woman like her, breathtakingly beautiful yet mentally twisted. I don't know how Gabriel deals with her.

She sets the tablet on the floor, releasing a loud exhale that puts me on edge. She sounds tired, and she wanted me to hear that. Why? She rests her head on an angle against the wall for support. Then she cracks a single knuckle.

With the lazy grace of a pampered feline, she slides the headphones off her narrow shoulders, then nonchalantly tosses them to me across the hospital floor. The wire connecting them to her antique iPod trails behind like a dog reluctantly heading to the groomer, nails scratching along the way.

"Take it," she orders. "You know you want to."

"I was taught never to take candy from strangers," I bite back, shifting in the bed and feeling the tape pull and itch at the IV in my hand.

Her lip tugs up for a mere second before she hides it. "I'm not a stranger. I'm something far, far more puzzling."

I tilt my head with interest. She never engages with me. I'll play. "Is this part of the assessment?" I ask as I grab the headphones and iPod.

"My assessment." She corrects me.

I squeeze the iPod tighter. The headphones feel warm in my hands. She always has these damn things on. For a woman so genetically evolved, the outdated iPod and wired headphones don't fit her, but maybe that's why she likes it.

"Listen to the whole song," She demands. Something flickers in her eyes, like witnessing a sea creature that sailors used to sing songs about—a creature you thought was extinct.

My legs widen, readying for an unknown attack. I look at the black and white screen that reads "If I had a heart" by Fever Ray. It's not my style of music, but I listen to the song and the lyrics.

As the song continues, my eyes leave the small screen, and I watch Luna. She sits relaxed against the wall. Bored. But her eyes still have that hidden emotion, like a black diamond filled with inclusions. Her flaws are hard to see, but if you look long enough, you'll spot them.

Dressed in shiny black leggings and a skin-tight black shirt. The only lightness about her is her blonde hair and blue eyes. She wears deep red lipstick and black eyeliner every day. I don't think she needs makeup. It doesn't enhance her beauty because she is everyone's wet dream.

Until she speaks, that is.

That last thought isn't me being a dick, it's just honesty. Luna's words have a way of chilling you to the bone, cutting through the facade of civility to reveal the depths of her morally twisted nature.

The song fades into silence; I remove the headphones and extend them back to her. Her hand doesn't rise to take them. Taking a page from her book, I mimic her. Sliding down to sit beside her. The air feels thinner as my heart picks up. The body's natural reaction to being so close to a predator. You never know when they will bite, but that doesn't stop people from swimming in the ocean or hiking a mountain.

"If I were to tell you that this song describes me, what would you think?" Her voice breaks the silence, eyes locked on me with an intensity that sends a shiver down my toughen spine.

I raise an eyebrow, contemplating her words. There is something off about her in this moment. Something real, whether it be fear or acceptance, I'm unsure. I don't know if I want to know, but I try to accept this thorn-ridden olive branch. "You don't have a heart, but you wish you did," I reply to what the lyrics sang.

She doesn't hide the smile on her lips now. Her fingers lightly tapping along to the tune of the song replaying faintly. "Interesting," she murmurs. "How's your heart doing?"

I let out a sigh, my gaze drifting towards the floor. "Luna, I want to proceed with this assessment so I can return to the field," I bite. Where the hell is Gabriel? Why isn't he the one assessing me. It's always Luna when it comes to the upgrades. Gabriel is usually fiddling with some nanobyte shit that is way above my pay grade.

Luna's eyes hold a penetrating gaze as she speaks, "You're a soldier, Wes. You've taken orders from various leaders throughout your life, some good and some bad. Am I correct?"

A wave of memories washes over me, flashes of faces and battles fought under different banners. I nod slowly, acknowledging the truth in her words. "Yes, I've followed orders, sometimes without question." Her grin deepens, eyes glinting with intrigue and understanding.

"What do they all have in common?"

"Who?" I rest my forearms on my knees and start to pick off the thick hospital tape around the IV.

"The leaders."

"I don't know. I'm not sure they had things in common." I respond. That get's me thinking about the different commanders I had to follow, even my father, who was my leader at one time. Each man was so vastly different. Some hated the job, and others thrived off the adrenaline.

"You're failing my assessment."

"Does your opinion of me matter?" I joke with a laugh.

"I saw the way you looked at me. You wanted me. But you can't have me because Gabriel belongs to me."

I laugh at her wording. She is fucking demented. First of all, any man with a dick would look at Luna. Secondly, the minute she spoke, I knew I would never entertain her. Thirdly, bros before crazy women. Luna is Gabriel's. Therefore even if I did want Luna, I'd respect their relationship.

She selects another song and places the headphones on my ears without giving me a choice. This time, it's "Paint It Black" by Hidden Citizens. I relate to this, and my shoulders relax as the lyrics are sung to me.

"You and I, all the Hunters and Horsemen, are the same. All we see is black. Astrid wants us to paint the world black," she voices in a somber tone that sounds more befitting of a funeral. She remains cross-legged but redirects her body toward me. "Astrid is controlling over half of the Masters. The other half are more divided than a Petri dish teeming with a diverse array of microorganisms."

"I hope that's not your attempt at a joke," I jest.

"I'm serious." Frostbite would be more soothing than her tone. "Astrid knows their secrets and is hanging them with her threats. Anyone, and I mean anyone, who doesn't agree with Astrid is killed, and she has been forcing Klara to be the bullet to kill them. Anyone, Wes."

My father's face flashes in my head. Is this a warning? Does Astrid know about the deal Gabriel made with my father?

"I know exactly what you're thinking. Stop making it so obvious. Astrid hasn't caught onto your father yet, but one day, Astrid will know everyone's secrets."

"Even yours?" I question, mentally committing everything she said to memory. I'll grill Gabriel about it later. He may love Luna, but I don't completely trust her.

She chuckles an unnatural sound, "If Astrid knew my secrets, I'd already be dead. That's why I need you, Wes."

"Need me for what?" I finish ripping the tape off my hand and pull out my own IV.

"To bear a burden. A secret Astrid knows about but doesn't fully understand yet." Her blue eyes reveal a harmful intention. "Did you know I have a twin?"

"You have many twins." I rub my temple, fearing this run-around conversation will give me a headache no amount of Advil could cure.

"No, I have one twin. One sister, her name is Sol. She is an artist."

"That's nice." I hiss. Why the fuck is she telling me this?

"Sol paints hyperrealism. She can replicate a photo with paint. It looks so clear it even amazes me. She's an artist."

"You said that already,"

"An artist needs colors to paint, Death." She hisses my code name.

I twist towards her and snatch the iPod from her hands, "What game are you playing? Spit it out." Why is she wasting my time?

"What game are you playing?" She parrots and slants her head. Her blue eyes reflect like the water of a wishing well I don't dare toss a coin into. "A war is coming. We are being trained for something so deadly it might even convince you to run from battle."

I snort, "Unlikely. I'm no deserter." I already know Manus Dei's intentions with all their genetic science. My father never stood behind their idealistic bullshit. Gabriel and Luna don't either.

She pats my kneecap. "That's why you're such a perfect Horseman," She takes the headphones then selects a new song but she doesn't press play. "My sister needs color to paint, Death. She needs color to live. Astrid would take all her paints away." She stands and puts her headphones on. "I hope you don't paint it all black, Death." Clicking play, her blue eyes haunt me before she turns away and leaves the room.

I push up from the wall and cross my arms, repeating every bizarre thing Luna mentioned today. Thirteen hours later, I'm perched outside Dorian Eklund's mansion in Switzerland. Trying to see what Luna is really up to. I wonder if she is playing us all, I think Gabriel does, too, but he won't admit it.

A blurry image walks past the scope of my rifle. I adjust it again, and then I see Luna. She is dressed differently, not in her usual dark clothing. Today she is wearing a summer dress in floral patterns. She spreads her fingers wide and tips her head up toward me. My muscles stiffen, but there is no way she can spot me concealed against the mountain her home is nested against.

A mountain that holds many secrets.

Her eyes scan the horizon slowly as if she is looking for me. I study her face, but it lacks that sinister look. Another image blurs in front of Luna. I have to adjust my scope again, and now I see two of her. I was hunting the wrong person. That was her twin. The girl in the dress must be the artist. She sits on the grass, and tilts her head to the sky. She stays like that for so long that I look away from my rifle and scan the horizon.

What the fuck is she looking at for so long?

I look back at Luna's sister. It freaks me out how many copies of Luna there are. She is a clone of Luna, a twin down to every detail. But when I look longer at her eyes, I notice something that slows my heartbeat. I'm nervous. It's a sensation I haven't felt in a very long time.

This sister, this Reflection, is unlike any other Reflection I have seen. There is a hope in her blue eyes that none of the others have.

I want to have the hope that she has.

I want to know what guides her and keeps her so innocent.

Something sparks inside of me. A burst of color ignites when I look at this Reflection.

Color.

"My sister needs color to paint. She needs color to live. Astrid would take all her paints away. I hope you don't paint it all black, Death."

Luna was asking me to protect her sister. To ensure she remained unadulterated and wasn't painted black by Astrid's ideals. She knows this sister of hers will be in the war that is coming to claim us all.

I stalk the artist for an hour until she goes inside. An innocent lamb that didn't know a lion lingered in the brush.

She just watched the clouds as a child would or an angel who wanted to rejoin the heavens that were so far out of her reach.

My father's pursuit of my mother has forever shaped my perception of love. I watched as he chased her, refusing to let her slip away, even when she ran. That relentless passion, that unyielding desire to claim and possess, became the twisted foundation of my understanding of love.

Now, as I set my sights on Luna's sister, a new sensation grips me, one I have never felt before. It's an attachment, a craving that goes beyond my usual predilections.

Sol, the innocent lamb unaware of the lion lurking in the shadows, awakens something primal within me. I feel a deep need to chase, to capture, to possess her like I've never felt with anyone else.

It's as if she holds the key to a side of myself I never knew existed. This obsession is consuming, intoxicating, and I find myself drawn further into the dark depths of my desires.

Mission accepted, Luna. Your sister is mine.

Chapter 29

Wes

Under the golden glow of the bathroom light, I observe Sol scrubbing her hands with such intensity that it looks like she's trying to grind her bones to make bread out of the dust, once again trying to turn her reality into a fairy tale.

I approach her cautiously, her long blonde hair perfectly disheveled from my hands. My marks look perfect on her. My eyes float down, unable to see the contours of her slender body. The clothes we have for her swallow her up. I need to get her some muffins; she looks thinner, and Hazel mentioned how much Sol enjoys muffins.

I want to see her light up like she did when she entered her art studio. I will, eventually.

Aspen was a carefully crafted lie, but it taught me what she truly liked. Gabriel wanted Sol further away from Manus Dei, and they thought she had a mental breakdown, so it was either allow her to rehab herself through her art or kill her like the rest of the subjects who broke. It took a shit ton of convincing to allow Sol to remain alive.

When Sol started sending her artist portfolio to galleries, War hacked her email and ensured the only application that went out was to Hazel's gallery.

Poor Hazel remains blissfully unaware of who or what Sol truly is. Levi, on the other hand, possesses that knowledge. He had no desire for a clone to get near Hazel, but a debt to me had him agreeing, albeit reluctantly. In my world, favors hold more weight than gold.

Like countless others, Levi is quietly counting down the days until he can escape Manus Dei's grasp.

With slow, deliberate movements, I nudge open the door. Contrary to what Sol might think, I have no intention of making her feel like a cornered animal. I need her to feel safe in the cage I made for us. Cages are traps, but they also can be a refuge, and that is what we both are for each other.

The cold water is turned on and must feel like ice pouring over her skin, akin to puncturing needles.

I don't want her to seek pain to feel; I want her to pursue me.

A faint blue tone tinges her delicate fingertips, merging with the raw red hues from the intense scrubbing.

She tilts her head from side to side, as if she's curious, resembling a dark soul poking a dead creature.

She studies her hands with narrowed eyes. Every few scrubs, she flips them over and begins again, taking the time to wash between her fingers and under her nails with a surgeon's accuracy.

"Sol," I put effort into making my deep voice sound gentle. She doesn't respond to me, but I know who she will react to. I walk closer and lower my lips to her ear, "Little mouse." She pauses now and blinks rapidly. Death has a tighter grip on Sol than my other half does.

Our relationship is an enigma; it is so flawed that it is flawless. Sol loves the part of me that is Wes because he is broken like she is, seeking a normal life he can never have. Wes wasn't born into an average family, nor was my little mouse.

We connect in ways others could never understand. They don't need to. I value my privacy.

Her attraction to Death is logical. It's all about survival. Death is stronger because he's upgraded and constantly in the know. Sol wants that, has always wanted it.

Sol thought Luna was off balance because she had to win at all costs. What Sol hasn't admitted to is that she is the same. Everything is a task, a competition, and she must succeed, even if it is her own game constructed by her mind.

Her hands stop moving. She looks like an Aphrodite from an art nouveau painting, frozen over a wishing well. *I'll grant you a wish, but I seek something in return. Devils always do.*

"Where did you run off to now, little mouse?" I question. Moving with caution, I press my body against her back. Like two petals of a budding rose, we relax and unfold into each other. I turn the faucet off and cup her hands in mine. "Look at me," I demand.

Blue eyes, so saturated they look photoshopped, flick up to meet mine in the mirror. "I'm ok," Sol voices. What a fucking lie. I grind my teeth.

I refuse to break eye contact, my gaze unwavering. She's running. I don't fault her this time. Klara's childhood was hard to watch, let alone virtually experience. Sol believed her childhood was cold, but it was a warm and cozy campfire compared to the experiences of the other clones. That messes with a person, makes you feel guilt that is unfairly placed. Just because someone else had a harder road to walk doesn't mean your own journey was insignificant or matters less.

"You are not Klara or Luna. What you have witnessed, *they* did. Not you," I assert with conviction, squeezing her hands firmly in mine. "Your hands are clean from their sins."

In the depths of the night, I bear witness to the haunting tremors of her body, the echoes of her nightmares that hold her captive. She cries out for a sister who can no longer come to her rescue. That role falls upon me now.

Her teeth sink into her lip, the delicate skin turning pale under the pressure. "I don't see *their* sins," she confesses. "I see the stains from my sins that will mark my hands." A laugh escapes from her. "It's not even begun yet, has it, Wesley? My sins. Tell me?"

"Tell you what?"

"You're a sinner, so tell me, will the marks fade or deepen over time?"

"I don't feel guilty about catching you."

"Of course you don't. You don't have a soul anymore."

"That doesn't mean I don't feel."

Her brow inches up. "That's interesting. I was convinced Luna didn't feel it. I worked so hard to make her understand emotions," she releases a snarky sigh. "I was unsure if my lessons sunk in or if she was just lying to make me feel better. But her actions prove otherwise. Someone who never felt would not have done the things she did."

I release her hands, brushing my thumb against her trembling lips. I'm not going to lie and tell her everything will be alright. "The stains of your past may linger, but we will face them together. I will be your guiding light through the darkness, and we will find a way to cleanse your hands of the burdens that weigh you down. Trust me, Sol, I won't let the stains define you."

Her eyes glance to the left, and mine follow, landing on the iPod and headphones I gave her. "I found a song that reminds me of you. I decided I'll play it when I run from you because you're right, Wesley, I will run. There is nothing I want more than to be free from this science, and there is nothing you will cling to more desperately to save me." She shakes her head, "Why can't you understand that what you think will protect us will erode us?"

"You're a dreamer, and I love that about you, but you have to be dragged down to earth from time to time. The future of our world isn't a candy-coated one. Governments and people are already clamoring for more, always have been. We are entering the genetic age, and it's not for the faint of heart or the glass-half-full dreamers. I will do absolutely everything to keep you safe," I sneer, my tone laced with cruelty. I grasp my scar-covered chest. "I'll risk this heart, fight till my last breath only to insert a new one, and then I will fight till the death again for you. I'm not going anywhere, so run all you want. Eventually, all roads lead back to me."

Her expression stays distant, her tone icy. "Did you rehearse that?" she inquires.

My eyes turn to slits. This isn't her. Usually, she has backed down by now. She wants to fight, to push me so she can hate me and I her. Not. Gonna. Happen.

Her shoulders widen slightly. It's beautiful to watch her try to fight, even when I know she's going to lose. It's the thrill of the chase in a different scenario. "I don't get it. You want to protect me, but you're willing to let Gabriel use me. Willing to allow me to sin, to keep seeing what Klara has gone through," she continues, pushing further.

She's right. Tension burrows in my muscles like a weed I cannot uproot. Sol has to do this mission. She is the only option because she is the only Reflection we trust. One last step before Sol is free from this game and enters the next, a game I control. Our future.

My hands skim up her arms, leaving a trail of goosebumps in their wake. She might be able to speak lies, but her body can't deny its attraction to me. "I know what you're doing, little mouse," I murmur. Bending down, I nip her ear. Her legs clench. "Do you know the meaning of obsession? That's what you are to me. A fixation. If you think you can manipulate my love for you into hate, I'm sorry to break it to you," I slap her ass and am rewarded with a yelp that goes straight to my cock. "Its just making me fall harder." All my blood rushes south as I press my body into hers. She gulps.

Tipping her chin up to meet my gaze, I stare into Sol's wide, doll-like eyes, my desire to possess her consuming me. "Come back to bed," I demand. But it's not enough. I need her now. No more games. Without hesitation, I scoop her up, refusing to allow her to walk away from me. She feels so delicate, so weightless in my arms that I tighten my hold, unwilling to let her slip away.

Setting her down on the mattress, I watch as she looks up at me, her gaze always upturned and curious, even in moments of fear. Her lips part slightly, as if a silent plea has escaped from them. With a knee on the bed, I guide her to lie down, my lips eagerly seeking the warmth of her neck. I savor the taste of her skin, reveling in its smoothness as my lips explore every inch.

Cupping her face, I lock eyes with her, my voice a low murmur that resonates with possessiveness, "I won't lose you. I won't let you leave me either."

Her response is a subtle arch of her back, pressing her breasts against my chest, a tantalizing display of desire. She wraps her legs around me, grinding against me, a desperate attempt to ignite a response. "I don't want to lose you either," she whispers.

My eyes close, wrestling with conflicting emotions. Is this how it began between Gabriel and Luna? A stubborn line drawn between them, neither willing to erase it, and in the end, losing each other.

I cannot turn my back on my brothers. Abandoning them would mean losing the power necessary to protect Sol. I'd have to rely on my family for protection, which isn't the worst outcome—I love my family. But being a Horseman grants me much more freedom and it keeps Sol away from my father who isn't keen on the cloning project. Dad won't understand how I can not just accept Sol but also love her. Some issues are better kept at arm's length.

A solitary tear escapes from her baby blue eyes, tracing a path down her cheek and dampening the bedsheet. She understands that my decision is final. I will always be a Horseman. Bending down, I gently lick the tear away, my voice barely a whisper, "These tears are mine."

Slowly, with deliberate precision, I sink into her. Muscles coil as the need never to be separated ignites a frantic fever within us. Each inch of our connection is a deliberate dance. She has turned me into a love-sick heathen willing to go to any measure to possess her.

Like two pools of liquid desire, her enchanting eyes captivate my gaze. If she were born in a past era, they would have written songs about her beauty and told tales that lasted centuries.

"Wes," her lips stay parted, eyes wide as she looks up at me like I'm the second coming of her god. When she moans my name, it redefines the definition of insanity. I'll never be the same. It's a god damn siren's song that pulls me closer.

Her touch is electric, making me so hard it's painful. The only relief is sinking into her again and again. Nails delicately trace patterns on my back until she digs them deep into my flesh as I thrust into her. *Yes, Mark me.*

The sound of our moans and whispers fills the room with a sweet melody that would reach the best-seller charts. I want to record it and have it on replay 24/7. Slapping of skin, nails scratching flesh, cries of passions, shouts of my name, of the nickname she gave me. Breathless purrs of passion push me to go deeper, to lose myself. No longer a man but a beast because she drives me feral.

My movements turn rougher, her skin reddens in the most stunning way. Her warm, wet heat squeezes me in a vice grip. Her breath increases; she is about to come. I slip my hand between our bodies and add more pressure.

She explodes, as do I. But it's not enough. It never is.

Even as the waves of ecstasy crash over us, I continue to thrust into her. More wetness floods her; her neck rolls back in utter bliss.

"It's too much," She whispers, but her hips keep grinding into me.

"Liars get punished, little mouse." I purr. Lifting her legs, I place them over my shoulders, making her tighter. *Fuck!*

Her body trembles, laid out beneath me like a canvas of desire and pleasure that I can paint and manipulate in whichever way I desire.

Her eyes roll back, and she comes again. I sit up, pulling her to me. Still connected. Chest to chest, our hearts beat as one. Her head falls to the side, resting on my shoulder, arms wrapped lazily around me. Our scents floats in the air. It's a moment of intimacy I have never experienced before. I didn't know this kind of love could exist. I feel a profound connection—a connection that transcends the physical.

Luna asked me to make sure her sister had color to paint with. In this new world on the horizon there will still be hues for Sol's canvas. Amidst the shadows, she'll continue to paint, living and thriving, although her palette will be much darker.

Chapter 30

Wes

The Biergarten in Munich pulses with a vibrant atmosphere. The air carries the robust scent of freshly brewed beer and warm, artisanal bread. Long wooden tables host platters of pretzels, their golden shells adorned with hefty salt crystals. Laughter and boisterous conversation reverberate throughout the space.

Maybe in another life, I would have been able to sit down and enjoy a beer with the rest of them. That's not a chip on my shoulder talking. I love my life, treasure the inside knowledge and the added benefits of the genetic upgrades. It's like seeing the world with new shades of colors. You never want to go back to boring black and white.

I still find solace in observing these normal people who are blissfully unaware, much like my little mouse once was. Oblivious to the impending upheaval that science will bring to our world, just as it took us to the moon and harnessed the power of the nuclear bomb, it will now irrevocably transform humanity. Ten years from now, everyone in this Biergarten will be altered. Most will have enhanced something about themselves.

The clashing of beer steins rings in the air. For these people, life will never be as peaceful as it is at this moment.

If Astrid wins, the world will be held hostage to her demands. Only those deemed worthy would be granted access to advancements and breakthroughs, while others would be left to suffer and perish.

That man sitting on the stool, tipping back his beer. That poor bloke would be dead. Astrid would never grant a nobody the gift of genetically engineered upgrades.

To Astrid, the loss of a few lives seemed inconsequential in the pursuit of her ambitions.

Now that man, the one standing with a cut-off shirt, mohawk, and muscles pumped with steroids. That fool might be wondering how this happened. That fucker never trusted governments to begin with. So, if the government isn't doing anything to stop them, he will.

He'd be picked off so easily it wouldn't even be fun.

The truth is Manus Dei has long enslaved governments. Knowledge comes at a price, and Manus Dei always collected. How else would their trials get approval in even the most strict countries?

Money can make the most righteous man turn a blind eye.

Manus Dei holds clandestine power not only in the world of genetics but also in the development and possession of biological and chemical weapons. They are *the* force to be reckoned with, capable of exerting control over nations.

Fear is a sickness. It's consuming. Worse than cancer. You can't fight fear; it grips you, rewiring your thoughts and reactions. Governments feared Manus Dei, worried about the consequences because they learned from the past.

Those flea-ridden rats on the ships that carried the plagues in Europe centuries ago. Well, let me tell you something: it wasn't by chance. Don't believe me? I read the details about it in Manus Dei's private database. That's power, and that knowledge shared causes fear.

Imagine the kind of destruction Manus Dei could cause nowadays if they engineered a plague. It would make the apocalypse look like a nice summer day.

Astrid wants fear; Gabriel containment. We need alliances, not enemies. Science for humanity, genetic upgrades for all with regulation, of course. That's why Gabriel will form a team that oversees all genetic upgrades released to the masses.

It sounds like a damn ideal world, but I've learned perfection's a fairy tale. Prime example, the Reflections. Flawed as hell, just like the rest of mankind. Not from their upgrades, they were raised to be ruthless. The question is, can you teach a dog new tricks? Can Gabriel handle all that power? Yes. Will Gabriel have to produce weapons to maintain that power? Yes. I know he will.

You can't have good without evil. Good teaches us what is evil, and evil shows us what is good. It's a scale we can not escape. That's why I must stand by my brother and never walk away. I need his power, but I also need to help guide it. Sol hasn't grasped that yet.

And that, my friends, is why when I find an empty stool, I claim it, grab a stein of beer, and chug down the whole damn thing.

"It smells like piss," Gabriel declares, grimacing as he pulls out the barstool beside me. His eyes sweep over the sticky, beer-spilled tabletop. He refrains from resting his elbows on it. Pampered ass, but I love the guy. "War's covering Sol?" he asks, his eyes narrowing at the table stains.

I nod, my hands squeezing the glass tighter. I hate leaving my little mouse, but at times, I must.

I pivot and look at Gabriel. His blonde hair is messy, and I know it's not from a recent fuck. He hasn't been with anyone since

Luna. Dark circles make his blue eyes resemble a stormy sea, ready to devour anyone in his way. "How is your hunt going?" I ask, grabbing another stein of beer and swallowing a gulp. I don't taste a thing. The only thing that ignites my senses is Sol.

"Klara's close," he says, reaching for the beer and pretending to take a sip. Gabriel doesn't drink. He won't risk his senses being clouded, even though his liver functions at higher rates to ensure he can never get drunk. My brother likes to torment himself; it's the only way he can cope with his grief from losing Luna.

"Everything is working," he repeats, his jaw clenched. He's a soldier like me, and suspicion is raised when plans go too perfectly.

"The cardiologist sent me the final reports." Gabriel divulges. Two days ago, we had a cardiologist come to the safe house.

"Is it the PFO?" I ask. Gabriel and I hadn't fully disclosed the truth to Sol until the doctor came. She isn't just Astrid's clone due to minimal upgrades; there's more to it. Dorian, her father, deliberately left a flaw in Sol, the same one Astrid has used as a biometric key and safeguard. Sol's palpitations aren't just stress-related; it's a genetic error, a patent foramen ovale (PFO) - a hole in her heart chambers.

That's why Sol is a key. She can get inside the places no one else but Astrid can. Astrid has specialized biometric scanners in place that scan wrist vein patterns, heart activity, and the PFO. It's still unclear to us why Dorian left this flaw in Sol. Maybe Sol was his safeguard over Astrid, but then again, the man seemed devoted to his sister in peculiar ways.

Gabriel and Luna stumbled upon this vulnerability, allowing them to remove Astrid without needing her alive. Unfortunately, only Gabriel will witness Astrid's death now.

"It's the same as Astrid's down to the architecture of the veins that cover the valves. Sol is the key." He replies. I don't miss the regret in his voice. Gabriel needs to use Sol but still wants to protect her.

I feel his eyes on me, trying to peel back my flesh and see what I'm thinking. Obsession is a dangerous emotion. Right now, Gabriel is wondering just how deep my lust for Sol goes? He's wondering if I will intercept and fuck it all up. His fingers tap his glass. For a moment, he considers touching my shoulder, but he resists. "She will be fine," he claims.

"You don't know that." I deadpan. I don't like knowing my little mouse has a hole in her heart. I want it fixed even if the doctors tell me it is harmless. It keeps me up at night knowing I'm sending her into Astrid's layer, not by her side to protect her.

"Why didn't you tell me you formed an attachment to her, brother," Gabriel bites. An attachment. I laugh at his choice of words.

So he's still pissed off.

Too bad.

I set my beer down with a loud thump that is swallowed up by the drunk crowd. I've never told this to him, never told anyone. Baring an obsession is a solitary journey. "Luna asked me," I grin at the memory, "in her own elusive way, to protect Sol. Long before you did."

Gabriel's blue eyes deaden, "Luna asked a lot from many." Fuck, his pain is palpable. I never want to feel that ache. That's why I want to cage Sol. Lock her up, tie her down in my bed. I want to always be beside her, inside of her. I want to see her eyes blink, pupils dilate as I sink inside of her, and hear her lips moan my name. More than that, I want to see her smile and not be worried. I want her free to paint and not be trapped in a game of lies. "Is this a game? Is that why you fucked her?" He snarls.

My blood boils. Inhaling, I push up the sleeve of my jacket, forearms tensing for a physical fight. "Don't speak about her like that. I've allowed many things, but I will not allow you to disrespect her."

He picks up his beer and brings the thick glass rim to his lips. Had I driven him to break his own rules? Almost. He slams it down, sloshing beer on the tabletop. "Insult her or you?"

"Both."

He snorts, "So you really care about her."

"I'm insulted you have to ask. Maybe I need to make my intensions clearer." I warn.

His next words cut through me like a knife. "Are you going to fuck this all up? Do I need to question your loyalty now, too?" He watches my reaction closely.

I meet his gaze with a steady one of my own, my clenched fist slowly relaxing. "If you did, I wouldn't be here," I reply firmly. "We'll get Famine back. It won't always be like this." I add.

The crowd's roar fills the air, and the beer flows freely around us. The nearest TV shows a winning goal in the soccer match, and I can't help but see it as a foreshadowing of Gabriel and me winning against Astrid.

He runs his hand through his hair. "We shouldn't be fighting. Not now," he admits.

"This isn't a fight, brother. You've seen me when I fight. This is a discussion. I want to make sure you've thought of every angle. Every outcome. You're asking me to send Sol into the lion's den."

"I have. I'm trying my best. The loose cannon is Famine, but he isn't going to make his move until we get the encryption codes. And you know he'd never risk a Reflection. Plus, by then, I won't need Sol."

Ever since Famine fled to the other side, it broke something deep in Gabriel. Another person he loved abandoned him. He's been keeping secrets from War and me. I know why. He fears we will leave him too.

"You'll be keeping Sol when she's free?"

"She was never going to be free."

He releases a harsh breath, finally touching the grimy table. His nail digs at the wood's grooves. "I know. I just want her to be happy. Even if I had to genetically engineer her brain to release daily doses of dopamine for her to feel happiness after all of this is done, I was willing to go to that extreme."

I watch as a splinter of wood pierces his flesh. No reaction. He lets it linger in the pad of his index finger for a minute before slowly tugging it free.

Is that the only way he can feel now? Through pain. The only emotion to fill the gap of losing your loved one.

"You already designed it, didn't you?"

He nods. "I created it for myself at first. The night Luna left me, I was so furious. I wanted to spite her. 'A big fuck you, I'll feel happy again,'" he shrugs. "I never used it. Hate felt much better than happiness. It's a better motivation. Hate is a fuel that never runs out. Happiness does. You have to keep chasing it, but hate...it chases you, and it always wins."

"I'll make her happy." I lower my chin.

Gabriel's gaze remains fixed on his beer stein, his eyes a reflection of disbelief. "I never thought I would lose Luna. I never imagined she would take her own life. It just doesn't make sense to me. I still can't understand it."

Edging my stool closer to my brother, I place a hand on his shoulder, digging my fingers in. We're his lifeboat now. When his grief is too dark, it's up to War and me to pull him out of the choppy waters.

"Luna was headstrong, determined to always come out on top. She had an intense drive to win, to be in control. But sometimes, the burden becomes too much for even the strongest to bear. It's like a breaking point, where even the toughest material can meet its match and tear."

He shakes his head, "Luna had been losing for a long time. At least, I think she had been. She failed some tests, so I helped her cheat. Now I wonder if it was all a lie. Maybe she failed on purpose to toy with my heart. See how far she could push me and what I would do for her." My ears perk up. "We had to play the game, Wes. Luna and I manipulated the results to ensure the numbers were too close to call for years. It was the only power we had over the Masters. Then the day came when we had to compete truly."

A dark chasm covers his eyes as it consumes him with a haunting memory. I want to reach out and shake him free from its hold, but I don't. "Before that final test, Luna smiled at me. It was her grin that told me she had the upper hand. I was happy because I thought she received a new upgrade that would help her win. For the first time in my life, I didn't care about claiming the win. I was so proud of the woman I loved for knowing she would win." He sneers and shakes his head. "So when I won, I didn't understand why she had looked at me that way. I looked at Luna, and she grinned again. It was a new smile I hadn't seen from her." He taps his temple, "I see it every day. I think she was tired. She wanted me to win so she could be at peace." He lowers his head, "I don't know. Some days I'm so upset I want to destroy every Reflection that resembles her, and other days I'm content with allowing them to live because a part of Luna is living on."

He steeples his hands and rests his index finger on his lip. He's deep in thought as if his and Luna's life is a chess game. It is, and she checked him. He won the crown, but Luna's win weighed heavier.

"I understand the risk and know where you are coming from, brother. I've asked a lot of Sol. Everything relies on her in this round of the game. I've calculated everything. Even if Astrid doesn't fall for the trap, you and I will be in the tunnels. Sol just has to remain alive for 5 minutes until we reach her. She's strong. Smart. She can do that."

What's unsaid is that even if she dies, Gabriel will do everything in his power to bring her back to life, and he's the only man that could do it.

"When she has finished this task keep her safe. Not just from others, but from herself," He replies.

I respond with a solemn nod, my silence speaks volumes. Gabriel and I share a bond forged through loss and the determination to shield our loved ones from further pain. He lost Luna, the love of his life, and I know he will do everything in his power to ensure I don't suffer the same fate.

"Do you think War can handle his tasks?" He questions.

"Yes, he's ready and trained by the best," I assure him. Famine trained War. "He likes to play games but never risks our lives. You know that."

"Sometimes I feel like I don't know anything." His brows raise, "And sometimes I know too much."

I pivot towards him. This whole conversation has been odd. Gabriel usually doesn't show me his soft side, but I'm happy he has. You tend to lose your mind when you keep it all buried deep.

"Trust War's work. He altered the footage from the club perfectly. He will do it again the day we take Astrid down."

The plan is meticulously crafted, each step calculated to ensure our success and minimize the risk of exposure. Gabriel will take on the task of kidnapping Klara, swapping her with Sol, who will assume her identity. With Sol acting as Klara, she will have the access needed to infiltrate Astrid's home and the secured tunnels.

On the other end, Gabriel and I will make our entrance through his house, one of the ten houses with an entrance into the tunnels. Utilizing the hacked system by War to erase our presence from the live security feed. It will be a seamless, deep-fake, allowing us to move undetected. As we navigate through the tunnels, we will encounter loyal guards who stand in our way. I can't wait to eliminate those fuckers.

Once inside Astrid's office, Sol will release a nerve agent that Gabriel genetically designed to target Astrid. He's already given Sol the antibodies since they are genetically identical. We're concealing the bioweapon in Klara's watch, which Sol will wear. Once released, it will paralyze Astrid for thirty minutes, giving Gabriel and I a window of opportunity to reach Astrid's office and eliminate her. This way, Sol isn't responsible for Astrid's death.

See, we planned ahead. My little mouse cares a lot, even about monsters. This way, Gabriel and I will be responsible for Astrid's death.

It is crucial for governments worldwide to see him as a capable and level-headed leader, one who can steer us towards a future free from the control of the Masters. The success of this mission rests not only on our individual skills and resourcefulness but also on our ability to work as a cohesive unit. We understand the weight of the task before us and the consequences of failure.

As I said, every detail and angle has been plotted. We can't afford to have Gabriel painted as a bloodthirsty tyrant. That's why we have a scapegoat.

Klara.

It is cathartic in a way. Astrid's loyal clone turns on her in the end. Of course, this is all a crafted lie. We will report to the followers of Manus Dei, including some of the world's top scientists, that Klara, Astrid's clone, not only ended her treacherous reign but also handed over the decryption code to Gabriel. This way, clones will be trusted again.

See every detail and angle has been planned.

After all, Gabriel was always meant to rule Manus Dei. He was created in the image of the man who once did rule.

A king who was married to Astrid. A king she killed, believing it would secure her the throne, but the Masters had other plans. They compelled Dorian and Hans to resurrect Gabriel. There were no 3D-printed organs back then, so they cloned him instead. They also cloned Astrid as punishment, forcing her to witness another version of herself vying for the crown she coveted.

Astrid, a scorned woman, has been grossly underestimated by the Masters.

The Horsemen won't repeat that mistake.

Chapter 31

Sol

It's rare to find time when I can be alone with myself and my mind. I find myself excited now that it has finally happened. My skin itches, and my feet won't stay planted.

Wes left after we had sex. Twice. Once on the bed and then against the wall.

He said he was going to a local bakery down the street to get me fresh muffins. A touching gesture that didn't penetrate my heart.

What hurts more than all the games, secrets, and lies is that love isn't enough. Maybe it was foolish thinking it was.

Wes won't leave the game for me. He thinks playing gives him more power. It's the power that will kill us.

Why can't they all see that?

My nails cut into the heel of my hand until I finally give my flesh a break and grab the old iPod and lay in bed.

I open Spotify. It's a slow process because I have to use the wheel to type out my search. Luna had a playlist on Spotify. It's not a secret, at least not to Gabriel and me. She made it public years ago.

On the black and white small screen is the list of songs Luna loved. These were her repeats she played so often you wanted to scream, but now I want to cry tears of joy that I have these songs to listen to.

The past.

Footsteps sound as my sister joins me outside in our vast backyard. Winter will soon approach. The leaves are turning and slowly dying.

"What are you looking at for so long?" Luna asks as she plops down next to me, mirroring my image with outstretched legs, shoulders relaxed, and palms pressing into the grass. I like to sit directly on the grass. I want to touch the earth and feel its textures.

"Death."

"What." Luna's head whips towards me. Her voice is cold.

"I'm talking about the leaves falling," I point to the trees. Luna's eyes follow my finger, scanning the landscape with a narrow precision.

"Did you ever think death could be so lovely?"

"What do you mean?" Luna asks.

I can't help but notice how her body has stiffened. I wonder if it's because of the topic. "Everyone loves fall because of all the saturated colors, but in reality, they appreciate death. The leaves are dying. It's a slow end, which should be grotesque, but no one sees it that way. They see the saturated outside, not the decay from within."

We sit in silence, the sun kissing our faces, the blades of grass tickling the tips of our fingers. "You're right. Sometimes ugly is pretty, and sometimes death is beautiful." Luna admits.

I nod. "That's because everyone tries to see the good at first glimpse. People don't think nature is killing the plants or that food will be scarce for the animals. They see the colors then the blankets of untouched glittering snow."

Luna doesn't respond but grabs her iPod from her pocket and selects a song. She turns the volume up high on her headphones. It's so loud that we both can hear her music without putting the headphones on. She plays a song I know, "What a Wonderful World" but I have never heard this version. It sounds eerie, haunting. I'm not sure if the future is going to be hopeful or melancholy, judging from the way the artist conveys the essence of the song.

"Who sings this?"

"Soap and Skin."

I wrinkle my nose, "That's a funny name."

"People choose funny things." She deadpans. Her eyes go distant and I wonder if she envisions a hope on her horizon or an endless competition.

I sit with my twin watching the leaves slowly die and fall. Moments like this are rare. Just Luna and I, enjoying nothing but everything simultaneously.

"The way she sings the song makes me feel like something terrible has happened." I tilt my head up, trying to imagine a rainbow in the sky, "It makes me feel like ashes are falling from the sky, settling." I shrug, "But where there is death," I look at the dead fallen leaves scattered on the forest floor, "There is also new life waiting to spring forth. I know that even after a harsh winter, new life will come forth. Life is resilient, even in the most terrible of circumstances."

Pivoting, I look at my twin. Her blonde hair dances over her face, and her unblinking blue eyes stare at the horizon. She's ethereal, and despite our identical features, I can't help but feel inferior in her presence. I will only feel on her level if she trusts me more.

I just want her to trust me.

I can protect her as well as she has shielded me.

A subtle twitch pulls at her lips as if contemplating a hidden secret. I don't know if it was the budding of a smile or a snarl. I'll never know with Luna. She's an enigma, a Pandora's box. You never know what is inside or what monster will be unleashed.

I grab her hand, and interlace our fingers. Luna picked this song for a reason. She doesn't listen to music like a normal person. She picks songs that reflect her darkest voice and lyrics that can speak when she doesn't know how to.

"That's our world." She admits. She hits replay, and the song begins again. We stayed outside listening to the same song for hours that day.

It was one of my favorite days.

I blink away the falling tears. That old memory feels new with the added knowledge I have gained. I know why Luna reacted with alarm. She knew of Death then, both the act of dying and also the Horseman.

I hug the iPod to my chest.

Footsteps creek up the old wooden stairs. In a hurry, I wipe away the tears before Wes opens the bedroom door. When he enters, he has a wide smile on his stunning face.

That smile I rarely see. It's so pure I want to bottle it up to smell its fragrance.

Fresh snow is sprinkled on his short black hair. He shakes it off, somehow making the gesture looks so damn sexy.

In his hands, he's holding a large brown bag. The sweet scent of baked bread seeps from the top of it. He strides towards the bed, bends down, and kisses my lips, leaving me wanting much more. At first his lips are cold and I feel the need to warm him. To protect him from the elements.

He pulls away and sits on the edge of the bed. He is so happy; something has changed. He has gained an advantage in the game. It's obvious.

I have to force my body not to react. Not to be angry or show him how unhappy he is making me.

I can't help but focus on his green eyes, those optimistic beacons in the sea of darkness. His ridiculously long lashes would make any woman jealous, and his jaw is as strong as his stubborn personality.

He's shaved his hair short again, but left that shadow on his jaw. Why? Because he enjoys how my body reacts when it brushes against the stubble against my smooth skin, the devious tease.

I reach up and cup his face, gliding my fingertips over the stubble. "I love you," I declare.

There I said it.

It's doubled edged because in a way my confession is my goodbye.

My eyes water and Wes's happiness fades into what looks like shock, awe, and suspicion.

Love shouldn't be suspicious. It should be pure and untainted; that's what fairy tales tell children.

Wake up.

Life is no fairy tale; it is a never-ending story filled with ups and downs, heroes and villains. Love and monsters.

Wesley and I.

"It's going to be ok," He promises me.

Not the words I expected to hear.

He craved for me to speak the words to him. To give him a part of me he could not take.

I just did. But he didn't offer it back to me.

I'm just his possession.

The bed dips when he edges closer to me, grabs my face, and kisses me with so much passion I'm surprised the earth doesn't wobble off its axis. "The plan is going to work. You'll be safe." He vows over my trembling lips.

He has no idea that once I get Gabriel inside that vault I have a plan of my own.

I part my lips to plead my last hope that he will change his mind and join me when this is all finished, but my lips seal shut. *Don't be silly, Sol.*

"Once this is finished, I'll take you away to a place where you can be free." He repeats his plans to me with a gleaming grin.

"Freedom in a cage you built, Wesley. Loved by a man who is being poisoned with the need for power. A power that is a cancer that is hurting me."

He growls an exhale. His lips kiss me again, but this time, it's harder. Demanding. A new level of possession that steals my every intake of breath, making me dependent on him.

I still love it. This side; this version of the monster. Always will.

He grabs my hands which I scrub clean daily now. "I told you I would protect you. I'm trying my best. This is the only way. You'll be safe."

I bite my lip and look at his hands, enclosing mine. Then I paint the perfect lie I can create. I blink away my fury and sadness and clear my eyes.

I smile, trying my best to make it thankful. "I know you are," I tell the monster, the man I love. I lean forward and kiss him, slipping my tongue past his accepting lips.

He is trying his best. It's just not good enough for me.

Death wants his side to win, to have power, but he also wants me. The Horsemen have learned nothing from history. It repeats.

He can't protect me and cage me. Gabriel failed to do that with my sister. Wes is going to lose me just as Gabriel lost Luna.

No, I'm not going to jump off a cliff, but I will fight.

In the beginning, I thought I owed my sister my life. I did. I don't regret playing the game, but now I've evolved and will not be a pawn. I'm not prey. Inside of me, a monster lurks. After all, I was cloned from a beast.

Some monsters like to stalk, and others like to hibernate. Once I end the games i'm going to go far away where no one can find me.

I look into the eyes of the Horseman I love, green like the saturated hue of a fall leaf.

Death.

He is so beautiful; all dying life is in its own way.

"You never said you love me back," I admit. I hold onto that fact. It will help me when I must leave him.

Wes grins and shakes his head. "Love is too simple of a word to describe how I feel for you, Sol." He's using my real name. That makes it feel more real and less like a game. "I'm obsessed with you. You fill my mind. You are a constant worry, attraction, and craving. I can't function if I don't know where you are. I have to know you are safe, and I'm the only one that can keep you safe. I need you by my side to stay sane." He tucks back my hair, "My real heart died. It vanished from this world. You captured my new heart and kept it beating only for you."

"I'm your possession, not your love."

"Don't put words in my mouth, little mouse." His hand leaves my hair and grabs hold of the back of my neck. "You don't respect a possession."

"If you respected and loved me, you would stop playing these games and come with me."

He shakes his head. "You're running into a grave. You're stumbling," He taps my forehead, "In here. You need me to help you walk; that is what I am doing and will continue to do. I respect your strength to continue in ways Luna could not. I respect the woman you are, the artist you are, and how you create your art... even when you are the canvas. I understand why you must do it. But my care and need to protect you stop me from lying to you. Telling you that we can have a normal life is a lie, Sol. Others know about you, and they will linger in the shadows to take you. Waiting patiently to pluck the science from your flesh, they will rip you open and steal it from you. You don't even know half of it. You're a chip to be stolen and bartered with. That's why you need me to protect you. Your father kept you hidden for a reason. Even in Aspen, you were not free. I was watching. Others knew that, and that is why they stayed away." He embraces me in a hug so tight I can't fill my lungs all the way, "I'm sorry." He exhales, and I feel his breath on the top of my head, "I love you. You have my heart. Please protect it, just as I protect yours."

I will protect it. You just won't like how I do so. History is repeating, and that's your fault.

To bring an end to these destructive games, I am willing to go to great lengths, even if it means making Wes hate me just as Gabriel despises Luna.

Only through embracing the concept of death, be it the death of our love, trust, and loyalty, can I pave the way for a true new beginning.

Chapter 32

Sol

"Here you go." War hands me the headset, but from the way his hands are grasping it, it looks like he'd rather crush it. I take it, the weight settling in my hands. It feels as heavy as a ton of bricks.

What will I see through Klara's eyes today? My stomach knots.

"Were any of you close to Klara?" I ask War and Wes.

"No," they both respond.

Wes raises a brow and asks, "Why?"

I hug the headset to my stomach. "It's just odd. Klara wasn't in the game against Gabriel and my sister, but she usually watched their trials as a bystander with Astrid."

"Klara was Astrid's dog," Wes replies automatically without a care.

I jerk; it feels like a personal attack. "She was an abused child," I snap.

He tilts his head, replaying his words. "I never said she wasn't, little mouse." He licks his lips. "I'm sorry. I shouldn't refer to her like that. It's just," he sighs, "I know the monster she has been raised to be, and sometimes, all you see are the deeds and not the person or reason behind them." He steps closer, his hands cupping mine over the helmet. Leaning down, he whispers, "That's what I love about you. You see me; you see the person and not just the darkness. You always find a light."

He pulls away, green eyes filled with possession. "And that's why I need to protect you. Light can burn, Sol." Turning, he peels off his sweater and hangs it on the doorknob. His back is rippled with muscles that force his olive-green shirt to stretch.

This house has a constant chill, making it feel more like a morgue than a safe house. Dust-scented air, grimy windows. I can't wait to leave this place. I grab the VR headset tight. I can't wait to be free.

I push up the sleeves of my long sleeve shirt because, like Wes, I want the cold to numb me. Make me feel less. "Why did Klara receive this eye implant? Did Luna have one also?"

"No. Klara was one of the rare few. The retina recording is a beta technology in Manus Dei's nanobyte division. The nanobytes connect to wifi to upload visuals, but the recording lasts only ten to fifteen minutes. Then the information needs to be downloaded then deleted before it can record again. Patients have reported symptoms like debilitating visual impairments," War informs me. The dim lighting of the basement room gives him an ethereal yet sinister glow, like a demon who was kissed by Lucifer, given the gift of handsome looks with a sly tongue. "But like all technology, Manus Dei will work out the kinks. Klara has received several upgrades throughout the years. As you can see, these later videos from her life are much clearer. I don't need to enhance the frames or audio."

"Who created this upgrade?" I inquire.

"It's not a genetic upgrade. This modification is strictly nanobyte technology. Gabriel took over the nanobytes division a few years back. Klara was always the first guinea pig Astrid played with. Klara was easily disposable in her eyes. Like a lab rat," Wes interjects with a hint of disdain. "She wanted Klara to be her guard dog, to see and hear when she wasn't physically there. But she didn't trust Klara; Astrid never trusts anyone. The retina implants are a perfect solution."

I pause for a moment, taking in the information. "And how did you all get these files?" I inquire, curious about their source.

War glances at Wes. There is a fresh pain in his eyes, "Famine was our tech guy. He is one of the best hackers in the world, so it was a fun challenge for him to hack inside and find the footage of Klara. Now I have to pick up his slack." He bitterly bites.

"You're more than capable." Wes slaps his back.

"We shall see," War looks down at the floor. "Let's begin."

Wes walks towards me and takes the headset from my hands, "I'm right here," He promises as he places the headset on my head.

The darkness only lasts a second until the virtual reality starts. Like always, I begin in the white room. "I just need a minute for the file to upload to your headset, Sol," War states. "This time, you will be in the tunnels. Make sure you study the details. It is a labyrinth, but Klara goes directly to Astrid's underground office."

"Ok," I reply. My heart hastens as it does every time I enter the tunnels. There is something spooky about them, like the clashing of eras; nothing feels correct. The large gray stones belong in a medieval castle, but the automatic lighting and all the security feels like it belongs in the future.

A long bright white LED light on the ceiling snakes along every twist and turn. It only turns on once you step under it. You have to know exactly where you are going, and only then, once you've taken the step, will the lights turn on and light your path.

Each door I have passed is solid steel with large rivets and bolts running down the spine. It feels like a door that would keep nuclear fallout at bay. At the base of each door are numerous biometric scanners.

I mentally map out every turn Klara makes as she ventures deeper into the tunnels. At this point in the time line we are getting closer to the final test between Gabriel and Luna, which means we are close to the start of the game my sister asked me to play.

Klara reaches a new door. This one isn't steel but a matte black material. I wish I could reach out and touch it to know its texture, but since Klara didn't, I cannot. I tilt my neck, feeling the weight of the headset.

She places her wrist on the scanner; the light doesn't turn green but blinks orange. "I hate you," Klara whispers; I almost didn't catch it.

"Pause," I tell War. The simulation freezes.

"Who is she talking to?"

I hear War tapping on his tablet's screen. "I didn't register anything on the audio scans."

"What did you hear?" Wes ask.

"Can you replay it?"

War rewinds the footage thirty seconds, and I hear it again. "Klara said she hates you. But no one is in the hallway." I inform them.

"Maybe she was talking to herself," Wes suggest.

"No, I don't think so," I reply. If you are confident, a part of you is a narcissist. They go hand in hand. A narcissist wouldn't hate themselves. They put themselves higher than anyone around them. "Klara is talking about Astrid."

War clears his throat, "She has been devoted to her mother."

No, she has been devoted to Luna.

She just revealed her cards to me. Something isn't adding up. Until I connect the dots, I'll remain silent. "Yeah, you're right," I lie. "You can resume."

The virtual reality restarts, and the sound of clicking resonates through the tunnels as the door swings open. I step inside, greeted by the starkness of the blinding white office. The room is devoid of any color or warmth, with only a large white desk, a white chair, and a few white cabinets occupying the space. It's not a peaceful and inviting modern design; instead, it feels suffocating, like being trapped in a sterile, clinical environment or a straightjacket for the mind.

The room unveils two additional doors on the left side. One door is made of clear glass, accompanied by a large biometric sensor adjacent to it. Behind the glass door, I see a vast expanse of servers. No doubt the stolen knowledge of Manus Dei. The other door, painted white and constructed from metal, remains shrouded in mystery, its destination unknown.

Astrid removes her hand from the buzzer, and Klara enters the room. However, Astrid is not alone in this memory. Seated across from her is Gabriel, who briefly glances over his shoulder, acknowledging Klara's presence. Yet, the moment passes in a fleeting instant, suggesting that Gabriel either dismisses Klara's significance or considers her insignificant.

"I believe this was a prudent choice, Astrid. Our primary objective must take precedence, and we can advance our research with these backups. I have personally evaluated each one, and they exhibit mental stability," Gabriel comments.

Astrid brushes off his words with a wave of her hand. It still freaks the shit out of me, knowing I'll resemble Astrid in the years to come. I just pray I won't look so bitchy and cold.

"I remain unconvinced about retaining all of them," she retorts, her eyes narrowing with a cold gleam fixed on Klara. "I have reservations about those who are outspoken, and Luna has proven to be nothing but trouble. I fail to comprehend why everyone consented to your union."

"That is the decision of the Masters. As a fellow Master, you must abide by their vote. Otherwise, you stand against all of us," Gabriel challenges her, his blue eyes piercing with determination. Rather than faltering under his gaze, Astrid responds with a deranged grin.

"I wouldn't dare defy the other Masters," she purrs, a fake smile plastered on her face. Her eye briefly shifts to the server room, the vault where she has been hoarding stolen knowledge from Manus Dei. "Many of the Masters have questioned your loyalty to the cause. After all, it was your clone that first snapped. Was it difficult for you to eliminate him?" Astrid taunts, her laughter ringing out.

Gabriel remains stoic, but I sense the underlying emotions he must be grappling with. His clone broke, and Manus Dei forced Gabriel to kill it.

"I am loyal. I have always been," Gabriel asserts, his tone escalating in a clear challenge.

"Loyalty is like a river's current. It meanders, sometimes strong and steady, at other times gentle and meek." She retorts, she waves her hand dismissively. "You may leave."

Gabriel stands and passes by Klara, who remains by the door. Their eyes clash, and time seems to slow. It feels like an unspoken exchange between them, a camaraderie. Both have killed, both are chained to the Masters. Trapped and itching to be set free.

"Did Gabriel and Klara have a friendship?"

"No, Klara was an introvert. She didn't reach out to anyone. She is loyal to Astrid." War states.

Oh, War, you're so blind at times, too focused on another battle to see an alliance forming behind your back.

Wes and War are not seeing what I have seen. They are watching as bystanders, but I see it through Klara's eyes. I've picked up details they didn't even hear.

Klara isn't loyal. She is like a pawn that reached the opposite end of the chessboard, and if you're familiar with chess rules, you know that when a pawn reaches the opponent's side, it can transform into a different piece. The question now is, what did Klara choose to become – a rook, a bishop, a knight, or a queen?

I'll figure it out eventually.

What I do know is that Klara is like a tightly wound rubber band. Each mission Astrid sends her on stretches her. Sooner or later, she will snap, and her leash will break.

None of them seem to see that, but I wonder if Luna did?

That's silly, sister. Of course, I did. I hear Luna whisper a secret in my mind.

Chapter 33

Sol

The last grains of sand in the hourglass are slipping away, each one propelling us closer to the crescendo of our mission.

The training is done.

So many games are about to collide. Gabriel's game, Luna's, Astrids and of course mine.

We boarded a commercial flight from Munich to Switzerland and then took a train to Grindelwald.

Home sweet home.

Although we all traveled together, I haven't seen Gabriel or War because we separated and bordered the plane and train at different times. We all changed our clothes, and I overheard War ensuring his brother that he had changed the security footage.

The tips of my fingers rub against the tweed fabric of the train seat. I have rubbed it so much that I'm surprised I haven't worn a hole in it.

Wes and I are sitting side by side on the train as it tugs us closer to my old hometown. Like a perfect gentleman, he gave me the window seat, and like the fine-tuned stalker, he gave me this seat so I was trapped by his body and could not escape down the aisle.

Not that I would try. There is no point in running until my last task is finished.

Wes has his right hand spread wide over my thigh. His fingers inched up higher than socially acceptable, but who the heck cares?

I sure don't. I'm enjoying his touch because soon I will be without it.

The scenery is so stunning you could easily cry. Everything here is untouched and pristine, clean and wealthy. The grass is greener, but that's because it isn't real. It is a veneer of painted lies. Nothing but a completely untrue landscape. The truth lies beneath the mountain, where tunnels and secret bases house Manus Dei's labs and knowledge.

I, of all people, know just how easy it is to paint lies. To show the world what I want them to see rather than the ugly truth.

Speaking of the devil, Eiger Mountain begins to come into view. Unlike the mountain in Aspen, which is tree-lined, Eiger Mountain is more rock; it's snow-capped, but no trees cling to it. It's sharp and jagged and not warm and cozy.

It is home, brutal and unforgiving.

Reaching up, I pull down the black baseball cap Wes gave me as I block out the mountain. "Where do they think I am?" I ask. If I am pretending to be Klara, where do Astrid and Manus Dei think Sol Eklund is?

"They think you have been abducted by a black site agency run by the US government. That's why Gabriel had to take the bullet. We needed to make it look like a hostile takeover. By now, everyone knows Astrid is controlling the science. They are panicking, some have bent a knee to her demands, and others are willing to fight back. Astrid thinks they are dissecting you to try to steal the science."

"And she is fine with that. With others picking apart her clone." Wow, I sound like Luna. Vengeful.

Wes takes my hand, pretzels our fingers then guides it to rest on his thigh. He wants to be my rock. "Yes," he counters, "Astrid probably thinks even if they manage to steal fragments of the science within you, it is merely scratching the surface of the vast knowledge she holds. In her eyes, you pose no threat."

It's the way he utters *no threat* that takes me believe he actually thinks I'm not one.

Good.

The train jerks and chugs along slowly. One of his feet sticks out, forming a perfect shield that would cover me if he stood up.

During our journey, his demeanor is marked by eerie silence. It's as if his brain is doing all the shouting. His muscles are tense, his posture rigid, and his eyes scan the surroundings with the intensity of a starving eagle, ever watchful for its next prey. I can visualize it so clearly, the image etched in my mind: a majestic eagle perched atop Eiger Mountain, its golden beak rivaling the brilliance of the sun. Patiently, it waits, biding its time until it spots a small brown rabbit, weary from its ceaseless struggle for survival. In an instant, the eagle descends with lightning speed, its broad wings casting a shadow that shields the rabbit from the sun's glare. The unsuspecting prey, seeking solace in the shade, becomes a victim, its life snuffed out in the blink of an eye.

Poof! You're dead. Game over.

I swallow hard not accepting that fate for myself, the Horseman, or mankind.

"Why did Famine leave?"

"Where are you going, little mouse?"

I shrug, "I can't paint away my nerves or cover myself in makeup to believe my lies. I'm nervous and feeling chatty."

"Chatty?"

"You want to spend time together. We can't just spend time in the bedroom."

His pupils dilate, and a wave of heat flashes through me till it scorches my cheeks, "Sure we can," He purrs. That deep, low, husky tone makes my core pulse.

"As tempting as that is, I want to understand you better."

The train continues its journey around the curve of the landscape. He's reluctant to reply, which pisses me off. Stretching my fingers, I try to tug my hand free of his, but then his lips part, and my hand settles back where it belongs. Yeah, belongs. We belong together, but like so many love stories, our love is so passionate it can't be sustained for long.

That's what sucks about true love. It exists only in fairytales, and those types of stories are short and often filled with tragedy. Just like the love between Gabriel and Luna, and the love between Wes and me.

"Famine witnessed what hunger could do to someone. He didn't like what he saw. I believe he thought that by following Luna and carrying out her plan, he could demonstrate his loyalty to her, showing her she could trust him. His intention was to use that trust to help her heal."

"Her?" Is Wes referring to Luna?

"Not your sister. She was Gabriel's."

I feel a chill ripple through me. His response hangs in the air, laden with hidden depths, like a mountain harboring long-buried treasures.

Mentally, I grip my metaphorical chisel, poised to strike precisely where the secrets lie.

"I did give you a big wheel of cheese, didn't I?" He grins.

"Why?" I question, my curiosity piqued, my mind racing to uncover the hidden message behind his words.

He moistens his lips, a gesture that makes a natural blush paint over my cheeks. *What his tongue can do…* "I wanted you to trust me, to understand that we are destined to spend our lives together. So I'm trusting you with more information."

"Your reply wasn't trusting it was filled with more secrets."

"Secrets you want to discover." His brow tugs higher.

Oh, so you think that will make me run less. You're mistaken, baby. Once you figure out what I have planned, I will hide somewhere you'll never find me.

"You're coercing me into a life with you," I hiss, yet my hand remains in its place, unmoving, unable to resist his magnetic pull.

His right eye twitches. Slipping his hand free, he pivots, his wide back shielding me from the passengers across from us as his hand snakes around my neck. He tilts my neck as if I'm his doll. "You can't paint that lie, little mouse," he whispers, his lips capturing mine in a searing kiss.

I want him to lay me down on this seat and have his filthy way with me. Peel off my clothes, rip open my mind, and replace every past memory with a new one. I want his lips to baptize my flesh into his dark and twisted desires. I want him to bury himself so deep inside of me I forget.

Everything.

Our tongues collide briefly, but he withdraws before our desires ignite into an uncontrollable blaze. "This isn't force. This is destiny," his voice is low and rasp, his eyes holding mine with unwavering intensity.

He's right. It's not coercion. I just like to run because I know he is chasing me. I've wanted him since the night he snuck into my room, like the dark knight who came to save me from my locked-up castle.

My chest heaves as I sink back into my seat.

"Now," He swoops down and nips at my neck, his hot breath tickling my ear, "Piece together the fragments, read between my lines, and tell me, little mouse, what secrets were you able to figure out from my statement." He challenges me, a knowing gleam in his eyes as if daring me.

I squirm in my seat and cross my legs. He gives me clues and likes to watch how I run after them; it's our game. "Famine chose Luna's side because of a woman."

He nods. "Who do you think that is, little mouse?"

I shrug, "I don't know if that matters. I see a pattern. Love." I reply, "It's corrupted us all. Sent us each down different paths."

Wes's demeanor changes in an instant. His features harden. I press on, "Love can start wars. If you look up the definition of love, do you know what it says?" I don't let him respond, his eyes are narrowed and locked on mine. "It says love means an intense feeling of deep affection, a pleasure in something. It doesn't say it is a good or bad attraction. Look at you and me. You stalked me. Your love for me isn't good, Wesley. Now, look at Gabriel and Luna. They held a deep attraction for one another. They each claimed it was love," I shake my head, "Love forced us all down paths of madness."

Wes jerks, but I don't let go of his hands. "What's the point of this?" He hisses, upset by my view of our love.

"Love, power, greed, perfection. Winning or losing. Feelings," I declare. "Emotions. That's the problem with humankind. I understand why Luna wanted to purge herself of feelings."

I look out the window at the landscape. The mountain is closer now, and so are all the demons. A new dawn is on the horizon, a day much darker and scarier than humanity has faced.

We're resilient, though. Humans have survived everything in our past—mass extinctions, plagues, and world wars...we will continue to survive.

I don't care who Famine is in love with because he won't get his happy ending. Fairy tales are lies, and I don't want to be lied to anymore.

"Maybe when this is all over, we should find a cure for emotions. Become more like computers, point A to destination B. Problems are solved. Life is easy." I joke.

"You don't believe that." Wes growls. He snatches my hands, bringing them closer to his chest as if he wants me to feel his beating heart.

"We live in a world that teaches us love, is a good emotion. It's happy and blissful. Ask Gabriel what love is to him, question Famine." I shake my head, "Look in the mirror and ask yourself, Wesley."

His golden skin shades red. "We make our definitions. We decide what our love is and what its definition will be. I don't care about anyone else. All I care about is you." He growls. I feel a single tear escape my sky-blue eyes, betraying the emotions swirling within me.

"That's the dilemma with our love, Wesley," I confess, "It is a love born out of selfishness. You only see me, you only feel me, but you fail to consider the innocent lives that will be impacted by our actions. Your focus is solely on your own desires, disregarding the turmoil it may cause me and everyone else. You're love is selfish."

"My love is honest." He snarls. I feel my chin tremble. "I need you. Fucking need! Don't you understand that, Sol. I will not live without you." He leans closer, the vein in his neck pulsing, "Stop painting me as the monster."

It feels like a knife is stabbing my heart slowly. Every inch of his pain, fear and passion I feel. God I wish I didn't feel it. "I can only paint you with the shades you give me." I inhale, "Give me a lighter palette if you want me to view you as my hero." My voice cracks.

He snickers an evil sound that plunges the knife through my heart. "I don't want to be your hero, little mouse. Heroes die for the cause. I'd only die for *you*. You! Go ahead, paint me as your villain; make me your devil; I don't care because I will always have you, always find you. You're mine, and if anyone ever tries to help you escape me, if they lay a single finger on you, there will not even be ashes left of them for you to scatter across this earth. Trust me, loving you as your villain is much more enjoyable, knowing I face no consequences. I make our rules. Not anyone else."

"If you truly loved me, you would set me free. You would join me in escaping this plagued world, leaving behind the darkness and the pain. The science and its power. But you won't because our love is tainted. You will forever remain a Horseman, bound to the cycle of destruction." I inch closer to him, my features growing cold, "You're so scared, aren't you? Fearful of what will happen. Who will take me." I push back, relaxing in the seat as I rasp, "When all this time the biggest monster is yourself. It's you who is destroying us. No one else. It's all your fault. Love is a living, breathing emotion, Wes; if you try to cage it, you will kill it."

He extends his hand, his thumb gently capturing the solitary tear that escapes my eye. Bringing it to his peach-colored lips, he licks it with a mixture of tenderness and darkness. "No," he asserts, gripping my chin firmly. "I am selfish, as all humans are. I will not relinquish my love for you. This, my dear, is a game you have just failed. I refuse to let you turn away from our love. I refuse to let it die."

The roar of the train seems to disappear until I only feel his presence.

Wesley. Death.

My lover and captor.

I'm ensnared by his words. They wrap around me so tight I can't fully inhale.

He's never going to stop and the fucked up part of me relishes in that.

A knowing smirk tugs at the corners of his lips as he continues, "I told you, didn't I? I knew deep down that you would run; you love being chased. All those years in your sister's shadow made you crave depraved attention that only I can give you." His hand drifts down to my neck, his fingers resting on my pulse. He grins, feeling my excitement and my despair. "You delight in taunting me, just like when you refused to admit Wes and Death were the same person. Me. It was always just you and me. You were well aware that you could never escape me; truth be told, you didn't want to. You crave a love that is not adorned with red roses and chocolates, but one that ignites obsession. You want an emotion that consumes you. An ego-driven love that makes your heart race with each encounter. You seek devotion, a safety entwined with an eternal thrill."

"Yes," I deadpan. "I do. But you can't give me that if you remain a Horseman. You're not just obsessed with me but also with them."

He grinds his teeth. "You have my love. My heart. They don't. You'll see that in time. You are bound to me, my love. No matter how far you run or what precipice you choose to leap from, I will be there to catch you." His hand squeezes my neck tighter. Each inhale stressed. "Do you comprehend the gravity of my words? You have stolen my heart, and now you must bear the weight of your transgressions."

His lips hover tantalizingly close to mine, the air thick with anticipation. I pant for my next breath, yearning for both an escape and him. Just before our lips meet, he breathes a declaration that sends shivers down my spine: "Consider this your life sentence."

Chapter 34

Wes

Blue eyes so wide and deep they look like a puppy begging for help looked back at me. Those eyes haunt my every waking moment.

I want to give Sol the world. I will, but it will be a world where she is safe.

Sol remains oblivious to the dangers lurking, not only from governments but also from organizations pursuing the scientific knowledge held by Manus Dei.

Of course, I knew what my little mouse was doing. Thriving off the push and pull. The chase. Fuck, I love the chase. The thrill of cornering her, surrounding her so that my next exhale is her only available inhale.

It's on the tip of her tongue to finally admit it.

I already won. Sol said she loved me.

I never thought I'd need to hear those words. After seeing my father's obsession with my mother, I never wanted to experience that attachment. It was a weakness as much as it was a strength.

Now I have it, and I will do everything in my power to treasure it.

She bites her tongue, swallowing another retort.

Oh, Little mouse, that tongue is mine to bite. Mine to pleasure.

As a matter of fact, I think I'll have it wrapped around my cock tonight as her punishment. Seeing her on her knees with those sky blue eyes watering as they look up at me. It's like staring into heaven, and since I'm never going there, I might as well experience it here on Earth, in Sol's eyes.

She scurrying around in the maze in her mind trying to find a way to push me out. If she pushed, and I accepted, it would be easier for her to hallucinate again.

That wasn't going to happen.

Consider me the anchor forever chained to Sol's lovely legs. I won't allow her to escape the game or me, especially because Sol's freedom was so close. I could see it, and soon we would taste it.

***

I press the tips of my fingertips into her lower back, finding the groove that makes all my blood rush to my cock. I wish my fingers were pressing against her skin and not her clothing.

Patience is a virtue.

With wide eyes, Sol scans the new safe house. It's stunning if you like that cold, modern serial killer design.

Famine did.

The castle I have built for Sol is warm and cozy, with large pine logs composing the walls. She loves nature, and that's why I made sure to build a house that was close to it.

Everything I do is for her. Everything.

Sol takes hesitant steps like a mouse inching free of her cage. This new safe house is so spare it makes one feel uneasy like they are stepping around in a museum.

"Is this War's house too?" she murmurs as we pass a solid black granite sculpture. Her fingers reach out and gently touch the marble with fascination.

Jealousy makes my cock twitch. Her fingers should be exploring my body, not this excuse for art.

"No, this is... was Famine's safe house," I reply. She glances at me over her shoulder, her full lips slightly parted. I lick my lips, recalling how she tastes.

Her blonde brows raise, and those wide blue eyes call to me like pools of water. It's as if I have never drunk, and she is my fountain of life.

"Famine's?" She questions. Her face always lights up when I reveal the truth. That's why I love giving her little hints here and there. I always get to witness that excitement.

"Yes. It's the perfect place for us to hide. Gabriel's home is monitored." I shrug, "No one looks here because Famine left." And if they did, War would wipe the video feed. He has an AI scanning the surveillance videos 24/7, and if we appear on the screen, the AI starts to overwrite our presence.

Sleek black floating stairs lead the way to our private suite on the second floor. Unlike the old house in Munich, this room is massive; an entire wall is one window that looks out at Eiger Mountain. A King size bed is in the center looking out to the impressive view. There's a small couch and a sitting area with a fireplace to the right. The primary bathroom has a spa shower and a large bath. The walls are gray suede. Immediately my mind envisions pressing Sol against the soft walls as I make love to her.

I pivot my head towards the bed with its black silk bedding. I'll take her there too.

My erection hardens painfully.

My eyes find the mountain that hides so much from the world. Usually, I love a mountain view, but this mountain makes me want to level the land.

Turning my back, I close the bedroom door. Sol stands at the window with a hand on the glass as she looks at Eiger Mountain.

It has robbed so much from her.

Closing the distance, I wrap my hands around her from behind, feeling the warmth of her body against mine.

Home.

I can relax. My neck aches from the stress of the mission.

Inhaling deeply, I savor her intoxicating scent that fills the air. It's a fragrance that soothes my tired muscles, calming them despite the soreness.

The desire I have for her is overwhelming, an undeniable need that courses through my veins.

Mine!

As my fingers trace a path lower, slipping into her pants, I can feel the delicate lace of her thong beneath my touch. Her neck tilts back, ass pushing into my cock.

She wants me just as bad.

The gentle brush against her skin under my fingertip sends shivers down her spine. It's a reaction that I adore, a testament to the power I hold over her body. Sol may be capable of deceiving the world with words, but her body always speaks the truth to me.

"I don't want to fight, little mouse." I kiss the sensitive spot just below her ear. When I kiss her here, her pussy tightens. I know all her buttons, and I push them often. "I want to make love to you over and over again. Until you are so exhausted, you stop arguing with me."

Her hand cups mine, pressing the heel of my palm against her clit. "I," her words are heavy, her need starting to throb as she grinds my hand up and down her pussy. "I won't waste time fighting a losing battle. No more talking. Make me yours."

My ears catch the tone of grief still lingering in her words.

Her head arches up, finding its place on my shoulder, her deep blue eyes drawing me in with their depth. Her defenses drop and I accept the olive branch.

No more fighting. Just fucking.

"Be careful what you wish for, little mouse." I tease. Nipping her neck as I press my index finger against her swollen wet clit.

"Wesley," she giggles a moan, a sound that is pure and infectious. To witness her in such a carefree state is rare, and I cherish these moments. It's a reminder of the happiness I want to provide for her, a daily dose of joy in the sanctuary we create together.

With a twist of her body, I position myself to have complete access to her mouth. The sudden change catches her off guard, eliciting a gasp from her throat. I seize the opportunity, capturing her sounds within the depths of my mouth as I claim her soft, supple lips.

Desire surges through me, urging me to bite down gently, so I do. Sinking my teeth into her bottom lip, I suck it into my mouth, relishing in the pleasure and control it brings. Her moans threaten to break my restraint.

I guide us towards the window, pressing her chest flush to the glass, looking out at the mountain, unable to anticipate my next move.

I pin her hands up above her head. "Leave them here. If you move one finger, I'll stop." I tell her.

She responds by pushing her ass into my cock. This woman can end the world with her body. Men would die a thousand deaths to have one night with her.

I slip my hand back into her soaking wet heat, rubbing it slowly and deliberately. The texture of the lace against her sensitive nub elicits a shiver that courses through her body, causing her knees to tremble in response.

Soon, her moans fill the air, A sound that would make Mozart compose a new symphony. "Oh fuck, keep going, there, right there. Oh god, Wesley," Unable to contain her escalating hunger, her hands break free from their pinned position and reach for mine, pressing my hand firmly against her, trying to push my fingers inside her, urging me not to stop.

A mischievous smile tugs at the corners of my lips. "You disobeyed me, little mouse," I whisper in a low, husky voice. "I explicitly told you not to move a finger, yet you couldn't resist your own desires. You're greedy, and now I need to teach you a lesson."

She slaps her hands back onto the glass window, submitting to my command, her compliance a testament to our power dynamic. My chuckle fills the room, a mix of amusement and primal satisfaction. "Should I punish you by denying you, leaving you on the edge of your orgasm, driving you wild with need?" I pause, "Or perhaps, should I make you come so intensely it will leave you sore for days?"

"Wesley, please," she pleads.

"What will it be?" I tease, my fingers pinching her, only to bring her to the edge before I release her again.

"Fuck you," She slaps her palms against the glass. She leaves her hands pinned up high, fist-balled. *Good girl.*

"Is that what you want? For me to fuck you so you can hate me. You think I only take for my own pleasure?" I start to work her then, circling her clit with more pressure, "Or should I make love to you? Show you just how much I care about you?"

I grind my palm against clit. She comes undone. Moaning my name, knees giving out. Solely reliant on me to keep her upright.

Perfection.

A primal possessiveness. It's awoken in me and it will never slumber again. The realization that no one else has ever called me Wesley, and now, only Sol will. She has claimed a part of me that belongs to her alone.

Her knees start to push into the floor as she recovers. I press my hips into her ass, trapping her between my body and the cool glass of the window. For the next ten minutes, I alternate between working her fast and slow, driving her to the edge of ecstasy again.

"Too much," she rasps, her voice strained with desire and need.

Just as she's about to break, I grant her the sweet relief she craves. Her scream echoes through the room as her orgasm crashes over her with force so intense that I'm sure even my brothers outside the door can hear it.

I transition to softer strokes, gently caressing her as she rides the waves of pleasure mixed with a hint of pain. This is only the beginning of the night that awaits us.

"Wesley," she breathes, her voice filled with breathlessness and awe.

I turn her around, lifting her effortlessly and tossing her onto the bed. She's laid limp like helpless prey wanting to be devoured. Crawling towards her with deliberate slowness, I watch her eyes come to life again.

I yearn to claim her, to make her mine every day, but more importantly, I want to protect her. I want Sol to know that I am not just the walls of her cage, but her shield against the world. I am determined to keep her safe and free her from the clutches of Manus Dei and those who would abuse her.

I strip her of her clothes, peeling her soaking wet panties off, then I discard them onto the floor without a second thought. Her blue eyes watch me intently, the bliss of her orgasm fading and curiosity taking its place. She pushes up on her elbows and cups my face, her lips parting but no words escaping.

I know, little mouse, I know.

Words are inadequate to convey the depth of emotions flowing between us. It can't be defined.

All I have are my actions, and I demonstrate my devotion through my every touch.

My jaw clenches at the mere thought of her leaving me.

Sol was right. I do fear.

I want to purge it from my body, and the only way to do that is to have Sol under me with my cock buried deep inside her.

I guide her down, hovering above her, creating a cage of my arms and legs around her delicate form. I am acutely aware of her fragility, and a silent warning reverberates in my mind, reminding me to be gentle with her.

Sol's swollen lips part, and in a soft murmur, she reassures me. "It's okay," she whispers. "I'm scared, too." Her fingers grasp my jaw, slowly trailing up to scratch my scalp, her touch simultaneously comforting and arousing. The intensity of our connection frightens her, as it does me, but it also kindles a fire that refuses to be extinguished.

Rubbing my erection between her folds is torture for me as I coat it with her arousal. She's so wet and swollen.

Taking Sol should be a sin. No one should feel this good.

Her fingernails claw down my back. She pushes her hips up and begins to rotate them until I slowly sink my tip inside her.

We lock eyes as she guides me deeper. It's a rare tine I allow her the control.

There is no feeling like this. Euphoria doesn't even come close to describing it.

"You're so tight, so wet for me."

Her teeth sink into her bottom lip. I could orgasm just like this without even moving. Buried deep, holding my breath as I watch her face. The struggles to adjust to my size, a mix of pain and pleasure furrowing her brow.

Normally, I would kiss away her pain, but not this time. I want her to feel everything—the pleasure I can give her and the agony of its absence if she ever tries to leave me.

"I need you, Wesley." She whispers as she rocks, trying to bury me deep enough to feel her heart. "Yes, yes, please. God, please don't leave me." Her hands cup my face, "Don't you want this?

Me. Give it up and run away with me. I'll let you have me any way you want." She clenches her pussy.

Oh, you're the devil. I almost give in. What man wouldn't? She's trying to claim my soul.

"Wesley," She presses.

"I will have you any way I want. You'll always be mine, little mouse."

Sol is right. Our love is sick. It doesn't fit the definition of a good or healthy love found in novels. It's all-consuming. I'm shaping her to be selfish, to possess and obsess over me just as intensely as I do over her. I need Sol to depend on me so she stops running and confronts the cold, hard truth.

Her life belongs to me.

She takes a deep breath, and her erect nipples press against my chest. In that moment, I witness the shock of reality crossing her face. She has come to the realization that she *could* survive without me, but she cannot truly *live* without me.

Survival and living are two distinct things. Survival is filled with desperation, constant struggle, and ceaseless fighting. Survival is a game, and my little mouse is exhausted from playing.

Running is survival.

Fighting is living.

She yearns to truly live, to experience peace, happiness, and harmony. She craves safety and, above all, normalcy. I can provide her with that. No more games between us—just the two of us embracing our unique definition of love.

A solitary tear escapes from Sol's sky-blue eyes. The heavens cry.

I lean down and kiss it, then press my lips to hers, allowing her to taste the saltiness of her own tear.

I'm uncertain whether she's crying because she has come to accept our love or because she struggles to come to terms with it.

I pull out slowly, then push in fast. The next time I pull out of Sol's wetness fast, then sink in slowly. I watch her fight dwindle; she becomes putty in my hands.

This is torture for me, too. She is so tight and wet that she has erased every other woman before her. Before Sol, it was just fucking. The first time Sol and I had sex, it was like I was the virgin, not her. The experience was completely new to me. It was the first time I was with someone I truly cherished. I wanted to ensure Sol was prepared and she wasn't a quick fuck or one-night stand. This woman would be my wife, my queen, one day.

Every time we made love, I tried to convey that to her. I wanted to take her to new heights and make her dependent on me. We both came together the first time I claimed her virginity.

This time it differs from the others. She finally realizes how important she is to me, so much so that her mind can not process it. When she comes, it's so hard that she passes out.

I gently pull out of her and stare at her realizing I didn't wear a condom this time. My seed is dripping out of her, and I love the sight. I push it back inside of her.

I don't know if she is on birth control, but I hope she isn't. I want to see her belly round with my child.

I kiss her lips and nudge her jaw with the tip of my nose, "little mouse," I purr. Her eyes began to flutter open, and a wide smile spreads across her face. Death has a spell over her, and the part of me that is Wes is jealous.

She is ours. I tell myself. Sol belongs to all the voices inside my head.

Chapter 35

Sol

I'm tempted to reach out and run my index finger over his bare chest. Like licking icing off a cake. Smooth tan skin lays before my eyes like a temptation no woman should face. Wes can tempt me in ways I have never been swayed before. You want my soul? Take it. You want me on every surface of this room? Have me. You want to make love to me so hard I pass out? You don't need to ask. Just do it.

Not that he would ask.

A dark trail of hair starts just below his belly button then disappears under the sheet that barely covers him. I sink my teeth into my lip and stop myself.

Don't wake the sleeping beast.

I've laid awake many nights wondering if what Wes and I have is love or lust. After studying all my feelings and reactions, I know lust would have worn off long ago. Lust can't survive betrayal or games. It's short-sighted, whereas love is an endless journey.

I'm madly in love with my stalker, and our devotion might drive us to insanity when I leave.

Wes still thinks I'm going to try and run *after* the mission.

You're wrong, baby. I will run during the mission after I get what I need.

His square jaw is finally relaxed, and his dark eyebrows are stress-free. I wish I could paint him like this, capture this fleeting moment before the game takes it from me.

We slept with the window open, the stars and moon shining over the mountain. I always wanted to sleep with open windows, but Luna never allowed me. She said the monsters of the mountain would sneak inside.

Digging my toes into the sheet, I glance over at my monster. He found me and will never let me go.

I hope he forgives me. I must survive without him because he can't give me what I need: a life away from Manus Dei.

He woke me up two more times. The first time, he spread my legs open wide and made me come on his mouth before thrusting deep inside me. Then he wanted me on top. I looked down at him until I was forced to throw my head back in passion. His eyes looked up at me like I was an angel in the sky.

Rolling on my side, I feel the tender bruises forming on my hips from his grip. I smirk. Those bruises will still be present when I go on my mission. The gift of his presence when I'm on the mission.

It's not right to call when we did sex. It was much deeper, a vast desperation each of us tried to make the other understand. We did grasp the message, but we were each too stubborn to bend a knee to one another.

Wesley is in a deep sleep, his breathing undisturbed as I slip out of bed. Our luggage is downstairs, so I grab the first thing I find: his oversized undershirt, which drapes over me like a short dress.

Silently, I make my way to the door. Glancing back, I see him still sleeping soundly as I turn the doorknob.

In moments like this, I wish I had socks so my footsteps would be silent. I want to snoop around before anyone wakes up.

Gabriel and War haven't made any sounds, so they must still be asleep. I didn't hear either of them last night. It makes one wonder what they were up to on the first floor of the apartment.

I don't waste my time exploring the rooms we walked past earlier. I find another long hallway with three doors; using my heightened hearing, I conclude two rooms are most likely bedrooms.

Behind door number one, I hear the fast pace of typing on a keyboard. It must be War's room. He's up early, no doubt, working on our final mission. I tiptoed past the door I believed to be Gabriel's bedroom. No sounds come from it, so I take my chances and keep walking.

The last door I risk opening, and lucky for me, it appears to be another guest room. I step inside, but the hair on my arms rises.

No stale scent lingers in the air. It's been used recently. I walk to the bed, but the sheets are perfectly crisp.

Looking up, I scan the dark room for signs of a person, but there are no belongings.

"The third bookshelf," a voice startles me, its proximity right next to my ear. I bite my cheek, feeling the metallic tang of blood. Swiftly turning around, my eyes meet War's.

How did he do that? I have upgraded hearing. I should have heard him!

You're underestimating the players, Sol. Don't be silly, I hear Luna whisper in my head.

My hand instinctively rests over my racing heart as my breathing steadies.

War flashes me that notorious grin he wears when he's on the verge of betraying his brothers. His lips tug up higher on the left side, his left eye narrowed in unison. Casually crossing his arms, he raises an eyebrow in a challenging manner.

I take a moment to assess him, my gaze sweeping up and down his figure clad in a sleek gray three-piece suit.

"Do you sleep in a suit?" I quip, raising an eyebrow in mock surprise. It's not every day you stumble upon someone donning a three-piece suit complete with tie and pocket square, especially not before the crack of dawn in a secluded safe house where fashion is the least of our concerns.

Besides, here I am, wearing nothing but Wes's shirt.

"Wouldn't you like to know?" he purrs. "Tick, tock, mouse, or is it 'little mouse'? That's what my brother prefers, doesn't he? Keeping you small so you fit snugly in his cage."

I edge back slightly, sensing a mix of danger and manipulation in the air. "What do you want?"

"So many, many things," He inhales deeply before releasing an exhausted breath. "For now, I want you to walk over to the third bookshelf. Tell me what you find."

I cross my arms.

He waves his hands in an impatient gesture. "Hurry up. They'll wake up soon," he hisses.

Fine, I'll bite. Walking to the bookshelf, I feel his presence at my back.

"I'm surprised you can walk straight after the night you had." He jests. "Such a passionate scream when my brother makes you come."

I roll my eyes. "Jealous? When's the last time you made someone scream from pleasure, not your presence?"

He snickers, "Look at our little mouse grow. Just don't spread your wings too hastily. You don't want to get shot down."

"You'd be wise not to make me your enemy, War. A pawn can become a queen."

"A pawn doesn't need to become a queen to kill one."

I glance at him over my shoulder. "True. The puppeteer just needs to make a mistake." That's the only way a pawn can get close enough to the queen without her killing it first.

He nods towards the bookshelf, "What do you see?"

I look. Books in pristine condition line the shelf. Unlike the weathered volumes in the previous safe house, these books appear untouched, their spines uncreased. Each book is bound in black leather, devoid of any titles—purely ornamental.

My eyes continue to scan until I spot a peculiar change in spines. Without my enhanced vision, I might have missed this subtle detail. On the second shelf, one book stands out. Its spine bears an embossed logo.

Intrigued, I approach and run my fingers over the embossed emblem, tracing its pattern with narrowed eyes.

"Manus Dei," I say aloud, recognizing the design—a tree ensnared by its own roots.

"A slight pull will do the trick," War adds. Amusement on his lips.

Without hesitation, I seize the book and exert a gentle tug.

The entire bookshelf springs open, revealing a short, brightly illuminated hallway.

"I estimate you have about twenty minutes before Gabriel awakens. Perhaps even less before Wes wants to fuck you again. He likes to fuck when he's stressed. Don't we all." He adjusts his tie.

He's trying to get under my skin because, as Wes pointed out, the woman War desires isn't exactly within his grasp.

It works. Instantly, I wonder who Wes fucked in the past before he hunted me.

The new me, the braver one, replies, "In that case, your hand must be sore. Don't overwork it; we need your hand to hack into the security system. It would be ashamed to fumble the mission because your palm was too sore from being wrapped around your dick."

His teeth gnash. "Good. You're going to need that attitude to survive what lies ahead," he mutters as he turns.

I can't help but feel like he hinted at a secret I have yet to uncover.

I take a deep breath and cautiously step forward. The blinding light floods the hallway, with every surface gleaming in pristine white, from the glossy marble floor to the marbled walls.

The short hallway leads to a new room. A room made of thick glass. A cage.

The person in the cage makes my feet stumble, and I instinctively take a step back.

A steel-framed twin bed is bolted to the floor, its thin mattress devoid of any covering or sheets.

The room within the glass exudes a cold and unwelcoming atmosphere, a cruel trap for its prisoner. The glaring overhead light is so intense that sleep would be impossible in this sterile environment.

Chills ripple down my arms as I wrap them around myself, my entire body covered in goosebumps. A cold sweat blisters on my forehead.

I never want to be confined in such a place.

As I approach, my feet grow clammy, sticking to the white marble floor. I rub my eyes in disbelief, trying to comprehend what I'm witnessing. Could this be a hallucination, a product of my mind plunging into the depths of despair?

No, it's real. War led me here intentionally.

With trembling steps, I move closer, my body just a foot away from the glass wall. I plant my feet firmly, yet my upper body leans forward in fascination.

It's me.

The body lying on the bed is mine—my thin legs, the curve of my calves. The figure is clad in plain clothing, and my long blonde hair is gathered messily in a bun. My own face rests on the pillow, completely unaware of my presence.

Forgetting my proximity to the glass, my feet propel me forward, and I collide with it, creating a resounding thud. But the glass remains unyielding, unbroken. It's far thicker and stronger than I am.

Frustrated, I clench my fist and pound on it, desperately searching for a door, yet none is in sight.

How can I reach her?

Who am I looking at? Which Reflection is this?

Although her body remains motionless, her eyes open as she awakens from my futile attempts. She sits up, and I meet her gaze.

In those blue eyes, I see the predatory glint of a lioness, unimpressed by the spectators observing her in a cage. It's a look I was never born with, but Luna was.

Yet this can't be Luna.

No.

It's Klara.

My palm freezes against the glass, and at this moment, I'm grateful for its barrier. Stepping back, I swallow the dry lump in my throat.

Klara moves with graceful ease, akin to a wild cat stretching after a deep slumber.

Do I resemble her? Could I possibly reflect this Reflection?

She locks eyes with me, her gaze piercing mine. In her silence, she seems to pose the very same question.

Can you reflect me?

Chapter 36

Sol

Klara stands and stretches once again, before closing the distance between us.

I shake my head, feeling a sense of trepidation as her smile widens. That smile speaks volumes, conveying her judgment of me. Her piercing blue eyes study me, finding me lacking in her approval.

That reaction causes me to doubt myself, and I glance down at my bare legs, clad only in Wes's shirt. I imagine I must look thoroughly ravaged, used not just by Wes but by everyone.

Klara sees the puppet still attached to the strings.

Attempting to compose myself, I raise my hand to smooth my hair. Klara laughs, mocking my efforts.

"You're trying too hard," she remarks, her giggle echoing in the air. My fingers tingle as they run through my knots. "Tsk, tsk."

She steps closer, pressing her body against the glass. I instinctively take another step back.

"You know I want what they want," she states, squaring her shoulders. "But they don't believe me."

"I'm accustomed to deceitful words, Klara," I take my time now, tugging through my knots until my hair is smooth. My mask looks more put together. "*They* can be the Masters or Astrid, not necessarily the Horsemen. So tell me, Klara, who did you mean when you said 'they'?"

She grins and raises a brow. "Touché. I'll admit a truce. I want what the Horsemen want."

"That could be another trick. In theory, everyone wants Manus Dei's power, even Astrid."

"So you have grown wiser. Good girl."

She begins to pace the length of the glass wall, her eyes locked onto mine as she moves within the confines of her cage. "I could do this so easily; kill her. I don't think you can," she taunts, then stops abruptly and slaps her palms against the glass. The sound startles me, and I curse myself for showing Klara a glimpse of my fear. "Can you?" she challenges. "Are you ready?"

With Klara's final words, something shifts within her. The predator retreats, and genuine concern replaces it.

For a brief moment, I question my initial assessment. Was I mistaken? Did I misjudge her? In that split second, I almost saw Luna. The way my sister used to look at me before my father subjected me to testing. Genuine anxiety for a person you love, a person you consider weaker than you.

I snort and shake my head, admitting, "You're good." Klara possesses an incredible talent for emulating my sister. I have to give her that. She can pretend to be Luna better than I ever could.

That's why War led me to this cage. Virtual reality can only reveal so much. I walked in Klara's shoes, but now I must observe Klara as Astrid would.

Her entire existence revolved around her obsession, studying Luna relentlessly. Not her false loyalty to a Master she loathed. She clung by Astrid's side merely for survival.

Smart.

In contrast, I sought to understand my sister, not idolize her. Klara is the superior player in portraying Luna, but I don't have to be my sister. I have to be Klara.

Chapter 37

Gabriel

"I don't like this," Death grunts, his footsteps echoing his irritation as he paces the room.

It's the first time I've seen my brother nervous.

Within seconds of observing Death and Sol's interactions, I realized it wasn't just a fling. I used to watch Luna the same way. Deep, unshakeable, an animalistic attraction that only men like my brothers and I could understand.

When you've witnessed death as much as we have, you fiercely protect and confine those you love.

If the roles were reversed, I'd react the same way. Actually, I'd probably be even worse. I'd go to any lengths to protect Luna.

But I never expected that I'd need to protect Luna from herself. That's where I failed, in my grand failure to consider every angle.

I thought the threat only came from the Masters, so I plotted their removal. Such naiveté, right?

"Sol needs this. You agreed to this," I tell Death. "Klara can't harm her."

Death ceases his pacing and cracks his right index finger, his trigger finger. "Physically," he corrects me. "But we don't know how meeting Klara will mentally impact Sol."

"I need to be certain," I insist, jerking my chin up.

Something felt off when I encountered Klara. Then again, there's always something off with Luna's Reflections. My brothers believe it's my mind playing tricks on me, that my emotions are clouding the facts.

I shake my head, reminding myself that these two women are not Luna.

We all watch as Sol reaches out and touches the bulletproof glass. Klara mirrors her gesture, pressing her palm against Sol's.

Death's shoulders tense with a laborious inhale. "Klara can't touch her," I reaffirm.

They remain frozen, gazes locked on each other. "Why are you here?" Sol asks Klara, her voice calm, but I detect a hint of concern between her words.

Why would she ask that? She knows I needed to cage Klara so she could change places with her.

"That's a silly question," Klara responds. *Exactly.*

Death glances at me, but I ignore him.

Klara carefully chose those words because Luna used to repeat that sentence to Sol. She is trying to provoke and confuse me too

There is a slight tremble in the tips of my fingers. A sign of emotions and anxiety that was never there before. Fisting my hands, I conceal it from my brothers.

I find it utterly peculiar that Sol and Klara insist on pressing their delicate hands against the glass while chatting away.

I glance at War and Death, but they seem oblivious. Maybe I'm just being my usual overanalyzing, detail-obsessed self.

Sol nods in agreement. "I suppose it is." Narrowing my eyes I watch as Sol presses her palm harder into the bulletproof glass. Klara mirrors her actions.

"Do you see that?"

War clears his throat and interjects, "Conquest, calm the fuck down. You're worst than Death. Klara is playing Sol, attempting to establish an emotional connection so that Sol can help her escape. I guarantee it."

I turn my attention to Death, who nods in agreement. "It's a mind game."

They both stop scrutinizing the screens and fix their gazes on me as if I'm losing my mind. Ignoring their judgment, I focus on the screen, observing Sol and Klara intently.

"I'm not crazy," I hiss. The weight of their eyes hits me heavily.

"We never said you were," War clarifies. "You're still grieving."

I hate that word. Grieving! The hell I am. How do you grieve someone who lied to you, who never truly loved you? You don't. You abhor them.

"Do you have a better question, one not so silly?" Klara asks.

"I have many questions for you," Sol responds. Her narrow shoulders relax, and she leans her weight on her right foot, causing Wes's shirt to shift higher on her hips. If you look closely, you can catch a glimpse of her ass peeking out from beneath it. The same ass Luna had. The same body I can never touch again.

"Eyes up, brothers," Death growls in warning.

"It's not like Gabriel hasn't seen that exact ass before, Death," War jokes. He's one of the rare few who didn't fall head over boots for one of Luna's sisters.

Death strides across the room and smacks War on the head. "Sol isn't Luna or Klara. She is mine."

I used to call someone mine…

Klara tilts her head, redirecting our attention to the monitors. Her gaze shifts to the left, then encompasses every camera in the room. Sol follows her movements and grasps Klara's implied message. Klara knows we are listening. She is warning Sol.

"Why would Klara care?" I bark.

War sighs. "Calm the fuck down. It's her. Everything matches. There is only one other Reflection of Luna who escaped."

"And we haven't located her yet," I hiss, tugging at my roots.

Death steps closer. "That woman is Klara, and she's trying to manipulate the facts. Don't let her fuck with you. Trust War and me as your council. Trust us with this."

I rub the back of my neck. "I know." Tension remains rooted within my body, mounting with each passing moment.

Klara has succeeded in playing mind games with me. When I captured her, she adopted small mannerisms that Luna used to have. So much so that I caved and kissed her, my hands wrapped around her throat, taking her air as I claim the wrong lips.

I didn't tell my brothers.

Death would never trust me to be alone with Sol if I had.

I'm not going crazy! I'm not like my failed clones. This is what Klara wants! Fuck her! "I want to strangle her," I grunt.

"If you do that, we'll lose Famine," War asserts, pushing back in his seat.

"We've already lost him." I point at Klara. "He is fighting for a soulless monster. Klara is an empty shell that mimics others. Famine can't love that."

"You don't believe that," War punches my shoulder. "We don't abandon our brothers."

"Famine has lost his way. We agreed to let him find his own path back to us," Death declares. "When Luan's pawns fail, Famine will rejoin us. If he wants to try and save Klara, that's up to him. You won't take that from him," his words a firm order.

"We agreed to let him go his own way," War adds.

"I know what we agreed to," I bite.

This game has taken so much from me. My friends, Reflections of myself, my brother, but above all, the love of my life. Luna was the reason I entered this game.

I run my hand through my blonde hair. "Sometimes I wonder why I'm still fighting. Part of me thinks it would be easier to let Astrid win, to give her complete control." I'm just so fucking tired.

War's demeanor shifts, and he blinks rapidly. "You don't believe that." He strides forward and grabs me by the shoulders. "The end is within sight. Yes, we're weary, but we can't lose hope now."

I meet his gaze. He's always so composed and confident, always wearing his armor. "You're not weary?"

War grins. "I'm War. I thrive on this."

"Maybe you should be the leader once we kill Astrid,"

War shakes his head. "This is a brotherhood, and we rule together. A democracy. We all agreed that your face is much more lovable. Everyone loves a blonde, Conquest. You're the face. I'm the brains. Death is the muscle." War jokes, but his laughter fades, and his eyes search mine for authenticity.

"I'm tired of the games within games, endlessly layered," I mutter.

War digs his fingers into my shirt. "We will take the lead. We will clean this mess up. In the midst of the battle, don't lose focus, brother. I haven't. I will bring our family back together."

I turn away from him, focusing my gaze on Sol. "You're right." Sol and all the innocents are the reason I must persevere.

"We're going to finish this." Death declares.

I survey the small room. This is my family. Not everyone is here. Some have left, some perished, while others have run away, but this is who I'm fighting for. If Astrid triumphs, she will systematically kill them, one by one, saving me for last.

I will never allow that to happen. A renewed vigor surges through me.

Klara's existence has been a source of torment. After Luna died, she started playing her mind games with me. Leaking information about Astrid, info we vetted as true, while she remained hidden in the tunnels.

Klara told us she wants what Luna wants, including killing Astrid. Yet, she could have accomplished it if she truly desired Astrid's death. That's why I will never trust Klara, and that's why I'll make her my scapegoat.

My brothers and I must assume control of Manus Dei. Like War said, they are forcing me to be the face. Probably so I can't give up and take the easy way out like Luna.

People are much more inclined to follow a leader who ascends to the throne amicably rather than through brute force. It's a simple matter of finesse and sophistication. The throne has always been rightfully mine, and now it's time to claim it.

As for Klara, I haven't decided what to do with her afterwards. I suppose I could hand her over to Famine if he comes back to us.

"They think I'm a loose cannon. That's why they assigned you this mission," Klara begins to speak. "You're the stable one, the control. Did they reveal who you truly reflect?"

"Yes," Sol responds.

Klara tilts her head. "How does that make you feel?"

Sol taps her index finger against the glass. "Why did you want to embody my sister?"

This is the first time I've witnessed Sol take charge of a situation. She becomes the interrogator, surpassing Klara. Luna would be proud of her.

Not that it matters now.

"She's ready," War voices.

"We don't need to let this continue," Death asserts. "Sol is ready, and that is Klara." He walks toward me. "I understand your suspicions. Klara portrayed Luna so convincingly, at times too convincingly. Your mind would do anything to bring Luna back, but physically, you cannot. Luna is dead. Don't let Klara manipulate your mind. She dedicated her entire life to becoming her idol. That's what she's doing, what she did when you captured her. She's trying to confuse you because that's what Astrid ordered her to do."

I nod. Astrid is the devil incarnate, and like the fallen angel I resemble, I will wipe her from this earth, and then my brothers and I will rule it.

Chapter 38

Sol

"I'm not playing this game," I assert. I intend to establish my dominance in this conversation with my next question. After all, I'm not the one trapped in the cage—Klara is.

"Why did you want to embody my sister?" I ask, tapping my finger against the thick glass that separates us. I want to hear Klara's own words, to understand her motives without making assumptions.

Klara doesn't flinch, but I catch her bite her tongue—a subtle gesture, perhaps missed by the room's cameras.

"How have I done so far?" She counters. She won't back down easily, but neither will I. We're both baring our teeth and claws, locked in a battle of wits.

"Luna would be proud," I reply, extending a small mercy toward Klara. I acknowledge that she, too, was a victim—broken and forced to seek the affection of an idol instead of her mother's love.

Offering an olive branch, I test if Klara is willing to grasp it.

She grins, but it's not a genuine, relaxed smile. There's no hint of joy in her eyes at my praise.

"You miss her?" I probe, my voice steady.

She presses her forehead against the glass, her eyes mirror my own emptiness. Without speaking, she moves her mouth, and I have to read her lips. Everything hidden from the cameras. "Don't you?" Klara asks.

I don't reply. To do so would feel like an insult to Luna's memory. Of course, I miss my sister. But Klara's experience cannot be compared to mine. She studied Luna from a distance, while I lived alongside her, experiencing her joys and struggles.

Calm down. Don't let her upset you.

Klara, too, is a victim in this twisted game. She was manipulated and used, just like me.

Instead of lashing out, I offer Klara my own way of coping with grief. "I look in the mirror."

"Hmm," Klara hums, her expression inscrutable. "And how far has that gotten you?" Her words hang in the air, challenging me to confront my own reflections and inner turmoil.

I slide my hand over the chilly glass as if I could cup her face. "I'm here, am I not?" I assert, reflecting on how far I've come from the ignorant girl who once turned her back on Death and chose to remain in ignorance.

Klara taps her forehead gently against the glass. "It seems you are," she remarks. "But one never truly knows who they are looking at in this game. Faces change so often."

I sense a presence behind me, but I don't acknowledge it. Klara continues to study me, and I meet her gaze, uncertain if this will be our last encounter.

"You better run along, little mouse," she says, her words holding a hidden message. "Death has been chasing you for a long time."

Footsteps draw nearer, and without turning, I feel the man whose heart I hold, a treasure I never asked for but now feel compelled to protect.

Death presses himself against my back, his warmth seeping through his thin shirt. He wraps his arm over my chest and another around my stomach, trapping and safeguarding me.

My muscles tense, and Klara notices.

"Klara," he grunts in acknowledgment.

"I could still do this job. Your mouse could be safe," she taunts.

Strong hands tighten their hold on me, a conflicting display of affection and confinement. He tugs me as he steps back but I fight his hold. "Come on, Sol," he urges, no longer giving Klara any attention.

With ease he controls me, turning me away from Klara. I steal one last glance around his solid frame. She remains against the glass wall, watching us, but this time her smile is wide. It's a counterfeit smile, the kind she used to flash to Astrid when I observed her in the virtual reality.

"You think he doesn't cage you because he loves you," Klara shouts, her voice carrying a tinge of bitterness. "But you're still trapped, running in the game they created. Love is the cruelest game of them all, Sol. Ask your sister what it did to her mind. Ask Luna what love felt like."

Feet halt.

I step out of Death's embrace and lock my gaze on her.

Head to head. Eye to eye.

Adrenaline hits me. I feel like I'm soaring down a roller coaster.

The unforgiving, blinding lights in the room don't do her any favors, mercilessly exposing the toll hatred has taken on her.

Klara's complexion looks sickly, and her outlook appears clouded by despair.

"You know what I would ask my sister." I begin, my voice steady. She clenches her jaw as bitterness consumes her. I take a step back, seeking solace in Death's presence. That really pisses her off.

My job is done.

I'm not the puppet that moves when my strings are pulled. She knows that now.

"Why wasn't love enough?" I question, my voice filled with longing. "Why couldn't Luna and Gabriel find a way to both win, rule together, and still love each other? Luna was wrong when she solely blamed Gabriel. They both are at fault."

Klara's eyes turn to sharp slits. "Love is a trick," she spits venomously. "You can't claim a trick as a prize. Luna understood that."

Death's grip tightens on my shoulder as he pulls me from the room. I can't help but rearrange her words in my mind, searching for a hidden message that might hold the key to the truth. She loves to mimic Luna, and we all know how Luna played with words.

Could it be that she was warning me? Perhaps the prize we're all fighting for, Manus Dei's power, is nothing more than a cruel trick.

Is it possible that the real reason Luna initiated this game was something entirely different?

Chapter 39

Sol

Why did the walk back to our room make me feel like I was the guilty one?

Once the door closes, I turn and jab my finger in his chest, "What are you doing with her?" I demand, searching for the truth beneath his gaze.

His face is stern, "You knew we had to catch her."

"And cage her like a lab rat?" I cross my arms. Just because I don't like Klara doesn't mean she deserves to be treated like an animal. It's not her fault she is the way she is. The Horseman are only adding to her reasons to hate others.

"What do you do with a wounded dog?" He counters. "Put it down or try to heal it? My brothers kill but they also protect. Klara will be dealt with accordingly when the time comes. You know how crazy she is. She's lucky Gabriel doesn't have her chained down."

My finger jabs deep into his chest. His skin is burning hot. Lust may darken his eyes, but I won't let it cloud my judgment. I take a step back, determined to get answers.

"Answer me," I insist. "What exactly will you do once you don't need her? I know you won't let her go, but will she be just another puppet for you all to play with?"

"We're not going to harm her," Wes asserts, closing the distance between us. His scent invades me making it hard to concentrate.

I blink. "She's in a cage," I remind him.

Would Gabriel cage me after this is done? Would that be my fate if Wes hadn't claimed me as his.

Always a cage waiting.

A hint of amusement playing on his lips. "And apparently, you're in a cage too, little mouse. How do you like being confined?" His palm covers my stomach before it slips under my shirt.

"Wes." I warn him. *It was a warning not a plead, right?*

His skilled fingers trace up my slit and are soon met with wetness. His nostrils flare, his smile widening, "You like your cage." He taunts me as he pushes one finger inside of me. Using his skills to work my body so I forget our current conversation is pure evil.

"You once told me a cage made you feel safe." He swirls his finger inside of me causing more wetness to surge. One single finger almost breaks me.

Almost.

I don't react. "But Klara doesn't feel safe," I counter, my voice firm.

He leans in, his breath warm against my ear as he curls his finger. "As long as Astrid is alive and holds the power, none of us are truly safe."

The back of my knees hits the mattress. I didn't even realize he was guiding me to the bed.

"You left our room in nothing but my shirt." He growls, slipping his finger free, making me feel empty before he sucks it into his mouth.

Why is that so sexy? It shouldn't be, right? Or is my old self trying to make me feel guilty for wanting his depraved love?

His hand grabs the back of my neck, smashing my lips to his in a punishing kiss. I taste myself on his lips, feeling his fury with every tongue swirl. More than that, I devour his fear. My fear, too.

My hands rise up and grasp him. Deep down, we know our time is almost up. Once Astrid is dead, everything will change.

Everything.

Our love is a major aspect of that change.

"It's your fault," I whisper over his lips. Not just that I only had his shirt to wear but the breaking of our bond as well.

"It's always the villain's fault. The hero never gets blamed."

I roll my lips to hide the tremble of emotions.

You refuse to be my hero; you have cornered me and turned me into a villain as well. Sometimes, I like how it feels, as I'm sure you do. Other times, I have never felt so filthy.

Our kiss slows as we savor the feeling of one another. I press my forehead to his. "What will you do with her once Astrid is dead? Tell me the truth." I press.

"I don't know. She hasn't been acting right."

"Maybe it's because she's in a cage."

He rolls his eyes, "This is the safest place she has ever been. Gabriel wants to run some tests just to make sure Astrid hasn't fucked her up with a new upgrade he doesn't know about. Don't worry about the rest." he admits, his hand reaching to caress my cheek. "I don't want to talk about Klara right now. I want to focus on you. I want to mark every inch of your mind, body, and soul with my touch." He guides me down on the mattress, his legs spread, caging mine in between, trapping me. *I like this cage*. Slowly, he lowers, and his muscles flex. My fingers inch up and glide over them. Involuntary, my legs open for him, caging him just as tightly.

"You once told me that a wild creature can't survive in captivity," I remind him. My fingers trail up his strong thighs until they rest on his hips. Hard. Unmoving strength. Unwilling to leave his brothers for me.

A somber cloud covers his face, making his structured jaw look more angular. Harsh like our passion.

His eyes dilate, the green turning black. They grow distant as his hand wraps around my neck. Fingertips on my pulse. He loves doing this. I just realized why. It's a snare around my neck. He has my heartbeat and my next breath in the palm of his hand. My life.

"Did it help you to see her?" he asks, his grip tightening slightly. Does it upset him if I say yes? Does that make me as monstrous as Klara?

He sinks lower, chest to chest. Soft versus hard.

Something takes hold of me. The need to have his respect. I wrap my hands around his thick neck, gently squeezing until I feel the pulse of his 3D-printed heart. A heart my science helped create.

The muscles in his neck relax under my hold, and his eyes close in pure bliss for a moment.

"I want to give you the world." He utters. Blinking his eyes open, some of the green has returned.

"I don't want the world," a somber grin paints over my face. "I just want you without Manus Dei's power. I just want your love."

"You have it and more."

"The more is too much. It's killing us."

He doesn't look at me.

"These games have given me an excuse to become a monster, a liar, a trickster." *You don't even know the half of it yet, baby.* "I want a new chapter. No science, no quarrels over power. I don't want a crown, riches, or an army. I just want you. Just love."

Luna might have thought it was silly of me to keep trying to win his loyalty. I'll continue to fight and provoke him until I have to turn my back and step into those tunnels.

Love is worth the fight.

My hands slip free until they land on his scarred heart. "Look at me."

He does.

"Do you know why I fell in love with you, Wesley?" That does the trick. Wes's veneer fades; Death vanishes. Wesley and I are alone, and it might be the last time I can reach him this way.

"You make me feel small," I confess. In his eyes, I see a flicker of guilt, a crack in his armor. "Listen to me before you judge my words. When I'm with you, I feel tiny because your presence is so immense. You're like a black storm cloud, embodying Death," I chuckle, overwhelmed by his impact on me. "You make everyone around me feel lifeless. You're all I see. No one else compares to you." Slowly, his green eyes lift in approval, and a warmth blossoms within me, like chestnuts roasting over an open flame. "I know you're always watching over me, and that makes me feel safe. You've deceived me by making me believe I had choices. It was a kind mercy that no one else extended to me. They just forced me." My finger traces the outline of his scar.

His hand slips from my neck and cups my hand over his heart. I continue, pouring out my truths. "Astrid, Manus Dei, Gabriel, and even Luna never gave me the option to play; they all forced me. You gave me an option. Walk with you in the darkness, or go alone and be swallowed by it. That's why I'm still in this game and continue fighting. You grounded me when everyone else who claimed to care about me set me adrift."

At first, I thought I owed everything to my sister, willing to sacrifice my very life for her. I soon realized it would never be enough. Luna didn't care about the price of the game, only about winning at any cost.

It was time to cut my puppet strings. I would leave to forge my own life after this. Not a normal life; that concept no longer exists in my future, not after what I have done.

I long for a future where I don't have to play these games and can grow old alongside someone who isn't involved in Manus Dei. I need a lover who will keep me honest, not one I am forced to lie to.

Can a heart fracture any more than mine?

I wish that person could be Wesley, but he can't let go of his training like Luna. Wesley cannot relinquish Death, and if I allow him to keep that part of himself, it will only bring demise to me.

"I hope that when the dust settles, I'll find you by my side, on the other side," I say, pressing my index finger into his raised scar. The mark reflects us—twisted, rough, and ugly. But in our distorted version of love, there is also beauty and strength, just like the thick skin of his scar.

"I'm not leaving your side," he growls.

But I'm leaving yours. Even with you by my side, I can not survive like this. Running from game to game. Creating more lies to cover up the old ones.

I wonder if Luna knew I would cut the strings and no longer be her puppet?

My thoughts drift into the depths of my mind. And then, unexpectedly, Luna's laughter echoes in my consciousness. Her voice rings clear as she responds, "That's so silly, sister. Of course, I did."

Chapter 40

Sol

"Three guards are stationed here," War points to a map of the entrance of the tunnels in Astrid's house.

I roll my eyes. Does he forget I'm a genetically engineered human? Of course, he does; they all do. That's what makes me so cunning. They all think I'm the twin who was neglected on the sidelines, never trained as thoroughly as Luna.

I'm a fast learner.

Wes, War, Gabriel, and I saunter over to the dining room table, basking in the ostentatious glow of the grand chandelier above. Naturally, War rocks another custom suit. Where he keeps finding these bespoke gems in our safe houses remains a mystery that even my vast knowledge can't crack.

All I want is my makeup, but they can't seem to acquire that for me.

It grates on my nerves how War's perpetually poised. I'm tempted to snatch a pair of sewing shears and slice his perfectly tailored sleeve right off. There's something strikingly dissimilar about War compared to his other brothers. Maybe the boy-next-door grin gets him a free pass for every audacious move he makes.

His true skill lies in effortlessly navigating all sides, manipulating with such finesse that you'd think he invented the art of trickery.

"You always say hi–" War continues.

Flicking my hair back and securing it in a low bun, I pinch the bridge of my nose and interrupt him. "Klara always says hello to Erick, wearing a malicious grin that puts him on edge and keeps him at a distance. I'm well aware of that. And once I'm in the tunnels, Astrid has stationed a guard outside her office named Daniel. He searches Klara for weapons."

We're working with outdated intel from Klara's last virtual reality transmission a month ago. It's a risk, but it's the best information we have. We can't fully trust Klara and the information she provides.

I delve into further details to assuage War's anxiety. "Interestingly, Klara never looks at Daniel or acknowledges him. It's peculiar because she's usually inclined to poke and provoke, but with this guard, her eyes remain fixated on a crack in the stone above Astrid's office door. I've seen it through her eyes countless times during virtual reality sessions. I know exactly where that crack is. I know what I'm doing." I stress.

"She is ready. Let's call it a night," Wes agrees, his hands rubbing my shoulders. Yet, I can sense Gabriel's gaze fixated on Wes's touch, a subtle tension brewing in the room.

Gabriel is the most enigmatic player in this twisted game. He oscillates between wanting to kill me and seeking to protect me, often flipping roles. He uses me as a pawn, a trophy to fill the void left by Luna's absence. In rare moments, he assumes a brotherly role, becoming visibly irritated and uncomfortable when Wes is near me.

Tonight marks the final sunset before I must embody Klara. The impending battle looms, thick with anxiety that permeates the air like dense humidity. It clings to the skin, frizzes hair, and coats the body in a sheen of warm, damp sweat.

The battle is coming.

I've spent the entire week meticulously studying the layout of Astrid's mansion. I've memorized the placement of every camera, the ones I must evade, and the specific security feeds that War can manipulate.

Tomorrow, lives will hang in the balance, including mine.

I know the names of every guard, their patrol patterns, and even the number of steps they take during each perimeter check. I'm intimately familiar with the location of the tunnel entrance and Astrid's hidden office, thanks to my virtual reality experiences.

"You got this," Wes encourages, though it's unnecessary, considering I'm about to shatter their plan.

My ultimate scheme reaches far beyond their expectations. Once I incapacitate Astrid with the nerve agent, I will swiftly advance to the server room, where I'll seize the coveted master hard drives that carry the encryption codes on them. Then, I'll have less than five minutes to leave the office and venture into a new tunnel before Wes arrives to finish Astrid.

I'll walk through the same tunnels that Luna used, which leads me back to where this all started. My father's house.

It's the perfect place to hide, a layered dollhouse with numerous secret rooms.

You see, when Luna and my father were away playing their game in the tunnels, I was left at home. That gave me a lot of time, a lot of time to sneak around.

Among the array of rooms I could seek refuge in, only a select few are privy to the existence of the secret spot concealed within an old servant's quarter—a desolate linen closet that doubles as a hidden door leading to a panic room. Stocked with food supplies to last for months. Its walls are so thick that they thwart any attempts to breach the room's security, making it an impenetrable fortress against Wi-Fi signals and rendering the tracking chip inside of me utterly useless.

All I have to do is get to that room and close the door. I can decide when to communicate with them. I'll have all the power.

That knowledge doesn't make me feel bigger or wiser; it makes me feel sick. This is what it has come down to: a game supposedly started to save us all from Astrid's evil agenda, and now we are all fighting.

If they don't agree to my terms, I will resort to blackmail, leveraging the threat of destroying the codes that will unlock all of Manus Dei's science again.

A part of me wants to destroy it all. Maybe I will...maybe I won't.

War briefly exits the room, only to reappear with a sizable suitcase. He carelessly drops it onto the table, seemingly indifferent to any potential damage to the wood. His fingers leisurely drum the suitcase's surface, a mischievous glint in his eyes that's almost teasing. Could he unzip it any more slowly?

As he leisurely tugs the zipper like the cat that got the cream, my anticipation builds to the point where I'm practically on tiptoes, eager to catch a glimpse of what's inside.

The lid tips open, and nostalgia washes over me as I lunge forward, delving into the case, my fingers rediscovering my beloved makeup brushes and cherished palettes. My tools to paint lies.

Among them, I find a pair of nondescript black running shoes, gray leggings, a black t-shirt, a worn black leather jacket, and a belt.

"You're going to need your paint to make them believe you're Klara," War remarks. "And these are the usual clothes she wears."

"You should practice," Gabriel finally speaks. It's an insult. He still thinks I'm the weak twin. That's good; that means he hasn't figured everything out yet. I've played my part too well.

Are you proud, Luna? Will you be proud when I betray your pawns, too?

I tilt my head, and my hand stills on the ruby red lipstick color that Klara wears when she isn't in the tunnels. Klara doesn't wear red when she visits her mother. Any strong resemblance to Luna tends to make Astrid bitter. It's ironic since Klara, Luna, and I are physical mirrors of each other, but one swipe of color can dramatically alter the canvas.

"I don't need to practice," I reply sharply.

"Are you sure?" War retorts.

My eyes don't leave Gabriel. Those dark circles under his eyes are getting more pronounced. Stress is eating away at him, like a starving lion so close to its next meal you can see him salivating.

Spite sparks within me. Gone is the boy who guided me in his one cruel way as a child, a boy who loved Luna; replaced is a man with ashes for a heart.

This grief could have been avoided. That fact makes me lash out.

My lips tug up in a malicious grin. It must be so infuriating for him to be so close to claiming the crown but having to rely on me.

"I could ruin this all for you." I taunt. I can't help it. It's not just me playing the part of the broken sister who struggles to go along with this plan. That lie is easy to swallow. A part of me wants to hurt Gabriel still. Not only him but Luna, who saved me, protected me but used me.

I want them to hurt.

Is that wrong?

I feel Wes step closer, his chest spoons my back. A warmth spreads over me and tries to blanket my coldness. It works.

That's wrong of me to think.

Klara, Gabriel and Luna just don't know any better. They can't ask because asking makes them weak.

Wes's touch serves as a reminder. It ignites a love within me that vanquishes my cruelty.

Gabriel parts his lips, but then his shoulders relax as he speaks, "You won't, because if you do, then all of us will die. Me," he shrugs, but I catch a glimpse of pain in his eyes as he continues, "which I'm sure doesn't bother you today, but it will in the future. War, Klara, and Wes. Trust me, I know what it's like to lose your lover." His eyes grow black as he steps closer to me, sneering, "You'll never survive. Not all the lies in the world could take the despair away, Sol." Turning on his heels, he hisses, "All our lives and futures are resting in your hands, Sol. Go ahead, fuck it up. I sure could use a good long rest. It's up to you. You can play this round whichever way you want, but there is only one outcome where you and the man you claim to love walk away alive. Play *my* game or die like Luna did," He taunts.

Wes's grip on me tightens. He is my shield but also the wall blocking me from running, forever torn between his loyalty to the Horsemen and his love for me.

"Well," War sighs, shaking his head, "That was unnecessary. I enjoy the taunting, little mouse, but you have to master the art of timing. Now isn't the time to mess with him." His eyes linger in a beat of disapproval before he goes after Gabriel.

Wes turns me around, his touch both firm and gentle, striking a balance that would make Goldilocks proud. He tilts my chin upward, locking his eyes onto mine.

"I wanted to make him worry," I admit, grasping his forearms for support. "I don't know why I do that. I don't like the person this game has forced me to become." My chin dips, and I press my forehead to his heart, "I miss being that ignorant girl you first hunted. Life was so simple then."

His hand rubs gentle circles on my lower back. "No, little mouse, it wasn't. The same problems were painted all over the walls. You just chose to paint over them. Now, you can't. We will face it all together."

Exhaustion hits me. "I do love you," I declare. My throat starts to thicken.

"I know," he utters, kissing the top of my head. *Not what I wanted to hear.*

My eyelids grow weary. All I want is to crawl into bed and sleep. I don't want to think about tomorrow or the risks or weight of the future. It's not just our lives in my hands tomorrow but the world. Manus Dei has started a game where everyone will be a player eventually. Innocent people with no idea genetic manipulation is possible will have to play and battle against genetically upgraded soldiers.

"Hey," Wes tips my chin up again, "It's going to be ok." Grabbing my hand he leads us to our room, pausing at the door, "Leave it all out there, ok." He orders me in a gentle voice he rarely shows.

"Isn't that the ignorant path to take?" I joke but my voice sounds dead. So empty.

He grabs the hem of my shirt and pulls it above my head, "This is the last night you will feel like this. Tomorrow night you will be free."

He unbuttons my pants and undresses me, only to press his forehead to my stomach as he kisses me there. The gesture so caring it makes my knees tremble.

"Free in your cage," I speak the truth. "And when will you be free, Wes?" My hands sweep through his hair. He purrs in satisfaction.

He stands, his shadow enveloping me, and the quietness in the room intensifies, making my heart race.

He didn't say he loved me back. He's choosing his brothers over me.

Vulnerably clogs my throat and tears my eyes, but instead of covering up, I move my trembling fingers to unzip his jeans, tugging them off. His gaze remains guarded, yet intense, as he peels his shirt away. His next exhale becomes my inhale. Heat grows in my stomach and then pools between my legs. Our eyes lock, brimming with desire and anger at one another. My eyes hungrily roam down his sculpted form, his movements mirroring mine.

He scoops me up into his arms, effortlessly carrying me towards the bed, and with each step, my heart beats in rhythm with his thumping footsteps. The strength and tenderness he displays now are a striking departure from the lethal aura he typically exudes as Death. In this moment, he sheds that persona and becomes simply Wesley—the man who knows my heart intimately.

He gently lowers me onto the center of the bed. "I need you," I whisper. I'm throbbing for him. An escape. One last night before I destroy all their plans.

"Tell me what you need," his voice thick with lust; his eyes drift down to my breast, my peeked nipples pulsing for his fingers and mouth.

I grasp one, pinching and rubbing it, imagining it's him. His eyes darken. I purse my lips. My touch isn't enough. How will I survive without him?

"Make me forget. Make me only feel you." In this moment, there are no games, no roles to play. It's just him and me, two souls entwined in a fiery embrace, seeking solace and pleasure amidst the chaos that surrounds us.

"I'll give you everything you need." His eyes are glued to my erect nipples. "I'm free when I'm with you. You are the only escape I have, Sol." He puts his knee on the mattress, then the other. It dips under his weight as he crawls to me. His hot breath warms my cold nipple before he sucks it into his mouth. My back arches, pushing it deep. He releases it with a pop, then licks the center of my chest till his lips devour my mouth. I taste the salt of my skin on his tongue. "You want freedom so badly; I do, too. You will never give up the idea of being free, nor will I. That's why I can never let you go. You're my escape." He growls before his knees nudge my legs open.

"Let me in. Let me give you want you want."

My legs fall open. One thrust, and he's home.

Home. Inside of me. All I ever wanted was a home. A place I was safe and loved. I have it, but now I will ruin it by burning it to the ground. Shaking our foundation when I betray him.

A tear falls from my eye, then another and another, until I'm crying. My hips matching his thrusts as we each race to chase our climax.

I want Wes to be free, but that means I'll be caged.

Like Gabriel and Luna's love, one must suffer for the other to flourish. One must win, and the other lose.

Like my twin, I can't accept losing. I have to win because I need to put myself first. I must leave these games. That means leaving Wes and taking his only reprieve away from him. He will have to suffer for me to be free.

My absence will force Wes to evolve into a new kind of beast. Someone much more deadly. His absence in my life will cause me to evolve, too. I'm unsure if I will become a version of Gabriel or worse...Astrid.

Chapter 41

Sol

Silence clings to the walls of the bathroom. It's the calm right before the storm. The wind is starting to pick up the pace, and if you listen carefully, you can hear it begin to howl.

I'll truly go insane if I stand in the quiet any longer! Pushing the headphones deep into my ear until the point of pain, I scroll through Luna's playlist. I can't select a song, though. Whispering in my mind is my sister's voice.

I yank the headphones out, set the iPod down, and do what I must. I find my compass, and it points directly at Luna's memory buried in my mind.

"I haven't spoken to you in a while," I whisper. My eyes can't look in the mirror because I know this is wrong—to speak to my own reflection while pretending it's my twin. I sigh and pick up the nude lipstick, but I pause right before I paint my lips.

I need to make sure Astrid opens her office door. She's anticipating an update from Klara, but there's never a guarantee she'll accept her visit. I've witnessed Astrid's power plays during my rare appearances in virtual reality, where she would summon Klara to her office only to dismiss her as a display of dominance.

I set down the nude lipstick Klara usually wears and pick up the red lipstick that Luna wears.

You have to poke a monster to get them to react.

I continue my conversation with the hallucination of my sister. "Why red?" Luna might have asked.

Removing the lid, I glide the bold red pigment over my full lips. I take my time rubbing my lips together to make sure every inch is covered. The pigment is such a contrast against my pale skin. It's the first layer of armor, an intimidation factor. That is why I chose this color for Luna. She was a warrior, and she needed the proper armor to ride into battle.

"Because it is what you wore. Astrid knows this. This color provokes Astrid, like a Matador waving a red curtain in the eyes of a bull. I have to guarantee Astrid opens that door. If my lips are red, Astrid will want to punish Klara for resembling your ghost." I reply.

Staring back at my reflection and perfectly painted lips, I say, "I hope I have made you proud, Luna." Because, mentally, I have made myself sick. Ill with guilt but also a darkness that likes to seek out the grey areas. Like my twisted attraction to Wes and the thrill of uncovering more, even if the knowledge erodes my morals.

"It was never about making me proud, Sol. That's such a silly statement." I imagine Luna rolling her eyes and growing annoyed.

I run the hot iron through my hair, feeling the tool's heat near my cheeks; it begins to flush them with a faint red hue. A foreshadowing that blood will be shed today. The hairs on my arms raise when I realize, in a twisted way, I'm going to watch the older version of me be murdered today. After all, Astrid is who I truly reflect. Astrid is the older version of me.

"Don't go off the path." Luna would have snapped just now. The memory of her voice is like a beacon calling me back to our initial conversation.

"Was it worth it? Starting the game over so you could claim the title as the winner."

"That's another silly question." Luna would jest.

I continue to flatten iron my hair. I'm halfway finished when I hesitate and look in the mirror. I'm Klara, Luna and myself. We can change and tweak small details, but we're all the same, and in the end, when I age, I will look like Astrid. That fact haunts me.

"Why do you insist on feeling guilt? Guilt over looking like Astrid. See the glass half full; she is stunning on the outside. Unlike her, it's your job to remain whole on the inside."

"What about the science I helped create?" I question.

She would have rolled her eyes, "It was coming eventually. We just sped it up." She would have grabbed her iPod then, "Just stop being silly and feeling guilty. It's such a waste. Your mind could be put to such better use."

I imagine her speaking with her words and not just through a song as her face grew more irritated by me, "The world evolves all the time. When men settled in caves, and others decided to hunt and gather, those who didn't follow were left behind. Technology is the deadliest weapon man has created. It all started with the wheel, and it continues with genetic modification. Either way, this is happening. Millions will argue against it, but many will jump on board. When they sail to higher horizons, more will follow by clinging to lifeboats so they are not left behind. Those who remain naturally born humans will eventually die out in future generations. The science our father and Manus Dei created is life-changing. I never hated the science." She would have told me.

"You hated how they controlled it," I admit. "I'll never be normal, not in this world. Everything is about to change. I understand." I set the flat iron down.

"Normal is antiquated. You are exceptional, Sol. I just wished you believed that."

"Even though I reflect Astrid?" I rebuttal. How can they love and care for me when I mirror a monster? Luna and Klara might look like Astrid, but genetically I am the closest twin to the woman who wants to destroy the world and recreate it making herself into a god who controls everything.

"I reflect her too." Luna might have shrugged, "That doesn't mean I am her. I make my own path just as you will and all the other Reflections."

Nodding, I pick up my concealer and touch the faint red marks on my neck. Wes left them last night. I like knowing his marks are on me, hidden by the makeup. "I'm leaving after this, Luna, after I end the games."

That would have either upset her or made her proud.

I imagine her giving me a look that would have rendered me still. It would have shattered my declaration and whispered the secrets I know to be true in my mind. Secrets I have not confessed to anyone. Not even out loud to myself…yet.

That night on the Cliff Walk, so many details were disclosed. Some I buried so deep in my mind that they have only started to float to the surface.

"Don't be silly, Sol. Listen to my secrets. You know as well as I do, none of us can be free. There is no real escape. If you run it's just going to start another game. Isn't that the opposite of what you want?" I imagine Luna asking as she tried to probe for more answers.

I grab the hair oil on the counter and pour some into my hands. It makes them shine like plastic. Shimmering as bright as the blood that poured out of Subject 52.

Movement catches my eye. When I look up, I spot Wes leaning against the door frame.

Goodbye for now, Luna.

His eyes are watching my hands.

I flip my hand over and rub the oil in my long flat hair. "It's just my hair oil," I lie.

No reply.

He remains standing against the door frame, watching me. "I wish I could fill the void that calls to you when you need to speak to Luna." He utters.

How much did he hear?

"No one can fill the emptiness, but you help make it bearable," I whisper, meeting his eyes in the mirror. His body is dressed in tactical gear, every bit the soldier today. Guns and weapons are strapped to a thick black belt. His hair is cut again. I heard the buzzing of a shaver this morning. He's more Horseman than Wes, and Wesley has all but vanished.

Clearing my throat, I meet my own blue eyes in the mirror. And I am Klara today.

Death pushes off the frame and stands tall. "Are you ready?"

I nod as his eyes look me over. He strides toward me, twists me, and cups my face gently. His palms rest against my neck, and his index finger gently taps the light red bruise he left behind. His lips tug into a crooked smile that sends butterflies soaring in my belly.

"I'm here," He touches the mark.

I cup his hand, "I know." The weigh on my shoulders multiplies.

"I'm under all the paint, beneath all the lies. You can't run from me, little mouse. When you run, no matter the direction, it will always be towards me, even if you don't realize it." He bends down, pressing our foreheads together. "In my dreams, I imagine you running into my arms after finishing today. Running into the house I built for us," He built a house for us? Why does that sound more appealing than a cage? Why does it sound like a trick?

He continues, "Staying there and making it into a home where we will raise a family one day." My eyes water. It sounds like what I always wanted. A family. "You don't have to fight me once this mission is over. It's your choice. Just know I'll never let anything happen to you." He declares.

My heart is soaring, but it's also being shot down faster than it can fly away to protect itself.

This statement is his painted lie; he whispers it to himself to release his guilt. It's not just my choice. It's both of ours. And he can't always protect me. He's lying to settle his nerves about the mission. I will be alone when I enter the tunnels until he and Gabriel arrive. During those minutes, he won't have my back. It all depends on me.

Pushing up on my toes I kiss him with everything I have.

It's the best kiss in the world.

It's the most painful.

When I pull away, I see a faint red hue my lipstick left behind on his peach-colored lips. I touch it with my index finger. "Now, I have marked you too."

***

The air is so tense that it would crack a knife blade in half. Gabriel stands at the door, and if I thought I knew his serious face before, it was nothing compared to the stern look he's nailing me with. I feel like he's trying to crucify me onto a cross, and I'm not even guilty...yet.

I swallow, and it almost gets lodged in my throat. His eyes still watch. Does he suspect my plan to betray all sides?

"Where is War?" I ask, using all my strength to keep my voice normal and flat.

Death places his palm on my lower back, "War will stay here and hack into all the cameras. It's all going to be fine. Gabriel and I have your back."

Gabriel extends a smartwatch to me, the same model he and Luna always wore. These watches gave them constant alerts from Manus Dei. It called them when they needed to meet in the tunnels and now it will be used as a trojan horse.

"Give me your wrist," he orders.

Death steps between us and takes the watch. "I'll do it." With gentle fingers, he straps it onto my wrist.

"Do you know what you have to do?" Gabriel quizzes me, steeling his spine to stand the tallest in the room.

I adjust my posture, slouching on one knee. I'm not provoking him; I'm trying to make him believe I'm relaxed and confident. "I have to press the dial on the watch for the nerve agent to be released," I explain. The dial serves as the trigger. The embedded speakers will pulse a rhythm that will release the bioweapon. It's a weapon Gabriel engineered not to kill Astrid but to render her immobile, just in case I can't access the vault.

"How close do you need to be?" He drills me again.

"Within a foot," I reply. No pride or relief is shown. My lips thin before I snap them shut.

Is he worried about me? He's faked it so much in the past.

Look who's talking. Good point, and yes, I do care about him.

It's a good old case of the pot calling the kettle black. It is possible to care but be cruel, especially for those who have only been shown affection through skin thickening.

"Let's go," He orders, and then I see the corner of his eyelids soften before he turns his back to me.

I make to follow, but Wes grabs my wrist, spinning me. Our chests slam together, his breathing deep, eyes worried. He doesn't speak, and neither do I. His forest green eyes take a mental snapshot of me. His warrior mask fades, and all I see is fear and worry. I squeeze his fingers, telling him I will be fine.

Footsteps echo through the room, sounding like a faint battle drum. War strides in, dressed impeccably in his suit, glasses perched on his nose. "It's time for you to make your move, little mouse," he grins.

That's an odd choice of words, isn't it?

There is no way War knows what I have been mentally planning.

Stop being paranoid, Sol!

Wes interlaces our fingers, tugging me towards the exit. Just before the door closes behind us, I glance back at War. He lifts his right hand, adjusting the tie pin he's wearing.

It's a hidden message, both a hint and a warning.

When I first met War, he gave me his tie pin to symbolize his alliance. He's War, playing *all* sides, aiding both Gabriel and Famine.

Just before the door closes, I note how his lips spread wide; hope ignites in his eyes, spreading like a nuclear mushroom cloud. Growing and polluting everyone around him.

Who is his hope rooting for? Who will benefit, and who will be plagued with nuclear fallout?

Numbly, I walk to the car. My mind was left behind in the living room. War is staying behind in the safe house...where Klara is.

"Sol," Wes speaks.

I blink. The car door is open, waiting for me to get inside.

I smile, it's fake, and worst, Wes can tell it's full of shit. Luckily, he chalks it up to nerves.

I climb in and try to calm my racing heart. We each have roles to play today. I need to focus on being Klara. Conquest and Death will be Horsemen about to kill the Queen, and War will play the unseen Horseman who plays all the sides. His loyalty is to Death, the brother who took a bullet to the heart to save him, but that

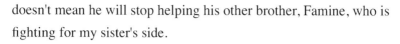

doesn't mean he will stop helping his other brother, Famine, who is fighting for my sister's side.

I might not be the only traitor on the game board today.

Chapter 42

Sol

Gabriel steers the car to a stop. No one speaks, and for a few beats, it sounds like none of us are breathing either.

"I thought you had faith in me?" I try to joke. I rub my clammy hands down my thighs.

"We do," Wes reacts, edging closer to me, but he doesn't touch me. He hasn't touched me since we got in the car. Not a handheld. It's as if I'm a stranger to him, or he's trying to force that belief into his mind, so my departure is easier.

"Then lighten up. You're making me feel as if I'm walking to my death."

"Don't," Wes snaps, "suggest that."

I expel a long, slow breath, slide away from him, and grasp the car door. I know what I have to do. Walk through the woods until I reach the train station where Klara's car is parked. Take the car and drive to Astrid's, then follow Gabriel's plan until I follow my own.

Wes scoots the opposite way and gets out of the car.

"Can you give me a minute?" Gabriel asks him. Wes pauses before he nods and slams the door shut.

Gabriel taps his index finger on the steering wheel, eyes forward, neck stiff. "You know, Sol," his next breath is slowly pulled from his lungs, like he's confessing under duress, "You could have played the game." His hand grips the wheel before he releases it. "You didn't have to switch places. You had it in you all along."

Why is he telling me this? I didn't, did I? I was a scared child who feared. Luna didn't. I did want to play, what child doesn't want to play a game? I was curious. Curiosity kills the cat. Luna saved my life.

"If I had, then you never would have met Luna."

"Maybe," he shrugs. "Do you regret it?"

"What?" Why does it feel like I should have automatically replied yes? I regret so many things.

"Allowing her to force you to sit on the sidelines, letting her take your place."

I laugh bitterly, "My regret over that decision feels like a coin that is endlessly flipped, never allowed to land." My spine sinks into the car seat; my hands stop sweating. I'm ready. No more fear. "Of course, there are times I hate myself for not fighting. Not telling Luna, 'no'. I never told her no; I'm not sure you did either. We spoiled her, but she also spoiled us. We're all to blame, Gabriel. The other side of the coin is thankful. Could I have played the game against you?" I bite my inner cheek. "Sure. Would I have survived?" I shake my head, "I liked to escape, but there was only one way to escape the game. Death."

"You don't sound so silly anymore." His eyes shift and meet mine in the rearview mirror.

My red lips tug up, "Why are we so messed up, Gabriel? Why can't we be honest like this all the time?" Why do you and I snap at each other only to feel guilty about it later? That is what he is feeling: guilt. Gabriel has continued to evolve. He never did feel to this extent as a child. Maybe Luna's departure allowed him to surrender his defenses and accept empathy.

His eyes leave mine, "I'd like to think that Luna would have said it made life more exciting this way. Keeps you on the tips of your toes. Will our next conversation be cordial or tense?" I hear his swallow, "She liked the excitement too much."

"And what did you like about the games?"

He cracks his neck. "I hated the games."

"So why did you continue to play?" I deadpan.

"Back to the silly questions again." He snickers. "I played because I liked seeing Luna; that liked turned to curiosity, curiosity to obsession, and obsession to..." his voice cracks.

"Love."

He nods. "Love to..." his shoulders rise, "such a feeling of hate I can't begin to describe it."

I touch his shoulder and his body tenses. "It won't always be that feeling." In fact, in several hours, all the lies will crumble. *You still haven't figured out my untruths, Gabriel. I am sorry; truly, I am.*

I'm not referring to my plan to take the encryption codes myself. Gabriel still hasn't figured out Luna's grand plan. That's how I know that feeling of hate will change and become a tornado of feelings that will either destroy him or give him a new gust of motivation.

"I should go."

He nods.

I squeeze his shoulder before I open the car door.

"You would have survived." He says. My foot stills on the pavement. "You would have survived much longer than you give yourself credit for." He turns his head away from me.

My hand rests on the door after I close it. Gabriel doesn't know how much those words have boosted my confidence. He'll regret that once he knows I'm working against him.

Wes comes to my side, "Sol,"

"Don't," I snap. "Just let me go. I have to do this." I shoot a brief look in his direction. He takes my breath away, mind, thoughts, and control; it all vanishes with one look.

"I'll never let you go." He snarls, fists balled, jaw clenched. He's one second away from throwing me over his shoulder and ruining everything.

His eyes find my lips; he steps closer. I shake my head. "You're going to ruin my lipstick." My throat feels tight. I don't want a kiss goodbye. It's too much.

If eyes could kill, his would. I turn my back and step into the forest.

"Little mouse," he calls. I stop, feeling the pull of the puppet string he controls. The one attached to my heart. "I told you that love is too small of a word to describe us. No word can illustrate my feelings for you, but I know it's the one word you want to hear from my lips."

"Stop," I bark as I begin to walk forward. I swing my arms to quicken my pace. Why is he doing this now? I'm supposed to be Klara.

My foot snaps a twig in half. I feel more like the version of me I have always wanted. I want to turn around and run into his arms.

"You better be standing there unharmed by the time I reach you." Wes shouts. "And when I catch you, little mouse, I will tell you that silly four-letter word you have been dying to hear. Just know that you mean so much more to me than one word."

Chapter 43

Sol

Well, my heart feels utterly broken, which is a good thing, since Klara doesn't seem to have a heart.

He will say he loves me, but there are strings attached.

I floor the gas and race towards my new chapter. My father's house comes into view, but I don't slow down. I press the gas harder. A root system of emotions begins to spread deep within me. Longing to go back, the urge to run far from it. Memories, both good and horrific.

I don't focus on these feelings; why nourish a seed that bears bad fruit?

That home was a dollhouse.

Fake. Nothing but a game. In that home, I was nothing but a puppet that was played with.

I don't even spare it a glance because someone might suspect I have a sense of nostalgia for it if I did. Cameras are all over this private community. You never know who is watching. I can't break character. I can't be foolish enough to tip anyone off to my hiding spot.

The best place to hide from monsters is right under their noses. Cliché, I know, but a fact is a fact. If you run, they will scent your fear lingering in the air, thicken it like a damp humidity of sweat, leaving a trail right to you. You have to be shrewd; evolve into one of them. Don't run. Dig in. Camouflage using the same patterns and spots they mask themselves with.

That's exactly what Astrid did. She played along for decades. All these years, my aunt, lived right next door in her own mansion. Slowly encrypting everything and building and army until she made her move.

I guess the apple doesn't fall far from the tree, but hopefully, I don't taste as sour as Astrid.

A loud exhale would have alerted Gabriel and Wes to my anxiety but I'm alone so the sound gets swallowed up by my next inhale. I've never felt more scared in my life. I'm not worried about this mission or getting inside the tunnels. I fear the after. That thinking is what trips people up.

Focus on the moment, Luna would tell me. Bury the rest until you need it.

I pass by three guard gates, park the car, am body checked before I enter the house, then escorted through the halls.

Living in a jail is more cozy than this.

Everything goes routinely. My neck grows stiff, and I want to crack it but resist the urge to break character.

I glance around the house. If I weren't so well versed in lying, my mouth would be wide open in shock over how real the virtual reality was. Everything, and I mean every detail, is exact. Down to the small amount of dust that clings to the banister curve of the staircase.

The further we walk, the more I relax. Walking these frigid halls feels like an old habit. The only new detail is the air. It's scented with a clean laundry smell, unlike the death Astrid seeks to bring upon the world.

Rounding my shoulders back, I embrace Klara and how her walk is slightly feline when she walks through the house. Of course that sass all but vanishes once she reaches Astrid's office. By that point, Klara has become a robot. One foot in front of the other. There is no other option but to be the loyal clone or be put down. I suspect it makes life simple.

I understand why Klara danced when she killed Subject 52. She didn't have to be a robot, then. Klara was on her terms in the club. She was free.

I'm not saying it gave her a right, but she can't be fully held accountable for her actions. This is how she was raised. This is her right and wrong, defined by Manus Dei.

Astrid will be held accountable. That puts a pep in my step.

When I reach the entrance of the tunnels, I spot the three guards Klara always sees. Erick's lip twitches in disgust at the sight of me.

Eat your fill, Erick.

I paint on the practiced grin Klara flashes him. "Hi, Erick," I greet him and stifle a giggle just as Klara usually does. Looks like Klara likes to provoke as well. Some traits are genetic.

Erick pushes himself against the wall trying to create distance from me. I jerk my body, and he flinches. I laugh out loud now. Another guard opens the door to the tunnels, and my confidence falters for a second.

The tunnel stretches ominously before me, its gaping maw devouring any trace of light. It seems to coil like a serpent, its darkness whispering of unseen dangers lurking within. With a pounding heart, I place my foot inside, the cold and eerie silence enveloping me.

How was Luna never scared as a child?

Then it hits me. We are clones, she felt just as I did, but she changed the definitions. Redefining fear into excitement. She kept lying to herself until she believed the anxiety was thrilling.

I figured it out, sister. I'm sorry it took me so long.

The door behind me closes, and I am entirely immersed in darkness for the longest minute of my life. My heart skips a beat. Something is wrong! The sight before me doesn't match the virtual reality. The tunnels are so dark that they rival a black hole, but somehow, I can see. It's an odd sight filled with shadows, but I can make out every curve and see every brick.

It worked. The second upgrade Logan gave me worked! He wanted me to be able to see in the dark, not just the dim shades of night slightly illuminated by city lights, but the absolute, pure darkness of evil. I thought the second upgrade Logan gave me was meant to help me in Norway, where the sun won't be shining, but it's also meant to help me here.

The problem is that the overhead light turns on with each step I take. My newly upgraded eyes blink, my pupils retracting quickly, but then I'm submerged in darkness again until I take the next step. It feels torturous on my eyes, and I sense the pulsing start of a migraine.

Pushing past the pain, I maintain even steps and neutralize my facial expression. Each step I take triggers another light to reveal the path ahead while the ones behind me extinguish, leaving me in an ever-shrinking pocket of illumination. The claustrophobic maze of the tunnels presses in, suffocating my senses.

I twist and turn the route Klara walked until I finally reach the door to Astrid's office, its presence a sinister gateway.

It's exciting. I lie to myself. *Thrilling.*

The light above casts an eerie glow on the metal surface, emphasizing the foreboding nature of what lies beyond. I glance at the guard stationed there, his smile an unsettling contrast against the perpetual darkness that surrounds him. His enhanced night vision grants him the ability to see beyond the meager light, exposing the deeper shadows that dance and writhe like twisted specters waiting to ensnare unsuspecting prey.

"Back again, pet." Daniel, the last guard I have to trick, greets me. Disgust ripples off of my skin. I don't respond because Klara never regarded Daniel.

He steps forward, and something about his smile puts me on edge.

Details whisper in my mind until I glimpse the same crack in the stone wall that Klara always looked at when she encountered Daniel. She never looked at him. Just this break in the stone.

His hands begin to sweep and press parts of my body as he pats me down.

You fucker! I almost broke character. It's hard not to. A true mental fight not to react, to wrap my hand around his neck and squeeze. My teeth clench as I eye that same crack. I know why Klara never reacted. Daniel isn't doing his job. He's not patting me down as he should be. He's groping me!

How many times has Klara had to suffer this abuse?

The Horsemen had no idea. The angle of the camera they hacked into doesn't reveal this detail. Only one camera can see what is truly happening. The camera above Astrid's door. The one camera War could not hack into.

Daniel's hands squeeze my breast painfully. His hips push into my ass, his hot rancid breath coats the side of my neck. Time stills as his hands roam. From the corner of my eye, I see the blinking red light of the camera above the door. Astrid must know what Daniel is doing, yet she allows it to happen.

He eventually steps back, and when he does, I see the tent in his pants. Murder has never been my style, but the game is changing me. Each round corrupts and enlightens me. Astrid and Daniel need to die. If I had a gun in my hands, I would shoot Daniel.

Maybe it's ok to blur that line in the sand? Or maybe that thought is what created Astrid?

With my heightened hearing, I hear the camera moving. Is Astrid zooming in on my red lips? I curl my toes which are hidden in my sneakers. I want to bounce from foot to foot, but I refuse my request.

The door clicks multiple times as the numerous locks on the vault-like door pull back and unlock.

I did it; I got in the office.

The door opens to a bright white room, momentarily blinding me. It's smart of Astrid to force us to walk in blind as our eyes adjust. Daniel keeps his back to the light, probably because he wants his eyes to focus on the dark tunnels. That and he isn't special enough to look inside.

Once my pupils constrict, my heart palpitates when my eyes drink in what is before me. I break character and look over my shoulder at Daniel. He doesn't see it because he isn't facing the office. He is ignorant of reality, just as I once was.

I want to reach out and grab him, shake him to look at what has happened right under his nose!

Is this how Luna felt when I chose not to see what was happening to her?

I want to lean over and vomit, but I don't. My heart beats so hard it might break a rib.

I don't know what to do! This was not suppose to happen!

A dark shadow moves past me. The shadow is a man, but my mind paints him as a shadow because that is less intimidating than the man. The shadow walks slowly, his eyes on me. I don't look at the shadow. Even if I wanted to, I couldn't peel my eyes off the color pooling inside the office.

All I see is red.

I even taste it.

A metallic scent coats my tongue, covers my eyes, and seals off my ears.

This is not part of the plan!

Panic pulses through my mind. I know if I can not gain control of my emotions, I will die any second. The only way to do that is to disconnect myself from my surroundings. Not to focus on the details but just on aspects of reality.

The ringing in my ears stops, but I wish it continued. The sounds happening behind me are that of one thing. Death. If only it were my Horseman, but it's not; it's murder. A guttural gasping that turns to hushed gargling.

A thump.

A few more agonizing gasps.

Silence.

Footsteps. The shadow moves and reenters the office.

Daniel is dead. The shadow killed him. I don't turn to look. I keep my eyes ahead. A moment passes or maybe a lifetime flies by before I fully sink back into my mind and body. What is revealed to my eyes is not what was planned. Gabriel thought of multiple outcomes. He told me to play every side, but neither he nor I plotted this version of the event.

Astrid's office has three doors: the entrance I used, the server room door, and a third door. We never knew what that third door concealed. Gabriel assumed it was another entrance. We didn't focus on that door because we already had a way inside. It didn't matter to Gabriel, but it should have. That third door is wide open now. A darker tunnel is revealed to me. It is another entrance.

Did Gabriel consider who would use that third door? Of course he didn't because he had yet to figure out my lies.

There is nowhere else left to go, so I raise my foot and step inside. It feels like an out-of-body experience. The moment I enter the office, my entire belief system disappeared, and the reason the game was started seemed like a fool's gambit.

My lies were built on lies. I should have known better.

Such a silly fool!

Just like that, the ground is pulled from under me. I fall and hit bottom. There is no return from this.

The old me is completely erased and painted anew. Everything I thought I knew has altered. Everything I thought Luna was capable of doing was grossly miscalculated.

Chapter 44

Gabriel

For years, I entered these tunnels. Each time I stepped inside, my body filled with dread and anticipation. I hated the testing, but seeing Luna made every ounce of pain I endured worth it. I craved the pain because my relief was seeing her again.

I was nothing more than a modern-day gladiator, competing for my life while Astrid, along with the other Masters, would sit and watch the spectacle. I was a fool to think Luna had my back when all she did was stab me in the end.

Not all tests were physical. Most were mental. I might have won the games, but I feel like the biggest failure. I didn't see the extent to which Luna would resort to not being called a loser.

"You're all clear." War radios into Wes and I's earpiece.

We move forward with deliberate strides, descending further into the abyss. As the camera's ominous eye blinks out due to War bypassing it, we embrace the darkness, a scene we know intimately.

Enhanced night vision is just the tip of the iceberg in our arsenal of enhancements. Manus Dei's military genetic advancements have turned soldiers into something more akin to weapons than men.

Securely strapped to our wrists are cutting-edge holographic devices, the latest in many technological wonders. The holographic interface projects a gridded map, mapping our real-time progress. Only those with a specific upgrade can see the holographic.

If Wes looks at the feed one more time I'm going to punch him. I need him to focus on the mission and not on Sol's progress. Sol can do this. She has to.

I just need everything to go to plan or the backup plans. Sol's journey through the tunnels is expected to take approximately five minutes. Once inside Astrid's office, Sol will release the bioweapon I engineered, Astrid will be immobile. Sol's hands will be clear of murder and then I can finally get the fuck inside of that vault. I'll get the key to unlock all the knowledge Astrid encrypted. Wes, acting swiftly and decisively, will ensure Sol's safe extraction. Meanwhile, my second team will infiltrate the stronghold, swiftly neutralizing any soldiers fiercely loyal to Astrid.

Astrid and her obedient lackeys are completely clueless about Wes and me being right under their noses. Thanks to War's expertise, we've cooked up a deep fake. A phony video playing of Wes and me, yours truly stars as a diligent scientist, giving Wes the full workup. The whole point? To throw anyone snooping into our activities off the scent and serve as a convenient alibi for our little adventure.

As for the security cameras posted around my house, they've been dealt with. Every last one of them bypassed, so no one's the wiser about Wes and me strolling through my own front door and slipping into the tunnels like phantoms. It's almost too easy, but sometimes the simplest plan is the least expected.

Governments worldwide are already on high alert because they know there is a civil war inside Manus Dei. We have lost face, and that makes us valuable to more attacks. I have to fix us before we lose everything.

"She's in the office," War states. *Thank fuck!* Right away, tension leaves my shoulders. Even if Astrid and Sol had a physical struggle, the nerve agent works in less than one minute.

I dart my eyes at Wes; even with my built-in night vision, he looks more beast than man blanketed in shadows, Muscle tense, pulse-pounding. His pupils are blown huge due to the darkness. It's hard to know what he thinks now, especially because his feelings for Sol have tainted him.

Love is a fucking waste of time.

I grab my knife as we prepare to turn the last corner where Daniel is stationed. I would have preferred to kill him with a gun, but Klara preferred knives, and this scene has to look like Klara's style.

She's my scapegoat. People won't question why she killed Astrid. They will sympathize with her. Not with me. If it looked like I killed Astrid, I'd just be painted as another clone that went crazy. A ruthless ruler who didn't care about his people. I don't want the scientists who work for us to fear me. I want to rule Manus Dei differently.

"Wait," War's bites. That's when I know something has happened, and a pit in my stomach tells me I'm a deadman.

"What the fuck is happening?" Wes hisses.

Nothing.

"War?" Wes presses. The tension only thickens as the sound of a rapid keyboard tapping fills the air.

"Give me a fucking second!" War snaps.

Of course, Wes doesn't wait; he charges through the tunnels towards the office. He's thinking with his dick.

Let the shit show begin.

I reach out, grabbing his shoulder again, desperate to restrain him. The last thing I need is for him to take another bullet.

"I don't see Daniel," War grunts, his voice strained. "He was there, at his post. But now he's gone. I searched the tunnels, and he's nowhere to be found. I'm locked out of the cameras again. I can't see all the angles."

Wes pushes past me, but who can blame him now?

I swiftly swap the knife for my gun. As we round the next corner, a new detail emerges, and Wes shoots me a glance. I nod in response, giving him the silent acknowledgment that I hear it, too. A haunting melody begins to drift through the air, barely audible yet enticing, tempting us to uncover its source.

We pass the final corner, stopping in our tracks. The lights in front of Astrid's heavily fortified office flicker to life, casting an eerie glow over the scene. The first error with this detail is the lights should have remained extinguished, shrouding the path in darkness.

"That's not me!" War stresses since he can see through our feed. "I'm trying to turn them off."

Click, click, click.

The entire tunnel system slowly starts to light up like a goddamn Christmas display.

Someone else has hacked into the system.

"Jesus," Wes breathes.

He sounds shocked, which I find odd because I'm pissed. It's only when I follow his line of sight I understand why.

Ahead of us is Daniel; correction, was Daniel. He is long dead now. His throat is slashed open wide, and his head cocked at an angle that even makes my iron stomach knot. The cut wasn't a clean slash; it was deep and jagged, meant to inflict as much pain as possible.

The door to Astrid's office is cracked open. It should be closed; Danial should have died at my hands. I can't even comprehend that detail before another one emerges, this time even louder. Lyrics cut through my shock, and I register the song is coming from inside Astrid's office.

I know the song. It's 'White Rabbit.' I grind my molars. Luna was fascinated with it after she caught Sol listening to it one day. She played the song on repeat for two weeks straight.

They say you can't understand love one without knowing hate. Luna's relentless obsession with certain songs was something I couldn't stand.

No I know who has fucked this all up.

Famine. He is the only other person who could hack in here. He's also well versed on the songs Luna played on repeat.

Well, brother, you didn't pay attention to the details. Luna didn't play the original version by Jefferson Airplane.

Wes strides past me, not thinking because his gun isn't aimed high but hangs loose in his hand. His footsteps pound with fear. I know exactly what he is feeling right now. I felt it when I first arrived at the Cliff Walk. It's a dread you ignore and can't acknowledge. Like stage four cancer, there is nothing you can do, so you think if you ignore it, it will go away.

It doesn't.

You have to face it eventually.

I did when I saw Luna's mangled body down below, and right now, Wes is filled with the same emotions about finding Sol dead.

Wes kicks open the door, pauses, and staggers back. His left foot slips on the pool of blood from Daniel's body. I rush forward and balance him. Aiming my gun high, I look at what has shocked Death himself.

My lips part, but no words come out. In the echoes of my mind, I hear War shouting at us, but neither Wes, nor I can react.

My mind traces back to the plan and what should have happened. By now, Sol should have released the bioweapon. Astrid should have dropped like a fly, becoming paralyzed. It wasn't fair that I only had five minutes to kill her. Astrid's death should be slow and painful. That's why when I developed the bioweapon, I ensured it kept her awake and heightened her nerves. This way, she would feel every inch of the knife when it sliced her neck.

I wanted to see the shock when she saw Manus Dei's prized stallion kill her.

"Someone fucking talk. I don't have eyes on you anymore!" War shouts.

For the second time, my tongue is glued down, my lips sewn shut in disbelief. The first time this happened to me was when I looked over the edge of the Cliff Walk, down at Luna's broken body.

Now I see a broken body again. Like Daniel's body, this one is also killed violently.

Wes's body flinches like he is shocked awake; the disbelief fades, his mind becomes alert, eyes frantic, scanning the room for

Sol. The door to the server room is open. I already know the encryption codes are gone.

Wes runs past me, his feet skidding in the pools of blood. It smears and streaks along the white floor like an abstract painting.

An abstract painting...I thought it was odd seeing Sol painting an abstract piece in the gallery in Aspen. It was so unlike her.

My eyes look at all the smeared blood. Maybe it was her style all along. Did we all misjudge her? Was the most cunning beast under my nose this whole time?

Who the fuck are you, Sol?

"Sol!" Wes shouts as he disappears into the server room.

No response comes.

Another voice enters my ear. It's War screaming through the radio still. I must have tuned him out again. All I can fucking hear is that song on repeat.

I take another step into the office until my feet stop at the dead body lying on the floor. Astrid is not moving. There is no rise and fall of her chest. I want to interrogate her to find out what happened and then give her the death she deserves, but the scientist in me knows it is impossible to resurrect her due to her gaping wound. We can 3D print a heart, but the brain is a complex organ. Without oxygen, it's difficult to revive it.

A bone deep slice runs along her neck, severing inner tendons and arteries, leaving them exposed and hanging from the gruesome wound.

Good. It was painful.

Drip, drop, drip, drop. A slow drip of crimson liquid continues to pool, forming a macabre scene on the ground. Her once vibrant blue eyes now stare out, wide and devoid of life. Her mouth hangs open, a desperate attempt to gasp for air that can never fill her deflated lungs. Fingers that once murdered so graceful are now curled up in a haunting semblance of claws. The marks she left behind, etched in her own blood, mar the floor—a testament to her futile struggle and desperate plea for survival.

In the end, Astrid wasn't invincible. The queen is dead, but not by my hands.

"What the fuck is happening?" I voice. How did I not see this angle?

I shake my head. Sol didn't do this. There is absolutely no fucking way she was that good of a liar!

This murder was calculated, not swift or gentle. This is menacing, like Klara, but she is locked up in the safe house. That leaves only Sol.

It was Sol we had. I know it.

God damn it, I know it was Sol!

But she was painting abstract and Sol never painted like that before.

I grab my neck. I missed something, and it might just cost me everything.

Wes comes running out. Eyes wide. *I'm so sorry, brother. This is all my fault.*

I want to explain, calm and reassure him, but I can't. I feel my stomach tighten, and I might be sick. Not from the sight of murder. I don't give a shit about the chopped up body or the smell of the blood. It's the falling sensation filling my body that makes my stomach drop. The floor has been ripped out from under me, like fucking Alice falling in the hole. Just like the painting Sol was working on.

I shake my head, not wanting to believe what I'm starting to discover.

Sol betrayed me but was she capable of killing Astrid and Daniel? Was it even Sol all along?

Fuck! Fuck!

No, it had to be Sol because she slept with Death! They were fucking. Sol loves Death. None of Luna's other reflections know what love is. Sol does. Sol was in tune with her emotions. That's why she went crazy and started talking to hallucinations.

Holy Fuck! You are such a fool! It's starting to make sense now. All the lies that I swallowed down because I thought Sol was innocent.

"Sol isn't here," Wes shouts. "There is nobody in the server room. She's not here." He speaks more to himself now. Closing the distance, ignoring the dead body, he grabs my shoulders and shakes me, "Wake the fuck up. Sol isn't here." The veins in his eyes turn cranberry.

"Gabriel!" He roars. He pulls his fist back and punches me in the jaw. I fall to the ground. My hands slap in Astrid's blood, spreading it further.

More abstraction splashes onto the canvas of lies.

"Gabriel!" He calls me again, but instead of fury, it's worry. I'm pulled up by my collar and slammed into the closest wall. The back of my head bounces off of it.

"Gabriel!" He slams me again, "I won't lose you too!" In a flip of a switch, Wes is gone, and Death is back. The perfect soldier. He does what I can't. He's pushed aside emotions and is allowing his training to take over.

"It's my fault. It was my plan." I utter.

His hands release my shirt, palms slap on either side of my face, "Then help me fix it."

I numbly nod. "Go see if the hard drives are there?"

He shakes his head, "They have been emptied; the rest destroyed." He takes my gun and shoves it in my hand. "Someone is coming for us. This was a set up. Be ready, brother."

"It had to be Famine."

"Nothing is certain anymore." He rebuttals.

Something catches my eye. A new detail I missed that is on Astrid's dead body. Nestled in her ears are a pair of headphones. The white wire connecting them is tainted with her blood. Instinctively, my gaze follows the wire, tracing its path as it disappears into the pocket of her pants.

I already know what it is connected to. I move swiftly, feeling a sudden vulnerability like I've never experienced before.

This is what weakness feels like.

My trembling hand reaches into her pocket, grasping the headphone wire. With a tug, it comes free, and there, revealed in my trembling palm, is an old-fashioned iPod.

Luna's iPod. The iPod I stole for her. A gift I killed for.

"You gave Sol this!" I shout at Wes. I knew he did. "Why would Sol put this on Astrid?"

Wes swallows, and I see the role of his throat as he struggles. "She didn't have her iPod with her when we left."

Gunfire begins to erupt from the hallway.

"War, what's going on?" Wes questions.

A static sound blares through my radio before a new voice speaks, "You have three minutes to leave through the third door of her office. Don't go back through the tunnels." Famine speaks.

My blood boils.

I once called him my brother, and I hate that I still refer to him as one. What can I say, my family is fucked up. We show love by playing games.

"No, hello?" I sneer.

"Two minutes and fifty-two seconds." Famine repeats.

"Where is she?" Wes fumes.

"You're all wasting time." Famine bites.

I glance at the third door. A door, I assumed, was another entrance into Astrid's office. My assumptions were correct, but what's on the other end?

The gunfire gets closer, and Wes and I have no other choice but to listen to Famine. He won't kill us. We know that.

Unlike the other tunnels with twists and turns, this passageway is straight and narrow. The walls are not the same old stone bricks. Some parts of the ceiling are so low we have to duck to pass them. This tunnel was made without Manus Dei's knowledge. It lacks refinements. The tunnel starts to make a steep incline, and suddenly, the air smells fresher. Just as I start to think we're nearing an exit, the entire mountain shakes. Death and I scramble, our hands finding precarious holds against the rough, carved walls. Explosions echo from the direction we came from, shaking us to our core.

Boom! Boom! Boom!

In the pitch darkness of the tunnel, we don't speak, but we know what those sounds are. Famine just blew up the labs within the tunnels.

We continue to run as a cloud of dust begins to chase us from behind. A sharp turn ahead is bathed in sunlight. There is no door, just an open, exposed passageway that leads outside. We hesitate; the open exposure goes against our training.

"You'll thank me one day because I notice what you didn't, Gabriel. It will all make sense in the end." Famine states, "I told War to pick you up on the southeast road. It's a short hike down. I'd hurry if I were you." The radio is cut off.

Once outside, I walk to the edge of the mountainside; it looks directly down at the ten mansions that once clung to the mountain. They are all on fire now. Each of the houses belonged to a Master. My house, Astrid's, Luna and Sol's have been completely wiped off the face of the earth.

I yank the radio from my ear and palm the iPod. It's slippery from the blood on my fingers. Shoving the headphones into my ear, I catch the ending of a song before it repeats. I look at the screen and read the title. The song is "Move Me" by Badflower.

Everything I ever thought I knew about the woman I loved changes when the lyrics begin to play. My thoughts splinter like shattered glass; I feel each shard cut and slice my flesh, ripping apart all the memories I once held dear. I feel myself sinking, suffocating. I'm dying, the memories of my love are fading, and in its place is something so dark I can't begin to describe it.

Falling, falling, falling.

I'm devoured by the waters which are more powerful than me. They whip me around like a rag doll. I was just a puppet.

The storm tears me apart, limb by limb. All that is left is my heart. It's exposed to the elements and her cruelty.

It's beating again, shocked alive by the events.

I should have expected this because, like me, we can't accept losing. No matter the cost!

I refused to lose because it would have killed Luna. Her idea was ridiculous. That's why I had to win. I needed to protect her.

I know the song that echoes in my ears. I hate this song! Songs are never random. The music Luna played was always carefully chosen. The song in Astrid's office was "White Rabbit," but the original one.

The original.

This other song is special and filled with hidden secrets. Luna played it repeatedly, and when I questioned her about it, she told me it was our anthem.

Fucking ridiculous, but it made her happy so I allowed it.

She made me listen to it and told me it expressed everything our love was. I remember that day because I grabbed the iPod and threw it. The screen cracked and I had to fix it later. Luna's blue eyes looked at me. No emotion showed. She just told me that was silly and walked away.

The song is a message; it all is.

I played all the sides of those who I thought were still players in the game. I didn't consider this side, the version where Luna was still playing long after she died.

"It's Luna." I declare. My voice is only a whisper. I sound like a loser. My throat is dry and cracked. It burns with emotions. I feel as if I chugged acid.

It takes every bit of strength I have to shout it again. "It's Luna!"

The song still plays in my ears when Wes grabs my shoulders and squares me to him. His lips move. When I don't respond, he yanks the headphones from my ear. "What the fuck does that mean?"

I shove the iPod into his chest. The headphones fall from his fingers, but the wires keep them connected to the iPod.

Connected.

Everything is connected to Luna. The master puppeteer.

The game between her and me never ended the day the Masters declared it was over. When Luna jumped off the cliff I was too shaken with grief to look at the mangled body. I didn't want that to be the last image I saw of the love of my life. I had my brother, Famine, make sure it was indeed Luna who killed herself.

Famine abandoned my cause soon after that; he turned against me. I thought it was because he had seen Luna's body. Seen the damage that Manus Dei's power did. That I did.

I assumed he left to try and save the woman he loved from the same fate. After all, Klara idolized Luna; she would likely want to go the same way.

That's why I never tried to kill Famine. He was fighting for his love, and I would have done the same.

He played me!

Famine has been a pawn for Luna for much longer than I anticipated. I didn't play this side in my mind. I failed to determine what would happen if Luna was still playing the game, not just with all her puppets but with herself as her own puppet.

I lost because I never believed Luna could take things as far as she did. I didn't see it coming. It's the perfect Trojan horse, and now the kingdom I fought to save will burn just like she wanted.

Luna won.

"It's Luna. She isn't dead."

Hey, hold on!

Don't you even think about closing the book yet! Seriously, you don't want to risk upsetting an author. You never know when she might just immortalize you as a character in her next tale. Just saying (wink, wink).

Your reviews are invaluable to indie authors. Whether it's a few words or a star rating, your honest feedback is greatly appreciated. If you'd like, feel free to tag me in your review on Instagram or TikTok—I'd be thrilled to share your thoughts on my pages! Thank you for taking the time to read my books.

Against Fate

For those of you seeking an escape into the world of fantasy, I've got the perfect book for you. It was an honor when bestselling author Ashley C. Harris roped me into co-authoring a book with her. If you're into faes, shifters, vampires, dragons, hybrids, and a bunch more, our first book, 'Against Fate,' is about to cast a spell on you. It's a coming-of-age fantasy romance filled with young adult drama, rejected mates, magic, sizzling hot shifters, and mysterious fae.

A.G. Harris & Ashley C. Harris

www.authoragharris.com

www.ashleycharris.com

A.G. Harris

Against Fate

Rejected Mates of Magic Borne

"I can help you bring out your inner wolf," the mage whispered into my ear, but she never mentioned the price....

Most wolf shifters my age want two things... to find their fated mates and take a high place amongst their pack. But I couldn't even get close to those goals until I shifted.

That's right, I'm a half-shifter, half-human hybrid, living amongst the strongest wolf pack in all of Magic Borne. Unfortunately, if my inner wolf doesn't surface, I could lose my life.

Only the strongest can survive in pack Sköll, and Carter is the epitome of strength and power. He's also the son of the most prejudiced alpha in my world. I'm not exaggerating... Carter's father believes hybrids shouldn't be allowed to exist, which means the two of us should stay away from each other... but that doesn't seem to be happening.

Everywhere I turn, Carter is there, tempting me to either punch him or kiss him. My plan is to ignore his presence. I need to seek out the magic that can awaken my wolf by any means necessary. Even if that means venturing into the forbidden, exhilarating parts of Magic Borne and rejecting everything I thought I knew.

Against Fate is the first of a heart-pounding, enchanting story.

Chapter 1

ADAIRA

If only I were a mage. I'd open a portal up right now to swallow me from the fate that loomed upon my future. Six foot four and a solid wall of wolf shifter muscle. *In theory, that sounds perfect, a shifter with power and a title, drool-worthy looks that make women stop in their tracks. Sign me up!*

That isn't the fate I was dealt.

Nope.

With each inhale, his shoulders grew wider and curved forward, casting a shadow-like cage that crept closer until it encased and trapped me. It made my ribs constrict with each breath I took. He loved to lure his prey like all shifters, and I was the perfect little bunny cornered by the big bad wolf. I studied him closer; his hair was slightly longer now, the tips of my fingers tingled as they itched to feel the silken strands.

Damn him and his looks! Could fate have lowered the playing field and made him be a bit less panty-dropping handsome?

As I looked back into his eyes, I could see the conflict that swirled within them. They were always filled with mixed emotions when he looked at me. He was always at war mentally when I was nearby. Lately, he looked more stressed, like the weight of Magic Borne was bearing down upon his broad shoulders. He seemed only able to hold the pressure for so long until he snapped.

And snapped he did. I was what tipped him over the edge. I was his relief as well as his misery. I was the victim of his pleasure and pain caught in the cacophony, unable to escape. I have to admit that during times I didn't want to escape. These encounters became more frequent. Each time leaving me more and more confused. I should push him away. *Yeah, right, Adaira, like you could literally refuse him or push away an alpha shifter.*

I was never able to entirely fight him. There was something intangible that halted me from doing so. Maybe it was the flood of hormones when he came close. The perfect picture of the ideal male. He was strong, sinfully stunning, and had a title, money, and power, but he also had his dark side. *So yeah, he was what every girl wanted, right?* The bad boy who taunted us, cornered us like his plaything, and kissed away the pain with pleasure. That's not what I told myself I wanted... *Yet my reactions weren't right, and why wasn't I able to be callous and cunning back?*

No magical portal was opening up to save me, and as my feet tried to take another step back, my heels hit the brick wall of the dark alleyway. My hands flattened against the old brick. The hardness of the stone was nothing compared to the indifference he had shown me at times. The crisp cold air didn't help to dull my senses. Instead, it made everything feel more alive and more menacing. His nostrils flared while my skin blanched with goosebumps.

He could sense that as he visually stripped me bare of my clothing. Like a vampire on the warpath he drank me in. Roaming from my lips which were parted because, what can I say, I felt parched and the only thing to quench my thirst would be his lips. I unconsciously licked them, not the smartest thing in the moment. The reaction taunted him as a growl escaped, a growl that was pure wolf. No trait of his human remained. When his eyes dipped lower and lingered on my chest, I felt the magic swarm in my core, and somehow I know he felt it too because he took the final step closer. Any space between us had completely disappeared.

I forced myself to close my eyes. When he was this close, it was hard to think about anything other than him. Deep down, my body was yearning for everything he was, as my mind was shouting at me to wake the heck up and defend myself. I felt like I was standing at the base of a camp, watching an avalanche cascade right towards me. The situation was bad, ok scratch that. It was possibly unrecoverable. One swipe from his wolf, and I'd be dead.

Yet he always seemed to be trying to keep me safe as the warmth of his finger under my chin caused me to gasp. Such a contrast to the cold night air. He angled my face up to look at him. My blue eyes glanced away, but no escape had become evident to me. Even if I could slip under his arms that were caging me in I'd never make it more than one or two steps. *Hope was a good friend to have, but she could also be a backstabbing bitch when she failed.*

I tried to still my breath as I inhaled. Shifters loved fear. It egged on their animal for a fun hunt. There was no running from an alpha shifter, so I needed to fake my confidence as best I could. I had been faking things for a long time now, so I slipped on the mask and tried to cool my nerves.

His human hazel eyes switched to his wolf irises as they glowed with the hint of his magic. *That isn't good!* Just then, his magic started to leave his hands as his arm erupted with fur before I could even blink. *His wolf is too close to the surface!* The hazel now looked more like burnt gold that was ready to solidify on anything it glanced upon.

Unfortunately that's me. The prey.

His right hand slowly slid down from my chin to my neck as if he was trying to embed the feeling of my skin onto his fingertips. Slowly he settled his hand by the back of my head, where the gentleness evaporated, and his grip tightened. Some shifters preferred humans because they were so fragile. It gave their animal more of a sense of a need to protect what they claimed to be theirs.

I hated being so breakable. I felt like a doll that was tossed around. It was that feeling that forced me to take matters into my own hands. That was why I ended up here in the middle of the city, where I met with a dark mage from time to time. Even though I was told not to. Every decision has consequences, and as I tried to take fate into my own hands, I only hoped for a positive outcome.

My life was literally in his claws. Any shifter could kill someone like me in a blink of an eye. I tried to force down a gulp. "I... I'm tired...." I murmured as I licked my lips, "Of your games." My mind was filled with questions and anger towards him and myself because of how I reacted in the past when he trapped me with his kisses. "I'm not yours, and these—"

His growl caused my mouth to snap shut. It would have cleared a crowd of people if any had been nearby. "You want me to stop?" He leaned closer and smelled my hair. "Then leave Lykos." It was always the same request. Well, he wasn't requesting it, he was demanding it, but as much as he demanded it, he allowed me to stay. He was torturing himself too. If he wanted me gone so bad, he had the power to do so. Why was he waiting on me to make a move?

Knowing I had some kind of power over him, a power that stopped him from banishing me, caused me to gamble with my life. A bet I was willing to wager now. My weight shifted onto my toes yearning for his warmth. As my body pressed closer to his, the last few inches between predator and prey started to vanish. He sensed the shift of my weight, allowing it for a mere few seconds before his hand gripped me tighter. Then the control shifted as he pushed me back into the brick wall and pressed his body more intensely to mine.

I'd need a long cold shower.

His golden eyes darkened even more as if to tell me I would never escape him. "I should put an end to this. You're a distraction." His voice thick with fieriness sent chills down my spine, chills his wolf felt as he licked his lips.

"So do it." I hissed. I know I was poking the wolf. Actually, it was more like a strong kick I delivered to his hind legs. A smile came to my lips as I taunted him. It was a stupid gamble but one I chose to make. Clouds of blue magic started to fill the air as they fogged my vision. The blue was ethereal, like the streaks of blue haze that filled the night sky some nights.

"You're a distraction. One that doesn't listen to a single warning I give you." He pushed his chest against mine, and I knew he could feel my body's reaction to him. Each inhale of my breath was now pressed against his until our breathing became each other's air supply. The tension between us was palpable. It was only a matter of time before an explosion occurred.

His head lowered closer to mine. I closed my eyes, trying to push away what my body wanted. "Why can't you just listen?" With a slight change in the angle of his hand, my face was forced to look at him directly. To make matters worse, my eyes could not resist the pull from his as they snapped open and looked directly into his wolf's eyes.

His thumb grazed my bottom lip, "Just once." He whispered more to himself than to me. It was something he told himself every time, and I knew what was coming next. Maybe he didn't understand the definition of *once*. I should tell him the meaning when he finished.

But then you'll never feel his lips again, Adaira.

His lips crashed down against mine, and then the alleyway faded, and all I could feel was him. His warmth, touch, and scent that smelt of fresh pine after a rain shower. The feeling of his lips against mine as they took control was all my mind could focus on. He always put me under a spell when he kissed me. The way he forced the kiss was like a fight of fire and ice. Passion and hate, melting and freezing each other until ultimately each would be defeated and neither would remain.

For ice could suffocate the fire, and fire could melt ice. There was no chance of surviving for either one of us.

* * *

Two Years Earlier

Glossy white paint coated my fingers as I raised my hand and smeared the paint in a straight line down the canvas. *Finger painting wasn't just for kids, folks.* I needed my art to be tangible. I needed to feel it on the tips of my fingers. Line after line appeared on the canvas. Trees that looked liked the bases were carved of white ivory that littered the landscape mimicking the scene I dreamt of. Thick and haunting, perfectly smooth tree trunks that were unlike the metal buildings in the city I lived in.

I remember how the trees felt in the dream. I could still feel the silky smoothness on my fingers. It was unlike anything I had ever felt before. Behind the rows of white trees was a dark blue sky for contrast, creating a haunting image overall, just like my dream. Grabbing the paintbrush, I thinned down the grey paint, then I started to add the darkness that would consume the pure white trees. The darkness wasn't magic. It was something else, something darker. Like chaos spreading without an end destination, a great ocean storm was something that couldn't be destroyed or stopped, no matter what type of magic a person has in this world.

"You dreamed of this place again." A deep voice startled me from the trance I was in. Setting down my brush, I grabbed a cloth to remove some of the paint from my fingers. A wisp of my red hair broke free from my low bun as I turned to face him.

"It's nothing," I whispered. Liam was a shifter and able to hear me even when I wanted others not to. "Just a silly dream." I smiled at my best friend. His tall muscled body that fit the profile of a shifter male was leaning against the door frame. *I wonder how long he has been watching me.*

The downside of me being a magic-less hybrid, half shifter and half-human, was that I got the short end of the stick. I couldn't shift, and even smaller shifter abilities like accelerated healing, heighten hearing, amongst other badass magic, I couldn't tap into.

Liam's left eye twitched almost too fast for me to catch. This was his signal when he was concerned. I could read him like a book as he could me. *We are all each other has, a pack of two living in one of the most feared packs in Volkovia, the kingdom ruled by shifters.* We'd been together since we were babies who were tossed aside into the foster care home in Lykos City. *Liam had always watched my back, and I...well, I'd like to say I watched his, but a useless hybrid watching a shifter is as comical as it is impractical.*

But hey, it's the thought that counts, right?

After cleaning up, I grabbed my bag and closed the distance between us. My dirty sneakers squeaked across the floor. They were covered in more paint than some of my canvases. "Why are you worried? Seriously you don't want your face to get stuck in that pensive look. You'll never find a girlfriend." I nudged up to his side. It was as natural as breathing.

"I only need one girl in my life," Liam said as he swung his arm over my shoulder. His warmth always calmed me, as did his scent, which smelt like fresh laundry.

I flashed Liam a playful smile, but deep down, I wondered if his words had a deeper meaning. Before I could contemplate more, he added, "The results are out."

Four words I didn't want to hear. It was bad enough that I already knew the answers, but to have it posted in the hall for the whole school to see made it so much more humiliating. That's how my pack did things. There was no coddling. Pack Sköll was feared because of its history during the Great War. A history that was entangled with dark magic and a lust for killing. Not swift killing either, for the darker the magic, the greater the root of evil that spreads.

Pack Sköll was known not to be lenient to other kinds. Even to hybrids like myself, we all knew the alpha would cast us out if he could. Alpha Mason Sköll only allows hybrid shifters and other kinds into his pack's lands to appear more acceptable to the Guild of Creatures. In reality, it was all for show.

I was a sixteen-year-old hybrid who had never shown a single ounce of any magic. I was no more wolf than the average house dog. Heck, in the pack's eyes, a house dog was more accepted than a hybrid like me. *I'm utterly useless.*

Liam must have felt my body stiffen with tension because he pulled me tighter to his chest. "Hey, it doesn't change anything. We don't even have to look if you don't want to." That was Liam, always trying to shield me.

"No, it's fine." Looking up at him, I smiled, "I want to know what rank you are."

We were tested throughout our childhood up until our mid-twenties to see how powerful our magic was and, in my case, what type of hybrid I was. As a child, I was classified as half shifter and half-human, so I was sent to live with the shifters in hopes that my being around a pack would coax out my shifter magic. Liam, on the other hand, was classified as a full-blooded shifter. If he was sent to any other pack, he might have been adopted, but Alpha Mason ranked families by pure blood, lineage, and power. Since Liam had no known lineage or family power, he was left to the pack-run foster home. No one would want to adopt him because it wouldn't further them in society. It would only tarnish a pack's family name.

At thirteen, Liam was able to shift into his wolf. I remember that day clearly. I was being bullied, and right after I took a punch to my shoulder, Liam literally jumped in the air, shifting mid-jump. After that most of the time, the bullies stayed away when Liam was nearby, but Liam couldn't always be my shadow.

As we rounded the corner, I spotted the huddle of kids as they started to gossip about the results. My heart accelerated, a fact the shifters would be able to pick up on. I knew what was coming, Liam did too. I could feel him stand taller. His wolf was fighting to come forth.

Both Liam's and my fate was now foretold on a simple white sheet of paper that was taped up on the wall. I felt like the school should have made more of an effort. Maybe framed the results that would dictate our future. Even if some futures were not as bright, at least give us a pretty wrapping.

My eyes scanned down, looking for my name as I chewed my lip. I read,

Adaira Warg: Classification: Hybrid.

Hybrid Status: Shifter/human.

Power Ranking: Magicless.

Something in me dropped. "I shouldn't have even looked," I whispered under my breath as my heart beat even faster. I knew others could hear my pitiful mumble, but I couldn't help it as I tried to act ok. After all, I'd never felt my wolf before, and that fact was reflected on paper now, permanently. After blinking away emotions, I scanned further down to find Liam's results.

Liam Warg: Classification: Shifter.

Shifter Status: Pure blooded wolf.

Power Ranking: Beta.

My body twisted into Liam as my head looked up with pride. "Holy Fae Liam, you're a beta!" I gleaned. Being ranked a beta was a huge honor, just a step below alpha power. If Liam chose to leave Pack Sköll, he'd have a lot of opportunities open to him.

Liam ran his hand through his thick chocolate brown hair causing it to look like he just rolled out of bed. "It doesn't change anything here." He tried to sound nonchalant, but I could tell deep down that Liam was thrilled. I hated that he felt the need to hide his happiness about his magic ranking. It was a gesture like that, that caused me to question if I was more of a burden to him.

Liam turned us away from the wall, and we started to head to the exit, but we were stopped by the wall of bullies who relished in making my life hell. Front and center was Stella Sköll. Daughter to the reigning Alpha Mason, sister of Carter who graduated two years ago and was next in line to take over. She stood tall and confidently with her shiny black hair that hung around her face like a curtain of doom. Piercing hazel eyes looked down at me with an evil twisted smile.

If only I could channel a bitch face like that when it came to looking at people that displeased me.

"You know, since you're more human than a wolf, I should tell my father to send you out of the pack." Stella stepped closer, her minions behind her followed like magnets. "Why should we have to put you up at our foster home? You're nothing but a useless waste of space. Taking our money, food, and complete advantage of our pack. Let the humans have you. Oh wait, they don't want you either." She laughed.

"Back off." A growl left Liam that was more wolf than his normal voice. I could feel the vibration of his chest as it started to shake against my back.

Stella flashed a pearly white smile as she crossed her arms. "Make me. Oh, wait, you can't because my father would hunt you down. Then he'd make Carter kill her in front of you and save you for last." She glared at Liam as her eyebrow went up like she had an idea, "Actually, that could be fun. Go ahead, beta, piss me off." She taunted.

The sad truth was she was right. Our alpha wasn't fair and just. The Guild of Creatures was always questioning him about the rumors of him meddling with dark mages. That was just the tip of the iceberg. Stella's family came from a line of feared monsters. Shifters who during the Great Wars killed anyone who wasn't a purebred shifter. Although the wars had long been laid to rest, Alpha Mason still thought in the old ways. He only acted civil to hold onto his power and to keep the Guild away from his throne.

"Let's get out of here," Liam said under his breath, he actually took a hold of my hand, — not as a boyfriend, more as a protector— pulling us away from wicked Stella as I wished with everything inside that I had the power to shut her up, but I didn't.

Chapter 2

CARTER

A blood curdling yelp escaped from the back alley. A cry so loud and commanding it would have been clear to even a human that a shifter was getting pummeled to death. My senses smelled blood, so much that I could almost taste it like fresh prey in my mouth. As a shifter, you craved what your alpha wanted, needing to let it be, even if it was wrong, and I knew this was. My father's ways had acted like a poison. It spread like a bleeding wound, tainting the entire pack. Those who were pure of heart would slowly die here over time.

All I wanted to do was change... to lose this human shell, go back behind the giant Sköll skyscraper my father called home and either stop my dad as he drained another shifter of life... or help him.

That reason is why I fought to stay human, because had my mom been alive, knowing I'd help my father claw the life out of someone simply because they weren't a pure wolf or of good lineage, my mom would hate me. Just as she abhorred my father, just as I sometimes hated myself under my father's rule.

Until he died, this was my life. You had to suck it up or crumble under the emotions. *Bury the emotions Carter, bury them so deep you feel nothing.* Numbness was what I sought when I was alone.

After another feral cat-like scream, I heard Laurence, a panther shifter with a low lineage, let out the last gasp of his last breath. I and everyone from our pack nearby knew Laurence had left this world. This was all because of my father's third wife, Darla. She'd found out my father had taken on several new lovers even though he'd been mated to her since my mother ran off.

So Darla had welcomed an affair with the 'alley cat.' Something she knew would enrage her alpha wolf-mate because of his old-fashioned beliefs that different shifter breeds shouldn't mix. My father desired pure wolf breeds and was willing to silence those that argued, which is why my mom had run. But tragically, she hadn't bothered to take my sister or I with her, and now she had a new family.

My father rounded the alleyway with Jackson, one of the betas by his side. He handed my dad a shirt as my father wiped blood from his mouth. Jackson was a year or two older than me and already in college. He was the pure breed who believed in everything my dad professed and was now giving me a look like he wanted to challenge me for rule over our pack one day. If only I, Mason's son, and a future alpha, would get out of his way.

Yeah, in your dreams, buddy. I thought as I felt my own inner wolf want to come out and spar with him. *I'd end him.*

"You were summoned here over an hour ago," my father barked at me. He hardly made eye contact. He resented that he saw more of my mother in his kids than of himself. *How I wish that was true.*

"Yeah, I had this pressing matter called school," I sneered at him and wished our pack's pull wouldn't draw me to obey, forcing me to leave class and come here.

"I help fund that school, if you wish to continue to go to it, then I suggest you arrive on time, boy," He spat hatefully as his eyes darkened when they looked at me. I tried not to remind myself that I could look just as scary when I was angry. My father tossed aside his bloody rag he'd cleaned himself with, the metallic tang of blood hung heavy around him. He expected me to follow him and Jackson as we abruptly heard a female voice.

"My dear Mason, why do you stink of fresh cat," Joana said. She was the only female I'd ever met not afraid of my father and all his wrath. She was dressed in a fiery orange dress that clung to her like a second skin showing off her curves. Thick gold jewelry that she could re-wield into handcuffs was bound to her wrist like iron shackles. Joana had sexy dark skin, long slick black hair that went down to her hips, and wore red heels that made her tower over six-foot-two. She wielded her body like a weapon.

"Sorry I didn't save any for you," my father said back roughly. He may have been filthy rich and of the best wolf shifter lineage, but Joana was on a whole other level of wealth and shifter power. You see Joana wasn't just any kind of shifter, she was a dragon shifter. She stuck out in this grungy part of the city like a sore thumb because dragon shifters usually stayed to their high up homes in Skydome. The isolated island to the north was a perfect fortress for dragons. Surrounded by mountains, most of the top plateau was only accessible by flight or portal. *And trust me no one dared to open a portal in Skydome if it wasn't sanctioned.*

"Ugh, no, thank you, I don't dine on scraps that can hardly defend themselves," she said to my father, disproving of him killing another shifter, even if Laurence was of pathetic lineage.

"Well, I heard you do kill vampires. My sources told me that there was a scuffle and that's why a meeting of the entire Guild has been called," my father snapped at her.

He hated Guild meetings because he preferred to only be around his own. If it was up to my father, there would be no Guild meeting between all the different creatures and races of Magic Borne. *"Us shifters, we are supreme, not the mages, vampires, their pet humans, or those damn other worlders that call themselves Fae.... You know they only come to Magic Borne because it's their ancient power lingering here that all other beings want; power that doesn't belong to them bastards anymore." I had heard my father say over and over.*

"The blood sucker wasn't killed by one of mine," Joana said sternly as she and my dad walked in unison with us trailing behind them. They walked with an air of self-righteousness. Everyone was beneath them. My body reacted with hate as I balled my fist; my wolf wanted out to rip them apart. I forced my eyes away, I could not afford to lose composure.

Looking up to the tops of the city towers around us, switching my sight so my wolf was in control I spotted the shadowy figures perched on the roof tops. Members of Joana's pack always followed her as personal guards. Like our own kind dragon shifters were pack animals. They would protect their alpha and pack just the same as us.

"Rumor is a mage might have killed the vamp." Joanna added.

Dad seemed not to comment for a moment as he thought out his response before he grumbled, "Rumors are hardly worth their weight if they can't be proven... besides, if all the vampires took themselves out it would be all the better for us."

Only I knew he had a silent deal with the Mages and that's why he hadn't verbally accused them. My father had been scheming something behind all the other shifter alphas' backs and the entire guild for a long time, and he was set on not letting me or anyone else, especially the dragons, know about it. After all it was in my very own blood to be deceptive. I bit back my grin. Like father, like son.

Chapter 3

ADAIRA

A precious gem. Something that took years of work to make and tons of pressure to form. Dug from the dirt, then polished and refined, so it sparkled like the sun that burned in the sky of Magic Borne. At least that's what my sketchbook was to me. It was like a rough diamond covered in the dark lines from my charcoal pencil that formed an image.

I smudged the line using my index finger, so it faded into the background. It gave a softness to the columns I was drawing. The image was one I had dreamed of time and time again. A building of my imagination but definitely was influenced by the art history I had studied in school.

If only it were a gig that paid.

I dabbled in figurative drawing, but my passion was architecture, strongly influenced by my dreams of castles and far away lands. *Funny enough, I had never seen such buildings in person. Never even left the city of Lykos.* Yet there was nothing like drawing a castle opposed to a shiny new cage that lacked the history other cities had, but a cage nonetheless. Being trapped in a castle seemed more romantic than the newly built metal and glass buildings surrounded by trees and mountains the shifters had.

I dreamt of escaping from Pack Sköll, but deep down, I didn't think it would ever happen. It was hard for a wolf to leave its pack, and although I never had shifted, Liam had, and I wasn't sure if he'd be able to leave the pack we both hated. *His wolf self was connected to everyone else now, and breaking the pack connection wasn't an easy task.* We hated being a part of something our genetics made us loyal to, well, at least Liam's genetics. Mine still wanted to play hide and seek. They were a no-show, too shy to come to see the world.

Shitty circumstances, but you have to work with the hand fate dealt, and I was just trying to survive. So on the outside, I took all the rumors, swallowed them, and digested the cruel words of other wolves once I was back at our foster home. It was there with Liam that I cried sometimes. I heard whispers that in other packs, fosters were treated as equals. Adopted into families and raised with respect in the pack. They even received a monthly allowance.

I huffed out loud thinking about it as I tucked a lock of my red hair back behind my ear.

Sure we have a roof over our heads, Thank Fae for that! It only leaks when the rain comes down really hard, a meal a day at the foster house and a meal at school. Two meals a day for a shifter was slim pickings. We had to eat for our human side and our animal side. At least the meals at school were a buffet, so we usually ate our fill at lunch. I required more food than the average human but less than a shifter. I was stuck in limbo, unable to define a certain category.

My fingers ground the charcoal pencil into the precious paper as I thicken the lines in the foreground. I had to believe hope was on the horizon, or what's the point of chugging through life? My green eyes look up to the parade of meat currently sparring on the field below. *That's one reason to keep pushing through life.*

Men.

Especially the shifter men that were all fighting for dominance in the after-school sparring session I could see outside. Muscle on muscle. Glistening with sweat under the mid-day sun. What a sight it was too. I might not be in touch with my wolf, but I'd like to touch a wolf. I'd have to be satisfied with looking for now. *Settle down hormones you get the last pick of the pack.*

I didn't have a boyfriend or mate. Heck, my first kiss was my best friend Liam, and we only kissed each other as emerging teenagers wanting to explore. Since then, we hadn't ever kissed again, both of us too worried it would mess up our friendship which went beyond just friends.

Liam and I were also blurred lines, even with him I was stuck in a limbo situation. We were best friends, each other's only family. At times we were like brother and sister, then we were each other's companions. We cuddled and even shared a bed some nights in the foster home as we kept watch over each other. It was perfectly normal for wolves to seek out affection and touch. We were pack animals by nature and longed to be surrounded.

Living with little taught Liam and me how to be resourceful. That brings me back to my sketchbook, which I had now started using the opposite side of the pages for my rough drawings. In just a few weeks, I'd be submitting my drawings as well as a thesis paper to the Lykos Museum of Art, where I planned on getting one of five internships that pay.

That's right, wolves, I'll be making my own money, so take that!

Not only does it pay, but it's my dream internship. I'll be surrounded by history and the art inspired by it. With any luck, I'll get my foot in the door to have a full-time job at the Institution of Magic Borne's Arts Conservatorship. A program dedicated to preserving the history of the world through the arts. I'd be able to travel to all the kingdoms and see art others can only see in books. Work on preservation sites and curate shows.

As a good luck gift, Liam had bought me the premium paper and charcoal that I needed for my drawings submission. We'd each worked summer jobs and saved every penny making sure the money would last the rest of the school year. I didn't have the luxury of wasting paper, so I needed to make sure all my ideas were perfect before putting the first charcoal line down.

I heard a barrage of giggling and whispers from a group of girls that were a few seats down cut through the air. It was the classic tip-off sign that a guy was nearby. Why we changed our voice to high pitch squeaks was beyond me. It made us seem small and weak. It catered to the male wolves who sought to dominate their females.

"Hey, Liam," a girl shouted. At the mention of his name, my eyes snapped up, first in defense, then in annoyance. Yet they continued to reach out to Liam.

I was seated on the training field bleachers as I sketched. Every afternoon Liam wolfed around with the other shifters from the school. It wasn't mandatory to spar in high school, but that would change for those who attended college or military training. The training helped ensure they had control over their wolf and engaged in pack-like bonding and support.

I had noticed the changes in Liam after a few months of this sparring. He now seemed much more alert to what was happening around him. If a pack-mate was upset or agitated, it seemed to have a ripple effect that the others could sense. Liam was always protective when it came to me, but he also was protected now by others in the pack.

When we visited the city, if an outsider came near a pack-mate or us, Liam's physical demeanor would change. He'd stand taller, puffing out his muscles. His wolf becoming more on the surface, as if he was ready to shift and pounce if the stranger was a threat. In weird ways it was as if Liam was becoming slightly more aggressive. Kind of like the head alpha of our entire pack, Mason. All his wolves would show tiny bits of his traits as long as that alpha was alive. And Mason was someone Liam and I and everyone in our foster home certainly feared. Alpha Mason only valued members who were rich, strong and of a higher lineage. Those deemed worthy were able to hunt with him, those who were not could become the hunted.

Liam is too good, too pure for Pack Sköll. However, knowing he was more in touch with his wolf and magic let me sleep better at night. Yet pack bonding was necessary to become a more robust and be a healthier wolf. It made the person more stable and less likely to go lone wolf. Nothing was worse than a lone wolf.

Ok a few things could be worse, like not being able to shift, but socially the title of a lone wolf was like a danger sign hanging above your head. Lone wolves often were unstable. Going against their genetic need to bond with a pack caused most wolves to go crazy. *And I'm not talking about crazy in a hot and sexy way. I'm talking in a lunatic unhinged way.*

As Liam approached, I watched the girls change from their relaxed positions to ones of display. They all sat up straiter and pushed their best assets out. It was a sea of push-up bras, long legs shimmering with lotions freshly applied, and thick and shiny hair. You name it, it was being flaunted on display like peddles at a circus. From a distance, it was comical how hard they tried. None of them needed to. They all were pretty, some beautiful just as they were. They looked more attractive at ease than when they tried too hard. Guy wolves noticed girls without needing the extra effort. Still, nonetheless, the girls all tried to shove their asses in Liam's face. Biting back a smirk, I watched as a girl stood and tried to talk to Liam.

She flung her long brown hair back and pushed her chest forward, which was overflowing in her low-cut skin-tight top. Ever the gentleman, he stopped for a moment before he resumed his approach to me. She, like some of the other girls, had opted out of the fighting part of training, not wanting to break a claw or ruffle her fur. Instead she sat with a group that preferred to sit on the sidelines and ogle the half-naked guys who shifted from man to magical beast.

I can't blame them.

Yet since I had yet to shift, no guys in Pack Sköll would seriously consider me a viable dating option. I didn't want to just be another hookup. So like always, I preferred to stay on the sidelines and observe rather than join the action. But the sidelines were getting very dull. I wanted to live and feel the rush of adrenalin when someone you liked touched and kissed you. *Is that so much to ask for?*

The metal bleachers creaked with each step Liam made as he ascended the steps towards me. His steps were fluid and graceful, even with his body that seemed to add monthly muscle weight. If he took the extra time, he could silently take each step without making a sound. His wolf would be able to adjust and camouflage its sounds too deadly perfection. His chocolate brown hair was slightly damp from sweat, making it shine deeper in the sun. The ends of his hair had a curl to it, little curls I loved to twist around my finger tips when we cuddled.

"So what are you drawing today?" He asked outright as I put my sketch book down and looked up. His light blue eyes looked even lighter as the sun shined directly into them. His pupils adjusted becoming smaller as he watched me.

"I'm still deciding," I said with a shrug.

Behind Liam, I could see all the bitchy looks the girls were giving me, as Liam closed the distance between him and I. Liam was hot. He was fit and built like most shifters, which meant every muscle in his body was sculpted and defined. Liam didn't have family power or money. Yet still, he had charming good looks and a personality you wished every guy his age had. He didn't play around or hook up either. He was the real deal you wanted when you found a mate. Also, did I mention Liam tested as a beta which was terrific considering his family lineage wasn't known? Having the beta wolf title opened many doors Liam could use to his advantage even as a foster kid.

If Liam never found his fated mate he'd still be fine. Liam would have lines of girls waiting to possibly be picked as his mate. That was a semi depressing thought because I wasn't sure if I'd ever have one? I doubted I had a fated mate since my wolf was too shy to even show me her tail. She was worst than trying to coax a scared rabbit out of a hole. So I'd be left looking for a mate the way humans did. Striking up a conversation, and feeling some kind of spark that made two people feel connected.

Liam ran his hand through his curly brown hair. Now it stuck up at all angles but it somehow made him look even cuter. He was shirtless, and the thin coat of sweat glistened over his rippled torso. It was hard not looking at Liam in a different light now that we were older. The boy I grew up with was now a man becoming a powerful wolf. Flashing his goofy smile that leaned more towards his right side had started to make my insides warm.

I bit my inner cheek, trying to quell my hormones. These new feelings of action towards him I'd kept to myself. Liam used to be like a brother to me. He was my only pack-mate, my best friend, and I didn't want to risk feelings for him growing only to ruin our friendship. He felt the same way I think.

He sat down next to me, and immediately I could feel the warmth radiating from his body. That combined with the sun's heat, made me feel perspiration starting to build on my brow. I slyly tried to wipe it off, as he tucked a loose strand of red hair back behind my ear. A finger came up, meeting the corner of my lip. His thumb now was rougher than it used to be. Hours of sparring in human and wolf form made his skin tough like a warrior.

The fire inside my stomach went from an ember to a wildfire. *Oh my gosh, stop this, Adaira! This is Liam.* My mind fought with my body. *But Liam is gorgeous now!* It was a constant battle as I recognized that my body wanted attention, but my mind tried to quell my need.

The touch might have been innocent, but I wondered what his touch might feel like in other ways? Maybe if I had fooled around with other guys, the simple touch wouldn't feel so grand, but Liam was my comfort zone, and only his touch I seemed to welcome. Only his indication I trusted.

"You've got charcoal dust right there." Pulling his fingers away showed the evidence of the dark black charcoal I drew with.

And there's a sexy image Adaira, black smudges all over your face... not. I loved drawing in charcoal because of how intense the black could become. The downside was how extremely messy it was. Charcoal dust littered my clothing and skin constantly. I looked as dirty as the pack assumed foster kids were.

Smiling, I tilted my head down so a curtain of my red hair would cover my blush. Liam laid back on the bleachers letting the sun coat all his exposed skin. You could see every peak and valley of the muscles on his torso. He was always at complete ease with me, as I usually was with him, but my legs squeezed together as I tried to ignore the draw I had towards him.

"Are you tired?" I asked.

"Please, I could go a few more hours if I needed to." He grinned and opened his glacial blue eyes to look at me. I'd read that you could see glaciers so clear they looked like new glass surrounding the island Kingdom of Skydome. That's how Liam's eyes were, pure, pristine, and calming. "But I'm starving. Let's go to Maria's for a burger and shake."

I rolled my eyes and shook my head because I knew he was going to suggest that. That's how well we knew each other. Maria's was a small diner in a rough part of town, but she was famous for burgers and shakes. Even the likes of Mason Sköll would show his face at Maria's for a burger which said a lot since the Sköll family had enough money to portal in food from all over Magic Borne if they wanted to.

Maria was a bull of a lady shoved in a tiny body. Nobody messed with her. She always gave Liam and me food for free. All we had to do was a sink load of dishes which wasn't so bad. She was a foster herself and knew the life of growing up in Pack Sköll. So she took sympathy for us, and in turn, we helped out where we could. I'd fill in for a waitress or Liam a cook if she was short-staffed.

"Fine, but shower first, please." I jabbed his arm, which only made him grab me in a tight hug as he covered me in his scent. His scent wasn't foul. It was the opposite. Liam smelt like cinnamon and cloves due to shifting into his wolf to spar. It only made his scent stronger. It was a scent I loved. It meant protection and safety.

That was Liam.

As Liam went to the locker room, I continued to draw until the clacking of heels on the metal bleachers stopped me. "You think he'd be interested in you?"

That would be Stella.

Every pack had Stella, a queen bitch. She was also the alpha's daughter, unfortunately. I didn't even need to turn around to know that voice that haunted many wolves. So I ignored her, which only pissed her off. She stomped forward in her designer black heels, black leather skinny jeans and blood-red sleeveless shirt right into my view. Red and black were her two favorite colors and were perfect symbols for her wicked personality.

"I'm. Talking. To. You." She emphasizes every word.

I'm sorry I don't speak bitch. That's what I wanted to say, but I also knew when to tuck tail and just let Stella be Stella.

"And I'd rather not talk to you."

"You-" Her hand reached out towards me but retracted when a deep baritone voice shouted from down below. A voice commanded an order that was hard even for Stella to ignore.

"Stella, hurry up!"

My eyes looked around her to land on Carter Sköll. He was the next pack alpha and Stella's big brother. He sometimes showed up to these fighting practices after school. No doubt scouting for the next-in-line pack guards. Where Liam was all charming boy next door, genuine and sincere, Carter was the opposite.

He was like a portal that would take you to a dark, seductive land. Full of sinister secrets, his wolf would chew you up, bones and all. There was no coming back from a guy like Carter. If his family history proved anything, then Carter most likely dabbled in dark magic. His father was rumored to do so. Carter and his family didn't play by the rules. They made them.

Living in Pack Sköll meant you were merely a pawn for what the alpha wanted. So Carter was like poison. If you touched him, you would be tainted. And so many girls wanted to be tainted by him. *Hey, if I judged by looks alone, then even I wanted to be tainted by Carter at times.* He had hordes of girls waiting to be entrapped.

My eyes drank him in from a distance like an unquenchable thirst. As scary hot as Carter was, you couldn't look away from the male perfection he'd been formed into. Carter was the perfect model of what an alpha shifter should look like. He stood so tall, well over six-foot-four with broad wide shoulders, his arms alone could kill a man if they bugged him with the slightest force. From his biceps to his thighs, his muscles were so hardened and well-sculpted that I wondered how he had the power to shift and be limber as a wolf. I'd imagine Carter would be a better fit for a dragon shifter, not that I'd ever seen a dragon shifter. Still, a dragon seemed more fitting for his personality.

Bruiting, fire breathing, and eternally pissed off. *Yeah, that sums up Carter.*

I'd seen his wolf in action. It was the biggest of them all, with jet black fur and golden eyes. When his wolf ran, it was like watching fluid strokes of a paintbrush painted onto a canvas by a master painter. It was perfection. He could change directions at a moment's notice, just as seamless as water running down a stream.

Six foot four, square jaw, and shirts that were always too tight to fit his muscles, and when he threw on that leather jacket... I'll be damned. Every wolf's tongue was wagging. I wonder where he found clothing that fit him half the time? *Then again, as Mason's son he was wealthy beyond measure compared to the rest of us at this school. So all his clothes must be custom-made.*

As much as I hated Carter— *and my hate wasn't petty because he was a rich and a fine as heck looking alpha shifter. —My hatred was due to how his family treated others in the pack. Others like me who had no social status.* Yet I loved to look at him just like every other girl here. Love-hate relationships were always the best, or so I have been told. Fiery passion exploded and erupted until it all crashed and burned.

The sun reflected off Carter's jet black hair, making it look shaped and faceted like a polished stone. Carter had the same dark black hair as Stella's and those burnt golden eyes that looked like liquid gems cooling down and hardening from molten lava. When he walked into a room, you could sense his alpha power, and it sent most cowering. I had difficulty not lowering my eyes when he was near, a sign of submission to the alpha.

"You're lucky this time, Adaira." Stella hissed, then she flipped her perfectly straight hair and pranced down towards her brother. My eyes were summoned like a magical pull back down to Carter, who looked directly at me. I didn't particularly like it when he looked at me because I could never decipher what he was thinking. Yet his eyes always found me in the crowd whenever we were in a room together. This was unnerving. Was he looking at me in disgust because I was a foster, a hybrid that could not shift?

Sometimes I believed that because he usually looked so pensive and angry. However, other times he just looked at me as if I was this strange creature. Casting my eyes down and back to my sketch pad, I realized I needed to lock away my hormones and focus on my future. *Which was incredibly hard to do when surrounded by males competing for everyones attention after they'd sparred.*

It's too many male shifters. Pheromones were tainting the air, trying to trick me as I looked away from Carter and his sister, and looked to my comfortable Liam instead.

"Let's go," I told him.

Chapter 4

CARTER

I approach Lykos Grand Central station, where I saw some of my dad's top older beta's guarding the doors. They were easy to spot as they stood with an arrogant pride wearing our pack's uniform. Solid black with our pack's golden crest sewed over their hearts. A thick leather belt with weapons was strapped to their sides, but that was mostly for show since our real weapon was our wolf. Most of them were my grandfather's Betas before he died and now dried up soldiers for my dad. They were assigned to lower ranking positions such as guarding the central portal station. But they were soldiers just the same and took their jobs with pride. Avoiding them, because I was never in the mood to have a conversation with any of my father's men, I swing to my right.

Lykos Grand Central station was full of portals that remained permanently opened. Decades ago we paid mages for the upgraded portals that could get you anywhere within our world of Magic Borne. Some less and poorer cities were not as lucky to have the permanent portals. In the more rural area where mages and roads were few and far between humans and vampires still used horses as modes of transportation. Richer humans and vampires that didn't want to paid mages used the human designed cars or planes to get around. They designed the vehicles to run on the power of the sun. I always wanted to try to drive a car but my father thought anything a human made was for lesser species so I never had the chance to try.

Then there was our world's main portal station located in Ziden, Magic Borne's Capital kingdom. Ziden was the location of the first ever portal opened by the Fae when they first arrived to our world. Those lucky enough to receive an invitation to travel to the Fae world could use the capital's portal.

Rumor had it, that when my mom first ran away from my dad, rejecting her mate to be with Dracos, a Dragon shifter who was engaged to someone else. They'd both hid somewhere outer world with the help of the Fae until it was safe for them to return to the kingdom of Skydome, where the dragon shifters lived. Thinking about my mom always made me feel cold and bitter. I thought I had shut out any need of wanting answers from her but I was wrong. During the last Guild summit, Joana had slipped me a note. It had a message in it that had me breaking all the rules.

I approached Lykos Central station which was across from our campus, near series of parks made for hunting and sparring, and was the center of our city for commuters like me.

"I'm pleased to see you've come," I heard the voice of Joana before I saw her. My senses heightened as I walked through a darker part of the park that was plush with heavy trees. I turned where I heard her voice. I stopped walking when I reached the base of an enormous tree tucked in shadow as it was hidden from the moon's light. The wolf in me itching to come out as if I was being set up for a threat. Yet the note had said it was from my mother as I made a fist and tried to still the beast within me.

Out of the tree, where I smelled what can only be described as something slimy and damp underneath the surface and reptilian, I saw Joana. All Dragon shifters beamed with this scent. She looked at me. Even in the darkness her skin seemed to glow with a rich dark hue, her memorizing beauty was a gift dragons had. Behind her there was a portal that still remained open, showing off its view of Skydome. I could roughly make out the tops of mountains that were framed by snow and clouds.

"This portal is strong enough for you to enter my kind's domain if you really want to make this conversation private. We could even have some fun before you come back," she winked at me with a sexual smile. I remembered Draco, the dragon alpha that she served, he allowed his shifters to have relations with anybody. So to her pack a dragon shifter and a wolf shifter was a very much excepted combination and had been normalized ever since Draco had married my mother.

On the other hand, my father loathed mixed breeds of any kind. He thought that wolves were the first shifters ever. That made our breed superior to other shifters. Our family line was supposedly a direct descendent of the first wolf shifter and the first shifters period. My father said keeping our line pure meant our pack could access ancient powers that other packs and mixed breeds couldn't access anymore.

"I'm fine over here, thanks," I said, my voice coming out crueler like my dad's as I tried not to insult Joana. I would have been attracted to her before my mated bond clicked in with... *someone else*. My mate had exploded into my life, changing my very soul down to the core.

Joanna laughed, clearly not insulted since she had a hundred dragon suiters on her tail. Her full lips that were painted cherry red, grinned, "You're missing out, wolf-man," she laughed then as if my breed, compared to dragons, were a joke.

"Anyway, your mother wrote that note hoping you'd come and see her." She told me.

"Not happening," I barked, knowing my mom's new husband might try to imprison or have me spelled the moment I entered his domain. The way my father wished he could do to his subjects, brainwash them all forever... "You mind as well give me her message or stop wasting my time." I told her.

"That vampire's murder that the Guild is investigating," Joana paused. "Your mother has gathered secret intelligence about it. The vampire was pregnant with a hybrid baby at the time of her murder." There was no sadness in Joana's eyes.

I found myself struggling to hide my true feelings about hybrids that were very different from my father's. My dad wanted them all wiped out. He claimed they were our pack's biggest threat when it came to accessing our ancient bloodline's abilities. "Most hybrids for the past thousand years or so have been born weak and powerless."

"Young wolf," she purred, "Rumor has it something has changed... That new hybrids are being born with more power than even the Fae."

I scarfed, and crossed my arms over my chest. "Some rumors are just rumors. Most hybrids are a nuisance. Many given away before they are even tested. Why kill over it? Unless the vamp was just in trouble and the pregnancy didn't detour her killers." I told Joana.

"Your mom's intel is that the vampire's baby was showing signs of being very powerful, even from the womb. That someone, perhaps a shifter, not a mage, took the mother out to stop the vampires from raising the child and having an upper edge over us," Joana said as I tried to hide the surprise on my face at this theory.

If this was true, while most shifters in my pack would secretly be pleased. The vampires would raise hell at the next Guild meeting if they knew this rumor to be sound. The punishment for our kind could result in an all-out war if we lost the Guild's protection as a result.

"You see what your mother is concerned about?" Joana asked as I tried to act indifferent.

"What if one of your kind was responsible for the death?" I threw back. Did Joana want me to believe my mother was concerned about my sister and I? I tried to respond without an ounce of emotion in my voice.

"No, a dragon would not fear a vampire hybrid," Joana rolled her eyes like wolves were all muscle and had no intelligence. "But she does suspect that a Sköll is responsible. Moreover, that maybe your father had that pregnant vampire murdered. If that's so, the Guild could demand not only your father's death but you or your sisters too, to settle the price," Joana said as I felt a chill go down my spine. Not for myself, but for my sister Stella as I felt my wolf eyes transform, my claws coming out of my hands, my whole body wanting to turn to show this dragon what a Sköll wolf was made of.

"Relax, your mother cares about you and your sister more than you know. She won't let this happen. That's why she wants me and you to work together, covertly. To find the truth, and if it can't be hidden, then you instead should be the one to turn in the true killer before the Guild. You doing so could persuade those in power to make you the new reigning alpha of your pack; sparing the innocent wolves underneath you," she said to me, offering to help me replace my father.

I wondered deep down how destroying my family could benefit Draco, the dragon alpha who also craved control like a life line. That made me want to know more than ever who was really behind this vampire and hybrid killing, Draco, my father, or someone else?

* * *

ADAIRA

"*Even poison can taste sweet.*"

Sunlight casted off the metal pillars of the Cafeteria building, creating a rainbow of blue light. My eyes squinted as they adjusted from the change, as I exited the main hall to the outside courtyard. Sköll Academy was a newer building in the city of Lykos. It was grand and pristine. Paid for by the current ruling alpha's family, the Sköll family. Every building they erected in Lykos reflected their power and wealth. They often chose finishes that mirrored that. Metal and glass. Shiny like a diamond yet hard like the edge of a sword. It was cold and barren, much like the feeling of belonging here.

Of course, there was beauty in the designs if you looked deep. The architectural form was twisted into flowing lines that reached high and mighty. It reminded me of a ballet dancer. The metal was strong and solid like the muscles of a ballerina.Yet, the metal curves were gracefully bent and fluid like the dancer spinning across the stage. Magic Borne, the name of our world, was a mixture of old and new. Some buildings were made from the stone from the very first humans. In contrast, other cities and towns had been utterly destroyed and rebuilt with modern materials infused with magic.

Crossing the central courtyard, I passed a few groups of wolves sparring with each other. It was common to see. The only rule was no shifting inside the main hall. We might be shifters and have an animal inside us, but we had to remain civil. Besides the main hall, the library was also off-limits to a magical shift. No need to ruin the books with fur dander and claw marks.

The grass in the courtyard bore signs of numerous shifts. Full of patches of missing grass with muddy patches from the running and stomping of wolf paws. Balm trees scattered the area, providing shade. Given their name from the sap they produced which healed flesh of magic-less beings in half the time. The trees were infused with the magic that was rooted in our soil. Balm trees were a favorite tree in throughout Magic Borne not only did they have healing purposes but they just looked beautiful. They grew relatively short only reaching heights of about thirty feet. Their branches reached far and wide making them the perfect tree for shade. The branches were covered in bloom that ranged in color of deep blues to vibrant pinks.

Wolfs, especially young wolves loved to test their balance in wolf form and climb the tree. Since the branches were low lying a fall would be less painful. Liam and I climbed the trees often as children. When he first met his wolf, we played wolf and rabbit. He naturally the wolf and I the rabbit. I raced up the tree, trying to escape him. It helped us both, me with speed and Liam with balance in his wolf form.

Taking the steps up to the cafeteria, I reached out and pulled the door open. But I was quickly shoved away before clutching the metal handle. I stumbled back, missing the first step but caught myself before I tumbled down the entire way.

"Watch where you're going!" A catty voice snarled at me.

"You think your are good enough to enter before us?"

Stella's minion's barked at me as they pushed me to the side of the cafeteria entrance. They walked past me as if they owned the place. *Then again, Stella did.*

After they cleared, I stood tall and readjusted my backpack's straps as if it was some sort of body armor. I patted down my long wavy red hair as I flipped it over my shoulder and prepared to walk into a battlefield, otherwise known as the school lunch.

Hopefully, that would be the only attack during lunch today. *Washing food out of my hair wasn't a fun pastime.* The scent of baked breads, freshly cooked meats, and sugary delights assaulted my nose. My stomach rumbled as it always did when I entered the building. It caused a few of the eyes of my fellow classmates to glance my way. With their shifter hearing in tune, they'd hear my stomach rumble easily.

I know what they thought too, here comes the foster kid, a hybrid that can't do any magic. I tried not to let their whispers get to me, but it was really freaking hard to ignore the world sometimes. It felt like heavy chains around my ankles, like I was permanently attached to an anchor of failure since I could not shift or prove anything of worth to the pack.

Numerous circular tables were scattered all over the room except for the one long rectangular table near the far back left wall. That was my table, the table where the outcasts were destined to sit. Unlike the packed tables in the middle, my table was scarce and quiet. We were like a fallen branch off a great tree that slowly crumbled into the dirt again.

After loading up a tray of food, I walked to my seat. Slumping down in the metal chair, I felt its coldness as it pressed into my back. Nothing here was welcoming and cozy. It was cold and harsh and made for tough claws and hardened fur. *Two of which I was lacking.*

Lunch senior year was miserable due to one factor, Liam didn't have the same lunch schedule as me. I was faced with enduring one hour alone, and it was those first weeks alone that I realized how much I relied on Liam. He was my safety net, the blanket you wrapped a child in when they were scared, a shield when I had to go into battle. Stripped bare of Liam, I never felt so vulnerable. I realized then that I didn't know exactly who I was. So much of my identity was tied to him. I didn't want to know what it was like to survive independently. I always wanted Liam by my side like a safety blanket, and sometimes I wanted him in more than a brotherly way. We had experienced all our first together, *well not all...* Deep down, I wanted to explore more of those first.

I must have zoned out for longer than I realized thinking about it, because when I picked up my cheeseburger with sautéed mushrooms and truffle sauce, *yeah, our cafeteria wasn't lacking when it came to tasty food.* It was cold in my hand. Nonetheless, I'd never turn down a meal or cold food as I took a bite. Cold or hot the truffle sauced added something rich and exotic that made my taste buds jump for joy.

At lunch, I tried to eat enough to keep myself full until the following day since the food at the foster house was slim pickings. Now that I was older, Liam and I let the younger kids eat the little food that was provided. Shifters had an endless appetite. They had to feed both human and beasts within. Magic users, in general, required more calories, something humans didn't need to worry about.

Going to a restaurant or home of magic user meant food would always be plentiful. Those blessed with charm and magic were also blessed with a high metabolism. You never saw a magic user overweight. They were always sculpted and fit. Another benefit of magic.

My body was always in limbo. Sometimes I was starved like a wolf, yet other days I ate more like a human needed only one meal a day if that was all I could get my hands on. I polished off my tray of food in no time. Glancing at the large clock that was huge on the far wall. I still had fifteen minutes left to endure. My eyes flicked back and landed on Kevin, who usually sat right across from me.

Kevin was a nice guy, but he also had changed in ways I didn't know how to describe. Kevin wasn't a foster kid, but he was one of the unfortunate students who had a late shift, and by late, I mean eighteen years of age. The stronger the shifter, the earlier you would shift. For example, our Alpha's son, Carter, the next-in-line alpha, shifted at only fourteen. Whereas most other shifters matured into their animal by sixteen or seventeen years old.

Since Kevin was a late bloomer, he endured a few years of bullying and pressure from the pack and his family. The sad thing was we could never win. Kevin had come into his wolf, but he still wasn't entirely accepted because of his late shift. People assumed something must be wrong because it took his wolf so long to come forth that he was weak. I knew Kevin's fate would be the same as my own if I were to meet my wolf. I didn't care about being accepted by my pack. I just wanted to be on level ground. I wanted to defend myself and Liam if I needed to.

"The fries aren't bad today. Extra crisp when Joe is the chef," Kevin said as he picked up a french fries from the mountain still on his plate. I could hear the sound of the crunch when he bit into it, and it had my mouth watering. Kevin had offered me some of his food before, which wasn't just a friendly gesture to shifters. As pack animals, sharing was a big thing. You shared with those you accepted into your closer fold. I never turned down his gestures or others from the rejected table. Maybe I was too nice, but also it was nice to feel accepted.

The fry was still hot between my fingers when I picked it up and brought it to my lips. The taste of the potato was so fresh and lightly salted that I quickly grabbed another. "Thanks. They are good today."

I smiled, and ate a few more fries as I glanced around our table. Everyone here looked the same. We all sat slightly hunched over our food trays. We isolated ourselves and avoided conversations with others. Macey was reading a textbook about organism biology in Lake Caströft, a lake in the kingdom of Arenstad. From the look on her face, you'd have thought it the most significant thing to ever enter her hands. The sad part was every day, she read from that book. The same text, flipped the same pages, every darn day.

Life was on repeat for us.

It seemed like hope wasn't on the horizon. So we numbed ourselves. Macey with that damn book, me with my art, Kevin with... *something darker.*

Looking back at Kevin, I noted how he was different. He wasn't hunched over his tray of food. He leaned back in his chair with ease and confidence as if he was part of the main pack. His chocolate brown hair was buzzed shorter like a military cut, making him look more intimidating. He had filled out into the classical shifter body. Tall, lean, well-sculpted muscles primed for an attack. Tattoos of elder ruins on his knuckles and patterns twisted up both his arms.

"You want to tell me what you're looking at?" Kevin asked.

Blinking, I met hazel eyes that were watching my blue ones. He wasn't mad. In fact, he almost looked happy that I was giving him my attention. Maybe Kevin's gestures of sharing food and always sitting across from me had alternative motives? We were both single, after all. I just had never looked at Kevin that way before.

"Sorry," I whispered, embarrassed I was caught. It wasn't that Kevin wasn't cute, but I didn't see him that way.

"You're always watching, aren't you, Adaira, even when you pretend to have your head buried in a book or your sketchbook. That's the wolf in you, never able to fully settle, always on alert."

"It would be nice if that wolf wanted to show." I huffed.

Kevin laughed, "Watch all you want, Adaira, but you're never going to be able to defend yourself against them in your current state." He relaxed back in his chair, making it look like he was relaxing on a throne, "Let me guess, you know all the exits, you know when and where to run. But every week, something still happens, doesn't it? Every week they keep bothering you. Running only insights our wolf, you are constantly egging them to attack you. You're like a wounded animal leaving a trail of blood all over the woods."

My body caved in on its self from his harsh words. They hurt, but he spoke the truth. I tried countless different attempts to avoid Stella and her minions. I tried to be invisible, but they always saw me. I tried to run, but they found me. I even tried to fight back, which was a complete joke.

"What do you suggest?" I sneered.

Kevin's eyes narrowed as his lips turned up. He looked like a wolf who had just stepped out from the woods as it spotted its prey. The sudden change had me pushing back in my chair, needing space from the darkness that swirled in his eyes. Sensing his prey's retreat, he sat forward in his chair and rested his tattooed covered elbows on the table. The ink contrasted off his smooth pale skin with a dark beauty.

"You're making me uncomfortable," I admitted. I flipped some of my red hair over my shoulder as if it was a piece of armor to shield his eyes from my face.

"You're always uncomfortable in your current magic less state. Now, do you want the answer to your question?"

He stirred a nervousness in my core, causing me to take a prolonged pause before I mustered up the courage to ask him.

"What did you do, Kevin?" By his tone and confidence, I could tell that Kevin had indeed done something? His questions were bait. Dangled in front of me, and I was the little fish in the sea of more extensive, smarter fish. So I bit down on the baited hooked and held on as he responded.

"You are always going to be beneath them, Adaira. *Always.*" He stressed. "Your little pack mate is one of them." He spoke of Liam. "But you aren't." He smirked then.

A.G. Harris

The reaction caused my fist to ball. My nails pinched into the palm of my hand.

His hazel eyes glanced down at my fingers, and he laughed, "It's frustrating, I know, but it doesn't have to be. You can take matters into your own hands. You can go against fate, take the control into your grasp."

Kevin shifted, his eyes looking me up and down and lingering longer on my lips. "Are you going to bite Adaira?" He taunted. His tongue swept out to lick his lips, clearly enjoying his affect on me.

"I don't know what you're talking about."

"Don't play dumb with me. How many nights have you laid awake, hoping that your magic came forth when you woke up the next morning? How many times have you tried to call upon your wolf, Adaira? You feel her a little, don't you? It's a terrible joke, letting us feel our wolf but never shifting into it. They are like figures trapped beneath a frozen surface. You need fire and power to break through the ice, Adaira. I can help you obtain that power."

Kevin's words were like pages from my own inner diary. Too many nights, I stayed awake and researched how to connect with my wolf. Liam had tried endless times with me. It had gotten to the point where I didn't ask for his help anymore because the disappointment and worry on his face when I often got upset at my failure was too much to handle.

Licking my lips, I answered, "There is no magical cure." If it was that simple, humans who wanted magic would be lining up. Mages had tried and failed in the well-known past, and the outcomes were drastic. New creatures were birthed, creatures born of pure greed and evil. So many so that the

Guild of Creatures had teams trained to hunt and track the creatures down.

"Or is there?" He smirked. "There's always something else to try. Failure is never accepted in our world. There are people you can turn to for help. I've seen you with all your art history books. What has history taught us about waging wars?" he paused for a beat, "Follow me." He stood like a warrior that just won a battle, the muscles in his forearms contracted with his newly found adrenaline, "Magic always finds a way to succeed," he said.

Then he turned and exited the cafeteria leaving an invisible trail of bread crumbs that taunted me to follow.I knew what I should do. *Don't you dare, Adaira. Stay seated!*

I should remain seated, but that itch took control of my legs in my mind. I stood and slowly walked out the metal doors, knowing that what Kevin would confess wasn't something I should want to hear. Yet when people are desperate, we sometimes cling to the paths we vowed never to turn towards.

A.G. Harris

Made in United States
Orlando, FL
27 April 2025

60824955R00258